KAT MARTIN

Royal's Bride

MIRA®

MIRA®

ISBN-13: 978-0-7783-2642-7

ROYAL'S BRIDE

Copyright © 2009 by Kat Martin.

Recycling programs
for this product may
not exist in your area.

www.MIRABooks.com

Printed in U.S.A.

Read what the experts are saying about

KAT MARTIN

"Kat Martin is one of the best authors around!
She has an incredible gift for writing."
—*Literary Times*

"A knockout! From the first page it pulls the reader in…
the plot is so rich with twists and turns that I couldn't
put it down…[Martin] is one talented writer and
Heart of Courage is one for the keeper shelf!"
—*Romance Reader at Heart*

"Kat Martin dishes up sizzling passion and true love,
then she serves it up with savoir faire."
—*Los Angeles Daily News*

"Ms. Martin keeps you burning the midnight oil as
she sets fire to the pages of *Heart of Fire*….Don't miss
this fabulous series! It is definitely a winner."
—*Reader to Reader*

"Kat Martin shimmers like a bright diamond in the genre."
—*Romantic Times BOOKreviews*

"[*The Devil's Necklace* is] full of spirited romance
and nefarious skullduggery [and] one of Martin's
trademark nail-biting endings."
—*Publishers Weekly*

"*Heart of Honor* sweeps the reader away on a tidal wave
of emotion, bittersweet, poignant romance and a tantalizing
primal sexuality that are the inimitable trademarks of
multi-talented author Kat Martin."
—*Winterhaven News*

To the Martin family, all such wonderful people.
I'm so lucky to have them!

Author's Note

I hope you enjoy *Royal's Bride*. It's the first in my new Bride's Trilogy, a series that revolves around the handsome Dewar brothers and the women they come to love.

Reese's Bride is next. Retired from the cavalry, Reese Dewar has returned to Briarwood, the home he inherited from his grandfather. There he intends to make a life for himself that does not include battle. Instead, Reese will be forced to confront his painful past and the woman who betrayed him, the beautiful widow Elizabeth Clemens Holloway, the woman he once loved.

Now Reese must face his toughest challenge— staying away from the lovely, lonely widow he could never trust when all he can think of is getting her into his bed.

I hope you'll watch for *Reese's Bride,* and that you enjoy!

All best wishes,

Kat

One

England, 1854

Royal Dewar crossed the massive oak-beamed entry of Bransford Castle, his tall black riding boots ringing on the wide-planked wooden floor. As he strode past the main drawing room, so impressive with its high, Tudor-style ceilings and heavy beams, he tried to ignore the worn Persian carpets, the way the bright reds and vivid blues he recalled from his youth had faded to shadowy, lackluster hues.

As he climbed the wide, carved mahogany staircase, he tried not to notice the feel of the wooden banister beneath his hand, once polished to a rich patina but now dull from years of neglect.

He had been home for less than two weeks, returned to England from his family's plantation, Sugar Reef, in Barbados, where he had been living for the past seven years. His father had fallen ill and the family solicitor, Mr. Edward Pinkard, had sent for him.

The Duke of Bransford is dying, the letter had said. *In all haste, my lord, please come home before it is too late.*

He was home at last, grateful to have this brief time with his father, but the house was dreary and in desperate need of repair, and he was unused to being cooped up inside. At dawn, after checking on his father's condition, he had headed for the stables. He hadn't ridden Bransford lands in the past eight years and he looked forward to becoming reacquainted with his home.

Though the winter wind was chill, the sky gray and cloudy, Royal enjoyed the ride immensely, surprising himself a bit. The hot climate of Barbados had seeped into his bones and his skin was sun-darkened from his work out in the sugarcane fields. Yet this morning, with the brisk wind in his face and the open fields stretching as far as he could see, he realized how much he had missed England.

It was late morning when he returned to the house, swinging down from the big gray stallion that had been a gift on his twenty-first birthday, a colt he had named Jupiter that now stood seventeen hands high. He handed the reins to a waiting groom.

"See he gets an extra ration of oats, will you, Jimmy?"

"Aye, my lord."

Feeling only a little guilty for leaving with his father so ill, Royal hurried into the house and climbed the stairs to the second floor. Striding down the hall, he paused for a moment to collect himself outside the door to the duke's bedroom suite.

A strip of light seeped from beneath the heavy wooden panel, indicating a lamp burned inside. Royal turned the silver handle, opened the door and strode into the massive, dimly lit chamber. Across the room, his father lay beneath the covers of a huge four-poster bed encased in heavy gold velvet hangings, the shell of the man he had once been.

The duke's valet and most trusted servant, George Middleton, hurried forward on long, spindly legs, his shoulders stooped from years of service and now resignation.

"It is good you are back, my lord."

"How is he, Middleton?" Royal pulled the tie on his long scarlet woolen cloak and allowed the valet to sweep it from his shoulders.

"I am afraid, my lord, each day he grows weaker. Waiting for Lord Reese to arrive is all that keeps him going."

Royal nodded. He prayed his brother, two years younger than his own twenty-nine years and a major in the British cavalry, would reach Bransford before it was too late. His third and youngest brother, Rule, had already arrived, home from his studies at Oxford.

Royal glanced toward the velvet curtains and saw Rule sitting in the shadows next to their father's bedside. Rule rose and started forward. Tall and broad-shouldered with the lean-muscled build of an athlete, Rule looked a good deal like his siblings: same straight nose, carved features and solid jaw, but unlike Royal, who had the dark blond hair and golden-brown eyes of their mother, both Reese and Rule were black-haired, with the brilliant blue eyes that belonged to the duke.

"He's been asking for you." Rule moved into the flickering light of the lamp on a nearby rosewood dresser, the dangling prisms throwing off a rainbow of colors. "He's been rambling a bit. He says there is a promise you must make. He says he cannot die in peace unless you vow to see it done."

Royal nodded, more curious than concerned. All three brothers loved their father. And all three had abandoned him years ago to follow their own selfish dreams. They owed the Duke of Bransford. His sons would do whatever he asked of them.

Following in Middleton's wake, his brother strode past Royal out the door and closed it softly behind him, leaving him alone in the gloomy, airless room. His father had suffered three separate strokes, the first three years ago, and each more debilitating than the last. Royal should have come back to England after the first, but his father's letters had assured him of his recovery, and Royal had wanted to believe it. He wanted to stay at Sugar Reef.

He looked down at the frail old man on the bed, once a man of unbelievable power and strength. It was sheer force of will, Royal believed, that had kept his father alive this long.

"Royal…?"

He moved to the bed, settled himself in the chair his youngest brother had vacated. "I'm right here, Father." He reached out and clasped the duke's thin, cold hand. Though it was warm in the bedroom, he made a mental note to stoke up the flames in the hearth.

"I am sorry…my son," the duke said in a raspy voice, "for the poor legacy…I have left you. I have failed you… and your…brothers."

"It's all right, Father. Once you are back on your feet—"

"Do not talk…nonsense, boy." He took a few wheezing breaths, his mouth drooping slightly, and Royal fell silent. "I've lost it all. I am not…not even sure exactly how it happened. Somehow it just…slipped away."

Royal didn't have to ask what his father meant. The furniture missing from the drawing rooms, the bare spots on the walls where exquisite gilt-framed paintings once had hung, the general dilapidated condition of what had once been one of the grandest houses in England told the story.

"In time, our fortune can be rebuilt," Royal said. "The Bransford dukedom will be as mighty as it ever was."

"Yes…I am certain it will be." He coughed, dragged in a shaky breath. "I know I can…count on you, Royal… you and your brothers. But it won't be easy."

"I will see it done, Father, I promise you."

"And so you…shall. And I am going to help you… even after I am dead and buried."

Royal's chest squeezed. He knew his father was going to die. It was only a matter of time. Still, it was difficult to accept that a man once as strong and vital as the duke would actually be gone.

"Did you hear what I said…Royal?"

He had, but only dimly. "Yes, Father, but I'm afraid I don't know what you mean."

"There is a way…my son. The simplest…of ways. Marriage to the right woman will give you…the money you need." His frail hold tightened on Royal's hand. "I have found her, son. The perfect…woman."

Royal straightened in his chair, certain his father must have returned to his former rambling.

"She is beautiful…" the duke continued. "An exquisite creature…worthy of becoming your duchess." The old man's strength seemed to grow with every word, and for a moment, the dull glaze over his eyes lifted, turning them the fierce blue of his youth. "She is an heiress, my boy…inherited a fortune from her grandfather. And the size of her dowry is incredible. You will be a wealthy man again."

"You should rest. I can come back—"

"Listen to me, son. I have already spoken to her… father, a man named Henry Caulfield. Caulfield dotes on her. He is determined…to give her a title. The arrangements have already…been made." He wheezed in a breath, coughed, but his hold on Royal's hand never weakened. "After a suitable period of mourning…you will marry Jocelyn Caulfield. With her fortune…and your resolve…you can rebuild the house and return our lands to their former glory."

The duke's grip grew fierce. Royal was amazed he had that much strength. And he realized his father wasn't rambling. Indeed, he knew exactly what he was saying. "Promise me you will do it. Say you will marry the girl."

Royal's heart was thumping oddly. He owed his father, yet deep inside, some part of him wanted to refuse, to rebel against a life that had been dictated for him. Though he had been trained to assume the duties of duke, he hadn't expected to face those duties so soon.

His mind rushed backward. At two-and-twenty, he had hied himself off to adventure in the Caribbean. He had taken over the running of the family plantation. The vast acreage had been of little value when he had assumed the role as owner. Through hours of back-breaking labor, he had created a domain he could be proud of, made the plantation the success it was today.

He had known one day he would be called back home. He had known he would face responsibilities beyond anything he had handled in the past.

But he hadn't expected his father to die so soon.

Or to inherit a title and lands that had been stripped completely bare.

His father's grip slackened, his energy drained. The corner of his mouth drooped as it had before. "Promise me…"

Royal swallowed. His father was dying. How could he refuse his dying wish?

"Please…" the duke whispered.

"I will marry her, Father, as you wish. You have my word."

The duke made a faint nod of his head. A slow breath whispered out and his eyes slowly closed. For an instant, Royal feared he was dead. Then his chest weakly inflated, and Royal felt a sweep of relief. Releasing his father's cold hand, he slipped it beneath the covers and eased away from the bed. He paused long enough to build up the fire, then left the suite.

As he stepped outside, he spotted Rule pacing the hallway. His brother jerked to a halt as Royal quietly closed the door.

"Is he…?"

"He is as he was." He released a breath. "He has arranged a marriage. The woman comes with an enormous dowry, enough to begin rebuilding the family lands and holdings. I have agreed to the match."

Rule frowned, drawing his black eyebrows together. "Are you certain that is what you wish to do?"

Royal's mouth barely curved. "I am not sure of anything, brother, except that I have made a vow and now I must keep it."

* * *

The burial of the Duke of Bransford took place on a windy, overcast, frigid morning in January. The proceedings had actually begun several days earlier, with a lengthy funeral service given by the Archbishop at Westminster Abbey. It was attended by a score of nobles and dozens of London's elite.

Afterward, the coffin was transported to the village of Bransford via an extravagant black carriage and four matching black horses for a graveside service and the final interment of the late duke's body in the family's private plot adjacent to the village church.

A number of family members were in attendance, including the duke's aging aunt, Agatha Edgewood, Dowager Countess of Tavistock, as well as numerous other aunts and cousins, some Royal hadn't known existed. Some, like vultures, had come to discover if they might receive a bequest in the late duke's will. Those few had a surprise in store for them since little unentailed property or monies remained in the family coffers.

Royal stared down at the gleaming bronze casket that held his father's remains and a thick lump swelled in his throat. He should have come home sooner, should have spent more time with the man who had sired him. He should have helped him manage his vast affairs. Perhaps if he had, the dukedom wouldn't have fallen into ruin. Perhaps his father wouldn't have worried himself into an early grave.

Royal gazed at the coffin, which blurred for an instant behind a film of tears. His father was gone. The sixth Duke of Bransford had passed away peacefully two hours after the arrival of his middle son.

Reese and the duke had been cosseted together briefly, and another vow was made. By no later than the date his twelve-year enlistment was up, Reese would leave the military and return to Wiltshire. He would take over the lands and manor at Briarwood, a nearby property Reese had inherited from their maternal grandfather. He would rebuild those lands and make them and his life productive.

Reese, the most stubborn of the duke's three offspring, enjoyed his freedom, his military life and his travels. He wanted nothing less than being bound to a chunk of land he saw as a place that would hold him prisoner. But in the end, as his father's life drained away before his very eyes, Reese had agreed.

Rule, the wildest and least responsible, had made his pledge before Royal arrived. The duke believed an alliance with the Americans was in the family's best interest. His youngest son had pledged to do whatever it took to make that alliance a fact.

The vicar's words cut into Royal's thoughts, turning them away from events of the past few weeks and returning him to the words being said over his father's coffin.

A sharp wind tossed his long woolen cloak and cut through his heavy black tailcoat and dark gray trousers as he stood at the graveside. Next to him, Reese wore the scarlet-and-white dress uniform of a major in the British cavalry, the breeze slashing at his thick, wavy black hair. He was the most sober of the brothers, his features harder, reflecting the life he lived.

Royal's gaze moved to his youngest brother. Rule had been an unexpected addition to the family, born almost six years after Reese to a mother in ill health who had been warned against having more children. Amanda

Dewar had died in childbirth, leaving Rule in the dubious care of a nanny, his two older brothers and a father who often drank to bury his grief or hid himself away in his study.

Rule had survived to become the most reckless of the three. He had a reputation as an incorrigible rake and he wore it proudly. He loved the ladies and seemed to make it a personal challenge to bed as many beautiful women as he possibly could.

Royal almost smiled. His own future had already been decided. He would marry a woman named Jocelyn Caulfield. A woman he had yet to meet. She was out of the country at present, enjoying a European tour with her mother. Royal was glad.

The period of mourning for his father would last a year. There would be time enough to arrange a marriage after that.

Meanwhile, he had money of his own, income from Sugar Reef, funds sufficient to keep the dukedom afloat, if not enough to rebuild the fortune his father had lost.

In time it would happen, Royal vowed. He would not rest until he saw it done.

In the meantime, he would learn what he could of his duties as duke, investigate his holdings, see how best to resurrect his father's flagging investments and try to make them profitable again.

As his father had said, it wouldn't be easy.

Royal vowed that by the time he was wed, he would know how to best use the money gained from the marriage his father had arranged.

Two

London, England
One Year Later

Jocelyn Caulfield stood in front of the cheval glass in her bedroom overlooking the gardens at Meadowbrook, her family's mansion at the edge of Mayfair in a district of larger, newer homes. Dressed in a corset, chemise and drawers, the garments as ruffled as the white silk counterpane on her four-poster bed and the crisscross curtains at the windows, she surveyed her curvaceous figure in the mirror.

"I hope I am not putting on weight." She clamped her hands on the bone stays that trimmed her waist to a scant eighteen inches and frowned, pulling her sleek, dark eyebrows together over a pair of violet eyes. "What do you think, Lily?"

Her third cousin and companion of the past six years, Lily Moran, laughed from a few feet away. "You have a perfect figure and you know it."

Jocelyn smiled mischievously. "Do you think the duke will notice?"

Lily just shook her head. "Every man who sees you notices, Jo." Though the women were both average in height, unlike Jocelyn, Lily was blond and slender, with pale sea-green eyes and lips she considered a little too full. She was pretty in a more subtle, less vibrant way, not at all like Jo, who was the sort to stop a man where he stood and leave him simply staring.

"Have you finished packing for the trip?" Jocelyn asked. Which meant, *Lily, have you also finished mine?* Jo didn't trust Elsie, her ladies' maid, to choose exactly the right wardrobe for a trip to meet her soon-to-be-betrothed, the Duke of Bransford. It was Lily she trusted, Lily, one year older, whom she had come to depend on over the years.

"I am nearly finished," Lily said. "I have everything but your undergarments laid out for you in your dressing room. All you have to do is have Phoebe pack the gowns away in your trunks before you leave."

Jocelyn turned to survey her figure from a different angle. "I wonder what the house will be like. Father says Bransford Castle is quite a dreadful place—though I gather, until the last few years, it was one of the grandest homes in England. It isn't truly a castle, you know. It is only three hundred years old. It is huge, Father says, four stories high, built in a U shape with an interior garden and any number of turrets and towers. It even has a hedge maze."

Jocelyn's smile displayed a set of perfect white teeth. "Father says I should have a marvelous time putting it back to rights."

Lily smiled indulgently. "I am certain you will." Though she imagined Jo would be bored with the project after the first six months and her mother would wind up finishing the remodeling and redecorating the newly titled duchess would require of her lavish country home.

"I hope Mother and I will be able to endure such quarters. I am glad we shan't be staying much more than a week." Just long enough for Jocelyn and her future betrothed to get acquainted. "I am so glad I decided you should travel to Bransford a few days early. That should give you time to make the place comfortable for us."

"I'm sure the duke will do everything in his power to see to you and your mother's comfort, Jocelyn."

Jo reached over and took hold of Lily's hand. "But you *will* take care of it personally, won't you? You know the things that please me…exactly how I like my cocoa in the mornings, how hot I like the water in my bath. You will prepare the servants, explain my special needs?"

"Of course."

Jocelyn started to turn away, then whirled back. "Oh, and don't forget to take the dried rose petals. They scent my bath just perfectly."

"I won't forget." Lily had been taking care of Jocelyn since the day she had arrived at Meadowbrook six years ago. It had been quite a change for Lily, who had been living in poverty since her parents had died of the cholera when she was twelve years old.

On her sixteenth birthday, her uncle, Jack Moran, had made the announcement that Lily would be leaving the attic garret where they lived. From that day forward, she would be residing with her wealthy cousin, Henry Caulfield, and his wife, Matilda, acting as companion to their fifteen-year-old daughter and only child, Jocelyn.

Lily hadn't wanted to go. She loved her uncle. He and his friends were the only family she had, once her parents were gone. She had begged him to let her stay, but he had refused. Jack Moran was a sharper. He earned his living by taking money from other people. Once Lily had begun to mature into a woman, he was determined she would escape the sort of life he led.

She remembered their last day together as if it were burned into her brain.

"It's just too dangerous, Lily," he had said. "'Twas only last week you dropped that man's wallet and nearly got nabbed by the police. You're growing up, luv, becoming a woman. I want you to have a better life, the kind your mama and papa would have wanted you to have. I should have done this long before now, but I…"

"You what, Uncle Jack?" she asked tearfully.

"But you're all the family I have, luv, and I'm going to miss you."

Lily remembered how hard she had cried that day and the awful, sick feeling in her stomach when her uncle left her at the door of Henry Caulfield's mansion. She hadn't seen Uncle Jack since that fateful day and Lord, how she missed him. Yet, deep down inside, she knew he had done the right thing.

Lily looked over at Jocelyn. "I shall be leaving first thing in the morning. The newspaper says a storm may be coming in, perhaps even snow. I want to get there ahead of the weather."

"Do take the traveling coach, dear. Just send it back once you arrive. If it should rain or snow, Mother and I will wait a few more days, leave as soon as it clears enough to travel. That should give you plenty of time to put things in order."

"I am certain it will." Lily walked over to the gilt and ivory dresser and began to sort through Jocelyn's night-wear, choosing what to include in her trunks. "I heard the duke's aunt Agatha will be there to act as hostess for our visit."

"So I gather. I've never met her. Apparently, she rarely comes to London."

"Nor does your duke."

Jo sniffed as if the thought was entirely repugnant. "I am certain, once we are wed, that will change."

Lily just smiled and pulled out a soft cotton night-gown with roses embroidered around the ruffled neckline. "They say your duke is quite something—tall and well built, with hair the color of ancient gold. I've heard he is incredibly handsome."

One of Jocelyn's dark eyebrows went up. "He had better be. I shan't marry him if he is unpleasant to look at—even if he is a duke."11

But Lily imagined that Jo would marry the man no matter what he looked like. She wanted to be a duchess. She wanted to continue the lavish lifestyle she was used to, wanted the attention and high-ranking social position that came with the title. In truth, Jocelyn wanted everything.

And thanks to a father who spoiled her no end, she usually got what she wanted.

"You are leaving, Your Grace?" The butler, Jeremy Greaves, hurried forward as Royal strode across the entry toward the door. "If I may be so bold, Your Grace, your visitors are expected to arrive at any moment. What will your betrothed think if you are not here to greet her?"

What indeed? "I remind you, Greaves, we are not yet officially betrothed."

"I understand, sir. Still, she will expect you to properly welcome her to Bransford Castle."

Undoubtedly. It was the height of bad manners to be gone from the house when the lady and her mother arrived. He glanced at his butler, a gray-haired old man with watery blue eyes, and kept walking. It occurred to him that few servants would be bold enough to gainsay a duke, but that didn't stop Greaves or Middleton, who had lived at Bransford since before Royal was born.

"If she gets here before my return," he said, "tell her I was called out unexpectedly. Tell her I will be back very shortly."

"But, sir—"

Pulling on his kidskin gloves, Royal continued toward the heavy wooden door. Greaves scurried ahead and pulled it open, and Royal strode outside.

A storm had blown in last night, but instead of raining, it had snowed. He paused at the top of the wide stone steps to survey the beauty of the frozen landscape, the sun shining down through the clouds, making the countryside glisten. The circular drive in front of the house was covered by several inches of snow and the naked branches of the trees along the lane glittered with a sparkling layer of gleaming white.

Royal took a deep breath of the clean, crisp air and descended the steps. One of the grooms had his gray stallion, Jupiter, saddled and waiting. Fortunately, his father hadn't had the heart to sell Royal's favorite horse. Dressed in riding breeches, a dark blue tailcoat and high black boots, he vaulted into the saddle, his heavy scarlet cloak swirling out around him.

He whirled the stallion, nudged the animal into a trot, then a canter, the sound of hoofbeats muffled by the thick layer of snow. As Jupiter carried him down the road, he cast a last glance at poor old Greaves, who stared worriedly from the porch.

He would be back at the house before Jocelyn arrived, he told himself. In the meanwhile, he needed a little time to prepare. The fact he'd had more than a year to ready himself for this meeting seemed inconsequential. He simply wasn't yet ready for marriage and certainly not to a woman he had never met.

Still, he would keep his word.

Royal urged the stallion into a gallop and turned off on a narrow dirt road that bordered the fields surrounding the house. It was white for as far as he could see, the trees twinkling in the sunshine as if they'd been sprayed with starlight.

Twelve thousand acres surrounded Bransford Castle. That much land meant dozens of tenants, all of whom looked to him to make important decisions. The acreage was entailed with the title, or much of it would probably have been sold.

Royal shifted in the saddle. He didn't want to think of his duties now. He simply wanted to clear his head and prepare himself to meet the woman who would share his future.

He rode for a while, took several different lanes and

crossed a half-dozen fields. It was time he returned to the house, time to accept what could not be changed.

He took a different route home, skirting a dense grove of yew trees and eventually winding up on the road leading from the village to the castle. As he rounded a bend in the lane, something glinted off the snow up ahead. With the sun reflecting off the ice, it was incredibly bright. Royal squinted and tried to make out what it was.

Urging the horse from a walk to a canter, he rode closer, began to hear an odd, creaking sound in the light breeze blowing off the fields. All of a sudden, the images all came together, a carriage lying on its side, one of the wheels spinning whenever the breeze pushed it. In the field to the left, the carriage horses, still in their traces, stood huddled together as if awaiting further instruction.

Royal spotted the coachman lying next to the road. He urged the stallion closer, rode up beside him and swung down from the saddle. Kneeling next to the driver who lay unconscious in the snow, he checked for cuts or broken bones. A nasty gash on the head seemed the man's only injury. Royal made a quick survey of the area, searching for anyone who might have been in the carriage and been thrown from the coach. He climbed up and looked through the open door, but saw no one and returned to the man on the ground.

Apparently sensing Royal's presence, the coachman groaned and began to awaken.

"Take it easy, friend. There's been an accident. Don't try to move too swiftly."

The beefy man swallowed, moving his Adam's apple up and down. "The lady…? Is she…is she all right?"

Worry gripped him. A woman had been in the carriage. Royal glanced back at the overturned conveyance, noticing for the first time the opulence of the gleaming black coach. His gaze shot to the four blooded bay horses in the field, animals of the finest caliber, and a chill went down his spine.

"Jocelyn…" Rising swiftly to his feet, he began a second search of the area around the coach. Vast fields of white blinded him and for a moment, he couldn't see. A further search and he spotted her, lying like a broken doll in the thick layer of white covering the field. She was dressed in a modestly cut gown of rose velvet, her fur-lined cloak bunched beneath her still figure.

Royal hurried toward her, knelt at her side. He checked for a pulse and felt a strong, steady throbbing beneath the soft skin at the base of her throat. She was unconscious, but he saw no blood or other obvious injuries. He gently checked her limbs for broken bones but discovered none that he could see. He prayed her injuries were not internal and that she would soon recover.

When a soft moan slipped from her lips, he took her cold hand and rubbed it between his gloved fingers, hoping to warm her, hoping she would awaken. "It is all right," he soothed. "I'm the Duke of Bransford and I'm going to take you home." He was hesitant to move her, but when her eyes fluttered, lifting long golden lashes away from her pale cheeks, he breathed a sigh of relief.

"Your…Grace," she whispered.

"Just lie still. There was an accident. You're safe now and everything is going to be all right."

For the first time, he allowed himself to look at her.

She was as beautiful as his father had said, with a slender figure and delicate features. Lying in the snow, her skin was nearly the same white hue. Her mouth was full, her lips delicately curved, though paler, he imagined, than they usually were. A bonnet fashioned of the same rose velvet as her gown lay several feet away. Her golden hair had come loose from its pins and tumbled around her slender shoulders. Her eyes opened wider, a lovely pale shade of green.

She moistened her lips. "I think I…must have hit my head."

"Yes… Perhaps when you were tossed from the carriage." He removed his glove and felt her cheeks, her forehead, as smooth and clear as glass. "Are you hurt? Can you tell where you might be injured?"

Her pretty mouth faintly curved. "I am too cold to know."

He almost smiled. He could feel her shivering and wondered how long she had been lying out here in the snow. He thanked God he had come along when he did. "I need to get you somewhere warm. I'm going to lift you. If it hurts in any way, tell me and I will stop."

She nodded and her eyes slid closed. Very carefully he lifted her into his arms and cradled her against his chest. The big gray stallion stood a few feet away. Royal set her sideways in the saddle then swung up behind her, settled her gently in front of him and eased her back against his chest.

"All right?" he asked, sliding his arm protectively around her waist to hold her securely in place.

She turned her head and her sea-green eyes fluttered open. When they settled on his face, something tugged deep inside him. Royal felt as if a hand had reached inside his chest and begun to squeeze his heart.

"Just a little…dizzy." Her eyes slowly closed, then flashed open again. "The coachman…Mr. Gibbons…is he…is he all right?"

Royal's gaze went in search of the man. The driver was on his feet and walking into the field to collect the horses.

"He appears to be fine. Was there anyone else in the carriage?"

"No, just me."

Her mother was to have come with her, he thought. It seemed odd she would be traveling without so much as a ladies' maid.

The explanation would have to wait. Royal rode toward the coachman, careful to keep a firm hold on the lady in his arms.

"Can you make it back to the village?"

The driver grunted a yes. "Just a bit of a bash on the head, is all. I'll ride the wheelhorse back to town, get the animals properly stabled till I can put the carriage to rights."

"Good man. I'm the Duke of Bransford. I'll see to the lady. If you need anything, just send word to the house. Everyone knows where it is."

"'Twere highwaymen," the man said darkly. "Tried to outrun 'em, but there were ice on the road. They were gone when ye got here?"

"I saw no one, just the overturned carriage." A jolt of anger followed his answer. Brigands had attacked the coach! Perhaps they had searched the overturned vehicle and taken anything of value. A similar incident had happened a month ago on the road outside Swansdowne, a nearby village. Royal had hoped it was a onetime occurrence.

He flicked a last glance at the coachman, caught a wave as the stout man began leading the horses onto the road then swung up on the back of the wheelhorse. Royal watched him ride away, thinking of the highwaymen who had caused the accident. He gazed out across the fields but saw no sign of them.

An angry sigh whispered out, turning white in the frosty air. He would worry about the highwaymen in due course. In the meantime, his lady needed care.

Royal returned his attention to the woman in his arms—the woman he was going to marry. As he looked into the serenity of her lovely pale face and recalled her sweetly feminine figure and soft green eyes, he thought that perhaps being married wouldn't be such a terrible fate after all.

Three

❧❧❧

Handing Jupiter's reins to a waiting groom, Royal eased Jocelyn off the horse and down into his arms. Greaves made an odd, sputtering sound as he opened the door and saw the Duke of Bransford carrying a half-conscious woman up the wide stone steps of the porch.

"There was a carriage accident on the road a few miles this side of town," Royal explained. "Miss Caulfield was tossed out of the vehicle. Send someone to fetch the physician." Greaves scurried toward a footman who stood at the back of the entry, one of only fifteen servants in the house, all that were left of the eighty-five men and women the household had once employed.

The footman bolted for the door while Greaves dispatched orders to various other servants, including instructions to fetch the lady's trunks from the overturned rig. Royal didn't slow, just continued up the wide, carved mahogany staircase, the lady nestled against his chest, her rose-velvet skirts draped over his arm.

"She needs someone to attend her," he said as

Greaves hurried to catch up with him. "Has Aunt Agatha arrived yet?"

"She sent word ahead. She should be here within the hour."

He nodded, looked down at his future wife. "Which room is to be hers?"

"The duchess's suite, Your Grace. It was the nicest in the house."

Because his father couldn't bear to sell the elegant furnishings in his beloved wife's bedroom. Though it wasn't quite the thing to ensconce a duke's future bride in a room adjoining his before they were married, it was probably the right decision.

Royal turned the silver handle on the door and kicked it open with his boot. Greaves raced ahead to turn back the covers on the big four-poster bed, then headed for the windows to draw back the heavy damask curtains. The chamber was done in a soft, sea-foam green with lovely rosewood furniture, a room his mother had loved.

He wondered if Jocelyn would approve, looked down at her as he laid her on the bed, and realized her eyes were open and that they were the exact soft green hue as the chamber.

"How are you feeling?" he asked. Pulling off his gloves, he reached down to take hold of her hand. It was icy cold and he realized she was shivering.

"The fire, Greaves. The lady needs warming." But the old man had already set to the task and low flames were even now beginning to lick the hearth. A soft knock sounded and, with his permission, the door swung open to admit one of the chambermaids, who carried a long-handled warming pan hot from the kitchen. Another maid appeared to help remove the lady's gown and get her settled beneath the heated sheets.

"I'll come back once you are at rest," he promised, stepping impatiently into the hall to wait. He could hear the maid chattering away while she warmed the sheets and found himself smiling at Jocelyn's sigh of pleasure as she settled into the deep feather mattress.

Another maid appeared. "I've a heated brick, Your Grace."

He nodded his approval and she disappeared into the room to place the warm brick beneath the lady's feet.

"It feels wonderful," Jocelyn said to the women as they quietly fled the room. "Thank you all so much."

Royal didn't wait for the door to close, just eased it open and walked back into the room. He smiled down at the woman in his mother's bed and tried not to think that once they were wed, she would be spending most of her nights in his. "I hope you are feeling a little better."

Jocelyn smiled up at him. "My head still hurts, but now that I am warm, I am feeling a good deal more myself."

"The physician should be here soon, and my aunt is due to arrive at any moment, so you will be properly chaperoned."

"I look forward to meeting Lady Tavistock."

"As she looks forward to meeting you."

She moved to sit up a little and winced.

"Are you certain you are well enough to sit?"

"I need to get my bearings."

He reached over and helped her adjust the pillows.

"Thank you. I appreciate your care of me, Your Grace. When the highwaymen attacked, I wasn't sure I would ever reach this place alive."

Instead of leaving as he had planned, he sat down in the chair beside the bed. "Tell me what happened."

Jocelyn nibbled her lush bottom lip and Royal felt a stirring in his loins it was far too soon to feel.

"I am not completely certain. It all happened so quickly. The coach was rolling toward the house and of a sudden I heard men shouting, then the sound of galloping horses."

"Go on," he gently urged.

"I leaned out the window and saw them. They were pounding down on us, four men, each wearing a cloth tied over his nose and mouth. They had almost reached us when the carriage hit a patch of ice. I remember the coach tipping sideways. I remember seeing the doors fly open. That is the last I recall."

He squeezed her hand. "It is over now. Do not think of it anymore. Just try to get some rest."

She smiled at him so sweetly his chest tightened. "I'm immensely grateful you came along when you did. If you hadn't, I should probably still be lying out there, frozen utterly stiff by now."

He smiled. "But I found you and now you are safe."

She gave him a last soft smile and her eyes slowly closed. Royal resisted an urge to lean over and press his lips against her forehead. "Sleep well, Miss Caulfield."

Her lovely pale green eyes popped open. "Oh, I am terribly sorry for the misunderstanding, Your Grace. But you see, I am not Miss Caulfield. I am her cousin— Miss Lily Moran."

Royal stalked down the hall toward his study. He shoved open the door and walked straight to the sideboard, dragged the crystal stopper out of a decanter of brandy and poured himself a liberal drink.

Upending the glass, he swallowed the burning liquid in one big gulp, hissed out a breath and poured another, then turned and started toward the fire blazing in the hearth.

"As you rarely imbibe before nightfall and not much even then, I take it your day has not got off to a very promising start."

Royal's head jerked toward the sound of his best friend's voice. Sheridan Knowles, Viscount Wellesley, lounged in a deep leather chair in front of the fire.

"So far, it's been a rotter."

"I heard about the brigands. Greaves says your lady was in the carriage that was attacked. I hope she is all right."

"The lady is going to be fine. Unfortunately, she is not mine."

Sherry sat forward in his chair, a tall man with light brown hair and a slightly long, aristocratic nose. His eyes were green, but a far more brilliant shade than the soft color belonging to the woman upstairs.

One of Sherry's finely arched eyebrows went up. "An interesting statement. Care to explain?"

Royal sighed. "The woman in the carriage was not Jocelyn Caulfield. Her name is Lily Moran and she is Jocelyn's cousin."

"I see… Well, actually, I don't understand a'tall. What exactly is your future fiancée's cousin doing here instead of your unofficial fiancée?"

"Apparently, Miss Moran acts as companion to Miss Caulfield. She came ahead to prepare things for her cousin and Mrs. Caulfield."

"Prepare things…? She sounds more like a servant than a companion."

Royal took a drink of his brandy, felt the comforting burn. "I am not exactly sure what role she plays. I only know she is beautiful and gentle and if I am to be married, I should have been happy to take her to wife."

"Ah, I think I am beginning to see." Sheridan rose gracefully from the chair, walked over and poured himself a brandy. "After meeting the lady, you had begun to resign yourself to the inevitable. Now you are back where you started, uncertain what might lay ahead."

"I suppose that's about it."

Sheridan slid the stopper back into the decanter, making the crystal ring. "Best to think positively. You were satisfied merely with the cousin. Perhaps your future bride will be far more beautiful and even more to your liking."

But Royal didn't think so. There was something about Lily Moran that had struck him from the moment he had laid eyes on her lying there in the snow. The feeling had grown stronger as he had witnessed her worry for the coachman and sensed her gentleness, a quality that would have complemented his more aggressive nature. And of course there was the powerful physical attraction he had felt the instant he lifted her into his arms.

He would have to subdue it. He would soon be betrothed to another. Miss Lily Moran was never meant to be his.

Royal lifted his glass and downed a goodly portion of his brandy.

"So what of the highwaymen?" Sherry asked. "That

is the reason I am here. As soon as the coachman reached the village, word spread like a snowstorm. As there was also an incident last month, I thought perhaps we should discuss what might be done."

Sheridan lived at Wellesley Hall, his country estate, lands that bordered Bransford to the east. Royal and his brothers had grown up with Sherry, who was Royal's same age. They'd been chums at Oxford, both of them members of the school's famous eight-man sculling team. Royal and Sherry and four others of the eight had remained close friends ever since. The other two team members had joined the military but still kept in touch as much as they could.

Sherry had even traveled to Barbados for an extended visit when he realized Royal did not intend a quick return home.

"I had hoped the first robbery might be an anomaly," Royal said. "I hoped the men might take their ill-gotten gains and hie themselves off somewhere to spend it, never to be seen or heard from again."

"Apparently that is not the case."

"No, apparently not."

"The sheriff has already been informed. He will probably wish to pay a call on your…excuse me, on Miss Moran."

Royal glanced upward, as if he could see through the ceiling into her bedroom. "I'll tell her. At the moment, she is still not feeling well enough for visitors."

"And the robbers?"

"It's been a month since their last attack. I doubt they will strike again anytime soon. Still, it wouldn't hurt to organize some sort of nightly patrol."

"Good idea. I'll see to it myself. My men will take the first two weeks. If nothing happens, yours can take the next."

Royal nodded. He felt better knowing the roads would be protected. He did, after all, still have a bride making her way to his house.

Royal swore softly and swallowed the last of his drink.

Lily slept the rest of the day and didn't awaken until the following morning. She glanced toward the window to see a dense layer of clouds hanging low in a gray-purple sky and a spray of white flakes floating down to earth. Noticing she lay in a huge four-poster bed and the walls of the room were a soft pale green instead of the cream color of her room at Meadowbrook, her mind spun, trying to recall exactly where she was.

Then it all came tumbling back: the trip to the country, the highwaymen and the overturned carriage.

The Duke of Bransford coming to her rescue.

His image came sharply into focus and her heart began thrumming as she remembered her first sight of him. Kneeling beside her, against the white of the snow, he looked like a tall, golden angel come to earth. If her head hadn't been pounding like the very devil, she might have believed she was dead.

Even now, if she closed her eyes, she could recall the way it felt to be held in his arms, remember his worry for her safety, his gentle care of her.

Lily shook her head to dislodge the memory, making her head throb again. The duke belonged to her cousin, a woman far more capable of dealing with a man of his power and social position.

Lily knew the duke needed money to rebuild his family holdings. It was the reason for the alliance being made between the Dewars and the Caulfields. Lily didn't even have a dowry. And even were she wealthy as Croesus, her past would never allow her to enter into such a lofty union.

Which, of course, didn't matter in the least.

Jocelyn would be arriving a few days hence and her cousin's stunning beauty and voluptuous figure would snare the duke's interest as it did most every male. One look at Jo would offset the brief flash of disappointment Lily had glimpsed in the duke's tawny eyes when he had learned she was not his future betrothed.

If it hadn't been entirely imagined.

Lily took a deep breath and reached for the silver bell the chambermaid had placed beside the bed. She rang it briefly and a few moments later the door swung open, admitting one of the young women who had attended her last night, Penelope, she recalled.

"Good morning, miss." The red-haired girl made a very proper curtsy.

"Good morning, Penelope."

"It's just Penny, miss."

"All right, then, Penny. Could you please help me get dressed? I am still a little weak."

"Aye, miss. Your trunks were collected from the carriage. I'll have them brought up to your room while I fetch tea and cakes for your breakfast."

"Thank you, that would be lovely."

It was less than an hour later that Lily was dressed and ready to face the day. Descending the stairs, careful to keep a hand on the banister in case she experienced a fresh round of dizziness, she went in search of the duke.

She looked much more presentable this morning, in another simple, remodeled version of one of Jocelyn's gowns, a warm russet velvet with cream lace trailing from the sleeves and running in small rows down the front. The maid had drawn Lily's silver-blond hair into a tight chignon at the nape of her neck and she had pinched her cheeks to add a bit of color.

At the bottom of the stairs, she encountered the butler, a thin, elderly man with milky blue eyes. "I am sorry to bother you, Mr…?"

"Greaves," he said, looking her up and down. "May I help you, Miss Moran?"

"I am looking for His Grace. Would you see if there is a convenient time I might have a word with him?"

"I shall inquire, miss. If you will please follow me, you may await him in the Blue Drawing Room."

"Thank you."

He led her in to a once-elegant room off the entry. It had high, molded ceilings, robin's-egg-blue walls that were in need of a coat of paint and heavy, dark blue velvet draperies. The Persian carpets, a deep royal blue in a paisley design accented with dark green and crimson, were worn but serviceable and immaculately clean.

Her bedroom had also been clean, she reflected, a concern she wouldn't have to address. She sat down on a blue velvet settee to await the duke's presence, wondering if he would truly be as handsome as she recalled.

Wondering if now that he realized she was little more than a servant, the duke would see her at all.

She shifted on the sofa, watched the hands on the ormolu clock slowly turn. She glanced up as he walked into the drawing room and her breath hitched. The golden-haired duke was even more beautiful than the angel she recalled. Now that her vision was no longer blurred and her head not throbbing, she could see that he was stunningly good-looking.

And even with his well-formed features and slanting dark gold eyebrows, there was no question of his masculinity. He wore it like the long scarlet cloak that had swirled around him when he had knelt beside her in the snow.

She rose to her feet a little uncertainly and dropped into a curtsy. "Good morning, Your Grace."

He strode toward her, stopped just a few feet away. "Good morning, Miss Moran." His eyes were as golden as his hair and as they skimmed over her, she thought she caught a glint of appreciation.

"You appear to be recovering very well. How are you feeling?"

"Much better, I am happy to say. Again, I thank you for your very timely rescue."

"I assure you it was my pleasure." The glint was there again, as if there was a secret meaning to his words. She basked in it as his gaze ran over her even more thoroughly. And yet in just a few days, once he met the incredibly lovely creature he would marry, that glint would disappear.

Lily lifted her chin. "I wished to speak to you, Your Grace, in regard to Mrs. Caulfield and your future betrothed, my cousin Jocelyn. The reason I traveled here ahead of time was to insure their visit would be comfortable. Both Mrs. Caulfield and my cousin have rather…specific needs. I am here to see those needs are met."

His eyebrows drew slightly together. "And your

cousin and her mother didn't believe my staff would be able to handle those needs?"

She had angered him. She could see it in the set of his jaw. "Oh, it isn't that—truly. Please, I didn't mean any insult. It is merely that they are used to having things done in a certain fashion. If you would be kind enough to put a few members of your household at my disposal, I am sure I could have everything arranged before they arrive."

"You are Miss Caulfield's cousin, is that correct—a member of the family?"

"A distant cousin, yes. The Caulfields were kind enough to take me in after my parents died of the cholera." She didn't mention it was four years later and they were barely aware of her existence until her uncle sought them out and asked them for help. Still, she was extremely grateful. It was one of the reasons she worked so hard to please them.

"So you were orphaned," he said softly, and for an instant she felt the burn of tears. Even after all these years, her parents' death remained a difficult subject.

"I'm afraid so, yes."

His look seemed to gentle. "I see…"

And to her humiliation, she thought that indeed he did see. That he realized she was merely a poor relation who lived by the Caulfields' charity, that she was utterly dependent upon their goodwill. Still, it was far better than living on the street, or in an attic garret, as she had done before.

"The servants won't be a problem. You may have the use of whomever you wish. Let me know if you need anything else."

"Thank you, Your Grace."

He studied her a few moments more, assessing her in some way, then he turned and strode out of the drawing room. The instant he disappeared, Lily released the breath she hadn't realized she had been holding. Her heart was clattering, beating a frantic tattoo.

It was ridiculous. Things were exactly as they should be. The duke understood her lowly position and his interest was now very properly fixed on Jo.

Ignoring the little pinch in her chest, Lily lifted her skirts and started across the drawing room. She had a great deal of work to do if she was going to be ready for the Caulfields' arrival. She had almost made it to the door when a frail, silver-haired woman stepped through the open drawing-room door.

"You must be Miss Moran." The woman smiled, digging creases into her powdered cheeks. "I am Lady Tavistock. My nephew told me I would find you in here."

Lily sank into a curtsy. "A pleasure to meet you, my lady."

"I arrived yesterday afternoon while you were asleep. I gather you had a rather nasty accident on the road."

"Yes, my lady."

"Dreadful thing. My nephew said your carriage was attacked by highwaymen and overturned, and that you suffered a head injury. I hope you are feeling better."

"Much better, thank you."

"Why don't we sit down in front of the fire. The weather outside is dismal. A cup of tea should be just the thing."

She had so much to do before Jocelyn arrived. And yet there was no refusing the wishes of a countess. "That would be delightful, my lady."

They sat down on the sofa in front of the fire blazing in the hearth and a few minutes later the butler arrived with the tea cart. Tea was served. Casual conversation was made. Lily tried not to glance at the clock on the white marble mantel, but apparently she failed to hide the urgency she was feeling.

"I can tell you are eager to begin your tasks."

Lily flushed and wished she had been more attentive. "It is only that I have a great deal to do before my cousins arrive."

"Are your cousins, then, difficult taskmasters?"

She rarely thought of Matilda Caulfield as a cousin, though by her marriage to Henry she certainly was.

"It is nothing like that. It is just that my cousin Jocelyn…depends on me. She trusts me to see to her needs, as I have done these past six years. I do not wish to fail her, or Mrs. Caulfield."

"I see. And exactly what did your cousin Jocelyn and her mother send you here to do?"

More color rushed into her cheeks. Taking over the duke's household and assigning tasks to his servants was hardly the proper thing. Still, it was what the Caulfields expected of her and she meant to see it done.

"Only small things, really. I—I need to inform the cook that Miss Caulfield prefers biscuits and cocoa up in her room each morning instead of a meal downstairs. And I'd like to make certain the room she occupies has a nice view of the garden."

She bit her lip, thinking of the endless items on her list. "My cousin doesn't do well with dust. I shall need to speak to the housekeeper, make certain the carpets in her bedroom have recently been beaten."

"I see."

"Just very small things, truly, my lady. I hope it won't be too much of a bother."

Lady Tavistock set her gold-rimmed porcelain cup and saucer down on the table in front of her. "You may do whatever you think is necessary to make our guests comfortable."

"Thank you, my lady."

The dowager rose from the sofa and Lily rose, as well.

The lady reached for her cane. "I suppose I had best let you get on with your work." She smiled. "I enjoyed our visit, Miss Moran."

Lily relaxed. "As did I, Lady Tavistock." She watched the dowager countess leave the drawing room, silver hair gleaming in the light of the whale-oil lamps lit to offset the dark, cloudy day, her head held high though her movements were slow and a little wobbly. She was the late duke's aunt on his mother's side, Lily knew, a widow who lived in a manor house on one of her late husband's estates.

Happy to have the meeting behind her, Lily made her way back out to the marble-floored hall. The list of tasks to be completed awaited her upstairs. It was time she got to work.

Four

~~~⌒◦⊙◦⌒~~~

The following day, Royal sat in his study, his elbows on the desktop, his head propped in his hands. A stack of estate ledgers lay open in front of him. His eyes burned from the hours he had spent reviewing the pages.

During the first nine months after his father's death, he had spent most of his time learning about Bransford Castle and its surrounding lands. Aside from the estate's own farm production, there were dozens of tenants on the vast acreage. Royal had met with each family individually to discuss what improvements might be made to help production, benefiting them and increasing their profits, a percentage of which belong to the estate.

During his years in Barbados, he had studied books on agriculture and used that knowledge to help make Sugar Reef the successful plantation it was today.

Since his return to England, he had been exploring the most modern methodology, trying to find the best way to stop the declining income stream from the agricultural production and instead turn a profit.

One of the ideas he had implemented was the construction of a brewery on lands in the nearby village of Swansdowne. He intended to brew very high-quality ale, which, he was convinced, was the most profitable use of the Bransford barley crop. As he had done with the sugar produced at Sugar Reef, he intended to market Swansdowne Ale as the finest in England. He also intended to increase the estate's sheep herds and perhaps put in a woolen mill. All of that took money, of course, of which—at least until he married—he had little.

Royal released a breath, the notion of money returning his thoughts once more to the ledgers on the desk in front of him. In the last thirty days, he had begun to study the accounts that reflected former Bransford holdings, including several mills and a coal mine, properties his father had sold in order to raise money.

He had also studied the investments his father had made over the last several years.

At first the amount the late duke had invested had been small, the losses of little consequence. About three years ago his father's health had begun to decline, though, at the duke's insistence, Royal had never really known how severely. In an effort to recover the money, larger, even more poorly chosen investments were made and the losses began to mount.

Good money followed bad, and the duke began to sell his unentailed holdings in order to pay off his debts. Even the house itself was not safe from ransacking, as evidenced by the sale of the priceless paintings and statues missing from the castle, and the estate's run-down condition.

Royal raked a hand through his hair, dislodging several heavy, slightly wavy strands. He looked up at the sound of a familiar rap on the door. The panel swung wide and Sheridan Knowles stood in the opening. Never one to stand on formality, he strolled into the study.

"I see, as usual, your nose is buried in those damnable ledgers. I suppose I am interrupting."

"Yes, but since I am not particularly happy with what I am finding in the pages, you may as well sit down."

Sherry walked forward with his usual casual ease, pausing for a moment at the sideboard to pour himself a brandy. "Shall I pour one for you?"

Royal shook his head. "I've too much yet to do."

Sheridan studied the rich golden-brown liquid in his glass, just a little darker than his hair. "I just stopped by to tell you the patrols have been organized. My men will start tonight, cover the area around Bransford and Wellesley, and also the road between here and Swansdowne."

"Well done."

Sheridan sauntered behind the desk and looked over Royal's shoulder at the big leather volumes lying open on top, some of the writing on the older pages beginning to fade. "So what are you finding that you do not like?"

Royal sighed. "I am seeing thousands of pounds draining away as if they were sand poured down a rat hole. For the last few years, my father made one bad investment after another. It is a difficult thing to say, but after he first took ill three years ago, I don't believe his mind was ever quite the same."

"A lot of rich men make poor investments."

"True enough, but up until that time, my father wasn't one of them." He turned several pages, glanced down at the writing in one of the columns. "See here, for example, money that quite literally went up in smoke. Last year, my father invested in a cotton mill near Bolton. Six months later, the mill caught fire and burned to the ground. Apparently, the company had no insurance."

Sheridan shook his head. "Certainly a thing like that wouldn't have happened to the shrewd, formidable man your father used to be."

"No, indeed. I've hired an investigator, Sherry. A man named Chase Morgan. Perhaps it's a waste of time and money, but I want him to look into the companies in which my father invested. I want to find out which men wound up with the late Duke of Bransford's fortune."

Sherry sipped his drink, pondering the notion. "It couldn't hurt, I don't suppose. And you never know, you might discover something interesting."

Royal shoved back his chair and came to his feet. "The money is gone. There isn't much I can do about it now. Still…"

"Still…it never hurts to find out what happened in the past. As they say, it is often the key to the future."

Sheridan walked over to warm his hands at the fire and Royal followed. "So where are you headed from here?" he asked.

"Back to Wellesley, I imagine. Though I rode over mostly to escape the house."

"I am feeling a bit closed in, myself." Royal clamped a hand on his friend's wide shoulder. "How about some company?"

"I daresay, I'd like that. I take it your Miss Caulfield hasn't arrived."

"I'm sure she is still in London, waiting out the storm."

Sherry set his brandy glass down on the sideboard and the men walked into the hall. As they did, the door at the opposite end leading to the kitchen downstairs swung open and Lily Moran stepped into the passage. Her russet velvet skirt was covered with white streaks of flour, and as she approached, her mind clearly elsewhere, Royal glimpsed a spot of flour on her nose. He grinned at the charming sight she made.

Her light eyes widened at the sight of the two men. "Your Grace," she said, her hands shooting up to smooth a loose strand of pale blond hair. "Oh, dear, I must look a fright."

"You look…" *Lovely,* he wanted to say but didn't. "Only a bit worse for wear." He smiled and turned to introduce Sherry. "This is my good friend, Sheridan Knowles, Viscount Wellesley. "Sheridan, may I present my houseguest, Miss Lily Moran."

Sherry's green eyes ran over her, taking in the gleaming hair, feminine features and lush, full lips. His gaze lowered to the curve of her breasts and the tiny waist beneath, and Royal felt an unexpected surge of jealousy.

"A pleasure, Miss Moran."

"It is good to meet you, my lord." Nervously, she brushed at her sleeve, also dusted with flour. "I hope you'll excuse my appearance. There was an incident in the kitchen—" She glanced up, her gaze shooting toward Royal as if she'd said something wrong and was worried he would scold the servants. "Nothing untoward, Your Grace, just an overturned flour tin—but somehow I managed to wind up in the middle of it."

Royal found himself smiling. "Just be careful you don't get too near the oven. You might turn into a loaf of bread."

Her laugher, like crystal prisms in the afternoon breeze, was so sweet his chest contracted.

"I shall heed your advice, Your Grace."

Sherry gave her a long, assessing look. "Should you wind up toast, I would like nothing better than to eat you up, my dear. You're even prettier than Royal said, Miss Moran."

Lily blushed and Royal wanted to throw a punch at Sherry.

"I really should go up and make myself presentable. If you gentlemen will excuse me…"

"Of course." Sheridan made a modest bow.

"I shall see you at supper," Royal said, though seeing Lily Moran was the last thing he should be wanting.

Lily slipped by them and continued down the hall, her velvet skirts swaying enticingly. Turning, she started up the stairs.

"You were right. The girl is quite lovely." Sheridan's gaze followed Lily's slender figure, his eyes remaining on the staircase even after she disappeared. Royal wanted to grab him by his starched cravat and shake him till his teeth rattled.

Sheridan smiled. "Then again, as I said, perhaps the cousin will be even more luscious." He grinned, exposing a pair of crooked bottom teeth that should have detracted from his appearance but did not. "Then you can leave Miss Moran to me."

Royal said nothing, but his jaw clenched so hard it hurt. He had no claim on Lily Moran and never would. If Sheridan wanted her—to hell with Sherry, he thought for no explicable reason, and started for the door.

"I thought we were going for a ride," he said darkly,

pausing in the entry to allow Greaves to drape his cloak round his shoulders.

Sheridan still gazed up the stairs. "Of a sudden, I would rather stay here."

Royal ground his jaw, jerked open the door and strode out into the falling snow. Behind him, he heard Sheridan chuckle then the sound of his boots coming down the wide stone stairs.

The following day at the end of an afternoon ride to check on one of his tenants, Royal returned to the house, his stomach pleasantly filled with the mutton stew and tankard of ale he had enjoyed at the Boar and Thistle Tavern in the village. Handing his cloak to Greaves, he looked up at the sound of a commotion going on in the corridor upstairs. Recognizing the sweetly feminine voice of his houseguest, he climbed the staircase and headed down the hall to find Lily, a pair of footmen and two chambermaids rearranging the furniture in one of the bedrooms.

She looked up at his appearance and a hint of color washed into her cheeks. Her silvery hair was tied back with a kerchief and she wore an apron over her dress. Still, she looked beautiful.

"I—I hope you don't mind, Your Grace. I moved my things into one of the other bedrooms. I thought Jocelyn should have the one that was meant to be hers."

He didn't say that he liked having Lily in the room adjoining his, where he could imagine her lying on the big bed in nothing but a soft white cotton nightgown, embroidered, perhaps, with tiny roses. He didn't say that last night he had imagined unbuttoning the row of pearl buttons at her throat and nibbling his way down to her breasts.

Instead he said, "As you wish."

"Also…your housekeeper, Mrs. McBride, suggested a very nice room for Mrs. Caulfield that also overlooks the garden. If you don't mind…I'd…um…like to exchange a few pieces of furniture with those from one of the other bedrooms."

Meaning the furniture in the room was worn or in need of repair. He knew Mrs. McBride had done her best, but until the house was refurbished, it would never exhibit the grandeur of the place he had lived in as a boy.

"As I said, you are free to make whatever changes you wish."

"Thank you, Your Grace." She returned to her task, ordering the servants about and pitching in herself to help with whatever needed to be done. It was clear she took her duties seriously, but Royal thought it a little unfair that the Caulfields should treat her more like an employee than a member of the family.

One of the footmen reappeared, carrying an ornate writing desk Lily had procured from a room on the opposite side of the hall. She directed the man where to place it in the room, then, realizing Royal still stood in the corridor watching her activities, a nervous smile appeared.

"Mrs. Caulfield will enjoy the desk," she explained. "She likes to keep in touch with her friends."

"It's a beautiful piece of furniture. I'm a little amazed it's still here."

She seemed surprised he would allude to his poor financial straits. "Yes…from the looks of it, a good deal of the original furnishings are missing."

"After my father fell ill, his finances took a turn for the worse. It was his greatest wish to see the house brought back to its earlier magnificence."

"Jocelyn seems eager to help in that regard."

"That would certainly please my father, God rest his soul."

"Would it also please you?"

His lips edged up. "I love this place. It bothers me to see it in such disrepair."

She glanced down the long corridor, the paint yellowed and the wallpaper peeling in places, the rugs faded and worn. "It must have been beautiful. I'm sure it will be again." The smile she gave him was warm and hopeful and his body flushed with heat.

Dammit to hell, an attraction to his soon-to-be fiancée's cousin was not at all what he wanted.

"Let me know if there is anything else you need," he said a bit more harshly than he intended. Leaving her to complete what other tasks she had planned, he made his way down the hall to change out of his riding clothes.

The afternoon was slipping away. Soon he would be joining his aunt for supper. Tonight for the first time since her accident, Lily would be joining them.

Royal swore softly as he stepped into his suite and firmly closed the door.

Five

She didn't want to go. Lily considered pleading a headache, as she had done for the past two nights, but she simply couldn't ignore her host and hostess any longer. Still, the notion of sitting through a meal with the duke made her stomach quiver. Every time she was around him, she felt nervous and flushed and not quite certain what to say.

It was ridiculous. He was only a man, after all, not the golden-haired angel she had imagined when she had been lying there in the snow.

He was handsome, yes. But beauty was only skin deep. At the balls and soirees she'd attended with Jo, she had met dozens of handsome men. It had never bothered her before.

Lily didn't understand it. As a child, she had been shy, but in the years she had lived with her uncle, she had learned to overcome it. Living in Jocelyn's shadow for so long seemed to have brought its return.

Still, she usually did quite well in the presence of the

opposite sex. Perhaps it was knowing this particular male belonged to her cousin.

As the little maid, Penny, helped her fasten the buttons at the back of her aqua silk gown, she wondered when Jo would arrive and hoped it would be soon. The sooner the duke met his stunning future bride, the sooner this ridiculous attraction Lily grudgingly admitted to feeling would be over.

One could hardly be attracted to a man who looked through her as if she were not there, and she knew from experience, once Jocelyn arrived, that is exactly what the handsome Duke of Bransford would do.

"Gor, ye look lovely, miss."

Lily smiled at the dark-haired girl. "Thank you, Penny." She turned in front of the cheval glass, pleased at the changes she had fashioned in Jo's cast-off dinner gown. She had removed the extra ruffles around the hem and across the bodice, leaving only a single flounce of aqua satin across the bosom, which she adorned with a spray of tiny seed pearls.

The gown looked brand new, which it practically was, since Jo rarely wore a dress more than once and was happy to hand them off to Lily to change in any way she pleased.

She moved to the dresser, lifted the lid on the small rosewood box she had brought with her and removed a lovely peach-colored agate cameo hanging from a black velvet ribbon. It wasn't an expensive piece of jewelry, but it was one of her favorites, a gift from the Caulfields on her eighteenth birthday.

She held it out to Penny, then turned her back. "Could you tie it for me, please?"

"Of course, miss."

Penny set the cameo at the base of her throat and tied the ribbon round her neck. With her pale hair pulled away from her face and pinned in a cluster of curls at her shoulder, she felt ready to face the duke and his aunt across the supper table.

Taking a breath for courage, Lily swept out of the room and headed down the wide mahogany staircase. She found the duke and his aunt conversing in an antechamber that led into the elaborate formal dining room. She had hoped for a more casual evening, but with the dowager in residence, she should have known it wasn't going to happen.

"Ah, Miss Moran," the duke said, striding toward her. "We were afraid you'd had another brush with the kitchen maids."

He was smiling, teasing her, but with his aunt in the room, she was embarrassed. "Nothing of the sort, I assure you." Her cheeks burned. "I hope I haven't kept you waiting."

"Not a'tall," the dowager said with a smile. "Royal was telling me about the flour incident in the kitchen. The last time I was here, I slipped and took a tumble into the bushes in the garden. They had just been watered. I came up looking like a half-drowned wren."

Lily laughed, feeling a sweep of gratitude for the old woman's effort to put her at ease, which seemed to work quite well. "I haven't been below stairs lately, but should I visit in the future, I shall attempt to be more careful."

"Accidents happen," the duke said, smiling.

"More often to some of us than others," the dowager added with a twinkle in her eyes, nearly the same tawny shade as her nephew's.

"Cook has supper ready," the duke said. "May I

persuade you ladies to continue this discussion in the dining room? I find I am nearly light-headed with the need for food."

As was she, Lily realized, and couldn't help wondering if the man was truly that hungry or if he had guessed she had been so busy she had eaten only the cakes and cocoa she'd had for breakfast. She had a feeling it was the latter.

Drat it, she wished he would be less congenial. Surely there was something to dislike about him. But as he moved beside his aging aunt, taking great care not to walk too swiftly and provide the supportive arm she needed, as he seated her and then Lily, one on each side of him, she couldn't think what it might be.

The first course was served, a delicious oyster soup, the creamy broth lightly seasoned with herbs and floating with lemon slices, probably grown in the estate's conservatory.

"Have you heard from your brother Rule?" Lady Tavistock asked, taking a hearty spoonful of soup.

"He is finishing up at Oxford," the duke replied. "He has been offered a job with an American company once he is out of school—a liaison position of some sort, I gather. If he accepts, he will be traveling there and back quite often."

He glanced over at Lily. "It was our father's wish that our family develop an alliance with the Americans. Rule promised to make that happen. And I think he may be excited at the prospect of seeing a different country."

"I would love to see America, myself."

The duke smiled. "So you crave adventure, do you?"

Lily smiled back. "Only in my head, I am afraid.

Mostly, I enjoy reading books about other people's travels."

"As do I," the duke agreed.

"Royal spent a good many years in the Caribbean managing the family plantation," his aunt added. "Did a fine job of it, too."

"I enjoyed the challenge," he said. "I hope I am up to it here at Bransford. There is far more at home that needs to be done than there was at Sugar Reef."

"With the right woman at your side," his aunt said, "I am certain you will manage quite well."

Royal looked down at his bowl of soup and Lily wondered what he was thinking.

"So you enjoy reading," the dowager said to her.

"Very much. I read just about anything I can get my hands on."

"There is a library full of books here at Bransford," the duke said. "You are welcome to borrow whatever you might find interesting."

She felt his golden gaze on her face and something warm settled low in her stomach. "Thank you."

"What have you heard of your brother Reese?" the older woman asked, breaking the strangely intimate moment. Lily wondered if that was the dowager's intent. Her nephew was, after all, practically engaged to another woman.

"Reese is fighting the Russians in the Crimea at the moment. Though I haven't heard from him directly for a while. Apparently, getting letters posted is difficult, but at last word he seemed quite healthy."

"I am glad to hear it. With your brother Reese, one never quite knows what to expect."

Royal turned to Lily. "Reese is a major in the cavalry—a true adventurer. Still, we are all hopeful he will eventually leave the military and return to a more settled life here at home."

They continued the meal in pleasant conversation and Lily was surprised at how comfortable she was made to feel.

Until Lady Tavistock turned the conversation to Jocelyn.

"So when do you expect the Caulfields to arrive?" the dowager asked.

"Soon, I should think. At least soon after the weather clears a bit and the roads become passable."

"Do tell us a little about your cousin. What sort of woman is she? What are her interests?"

"Jocelyn is beautiful," Lily said without pausing to think. "Outrageously so." It was the first thing anyone noticed about Jo. "She has very dark hair and the most amazing eyes. They're the color of violets, you see. I don't believe I have ever seen anyone with eyes that exact color."

"Go on," the countess urged, obviously intrigued.

Lily faltered a moment, trying to describe a woman who was completely indescribable. "Jocelyn loves parties. She is extremely outgoing. She enjoys dressing in the height of fashion and she looks marvelous in whatever she chooses to wear." She glanced up. "Oh, and she's a very proficient rider. Her father made certain of that."

"Well, that is good news," the dowager said with a smile, "since Royal has a great love of horses."

But Jo didn't particularly like animals, just the thrill of speed and the feeling of mastery over a beast much larger than she.

The dowager looked over at her nephew. "I daresay, if Miss Caulfield enjoys parties, then perhaps we should have one here at Bransford. A small soiree, perhaps? A bit of music and dancing, just a few of our neighbors and some of our friends. What do you say, Royal?"

He took a sip of his wine, set the crystal goblet back down on the table. The house was no longer the showcase it once was, but Lily thought it could be made quite presentable.

"If you and Miss Moran are up to the challenge, I think it would be fine."

"Well, what do you think, Miss Moran?"

"I would be more than pleased to help."

"Marvelous. We'll begin making plans on the morrow." The old woman delicately sipped her wine, the goblet shaking in her frail hand. "Anything more you can tell us about your cousin?"

Lily dredged up a smile. "To be honest, Jocelyn is not easy to describe. She is a very unique person. You will understand once you meet her."

Lily couldn't help wondering how that meeting would go. She wasn't concerned with the duke, who wouldn't be able to see past Jo's alluring exterior. It was Lady Tavistock she wondered about. The old woman seemed extremely intelligent and keenly perceptive. Lily tried to imagine what the dowager would think about the woman meant to wed a nephew who seemed to hold a very special place in her heart.

A warm sun brightened the landscape, melting the last of the snow. Eager for a ride, Royal strode down a corridor near the back of the house on his way to the stables, passing several little-used drawing rooms along the way.

Rounding a corner, in a portion of the hall whose rooms faced the garden, he noticed the door of the Daffodil Room, one of the smaller drawing rooms, stood open.

He paused in the doorway, saw that a low fire burned in the hearth. His eyes widened as he recognized the woman perched on the yellow damask sofa. Sunlight streamed in through the windows, turning her hair a silvery gold.

Royal's gaze took in her surroundings. Swatches of fabric in a variety of colors and textures were strewn over the backs of the chairs. The table next to one of them was littered with yarn, streamers of ribbon, bows, feathers and imitation fruit.

Though he made no sound, Lily's head came up as if she sensed his presence. Her gaze snared his and he felt the familiar stirring of heat. This time it settled low in his groin and his sex stirred to life. The air seemed to thicken and warm between them until his shaft rode hard against his belly. Royal was glad he was wearing his riding coat to hide his unwanted desire.

A door closed down the hall, breaking the moment, and Lily jolted to her feet. "Your Grace…I—I hope you don't mind… Mrs. McBride said it would be all right if I used this room for my sewing. She said it was rare anyone ever came in here."

"It isn't a problem. You are welcome to use the room for as long as you wish." He glanced at the array of items that seemed in no way connected to any given purpose. "But if I may ask—what exactly is it you are sewing?"

She held up the item in her lap. "Hats, Your Grace. I fashion ladies' bonnets." She retrieved a finished product off the table in front of her, a bonnet of mauve silk with a wide brim surrounded by dyed feathers and velvet bows. The hat should have looked gaudy, but it did not.

"I think you must be very good at making hats, Miss Moran."

She smiled and it felt as if something pulled loose inside him.

"I believe I am, Your Grace. Not to be immodest, but I sell a very good number. Usually I have trouble finding time to fill all my orders."

"Good for you."

"I suppose making hats isn't exactly *the thing*, but I hope one day to open my own millinery shop."

"I think if you want your own shop, you will have it. I believe you could have whatever it is you want, Miss Lily Moran."

She stared at him and something flickered in her sea-green eyes, then it was gone.

"I hope you are right. I can hardly live with the Caulfields forever. Once you and Jocelyn are married, I shall wish to go out on my own."

He didn't offer a place for her there. If he did, sooner or later, he would give in to the powerful temptation she posed. Lily deserved more than a brief seduction and so did the woman he intended to wed.

"Most women think to marry," he said softly. "They want a husband and children."

"I want that, too…someday." She grinned, giving him a saucy look that made him want to kiss her. "But not until I have my shop!"

Royal laughed and so did she. He cleared his throat. "I suppose I should leave so that you can get back to your work."

She looked down at the bonnet in her hand. "I suppose you should."

"Have a good afternoon, Miss Moran."

"You, as well, Your Grace." Her eyes held his a moment longer, then she jerked her gaze away and sat back down on the sofa. Royal watched the delicate hands, the slender, feminine fingers working the needle through the fabric, and clamped down on an image of those elegant hands skimming over his naked body.

Turning away, he strode to the door of the drawing room without looking back. Silently he prayed God would see that the woman he meant to marry arrived at the castle very soon.

Six

⊱⊷⊶⊶⊷⊰

Amid great fanfare and household commotion, the duke's future bride arrived. A boy from the village rushed in with the news, giving the duke and his meager staff time for last-minute preparations, his aunt to make her way to a seat in the Grand Drawing Room—and Lily time to compose herself.

She was grateful for that. She knew what would happen when Jocelyn arrived. His Grace would be stunned by the beauty of his future wife and Lily would become invisible. It was inevitable and yet just thinking about it made her ache a little inside.

Half the household hovered in the entry as the Caulfields' fully restored, elegant black traveling coach rolled up in front of the castle. Footmen rushed down the steps to unload the carriage, a groom appeared to help the driver with the horses, and the housekeeper, Mrs. McBride, a short, stout woman with iron-gray hair, appeared in the entry to assist the guests.

The butler held open the heavy wooden door and

Matilda Caulfield marched into the entry like the duchess she meant for her daughter to become. A few steps behind her, Jocelyn swept into the house.

One of the footmen stopped dead in his tracks.

The butler's watery blue eyes focused and stared.

Dressed in an amethyst gown that matched the brilliant color of her eyes, Jocelyn was stunningly beautiful, her features perfectly symmetrical in her pale, exquisite face. Her nose was straight, her lips the shade of roses. Her thick chestnut hair, pulled back in glossy curls, nestled against her shoulders.

Perhaps she had stopped at the inn in the village to freshen and change, for her gown was the height of fashion and not the least bit wrinkled or travel-stained. High-necked and long-sleeved, it showed not the slightest glimpse of her voluptuous bosom and yet the tempting swell beneath the gleaming silk was apparent above her tiny, corseted waist.

Jocelyn spotted the duke, standing in the entry to greet her, and her eyes widened in pleasure at his tall, golden masculinity, equal and opposite to her own feminine appeal.

Lily felt a sickening lurch inside her as the duke stepped forward. He bowed slightly to Matilda Caulfield and then to Jo. "Welcome to Bransford Castle," he said. "My aunt and I have been eagerly awaiting your arrival."

Matilda Caulfield, tall and broad-hipped, with the same dark hair as her daughter's but now streaked with silver, managed a pleasant nod of greeting. "As we have been eager to get here."

Jocelyn graced him with one of her heart-stopping smiles. "Thank you for inviting us, Your Grace."

Formal introductions were made all round. Lady Tavistock was smiling, looking pleased with the bride the late duke had chosen. All Lily wanted to do was run away.

"I am glad you arrived safely," the duke said. "I hope your journey was not too unpleasant."

"Not at all," Matilda said.

"The roads were dreadful," said Jo with an airy wave of her hand. "I told Mother we should wait another few days, give the roads a chance to dry out, but she wouldn't listen. We suffered for it, I can tell you. Wet, cold and miserable all the way here." She sighed dramatically. "At any rate, we are here now and that is all that matters."

The duke's tawny eyes assessed her. "Indeed," was all he said. He turned to the housekeeper. "I am sure the ladies are tired from their journey. Mrs. McBride, would you please show our guests up to their rooms."

"Certainly, Your Grace."

The household once more scurried into action, footmen running up the stairs, hauling trunks and satchels and hatboxes, the upstairs chambermaids making a final check of the guest rooms.

"I hope you will find your accommodations satisfactory," the duke said. "Your cousin, Miss Moran, has made every effort to make sure you are comfortable."

Matilda tossed Lily a glance. "I am certain we will be."

Jocelyn hurried over to Lily and took hold of her hand. "I've missed you, Lily. Come upstairs with me, won't you? You can help me unpack and decide what to wear down to supper."

Lily just nodded. Waiting for the group to follow the housekeeper up the stairs, she fell in behind the assembly making its way to the second floor. As she passed the duke, she wasn't the least surprised to see his tawny gaze following Jocelyn's sensuous figure up the wide carved staircase.

Her stomach quivered. Ignoring a ridiculous feeling of abandonment, she continued up the stairs behind her cousin.

That night, Lily took supper in her room. Though Jocelyn tried to coax her into joining the group in the dining room, it was time she returned to the shadows.

Matilda Caulfield did not press the issue.

"My God, man." Sheridan Knowles stood next to Royal in the entry. Halfway up the staircase, Jocelyn made her way to her room on the second floor. Sherry had arrived unannounced, as usual, two days after the Caulfields' arrival. Royal had introduced him to Jocelyn, who afterward excused herself and was now on her way upstairs for her afternoon nap.

Both men watched until she disappeared.

"My God." Sherry still stared.

"You've already said that." Turning, Royal walked past him down the hall into his study. Sherry followed him inside and closed the door.

"She's the most beautiful woman I've ever seen."

Royal paused at the sideboard and poured himself a liberal shot of brandy, which seemed to be a habit these days. "She's beautiful. I can hardly argue with that."

He had just finished luncheon with his aunt, his future bride and her mother, an affair that seemed to have no end.

"Your father certainly came through for you."

Royal took a swallow of his drink. "He certainly did."

Sheridan tipped his head back, studying Royal down the length of his slightly too-long nose. "She certainly won't be a burden to bed."

"I'm a man. She's an extremely beautiful woman. It will hardly be a burden."

Sherry eyed him shrewdly. "All right, so what is it you don't like about her?"

Royal blew out a breath, raked a hand through his dark blond hair. "Nothing. At least nothing that would keep me from marrying her. It is merely that we share very few common interests."

"What does that have to do with anything? You will marry her, bed her and she will give you children. On top of that, you will have the luxury of making every man in London jealous of your incredibly beautiful wife. Along with that neat little package, you will also gain control of her incredible dowry and very sizable inheritance. What more could any man ask?"

He shook his head. "Nothing, I guess. Jocelyn will make the perfect duchess, just as my father said."

Royal took another drink, set the brandy snifter down on his desk. "Apparently, she's a very good horsewoman. After her rest, I'm showing her a bit of the estate."

His future bride seemed to require a good deal of rest, he thought, sleeping late in the mornings, then napping half the afternoon. He tried not to think of Lily, working dawn till dusk to prepare the house for her cousins. When she wasn't moving furniture or seeing that the rugs were beaten, she was fashioning bonnets for her wealthy clientele. He couldn't remember Lily every complaining about being tired.

"So she likes horses, does she?"

"Apparently."

"There—you see, you do have something in common. Tell me, how do you think she feels about you?"

How did Jocelyn feel? He wasn't sure. His future wife wasn't an easy person to read. Either she was good at controlling her emotions or she didn't have any.

"I don't know her well enough to tell. Perhaps she will open up a bit more this afternoon, when we are away from her mother." They would be riding with a groom, of course, since neither Mrs. Caulfield nor his great-aunt Agatha could act as chaperone. He was actually looking forward to the ride, hoping he would discover something in his bride-to-be that would draw them together.

Sherry sank into one of the leather chairs in front of the fire, draped a long leg over the arm. "Well, if you decide you don't want her, let me know. I'll be happy to act as a substitute groom."

Royal grunted. "I thought you wanted Lily."

Sheridan grinned, exposing his crooked bottom teeth. "She doesn't come with a fortune, my friend."

Royal downed the last of his drink. "That I should marry Jocelyn and rebuild the Bransford fortune was my father's dying wish. I promised him I would see it done and there is nothing on this earth that could stop me from keeping my word."

Sherry rose from his chair. "Then I shall hold good thoughts for you this afternoon. May you find in your delectable companion whatever it is you seek in a suitable bride."

Royal gave a faint nod of thanks, knowing Sherry

meant every word. He was a man whose friendship Royal valued greatly.

"I suppose I had better go out to the stable and find the lady a suitable mount. Thank God my father didn't sell all of his blooded horses."

"One last piece of advice?" Sherry offered, not really seeking his permission. "Kiss the lady. That ought to give you some idea of how the woman feels."

Royal smiled. It wasn't a bad idea. As Sherry followed him out of the study, Royal thought that for once he might actually heed his friend's advice.

"Help me with the buttons, will you, Lily?" Jocelyn presented her back then stood impatiently as her cousin buttoned her sapphire velvet riding habit. It was cut in the military fashion, with rows of small brass buttons marching up the front. Jocelyn had only just received it, along with her latest order from the modiste. Lily had fashioned the matching miniature top hat, which Jocelyn thought complemented the outfit quite nicely.

She settled it at a jaunty angle on top of her head, pinned it in place and pulled the tiny scrap of veil down just enough to cover her forehead.

"How do I look?" She turned to give Lily a better view.

"Hold still." Lily walked over and shoved a pin into Jocelyn's hair, fastening a stray curl in place, then stepped back to assess her. "You look perfect. The duke will not be able to take his eyes off you."

Jocelyn frowned. "Do you think he is truly pleased with me? It is difficult to tell how he feels."

"The man is a duke. He is trained not to show his emotions. I am sure that is all it is. This afternoon, he will have you mostly to himself. Perhaps he will let down his guard a bit."

Jocelyn certainly hoped so. She had been sure the duke would be far more impressed with her than he seemed to be. He hadn't made one comment about her beauty, as most men did. In fact, he seemed to have only marginal interest in spending time with her.

Perhaps he was simply busy with his affairs. His estate was vast. There was surely a good deal to do to keep it running smoothly. Today would be different, she told herself.

"Have a nice time," Lily said as Jocelyn made her way toward the door.

"Are you sure you don't want to come with us?"

"You know I don't ride very well. Besides, this is your chance to get to know him."

Jocelyn nodded. She was looking forward to the afternoon, of course, but there was something about the duke that made her nervous. She flirted and teased as she usually did, but he seemed to pay little attention. At luncheon she had told a very funny story about a house party she had attended where one of the chambermaids took a tumble down an entire flight of stairs and landed in front of very proper Sir Edward Marley.

Instead of appreciating her humorous tale, the duke had asked if the woman had been seriously injured.

"I was trying so hard not to laugh I didn't notice," she had replied. The duke made no comment.

He was waiting for her in the entry, she saw as she descended the stairs. He was certainly handsome enough, dark blond and fair and amazingly masculine, considering the beauty of his face.

"The horses are waiting out front. I've chosen a gelding named Vesuvius I thought you might like. He is spirited, but not difficult to handle."

"I'm sure I shall enjoy the ride."

They descended the wide stone steps to where a groom waited with the horses, one a tall bay gelding with a white patch on his forehead, the other a magnificent gray stallion. Ignoring the bay, she walked straight to the stallion.

"I think I would rather ride this one. What is his name?"

The duke's dark blond eyebrows drew together. "His name is Jupiter. The gelding is wearing the sidesaddle."

"Surely it would be easy enough to change."

He hesitated only a moment, then motioned to the groom, who rushed forward. In just a few minutes, the saddles were exchanged. The duke lifted her onto the gray, then went to the gelding and swung up on its back. A short while later, they were trotting along the drive, heading off toward the fields, the groom following along behind them.

Jocelyn rode a little ahead, saw an open field and kicked the stallion into a gallop. Following, the duke urged his mount forward and caught up to her easily. Laughing, she urged the stallion faster. He was a magnificent beast, clearly capable of handling the terrain. She spotted a low stone hedge, and the stallion took it easily, landing neatly on the opposite side. She could hear the duke behind her.

"Miss Caulfield, wait!"

Jo nudged the stallion even faster, aiming at a hedge off to the right.

"Miss Caulfield—Jocelyn, wait!"

Jo laughed and neatly clipped the hedge, landing perfectly on the opposite side. Unfortunately, in a shady spot some of the snow had melted into a puddle she hadn't seen. The horse hit the mud and nearly went down. Jocelyn kept her seat, but just barely, and she was furious that the animal had made her look bad in front of the duke.

He caught up with her just as she raised the crop to slam it against the horse's flanks, reached over and jerked it out of her hand.

"What do you think you're doing?" he asked sharply.

"The stupid horse missed my command. You saw him! He nearly unseated me."

"I tried to warn you. The fields are wet. You were riding too fast. It's a wonder you both didn't go down. It's a miracle you weren't injured."

"It was the horse, I tell you. If he had obeyed my command—"

He seemed to be drawing on his self-control. His jaw looked hard, but his words came out softly. "Why don't we ride south. You can see a bit of the forest. There'll be snow left on the branches. It's beautiful this time of year."

Jocelyn sniffed, placated but barely. She could have been injured. The duke should have taken her side, should have whipped the blasted horse for not obeying her command.

She looked up at him, sitting on the bay, tall and broad-shouldered, unbelievably handsome. She supposed she could forgive him. He was going to be her husband, after all.

"I believe we have lost our chaperone," she said, glancing around, but seeing no sign of the groom.

"He'll find us. He knows where we're going."

But Jocelyn was glad he was gone. She wanted a little time alone with the duke. When he reached the forest and suggested they walk for a bit, she readily agreed. The duke tied the horses, lifted her out of the saddle, then took her hand and led her down to a small, bubbling stream.

He stopped at the edge of the water, looked out over the landscape, a very blue sky over rolling hills that held the last traces of snow.

Jocelyn's gaze followed his. "It's lovely, Your Grace."

"I would like it if you called me Royal—at least when we are alone. May I call you Jocelyn?"

She smiled. "I would like that very much."

His gaze roamed over the countryside. "This land means a great deal to me. Once the house is refurbished, do you think you could be happy here?"

She returned her attention to the winter-barren fields stretching as far as she could see and thought how bleak it was. Pretty, in a barren, empty sort of way, but life in the country simply wasn't for her. "I presume we will also be spending time in London."

"If that is your wish."

She smiled with relief, thinking that once they were married, a brief, once-a-year trip to the country would be more than sufficient. "Then of course I could be happy."

Royal reached for her and she didn't stop him when he drew her into his arms. She closed her eyes as he bent his head and kissed her. It was a soft, gentle meeting of lips, a respectable kiss until she opened for him. Royal hesitated only a moment, then deepened the kiss, tasting her more fully, letting her taste him.

He was good at kissing, she thought in some far corner of her mind, his lips soft yet firm, moist but not sloppy. Once they were married, allowing him his husbandly rights would not be a difficult thing.

Royal was the first to end the embrace. He looked up, saw his groom riding over the top of a distant hill. "I think it's time we returned to the house."

Jocelyn glanced over his shoulder and saw their chaperone approaching. "Of course."

He helped her remount, setting her easily in the sidesaddle, then swung up on the back of the bay.

They rode in silence to the front of the castle and a groom rushed forward to take the reins. Royal lifted her down and they climbed the front stairs together. The butler opened the door and they walked into the entry.

Jocelyn spotted her cousin coming down the stairs. "Lily!" she called out to her, catching her by surprise. "Where are you headed in such a hurry?"

Lily turned. "I was just collecting a bit more trim for the hats I am sewing. How…how was your ride?"

"Lovely." Jocelyn thought of the kiss they had shared and beamed up at Royal with a hint of mischief in her eyes. "Quite lovely, wasn't it, Your Grace?"

But he seemed not to hear her. His entire attention was focused on the woman at the foot of the stairs—her cousin, Lily Moran.

Seven

―――∽⤳⟋⤳∾―――

"All right, Lily—" Jocelyn paced back and forth across the Aubusson carpet of the duchess's suite. "I want to know exactly what went on between you and the duke before Mother and I arrived."

Lily just stood there, her insides humming with nerves. "I can't imagine what you are talking about. Nothing the least untoward went on with His Grace. Mostly, I worked all day trying to make things right for you and your mother. The duke was polite to me, but that is all." *Unfortunately,* she thought with a twinge of guilt.

Jocelyn eyed her sharply. "Are you sure, Lily? You certainly seemed to grab his attention when we walked into the house."

Lily worked to keep her mind from straying to that one single moment, that beautiful instant when the duke's gaze seemed focused entirely on her and for once Jocelyn was the one who was invisible.

It couldn't have meant anything. It was merely a trick of the mind.

"You are completely mistaken, Jo. Since when has a man ever given me the slightest glance after he has been introduced to you?"

Jocelyn flopped down on the bed and gave up a little sigh, mollified a bit at the truth of Lily's words. "He kissed me this afternoon."

Lily's stomach tightened. "Did he?"

"He's a very good kisser. I would rate him a nine out of ten."

Jo had a kissing scale? Lily knew her cousin had kissed a number of gentlemen, but she hadn't realized each of them was being rated. "Have you ever kissed a ten?" she asked.

Jo rolled onto her back and gazed up at the green silk canopy above the bed. "Only one. Christopher Barclay. You remember him, don't you? He's the fourth son of some obscure baron. He's a barrister—young, though, not old. We danced at the Earl of Montmart's ball and later we walked in the garden. Christopher kissed me. I should have slapped him, I suppose, but his kiss was definitely a ten."

Perhaps that was so, but Lily couldn't help thinking that if Royal Dewar ever kissed her, it would also be a ten.

Royal. She had never said his name aloud, but lately she had begun to think of him that way, as Royal, instead of His Grace or the duke. It was dangerous, she knew, but she couldn't seem to help herself.

"So how was your ride?" she asked. "Aside from the kiss, I mean."

Jocelyn's lips thinned. "His bloody horse nearly threw me—that's how it was. I couldn't believe it. And he didn't do anything about it."

"What did you expect him to do?"

"It was the horse's fault. I expected him to do *something*."

Lily ignored the outburst. Jo rarely took the blame for anything that happened. Lily wasn't surprised she would blame the horse. "Did you talk about anything interesting?"

Jocelyn shrugged. "He asked me if I could be happy here. I said that I could—as long as we also spent time in London."

Lily thought of the lovely rolling fields, the yew forests and the stream that trickled along the edge of the garden. There was nothing she would like more than to live out here in the country. "I wonder when he'll ask you to marry him."

"Soon, I imagine. We'll only be staying a week, perhaps less. Mother and I decided a shorter visit would be better. She thinks a six-month engagement will be long enough to make all of the arrangements for the wedding. I'm sure the duke will make a formal proposal before we leave for home."

"You don't sound terribly excited."

"Oh, I will be—once our engagement is officially announced." Lying on the bed, she scooted back until her shoulders rested against the elaborately carved wooden headboard. "Can you imagine what people will say? I shall be the envy of every woman in London."

"That is certainly true enough, but have you given any thought to your feelings for the duke? Aren't you the least concerned that you might not love him?"

Jo laughed. "Don't be silly. I don't believe in love. Besides, once I give him an heir, I can take a lover if I wish. I can choose whomever I want and perhaps I will fall in love with *him*."

It seemed so coldhearted. Lily sank onto the stool in front of the dresser. "You can't really mean that."

"Oh, but I do. That is the way it works, cousin, in marriages that are arranged."

Lily swallowed. "I see." But she didn't really see at all. She only saw that Royal would be marrying a woman who didn't love him and had no intention of being faithful. The sick feeling returned to her stomach.

Royal headed down the hall and walked into his study. A man stood in front of his desk. He turned at the sound of Royal's footfalls—medium height, a solid build, jet-black hair and hard, carved features.

"I presume you are Chase Morgan," Royal said, speaking of the man he had hired to find out exactly what had happened to the Bransford fortune.

Morgan made a slight bow of his head. "At your service, Your Grace."

"Have a seat." Royal sat down behind his desk and the investigator sat down across from him. "You've brought news, I take it."

"Indeed, very interesting news. I thought it might be more productive if we could discuss the matter face-to-face rather than trying to communicate by letter."

"I appreciate that. So what have you discovered?"

Chase rose from the chair and retrieved a leather satchel Royal hadn't noticed before. He set it on top of the desk. "May I?"

"Of course."

The investigator opened the case, pulled out a sheaf

of papers and spread them on the desk in front of him. "Each of these pages represents a company in which your father invested. There are millworks, railroads, shipping lines and various trading commodities."

Royal grunted. "None of which managed to earn a shilling in return."

"Exactly so." Morgan singled out one of the papers and slid it in front of Royal. "The interesting thing isn't so much which companies your father chose to invest in, it is who owned these supposed companies."

Royal arched a brow. "Supposed?"

"That's right. None remained in business for more than six months. Most were closed down sooner than that—if they were ever more than merely accounts on paper."

"You are saying they were fraudulent?"

"That is the way it appears."

His mind ran over the implications. "But you don't know for certain."

"Not yet."

He tapped the paper. "How do we find out?"

Morgan pointed down at the paper. "We need to investigate the people listed as owners of these businesses—the Southward Mill, for instance, and the Randsburg Coal Mining Company. There are also corporations named that supposedly own shares in these businesses, which means we need to find out who owns those corporations, as well. I was hoping you might recognize some of the names, be able to tell me something we could use."

Royal sat there a moment, trying to absorb the news as he scanned the list on the page. He reached for another sheet, and another, and finally shook his head. "I am sorry. I don't recognize any of these names."

"I didn't really think you would, but it was worth a try." Morgan sat forward in his chair. "What I need to know is how far you want me to take this?"

Royal tapped the paper. "If these investments were shams, then someone or several someones took advantage of my father in his weakened mental condition. I want to know who these men are."

Morgan nodded. "All right. It may take some time, but sooner or later, I'll find out who brought these investments to your father's attention. There may be any number, but more likely just a greedy few who saw a golden opportunity and seized it."

Royal stood up from his chair. "I want those names, Morgan. Do what it takes to find them."

The investigator stood up as well, an imposing figure with his whipcord-lean body and thick black hair. "I'll send word as soon as I have further news."

Royal walked the man to the door of the study then watched him disappear down the hall. He'd had his suspicions that perhaps his father had been duped, but until today he hadn't been sure.

Unconsciously, his jaw hardened. He would find out who was responsible for the terrible losses his family had suffered. The question then would become—what should he do?

Jocelyn sat in the Blue Drawing Room taking tea with her mother and the Dowager Countess of Tavistock. She would rather have been shopping or perhaps gossiping with some of the young women in her social circle about the ball last night at the Earl of Severn's town mansion, which she had been forced to miss. But after she became a duchess, she could do whatever she pleased.

She nodded at something the dowager said, though she wasn't paying all that much attention. She wished the duke would make an appearance. Plying her charms on a handsome man was always entertaining. Perhaps he would rescue her from the tedious afternoon.

She took a sip of tea from her gold-rimmed porcelain cup, thinking that at least she was enjoying the chance to wear her new striped-mauve silk gown. It was a lovely dress, the skirt fashioned of deep flounces edged with mauve velvet ribbon. She started at the mention of her name and realized the countess was addressing her.

"I'm sorry, my lady, I must have been woolgathering. What did you say?"

"I said my invitation to tea extended to your cousin, Miss Moran. I expected she would be joining us. She isn't ill, is she?"

Jocelyn waved a hand. "Of course not—Lily is almost never sick. She is merely busy making her silly hats. Mother thought it best to leave her to it."

One of the dowager's silver eyebrows went up. "Miss Moran makes hats?"

"Unfortunately, yes." Mother set her teacup down a little too firmly, rattling the porcelain against the saucer. "I am embarrassed to say our dear cousin has ambitions of one day owning a *millinery shop*. I vow, I have never heard the like. I told her it simply wasn't done."

"What sort of hats does she make?" the dowager continued as if the topic was actually of some importance.

"Why, all sorts of hats, ma'am," Jocelyn answered.

"In fact, Lily made the velvet cap I am wearing this afternoon." She turned her head to show off the lovely mauve creation with its clusters of velvet ribbons that matched her outfit.

The countess looked intrigued. "Why, it's lovely. You say she is making hats at this very moment?"

Jocelyn nodded. "In a room somewhere down the hall. She sews hats every afternoon."

The dowager slowly rose to her feet. With a knobby hand, she reached for her cane and used it to steady herself. "I love hats. I believe I should like to see your cousin's handiwork."

Her mother's mouth thinned. Jocelyn merely followed as the old woman made her way slowly down the hall.

"The Daffodil Room, I believe it's called," Jocelyn said. "I think it is at the back of the house."

"I know the room. It has a lovely view of the garden."

A garden that needed a good deal of work, Jocelyn thought. She would hire the best landscape designer in England to modernize the pathways and replace the plants and bring the overgrown mess back into vogue.

The countess paused outside the door to the drawing room, peered in, then walked inside. "So this is what kept you from taking tea with us." She gestured toward the swatches of cloth, ribbons, lace and imitation flowers stacked on the tables and strewn over the backs of the chairs.

Lily shot to her feet, dumping the bonnet in her lap to the floor. She bent and quickly retrieved it. "My lady. I didn't realize you expected me to come. I apologize."

The old woman flicked Mother a glance. "It's all

right, my dear. Now, tell me what you are doing with all of this frippery."

"Making hats, my lady. It is…sort of a hobby of mine."

"Hobby or business?"

Lily glanced at Jocelyn, clearly not wanting to embarrass her.

"The truth, young lady."

"Making hats is my business, Lady Tavistock. I have a number of clients who purchase my designs. I hope to own my own shop one day."

"So I've been told." The countess strolled about the drawing room, using her cane only occasionally. There was a row of finished hats up on the mantel: a dress cap of pearl-gray silk trimmed with moss-green velvet leaves, a headdress of lace and violet ribbons, a leghorn hat with a cap of blond lace.

"I must say, these are quite lovely." She turned to Lily. "I should like very much to commission a hat for myself. Perhaps later this afternoon we might discuss it."

"Oh, my lady, I would be honored to make you a hat."

Mother looked as if she had swallowed an apple core and it was stuck in her throat.

"I realize you are busy with your work," the dowager continued, "but perhaps you might join us for a bit. We shan't be much longer, but a cup of tea would surely do you good."

Lily cast Mother a glance but there was no real way to decline. "Thank you, my lady. That would be lovely."

The old woman leaned on her cane and began a slow shuffle out of the Daffodil Room, returning to the drawing room down the hall. Jocelyn was hoping she could go upstairs for a nap. She was used to late nights attending parties and balls, and all of this country air seemed somehow tiring. She sighed as she walked back into the Blue Drawing Room and resumed her seat on the sofa.

A single thought kept her from yawning. Tonight might very well be the night the duke proposed.

Once he did, she could go back to London.

Royal stood at the window of the sitting room in his bedroom suite. Below him, the infamous Bransford hedge maze formed intricate patterns that culminated in a large marble fountain with cherubs spouting water out of their mouths.

The fountain wasn't easy to find. First, one had to meander along deceptive pathways that seemed to have no end, making dozens of false starts and stops, each avenue enclosed by hedges that took up nearly two acres, and over the years had grown more than ten feet tall.

He grinned as he watched the lady who had made the mistake of entering the maze. His great-grandfather had taken great pride in making it one of the most difficult in the country.

She made a turn, reached a dead end and backtracked, turned the wrong way and started along a path that led nowhere and would propose three alternate routes that also led nowhere. She could be in there for hours.

Royal grinned again. Unless he showed her the way out.

Taking his woolen cloak off the hook by the door, he headed downstairs.

The day was sunny, but there was a crisp, late-January chill in the air, and the grass, brown from the winter frost, was spongy and damp. He stopped at the entrance to the maze, mentally went over where he had last seen Lily and started inside. A couple of turns and he could hear her, mumbling something that sounded oddly like a curse. She started forward, her slender feet padding along on the spongy grass.

"Miss Moran!" he called out. "Lily, where are you?"

"I'm over here!" she called back, relief in her voice, which was coming from a long passage two turns to the left.

"Stay where you are," he instructed. "I'll come and get you."

He knew the maze by heart. He and his brothers had played there since they were boys. He made a couple of turns, took a little-used shortcut and walked quietly up behind her. She jumped when he settled his hands on her shoulders.

Her hand came up to her heart as she whirled to face him. "Good grief, I didn't hear you a'tall."

"The element of surprise. It comes in handy at times." She smiled. "So you came here to rescue me?"

"Just like a knight in shining armor."

"How did you know I was in here?"

"I saw you from my bedroom window."

She gazed down the path in front of her. "I wanted to see the fountain." Her bottom lip turned down in a pout that was rare for her and quite charming. "I thought I could find it."

"Actually, I usually warn our guests not to enter the maze unless they have plenty of time. It's very large and extremely complex. My great-grandfather got an almost demonic thrill out of getting someone lost inside."

She looked up at him with those lovely sea-green eyes and his chest tightened.

"Since you found me, I guess you know how to get out."

"My brothers and I played in here all of the time."

She flicked a glance toward the center of the maze and he read her disappointment. "I guess we should go back."

He knew he should take her back straightaway. Instead, he said, "I thought you wanted to see the fountain."

Her pretty eyes brightened. "Oh, I do!"

Royal held out his hand. "Come on, then, and I'll show you."

Lily hesitated only a moment then clasped the hand he offered. A lightning bolt seemed to arc between them and for an instant he couldn't make himself move. Lily must have felt it, too, for her gaze jerked to his face and warm color washed into her cheeks.

She tried to pull her hand away, but his great-grandfather's blood ran through his veins and some demon inside him wouldn't let go.

"Come on," he urged, his voice a little gruff. Tugging her forward, he led her deeper into the maze. Lily had no choice but to fall in beside him, and for a time they strolled quietly along the narrow paths.

As the minutes ticked past, she began to relax and they strolled along as if they were a couple, instead of two people fighting a forbidden attraction. It would be unseemly if they were discovered, but at the moment, Royal couldn't make himself care.

Eight

Lily felt the tug of Royal's hand and followed once more in the direction he beckoned. The maze had suddenly become more exciting, the solitude more intriguing. Royal seemed even taller in the narrow confines of the hedgerows, his presence all the more powerful out here where they were alone.

She could tell he knew exactly which way to go to reach the fountain in the center of the maze, stopping where it seemed the least likely, turning one way, then heading another. He took another avenue, chose an unlikely path that seemed to lead nowhere and pulled her that way. When they came to a choice between three paths, he stopped and looked down at her.

"All right, you choose which way we should go."

She bit her lip, studying the different routes, deciding on the least obvious one. "The path to the far left."

He laughed. "We could get there that way, but it would take us a whole lot longer. This is the way." He drew her forward and she smiled as she came up beside him. They followed several more twists and turns and finally stepped into the clearing in the middle of the garden.

The fountain loomed ahead and Lily let go of his hand and hurried toward it, thinking the journey had been worthwhile.

"It's lovely," she said, running her fingers round the rim where the water slipped over the edge onto the level below. "I love the sound. There's a fountain in the gardens at Meadowbrook and I go there whenever I can. The sound of the falling water helps me forget my cares."

One of Royal's dark blond eyebrows went up. "You seem happy in your circumstance. What cares do have, Lily Moran?"

She sat down on the bench that encircled the base of the fountain, and Royal sat down beside her.

"I worry about my future after I leave the Caulfields'. I worry that what I've saved won't be enough to open my shop. I worry that if somehow I do manage, the shop won't be a success."

"I don't think you need worry in that regard. My aunt told me how good you are at what you do. She said your hats are quite amazing. I gather she commissioned a bonnet for herself."

She smiled. "In fact, she ordered several. I'm hoping she will like them. It would certainly help my reputation as a milliner to have a countess among my patrons." She looked up at him. "Your aunt is a lovely woman."

"She's very dear to me. To all of us."

"I think you are very dear to her, as well."

A long sigh whispered out, his mood abruptly changing. "She wants me to be happy, but—" He broke off as if he worried he might say something untoward.

"It's Jo, isn't it? You are afraid the two of you won't suit."

Royal raked a hand through his hair, dislodging the gleaming strands. "It doesn't really matter. She's beautiful and charming, well schooled in the things a woman should know in order to become a duchess. The marriage has been arranged. All that's left are the formalities."

"I—I'm sure it will all work out. You and Jocelyn make a lovely couple."

He scoffed. "On the outside, perhaps. But inside…"

Lily's heart went out to him. She couldn't imagine marrying a person someone else had chosen. "Tell me what it is you fear."

His golden eyes came to rest on her face. "Inside it seems as if we are two completely different people. It is difficult to explain. It is just that we seem to think differently, view the world in a different manner." He sighed and shook his head. "As I said, it really doesn't matter. We shall marry and afterward we will make the best of things. Jocelyn will gain a title and high-ranking social position and I will gain the money I need to rebuild Bransford Castle and reestablish the Bransford fortune. That is the way it works."

But he was looking at her as if he had hoped for much more. Looking at her as he had that single instant when their eyes had met that day in the entry. Looking at her as if she was the one who could give him the happiness of which he had dreamed.

Lily's heart twisted. Dear God, even were there the slimmest possibility those were his thoughts, she had to stop them. She wasn't the person he believed her to be.

She wasn't worthy of marrying a duke. She had to tell him the truth.

"I think your father chose very well," she forced herself to say. "Jocelyn was raised in society. She knows how to behave in those circles, how to mingle with people in the upper classes. I, on the other hand, was raised by a poor schoolteacher and his wife—and an uncle who stole for a living."

His head came up. "What?"

Lily took a deep breath, determined that she would tell him all and end this mad attraction they both seemed to feel.

"My mother's grandfather was the Earl of Kingsley. The way Mother told it, the earl's daughter—my grandmother—ignored her father's wishes and ran off with a commoner, a farmer, I believe. The earl disowned her and she never saw him again. My mother also married a commoner—as I said, my father was a teacher." She managed a smile. "Thanks to him, I had a very happy childhood and a wonderful education, but then he and my mother fell ill and died of the cholera, and then…" Her voice trailed off at the tightness constricting her throat.

"Go on, Lily," he gently urged. "Tell me what happened after your parents died."

She swallowed past the lump in her throat. "Then I went to live with the only relative I knew, my father's brother, Jack Moran. The problem was, Uncle Jack had even less money than my parents. Where I had lived in a neat little cottage in the country, Uncle Jack lived in a tiny attic garret above a tavern in London."

She looked up at him, bracing herself to finish the story. "Uncle Jack was a sharper, Your Grace. From the time I was twelve until he left me on my cousin Henry's doorstep, I lived the same sort of life he did."

Royal straightened on the bench, his tawny gaze searching her face. "You aren't saying—?"

"I was a pickpocket at thirteen—one of the very best. I could run a three-card monte and never get caught. I was an accomplished thief who stole whatever we needed in order to pay the rent. When Uncle Jack ran a confidence game, I helped him by playing whatever role he needed. I had always been shy, but I learned to overcome it. By the time I was sixteen, I could play a dozen different parts and in time, I got very good at those, too."

Royal said nothing, but his jaw looked tight. Lily steeled herself against the disgust she knew he must be feeling. Fighting back tears, she forced herself to go on.

"I had hardly been raised to be dishonest and at first I was sick at the thought of stealing. But then we ran out of food and it looked as if we were going to be cast out in the street. Hunger is an amazing motivator, Your Grace. Though Uncle Jack did his best to take care of me, I realized if I wanted to survive, I would have to learn the things my uncle wished to teach me. I would have to do whatever it took to make ends meet. And so I did."

She forced herself to smile, but her bottom lip trembled. "So you see, Your Grace. At least with Jo, you will get exactly the woman you see. With me…I am not at all what I appear."

Her eyes welled. She thought that he would look away from her, perhaps even leave her there in the maze, but instead his big hands reached out and very gently framed her face. "Lily…"

The tears in her eyes rolled down her cheeks. Royal tilted her head back and his mouth covered hers in an achingly tender, breath-stealing kiss. A little sound came from her throat at the jolt of yearning that tore through her, the fierce rush of longing. And though she knew what they were doing was wrong, she couldn't stop her fingers from curling around his lapel, from leaning closer to press herself against him.

Royal groaned and deepened the kiss, their lips melding perfectly together. Lily had kissed men before. As she grew older, playing the role of seductress was sometimes part of a confidence scheme. But Uncle Jack was ever protective and never let things get out of hand.

Lily knew the feel of a kiss, but she had never been touched by one, never felt the sweet unfurling that blossomed inside her now.

"Lily…" Royal repeated, kissing the corners of her mouth, her nose, her eyes, then returning to her lips. The kiss turned wild and reckless, his tongue gliding over her lips, sliding inside to taste her. She could smell the lime of his shaving soap and the starch of his cravat. His woolen riding jacket warmed the tips of her fingers.

A soft moan escaped as he moved to the side of her neck, trailed kisses along her throat, gently nibbled the lobe of an ear. Pleasure washed through her and a deep, burning desire. Royal kissed her one way and then the other, kissed her and kissed her, branding her with the heat of his mouth as if he claimed her in some primal way.

Lily trembled. She slid her arms around his neck and clung to him, felt the solid muscles across his chest where her breasts pillowed against him, and inside her chemise, her nipples went hard. The insane thought occurred that she wanted no barriers between them, wanted to press her mouth against his skin, learn the texture, the scent of him. It was madness, she knew, but the thought remained until her body took over and it became impossible to think, and all she could do was feel.

She had no idea how long the kiss went on, or what might have happened if she hadn't heard a man outside the maze calling Royal's name. She recognized the voice as belonging to his friend, Sheridan Knowles, and the knowledge of what she was doing hit her like a harsh winter wind.

Lily jerked away. She stared into Royal's face, saw that he had also been jolted into awareness. His cheeks were flushed, he was breathing hard, and Lily realized her breathing was as ragged as his.

"It—it is your friend."

He glanced in that direction, his body tense. "They must be looking for us. Sherry came to warn us." He rose to his feet and adjusted his coat over the front of his riding breeches, reached for her hand and urged her up off the bench. "This shouldn't have happened. It was completely wrong of me to take advantage. I am terribly sorry, Lily."

She glanced away, her eyes stinging. "It wasn't your fault. I should have stopped you. You belong to Jocelyn and she is my cousin. Once you knew the life I had led, you must have presumed that I—"

"God, no! I just…I wanted you, Lily. Hearing what you had been through made me ache for you. I wanted to erase those years, protect you in some way." He laughed bitterly. "I certainly did a fine job of that."

He surveyed her dishevelment, wiped the wetness

from her cheeks, reached up and straightened her bonnet, tucked away a lock of her pale blond hair.

"We've got to go." Taking her hand, he started walking, leading her rapidly back through the maze. He stopped just before they reached the entrance. "I'll leave first. Sheridan and I were supposed to go riding. Wait a few minutes then go back inside the house."

Lily nodded. Royal didn't say more, but guilt was stamped into his face. Clearly, he regretted his momentary lapse in the maze.

Lily didn't tell him that long after he was married, she would remember his passionate kiss. And though she would suffer a small ache at the memory, she would know deep in her heart that his kiss was an eleven.

Royal walked up to Sherry and the men exchanged glances. Sheridan was dressed in his riding clothes for their trip to see Squire Brophy. The squire was among several village residents who had volunteered men for the nightly road patrols. Some of the locals had even volunteered to ride themselves.

"I was waiting in your study when I heard the women talking," Sherry explained. "I realized they were looking for you, and that Miss Moran was also missing. Your fiancée-to-be's mother did not seem happy about it."

"What about Jocelyn?"

He shrugged. "She said she imagined you were out in the stable and that Lily was probably in the village buying something for her hatmaking. I don't think she sees her cousin as much of a threat."

Royal just grunted. *If she only knew.* His body still throbbed with desire for Lily. When he moistened his lips, he could taste her there. She had the softest lips he'd ever known, the smoothest, silkiest skin. He hadn't wanted a woman so badly since he had been a green lad lusting after one of the milkmaids.

Royal sighed as he walked next to Sherry toward the stable. It had taken the full force of his will not to open Lily's bodice and slide his hands inside to explore the shape of her breasts, not to make a bed of his cloak, bear her down in the grass, slide up her skirts and bury himself inside her.

If it had been any woman but Lily, he might have continued his unplanned seduction. But Lily wasn't that kind, no matter the years she had spent with her uncle. Royal knew women and this one was innocent of a man's passions. If he'd had any doubt, her untutored, sweetly arousing kisses today would have convinced him.

His body tightened, the memory of her soft mouth under his making him hard all over again.

"So the two of you were in there together, as I thought," Sherry said. "I am beginning to understand the way the wind is blowing. Are you ready, then, to give up your heiress?"

Royal sliced him a glare. "It was only a kiss and it shouldn't have happened. I'm marrying Jocelyn, just as I planned."

"Well, then, I suppose I shall have to settle for her very lovely cousin."

Royal stepped in front of him, blocking his path. "Leave Lily alone."

Sheridan's lips curved in a mocking half smile. "Jealous, are we?"

Royal turned away, determined to convince himself

it wasn't true. "Marriage to Jocelyn will make Lily a distant relative. That means she falls under my protection. She deserves a husband and children—not seduction by a rogue like you."

Sherry straightened. "I wouldn't dishonor the lady, my friend—no matter my past indiscretions. If anyone is at risk of doing that, I believe it is you."

Royal clenched his jaw, but he didn't argue. His best friend was right. Every night as he conversed with the beautiful Jocelyn, he thought of Lily. Lily sitting on the yellow damask sofa with the sunlight silvering her pale golden hair. Lily's crystalline laughter. Lily smiling as they held hands and made their way through the hedge maze.

From now on, he vowed, he would stay as far away from Lily as he possibly could. Better yet, he looked forward to the day she went home.

He glanced over at his friend. "Your point is well made. I have postponed the inevitable too long already. Tonight after the soiree, I am going to propose. Once Jocelyn agrees, I'll go to London to formally ask her father's permission and finalize the arrangement he and my father made."

Sheridan slowed on the path to the stable. "Once you do that, you'll have no choice but to wed her."

"I never had a choice, Sherry. Not since the day I agreed to my father's dying request. I thought you understood that."

It was only a small soiree, no more than twenty people. Lily had helped the dowager countess pen the invitations from a list that included Squire Brophy and his wife, their two sons and their wives; Royal's friend,

Sheridan Knowles; Vicar Pennyworth, his wife and daughter; and Jocelyn's father, Henry Caulfield. Lady Tavistock had invited several widowed lady friends who lived nearby, including the Dowager Baroness Bristol and Lady Sophia Frost.

The pace of living in the country was slow and people looked forward to any sort of social event. Which was the reason that with little more than a week's notice, almost everyone who had been invited had accepted the invitation, all but Jocelyn's father, who was, as always, simply too busy running his numerous businesses to leave his offices in London. Even the incredibly wealthy Marquess of Eastgate, in residence at his country estate near Swansdowne, would be attending, accompanied by his daughter, Serafina.

Lily had been introduced to Lady Serafina Maitlin at several affairs in London. In Lily's opinion, the girl was even more spoiled than Jo, with a far nastier disposition. There was never a man she couldn't enthrall, she believed, which meant, since Jo felt much the same, that the women were bitter enemies.

Lily smiled. At least the evening would be entertaining.

Turning, she took a last survey of the Gold Drawing Room, a room that had been redesigned by the late duke's wife before she died. A lot of wear had taken place since then, but by exchanging some of the worn Persian carpets with rugs in other parts of the house, and bringing in bouquets of fresh flowers, the salon had been made to look quite elegant. The walls could use a fresh coat of paint, but the sienna marble columns and exquisite molded ceilings were as lovely as ever.

The cook and her helpers had worked all day on the buffet to be served in the adjoining Long Gallery, another room that had fared relatively well, since the paintings on the walls were of long-dead family relatives and had not been sold. All was in readiness.

Lily couldn't put off the inevitable any longer. She would have to go upstairs and ready herself for the evening. Last night, she had declined supper and hadn't seen Royal since the interlude in the maze, but she had to face him sooner or later.

By now he would have realized the mistake he had made and banished any affection he might have felt for her. He would see Jocelyn in a different light and be resigned to his upcoming marriage.

Lily told herself it was best for everyone and ignored the heavy weight that had settled in the middle of her chest.

Nine

The duchess's suite was littered with petticoats, drawers and an array of different evening gowns: a yellow silk, a mauve organdy, a silver-gray *peau de soie*. A corset lay open in the middle of the big four-poster bed next to where Lily stood waiting to leave for the party downstairs.

Jo had finally settled on a deep blue velvet gown with an overskirt and puffed sleeves of shot silver netting, a dress that made her eyes seem to change from dark blue to their unusual violet hue. The gown accented her cousin's lush figure and ivory skin and rode low on her shoulders, displaying an intriguing amount of her generous bosom.

Lily eyed her from head to foot. "You've made the perfect choice. You couldn't look lovelier, Jo."

Jocelyn grinned at herself in the mirror. "I'll show that witch Serafina. Hand me my slippers, will you?" She surveyed the silver overskirt gleaming in the lamp-light. "Royal won't even look at that woman once he sees me in this."

Lily felt a tightening around her heart. "I'm sure he won't." No matter the uncertainties he might be feeling about his marriage, no man could keep from staring at a woman who looked like Jo. *Beautiful* was far too dim a word to describe her. *Radiant* was closer, but still not enough. "At any rate, I don't think Serafina is his type."

Jocelyn rolled her eyes. "How naive you are, Lily. Every woman is a man's type—as long as she is willing. And I know for a fact, Lady Serafina Maitlin has been willing on more than one occasion."

Lily's eyes widened. "Truly?"

"I know she took Lord Holloway as her lover and I am fairly certain she had a tryst with Christopher Barclay."

"Did he tell you that?"

"No. Christopher is a gentleman. But there's a special way a man looks at a woman he's had. I could tell by the way Serafina looked at Christopher and the way he looked at her."

"You mean, like they both knew a secret about each other."

Jocelyn nodded sagely. "Exactly so." Seating herself on the stool in front of the mirror, she waited for Lily to fasten the clasp on the extravagant diamond necklace her father had given her on her nineteenth birthday.

Jocelyn rose to her feet and took a last assessing glance in the mirror. "You go down first. I'll come down a few minutes later."

Jo liked to make an entrance. Lily was certain that in the gown she was wearing, she would.

"I'll see you downstairs," Lily said, feeling as if she would rather face a hangman's noose than spend the evening with a roomful of people she did not know. In truth, though she worked to hide the fact, she was more of a country miss than she appeared, happier to be sewing than dancing.

She left the room and headed downstairs, pausing at the top of the ornate staircase to straighten the bodice of her apricot silk gown. She had remodeled it to fit her more slender figure, removed several pearl buckles and some of the extra moss-green satin trim, leaving a simpler version she thought more becoming on her.

She tried not to wonder if Royal would like it, but when she looked down, he was standing in the entry staring up at her, his handsome face creased with a smile of approval.

It quickly disappeared as she reached the bottom of the staircase, and his manner turned formal. "Miss Moran. You look lovely this evening."

"Thank you, Your Grace."

"I hope you are looking forward to the evening. You and my aunt did a great deal of work putting things together for tonight. You deserve to enjoy yourselves."

If he were someone else, she might simply have said that she was excited about the night ahead, but when she spoke to Royal, somehow the truth just seemed to slip out.

"I am basically shy, Your Grace. I endure these affairs, but in truth, I should rather be sewing or reading."

He smiled. "A true homebody."

"Mostly, yes."

"Unlike your cousin, I imagine."

"Completely unlike Jo. She is always the life of the party." She thought he would find the words reassuring, but instead he began to frown. He might have said something more but Matilda Caulfield walked up just then.

"Lily—where on earth have you been? Lady Tavistock has been looking all over. She is waiting for you in the drawing room."

It was a ruse to get her away from the duke, but for once, Lily was glad for the woman's interference.

"Then I shall go to her at once." She looked up at Royal, immaculately dressed in his perfectly tailored black evening clothes. Hair the color of pirate gold gleamed in the light of the crystal chandelier. "If you will both please excuse me…"

He made a formal bow and Lily hurried off to the drawing room. A trio of musicians in scarlet knee breeches and wearing white periwigs were playing. Most of the guests had already arrived. There was less formality in the country and everyone there was a bit more relaxed than in London, and laughter and good humor filled the drawing room.

Lily plucked a glass of champagne off a passing waiter's tray and went in search of the dowager countess. The woman was engaged in conversation with several of her friends, and Matilda's ruse was clear. The dowager hadn't even noticed Lily's absence.

She was meandering around the drawing room sipping her drink when Viscount Wellesley stepped into the path she traveled.

"Miss Moran… If I may say so, you are looking quite scrumptious this evening."

She smiled. She liked Sheridan Knowles. He always went out of his way to make her feel comfortable, and he was also quite charming. "You look extremely dashing yourself." And he did. Even when he wasn't dressed in black evening clothes, there was something elegant and sophisticated about Wellesley, and yet that elegance was tinged with a subtle masculinity that could not be mistaken.

"Would you allow me the privilege of introducing you to some of the guests?"

She would rather just slip into a corner and pretend to be invisible, but he wasn't giving her a choice.

"That would be very kind of you."

But the viscount wasn't looking at her with kindness. She knew enough about men to recognize the warmth in his green eyes and the faintly sensuous curve of his lips.

At least until a commotion in the doorway drew his attention and Jocelyn swept into the drawing room. Her blue velvet gown heightened the milky whiteness of her skin and emphasized the voluptuous swell of her breasts. Chestnut curls gleamed against her shoulders and her full lips curved into a breathtaking smile.

All conversation ceased. Even the servants stopped where they stood and just stared.

"Good Lord."

Lily laughed softly. "She is quite something, isn't she?"

Sheridan dragged his gaze away from her and back to Lily's face. "I do beg your pardon. That was not well done of me."

Lily just smiled. She was used to the effect her cousin had on men. "Perhaps not, but it was expected. You have only seen her a couple of times. You will get over the shock after a while."

Sheridan looked back at Jo, who, though escorted by the duke, was already surrounded by a group of male admirers.

"I am not certain I would want a wife whose beauty

drew such lavish attention," Sherry said, "a woman who was never completely mine alone."

"Ah, so you are a romantic, my lord."

"Perhaps I am, though if you tell anyone, I shall have to call you out. Whom will you choose as your second?"

Lily laughed. "I suppose it would have to be Lady Tavistock. Despite her age, I imagine she is game for most anything."

Sheridan chuckled and Lily glanced back at Jo. "She may be a bit of a handful, but even so, I should think the advantages would out-weigh the drawbacks."

One of the viscount's eyebrows went up as he correctly assumed she was referring to the pleasure a man would derive from bedding such a woman. Lily blushed.

Sheridan noticed and smiled and she realized he had several crooked bottom teeth. "You are quite sweet, aren't you? As I said, it would be my pleasure to introduce you to some of the guests." He extended his arm and Lily took it. "Shall we?"

For an instant, her glance strayed across the room to Royal and she was surprised to see him gazing back at her. A little tremor went through her that Lily entirely ignored.

Turning, she let Sheridan lead her round the drawing room, careful to keep her attention on the tall man at her side instead of the even taller man across the room.

Jocelyn was surprised to discover the evening was turning out to be far more pleasant than she had imagined. Her future bridegroom had been extremely attentive, introducing her to the guests and rarely leaving her side. Jocelyn had flirted madly as the duke had waltzed with her and escorted her round the room, making certain she gave him even more attention when she spotted tall, statuesque, red-haired Serafina Maitlin.

Jocelyn particularly enjoyed the bone-in-her-throat look that came over Lady Serafina's face when she realized the duke's attention was fixed firmly on Jocelyn and he was not going to stray.

As Royal went to fetch her a cup of punch, there was a momentary encounter.

"So you are setting your cap for the duke, are you?"

Jocelyn shrugged her shoulders. "I suppose I could hold out for a prince, but I am willing to make the sacrifice for a man as handsome and charming as Royal."

"You think to buy him. He needs your money."

Jocelyn just smiled. "Can you think of a better use for it?" Spotting Royal striding toward her, she moved in that direction, accepting the punch and casting her enemy a final triumphant glance.

All in all, so far it had been a pleasant, satisfying evening, and yet something seemed to be missing. Never once had her heart skipped when the duke touched her. Never once had a glance from his golden-brown eyes made her feel light-headed.

A year ago, she wouldn't have noticed. But that was before she had danced with Christopher Barclay. Before he had led her into the garden and kissed her. Silently she cursed herself. Now she knew what a man could make her feel. She had tasted the wild exhilaration.

It really didn't matter. Royal was a duke. With his golden good looks and impressive title, he was the most sought-after bachelor in England. Royal could give her everything she had ever wanted. And she meant to have him.

She looked up at the sound of his deep, masculine

voice, coming softly from beside her. "The hour grows late, Jocelyn. I should like a moment with you, if I may, out on the terrace."

She smiled and nodded, hoping he would speak the words she wished to hear and her future would be secured.

He took her gloved hand and settled it on the sleeve of his black dinner jacket and they walked out the French doors into the cool night air, careful to stay well in sight of the guests in the drawing room. Royal removed his coat and draped it round her shoulders.

"It's colder out here than I thought."

"It's all right. Your coat has absorbed the heat of your body and it is keeping me snuggly warm."

Something flickered in his eyes at the mention of his body and she thought that perhaps he was imagining their wedding night. Royal was a virile, masculine man and Jocelyn had always found the notion of bedsport intriguing. She was looking forward to it herself.

Royal took her hand and turned her to face him. "During the time you've been at Bransford, we've come to know each other a bit. Enough, I believe, that if you are willing, we might take the next step toward a future together." He went down on one knee in front of her. The torches burning near the balustrade illuminated his high cheekbones and gleamed on his thick golden hair.

"Miss Caulfield, will you do me the honor of becoming my wife?"

She smiled brightly, overcome with relief. It was going to happen. She was going to become the Duchess of Bransford. She couldn't wait to tell her mother! And her father would be utterly thrilled!

"I would be honored, Your Grace."

He came to his feet, lifted her chin with his fingers and looked into her eyes. Leading her into the shadows, he bent his head and very softly kissed her. It was a very proper kiss that lasted only moments but still she felt a faint rush of heat.

A second shot of relief swept though her. At least Christopher Barclay wasn't the only man who could make her feel like a woman.

Royal led her back into the light of the torches, where they could once more be seen. "Once you are back in London, I shall come to the city and speak to your father. We'll go over the marriage settlement and decide when to formally announce our engagement."

"Mother is going to be so excited!"

He studied her face and she wondered what he searched for. "I had better get you back inside," he said, "or we shall surely create a scandal."

Before they went in, he removed his coat from her shoulders and shrugged it back on, then took her hand and led her back into the drawing room.

Across the way, she caught her mother's eye and beamed. The signal was read correctly and her mother grinned broadly.

"The guests are beginning to leave," he said as he walked beside her. "I need to find my aunt so that we may bid them farewell. I shall see you in the morning."

He returned her to the group of women in conversation with her mother and she gave him a last warm smile.

"Good night, Royal," she said as he bent over her gloved hand and pressed a kiss on the back. Bidding a polite farewell to her mother, he went in search of his aunt. As soon as he was out of sight, her mother whirled to face her.

"So he asked at last!" Her mother looked radiant, her plump face wreathed in a smile.

Jocelyn grinned. "Everything is set. As soon as we get back to London, Royal is coming to speak to Father."

"Oh, that is splendid news. We shall plan a grand affair. We can make the announcement while the duke is in the city."

"It truly is exciting," Jocelyn said, getting caught up in the joy on her mother's face.

"Isn't it, though? My daughter a duchess! Henry will be so pleased. And you will be the toast of London!"

Her Grace, the Duchess of Bransford. It was like a true-life fairy tale. Jocelyn surveyed the Gold Drawing Room, noticing the signs of aging. "Tomorrow, I think I shall wander about the house, begin to think how we should manage the restoration."

"Good idea. I believe I'll join you."

Jocelyn nodded, glad for her mother's help. "I think we should leave for home the day after. One can only stomach this dreary country life for so long."

Her mother nodded, moving her double chins. "I couldn't agree with you more, dearest. And the sooner we get back, the sooner His Grace will come. Once that happens, your engagement will become official and the Ton will know you've been chosen to become the next Duchess of Bransford."

Jocelyn glanced toward the doorway where the duke had just disappeared. For an instant, her gaze snagged on Lady Serafina Maitlin. Jocelyn gave her a catty, triumphant smile.

Satisfaction rolled through her. Along with Serafina, soon all of London would know. Jocelyn could hardly wait.

Ten

The deed was done. Only the formalities remained. Royal sat at the desk in his study, contemplating his future as a married man. The woman his father had chosen was beautiful and desirable and yet she stirred him little.

She had left just after first light, along with her mother, grumbling at the early hour but obviously eager to get home. Lily had accompanied them.

Lily. He'd had no time alone with her since the day he had kissed her in the maze and for that he was grateful. After last night, he could never speak to her again as other than a friend, and friendship was the last thing he felt for Lily. The women were gone and Royal was relieved.

"I am sorry to interrupt, Your Grace, but it seems you have a visitor."

At the sight of Greaves's tall, bony countenance standing in the doorway, Royal straightened in his chair. "Who is it?"

"Mr. Morgan, sir. Shall I show him in?"

He hadn't expected the investigator to return so soon, but he was anxious to hear what the man had to say. "Yes. Thank you, Greaves."

Chase Morgan strode into the study, lean and black-haired, his hard, carved features reflecting the sort of work he did.

Royal rose behind his desk. "Have a seat."

Morgan complied and Royal sat back down.

"Your visit comes as a surprise," he said. "I didn't expect to see you again so soon."

"The task wasn't as difficult as I had imagined. Once I began digging, the pieces of the puzzle all seemed to fall together." He lifted his black leather satchel and set it on the desk, slid out a sheaf of papers. "If you dig deep enough, it's amazing the things you can learn."

"And exactly what have you found?"

Morgan separated several sheets of paper from the rest. "This is the list I brought with me the last time I was here, names of people who owned the companies in which your father invested, or at least owned shares." He looked up. "I couldn't discover the whereabouts of a single one of them."

Royal frowned. He leaned over the desk to examine the names on the list. "You are saying my father put money into companies that didn't actually exist?"

"I'm afraid I am. The corporations in which he purchased shares were also nonexistent. The documents were forgeries."

Royal took a moment to digest the information as he sank back down in his chair. "Then there really was no

Randsburg Coal Mining Company, no Southward Mill or anything else."

"No. Your father was too ill to visit the companies himself. He never delegated anyone to investigate, so he never knew the truth."

"If the companies weren't real, who got the money?"

"The bank drafts from your father's accounts were written to a single person, a solicitor named Richard Cull. It was Cull's job to distribute the funds to the various companies. Cull's office closed and the man disappeared around the time your father died."

Royal could hardly believe what the investigator was saying. It was all a total scam to divest the ailing duke of his fortune and it was managed brilliantly. Royal's jaw hardened. "I'm going to find him."

"Perhaps you can," Morgan said, "but here's the interesting part. According to my sources, the bank drafts were written to Cull, but ultimately the money went to a man named Preston Loomis. He's the fellow who convinced the late duke to invest in these projects. He is also the man who invented them. Ever heard of him?"

Royal's hand unconsciously fisted on the top of the desk. "He was a friend of my father's. My brother Rule mentioned him in a letter he wrote to me several years back while I was living in Barbados. He said the two of them were becoming very good friends."

"If I am correct, that would have been not long after your father's first stroke."

"About that time, yes. None of us really knew how severe it actually was, not until we arrived home just before he died. At the time it happened, we all assumed he would fully recover. I remember when I read the letter, I was glad my father had a friend to keep him company during his convalescence."

"Did your father ever personally make mention of the man?"

"After the stroke, he had trouble using his right hand, so his valet wrote his letters for him. Loomis's name wasn't in any of the letters." He sighed. "He was extremely perceptive. If it hadn't been for his illness, he would never have fallen prey to a charlatan like Loomis." Royal glanced back down at the papers. "How did you find out Preston Loomis was the man behind the swindle?"

The ghost of a smile curved Morgan's hard lips. "I have my sources. It's amazing what one can discover when the right palms are greased."

"Where is Loomis now?"

"In London, living like a king. If you had simply accepted the estate's financial losses at face value, merely as your father's poor judgment, none of this would ever have come to light. In town, Loomis is considered quite an astute financial adviser, though he claims to be mostly retired and extremely selective in his clientele. Undoubtedly, this isn't the first time he has taken advantage of an infirm individual, nor will it be the last."

Royal raked a hand through his hair, barely able to contain his anger. "I see no choice but to go to the authorities."

"With what? We can prove there was a fraud since none of the companies exist, but all of the evidence points to Richard Cull. Cull has disappeared as if he never existed. He may not even be in the country, and even if he were, he would be using a different name."

"What about the people who told you about Loomis?"

"Blacklegs and sharpers. Not a one whose word would hold up against a staunch citizen like Loomis. Even if you went to the authorities, you would never see a farthing of the money returned. Loomis would see it squirreled away until he was cleared of the charges—which he undoubtedly would be."

Royal leaned forward in his chair. "If we don't have proof, we'll simply have to dig until we find some. I refuse to sit by and let a man like that get away with the Bransford fortune."

Morgan eyed him with speculation. "You may be throwing good money after bad, but if you are certain that is what you want, I'll keep looking, though I warn you, it will likely be a waste of time. The man hasn't got as far as he has by leaving a trail that will send him to the gallows."

Royal said nothing. What Morgan said made sense, yet he refused to give up without a fight. He owed that much to his father. Finally he rose from his chair and Morgan stood up as well.

"Keep searching," Royal said. "Look into his background. Perhaps you will find something there."

"I intend that to be my next effort."

"We need solid evidence against this man. Let me know when you find it."

Morgan made a faint bow of his head, collected his things and left the study.

Royal thought of his father and felt sick inside. Sick and unbearably guilty. He should have been here. If he had come home, his father would never have been cheated. His family's fortune would have remained intact. He clenched his jaw. He would find a way to make Preston Loomis pay for what he had done.

Somehow, he would make him pay.

Lily heard the news with a sinking heart. Royal was coming to London to meet with Jocelyn's father. It had been nearly two weeks since she had left Bransford Castle. In that time, she had forced thoughts of the duke to the back of her mind. Then this morning, a messenger had arrived with a note informing Jo of the meeting Royal had arranged with her father to take place at the house at three o'clock day after the morrow.

Lily had no right to feel morose, to feel as if she was losing something precious that was meant to be hers. She had known from the beginning that Royal belonged to Jo—and they were a perfect match, both sophisticated and beautiful, both with a presence so powerful, so magnetic it made them the center of attention the moment they stepped into a room.

Not like Lily, who preferred to remain in the shadows. In time, she hoped for a quiet life filled with the love of a husband and children, though that was a distant dream, a hope that somewhere down the road she would meet her own handsome prince who would sweep her away on his magnificent white charger and they would live happily ever after.

In the meantime, she would take care of herself, support herself with the money she earned from her millinery shop. It was a different, more immediate dream, and in that regard, she was on an errand now she hoped would begin her future as a businesswoman.

Walking down Bond Street beneath an overcast sky, her wide-brimmed bonnet and woolen pelisse shielding her from the first light sprinkles of rain, she turned off onto Harken Lane, a small street also lined with fashionable shops: a clockmaker; a china shop; Winston's, the chairmaker's shop. A well-known modiste had a shop just round the corner.

She reached the small, empty, mullion-windowed store, and paused for a moment to collect herself. Taking a breath, she turned the knob, found the door unlocked and walked into the narrow, recently repainted space that would be perfect for what she intended.

A bell above the door rang as she entered. She started to call out when a tall, big-boned woman came toward her with a smile.

"May I help you?"

"I do hope so. My name is Lily Moran. I'm a hatmaker. I happened to notice the For Lease sign on the door when I passed through the neighborhood yesterday delivering some of my hats. No one was here at the time, but the monthly rent posted on the sign seemed reasonable, so I came back today hoping I might find someone to speak to about leasing the space."

The woman's smile broadened, splitting the wide circumference of her face. "A milliner, are you? I'm Hortense Siliphant. My husband and I own the building. I am very glad to meet you, Miss Moran."

"A pleasure meeting you, as well. Then the shop is still available?"

"It is. You're aware there is a small furnished apartment located upstairs?"

"Yes. I should very much like to see it."

The woman hesitated. "Are you planning to live here alone?"

"My current situation is changing. My cousin is getting married, which means I will have to find a place of my own. I can get you a letter of good character from my cousins, Mr. and Mrs. Henry Caulfield. I assure you I would be quite a respectable tenant."

"Henry Caulfield owns the bank just down the block, does he not?"

"Why, yes, he does."

The landlady nodded, seemed satisfied that Lily wasn't going to open a house of ill repute or take in disreputable boarders. "If you will please follow me, I will show you the living quarters. They are small but adequate."

Lily climbed the stairs at the rear of the shop, following Mrs. Siliphant's wide, swaying hips. The apartment had a cozy sitting room warmed by a coal-burning hearth. There was a horsehair settee and matching chair in a dark rose hue, and a kitchen at one end furnished with a round oak table just large enough for two.

"The bedroom is through there." It was tiny, the bed filling most of the space, but there was a nice oak chest of drawers and a dressing table with a mirror. The smell of fresh paint still hung in the air and the Aubusson rug looked newly beaten.

"It is very nice."

They returned downstairs, stopping when they reached the counter at the back of the shop. Mrs. Siliphant assessed Lily's stone-colored taffeta bonnet piped with scarlet that matched her walking dress.

"May I assume you fashioned that lovely creation you are wearing?"

Lily smiled at the compliment. "Why, yes, I did."

"It is quite charming, and with all the shopping in the area, I believe a milliner who produces such fine-quality merchandise would do very well in this location."

Lily barely suppressed a grin. "I am glad you think so."

"Then let us get started, shall we?"

Without further ado, they began discussing the terms of a lease on the narrow shop and small apartment. Knowing the price from the information on the sign, Lily calculated she had saved enough to pay the first six months' rent, even if she didn't sell a single hat—which she was certain she would.

"That sounds quite acceptable," she said when the woman had finished. "I've brought the rent for the first and last months plus a deposit, as your sign required." Lily drew the money from her reticule and handed it over.

Mrs. Siliphant counted the banknotes, slid them into a pocket in her skirt, then stuck out a wide hand, which Lily accepted, confirming the deal.

"Tomorrow is the first of February. Your lease will begin that day."

"Thank you so much, Mrs. Siliphant. I am so excited."

The woman smiled. "We're happy to have you, dear." She handed over a key, which Lily held like a treasure against her bosom.

She left the shop walking on air. It was happening. She was going to become a bona fide shopkeeper. She wouldn't be leaving the Caulfields until after the wedding, of course, since Jocelyn would surely need her. Which meant it would yet be some months away, but she planned to open her shop—the Lily Pad, she intended to call it—and begin making and selling hats right away.

Even the light spattering of rain that threatened to grow worse couldn't dampen her buoyant spirits. She was grinning, swinging her reticule back and forth, thinking of the day she would become completely independent, when a gleaming black coach pulled by four high-stepping grays rolled up beside her.

Her breath caught as she recognized the Bransford ducal seal on the side, the gilt paint worn off in several places.

Then Royal opened the door and descended the narrow iron stairs like a golden god come to earth and walked right up in front of her. Her heartbeat quickened and inside her gloves, her palms went damp. How could she have forgotten in so short a time how utterly magnificent he was?

Lily dropped into a curtsy. "Your Grace." She rose and looked into his handsome face. "I—I thought you weren't arriving in town until tomorrow."

"I've been in London several days. I have a meeting with my future father-in-law on the morrow."

"Yes, I know." The rain was beginning to fall more heavily, forming a spray of droplets on her taffeta skirt.

Royal looked up at the darkening sky, the dense clouds roiling overhead. "Come," he commanded in that soft-firm voice of his. "It is beginning to rain quite hard. I'll give you a lift to wherever it is you're going."

She could hardly refuse. Accepting the hand he offered, she climbed the carriage steps and settled herself inside, fluffing out her skirts mostly to have something to keep her hands occupied.

Royal sat down in the seat across from her, stretching his long legs out in front of him as best he could. "So where, then, are you off to?"

"Actually, I planned to stop somewhere for a bite to eat and celebrate my recent good fortune, then head back to the Caulfields'."

Those golden-brown eyes fixed on her face. The edge of his mouth began to curve, and the bottom dropped out of her stomach. She tried not to recall that day in the maze, the feel of his lips moving so hotly over hers, but it was impossible to do. She prayed he wouldn't notice the faint color rising in her cheeks.

"So if I may ask, what good fortune were you planning to celebrate?"

She thought of the shop she had just rented and couldn't keep the excitement out of her voice. "I am opening a millinery shop, just as I've always dreamed. I just finalized the lease. It becomes effective tomorrow."

He smiled and a dimple she hadn't noticed before appeared in his right cheek. Dear Lord, it simply wasn't fair for a man to look that good.

"My heartiest congratulations, Miss Moran. I know how much this means to you. I wish you the utmost success."

"Thank you."

"And you're right—you deserve to celebrate. I shall take you to luncheon and we shall celebrate together."

Her heart kicked up another notch. She gazed down at the reticule she clutched in her lap. "I—I don't think that is a very good notion, Your Grace. Someone might see us. What would the Caulfields say?"

His eyebrows, a darker shade than his golden hair, pulled slightly together. "I suppose you are right. It would be highly unseemly, considering I am about to become engaged. Still, I am yet a free man…"

He looked at her as if he tried to decide how far he should go. Then the gold in his eyes seemed to glitter and his mouth turned up at the corners. "There is a place I know, a small restaurant not far from here. There are a number of private rooms and the food is quite delicious. The owner is a friend of mine. We can go in through the backdoor. What do you say?"

Eleven

No, was the proper reply. It was madness to accompany him, madness for him to ask. "Yes," is what Lily said. "I would be delighted to accompany you to luncheon."

Royal flashed a brilliant, white smile. "All right, then." Rapping on the roof, he slid open the panel beneath the driver's box and commanded the coachman to take him to the Fox and Hen in Mulberry Street. "Drive round to the back," he finished.

They arrived a few minutes later and Royal helped her down from the coach and escorted her inside. The owner, a thin, black-haired, mustached man, appeared out of nowhere.

"Your Grace," the man said, beaming at the duke's arrival. "Always a pleasure to see you."

"You as well, Antonio."

Antonio flicked a glance at Lily, but kept his attention fixed on the duke. "I've a nice dining room for you just down the hall." His mustache turned up. "The special today is steak and kidney pie. If you will please follow me."

Though she could hear the sound of patrons rattling glassware and dishes in the main dining hall and servants bustled past, Lily grew more nervous, not quite sure what to expect. The room into which Antonio led them behind a gold velvet curtain was comfortably furnished with a table and two padded benches in an L shape along the walls. Clearly more happened in the private rooms than just eating.

As the man departed and the curtain fell behind him, Lily gazed at the intimate surroundings and blushed.

"It's all right," Royal said softly, guiding her over to take a seat. "I didn't bring you here to ravish you—though I cannot deny the notion intrigues me far too much."

Lily looked up at him. "I trust you, Royal." The name just popped out. "I—I'm sorry, Your Grace. That was quite inappropriate."

"Please…don't apologize. I like the way my name sounds when you say it. Besides, we are friends, are we not?"

She smiled broadly, relieved and beginning to feel once more at ease. "Why, yes, we are. And today we are celebrating."

"Indeed, we are." From that time on, the duke was careful to keep the conversation light. They ordered the special steak and kidney pie for lunch, along with a bottle of wine. Royal proposed a toast to her success and each of them took a drink.

"So where were you headed when you came across me getting soaked in the rain?" Lily asked between bites of the delicious food.

"On my way to a meeting with a man I hired, an investigator. He has been looking into a terrible fraud that was perpetrated against my father."

"Good grief. What happened?"

Royal hesitated only a moment before launching into the tale. The two of them had always had a certain ease of conversation between them and apparently that hadn't changed. He explained how a man named Preston Loomis had preyed on his father after he was taken ill and managed to steal a large portion of the duke's fortune.

Lily was outraged. "This man, Loomis, is nothing more than a confidence artist. A sophisticated version of a man like my uncle Jack."

Royal shook his head. "I'll never see a nickel of our money returned, I don't imagine. There is no possible way I could ever get it back. Still, I am determined to see justice done."

The words rolled through her, opened some part of her mind she had carefully locked away. Old memories stirred to life of the years she had spent with her uncle, shams he had invented, schemes they had managed to pull off. Nothing so incredibly bold as stealing a man's entire fortune, but still…

"I wonder…" she mused aloud, but let the thought trail away. Royal drained the last of his wine and set the empty goblet down on the table.

"What is it you wondered, Lily? Go on, you don't have to feel shy with me. Tell me what you were going to say."

Her chin came up. "All right, I will. You said there was no way to get the money back, but I was wondering if there might not be."

"What are you talking about?"

"I haven't seen my uncle in years, but I am certain I could find him. Unless he got involved in something that required him to leave the area, Uncle Jack never strays far from his old neighborhood. He feels safe there."

"I'm afraid I am still not following you."

"Well, I couldn't help thinking that if this man Loomis swindled your father out of his money, why couldn't we figure out a way to swindle him out of his?"

Royal laughed, his eyes crinkling in the corners. His laughter slowly faded. "You are serious."

She shrugged. "It was probably a ridiculous notion…" And yet she was already beginning to sort through possibilities. She summoned her courage. "I think we should talk to my uncle. He might know a way. I am sure he has never gone after anything remotely this big, but with your help and mine, we might find a way."

"And your uncle would help us because…?"

"Because he loves me and because you would be willing to cut him in for a percentage of whatever you might get back."

Royal just stared.

Lily felt hot color rising in her cheeks. "I am sorry. I tried to tell you before that I wasn't what I seemed. I apologize for bringing this up. Of course, you wouldn't wish to do anything illegal. I have shocked you and—"

"I want to meet him."

"What?"

"Your uncle. I want to meet him. Can you arrange it?"

"I—I am not sure, but I think so."

"I want Preston Loomis brought to justice. I can think of no richer justice than for him to lose at least some portion of the money he stole from my family."

He reached over and caught her gloved hand, brought it to his lips. "And you are exactly what you seem, Lily Moran. You are sweet and caring, and you are sincere. I appreciate your friendship and any help you might be able to give me."

Something burned behind her eyes. Lily managed a wobbly smile, then took a steadying breath and straightened in her seat. "I shall begin looking for my uncle immediately. Once I find him, I will send word. Where are you staying?"

"My town house in Berkeley Square."

"A note to you there, then." She glanced at the clock on the wall. "What time is your meeting?"

He followed her gaze to the hands on the porcelain face of the clock. "Half an hour. I suppose I had better get you home."

Royal rose and helped her to her feet. Leaving several coins on the table, he guided her out the back way into the alley where his big black coach sat waiting. He gave instructions to his driver, then helped her climb in and settled himself on the seat across from her.

The curtains were drawn to keep in the warmth. The flickering light of the carriage lamps made the red velvet interior far too intimate, and for several moments neither of them spoke. The only sound was the patter of the rain on the roof and the churning of the carriage wheels.

Lily did her best to think of Royal as her future cousin-in-law, but when she remembered the feel of his mouth over hers, his silky hair brushing her fingers as her arms went round his neck, it was impossible to do.

It was close inside the carriage, their knees brushing slightly, her full skirts wrapping around his long legs.

Lily found herself fascinated by the length of them, the muscles outlined beneath the snug fit of his trousers. Her gaze moved upward, over his dark brown tailcoat, then higher. When she looked into his face, Royal's gaze locked with hers, and his nostrils flared.

The atmosphere inside the coach began to change. A subtle tension crackled in the air that seemed to thicken and swell around them. Lily's heart pounded. She nervously moistened her lips, and Royal's whole body went taut.

"Lily…" he said, and then he was moving, reaching for her, lifting her off the seat and onto his lap. "I know I shouldn't, I know it's wrong, but God forgive me, I can't help myself." And then he kissed her and every other thought simply faded.

A small sound escaped and her hands fluttered up to settle on his shoulders. Royal deepened the kiss and sweet fire rolled through her. Any notion of resistance slipped completely away and Lily kissed him back, opening to allow him entrance, pleasure swamping her at the slick feel of his tongue. He took her deeply, drinking her up as if he had an insatiable thirst only she could quench. Lily felt light-headed, her body awash with sensation.

Hot kisses followed, seemed to have no end. Royal untied her bonnet and tossed it onto the seat beside her, framed her face with his hand and kissed her deeply again.

Trembling, Lily swayed against him, her breasts swelling, her nipples budding and beginning to throb. She didn't realize he had untied her pelisse and pulled it away, then unbuttoned the back of her gown until the dress tipped forward and he lowered his head and captured one of her breasts in his mouth.

Lily whimpered. Her fingers combed through his hair as he suckled her, tugging gently, his teeth lightly grazing her nipple. Dear God, the most exquisite sensations burned through her. Her body seemed to catch fire and there was no way to put out the blaze. Lily clutched Royal's shoulders and arched her back, giving him better access.

"Lovely," he whispered, pressing kisses against her tingling flesh as he nipped and tasted. "Exquisite as ripe fruit, even more perfect than I imagined."

Lily gasped for breath and clung to him, silently urging him on, and he turned his attention to her other breast, laving and tasting with the same gentle care as before. Her body tingled, dampened, pulsed with hot need.

A noise sounded above them. "We're almost there, Yer Grace," the coachman called down.

Royal's concentration didn't falter. "Keep driving. Don't stop until I tell you."

When she opened her mouth to protest, he silenced her with a deep, drugging kiss. For an instant, she kissed him back, breathing him in, reveling in the feel of being in his arms. But the present had begun to intrude. Realty could no longer be denied and harsh reason doused the flames of her desire.

Breathing hard, her heart pounding as if she had been running some mad race, she pressed her hands against his chest and pushed him away.

"Royal, please…we…we have to stop."

He bent to kiss her again, but Lily turned away. "We…we can't do this, Royal."

He blinked, seemed to awaken from a deep erotic dream. Slowly his mind began to clear. "Lily…"

"We have to stop, Royal. We can't go on any longer."

He shuddered, pulling himself back from wherever he had been, raking a hand through his thick golden hair, shoving it back from his forehead. "No…no, of course not." His jaw clenched as if he was in pain. With unsteady hands, he turned her back to him and refastened the small pearl buttons closing up her gown. He drew her pelisse back into place and reached for her bonnet.

Lily took it from his grasp with shaking hands and pulled it on over the disheveled mass of her pale blond hair.

Royal set her back on the seat across from him, his jaw iron hard. "I know I should apologize. I know this never should have happened. But it did, and I cannot say I am sorry."

Lily stared up at him, torn by guilt and despair, trying to hold back tears. "We mustn't…mustn't be alone together again."

A muscle flexed in his cheek. "I know." He started to reach for her hand, then caught himself. "If things were different…if the course of my life weren't already set…"

Lily swallowed. "Please take me home, Royal."

His eyes held hers a moment more, then he nodded. Reaching up, he rapped on the roof of the carriage, then shoved open the panel below the driver's box. "Take us back, Mason. Stop a block before you get to Meadowbrook."

"Aye, Yer Grace."

Lily closed her eyes against the sharp ache in her chest and leaned back against the velvet seat. She had been so happy. How could a day of celebration end up being so full of pain?

* * *

Lily wished she never had to see him again. It would be so much easier. But no matter how guilty she felt for what she had done, she had promised to help him and, like the duke himself, Lily wasn't one to break her word.

Dressing early the following morning in a simple gray wool dress, the hood of her cloak pulled over her head against the light wind and drizzle, she set off for an area in St. Giles, a rookery between Farley and Bunbury Lane. She was returning to the small flat above the Fat Ox Tavern she and her uncle had occupied six years ago, before he left her in the care of her cousins.

She had no idea if he would still be living there, but Jack Moran was a man of habit and likely he would be somewhere in the neighborhood.

Lily closed the iron gate in front of the Caulfields' mansion and walked along the street until she came to a corner where she could hail a hansom cab. She waited until she spotted an old horse plodding along the road and waved the conveyance down, then gave the driver directions to the area to which she wished to go.

The man, long-haired with a pockmarked complexion, cast her a look that asked why in the world she wished to go to a place like that, but made no comment, just waited for her to climb in, slapped the reins on the ancient horse's rump, and the cab lurched into motion.

It took a while to get there, traveling at the speed of a snail, but eventually she began to recognize familiar surroundings. A weathered board walkway in front of a line of run-down houses, a gin shop named the Blue Ruin, a blacksmith shop ringing with the pounding of an anvil. It wasn't a very good neighborhood, but it was better than some.

She spotted the sign for the Fat Ox Tavern and asked the driver to let her off in front.

"I'll pay you extra if you wait. I am looking for someone. I am hoping to find him here, but I am not sure."

The driver glanced at his surroundings. A spotted hound sniffed garbage at the entrance to an alley. A light-skirt plied her trade on the corner and a drunk shoved his way out the doors of the Fat Ox and staggered off down the road.

"I'll pay you double your usual fee," she said, reading the man's uncertainty.

"All right, miss, but don't be long."

She nodded. "I'll be right back."

The tavern was as loud and raucous as she remembered, the customers half-drunk and it was not yet noon. By the time she had turned sixteen, she had grown used to it, even knew many of the patrons. After six years away, six years of living in a completely different world, being here now stirred a hollow feeling in the pit of her stomach.

Lily squared her shoulders and walked into the taproom.

"Jolly!" she called out, spotting the big man with an even bigger belly who owned the tavern. "Jolly, it's me—Lily Moran."

He gaped at her, slack-jawed, his gaze running over her expensively fashioned garments, the simple woolen fabric finer than anything she had worn when she had lived in the room upstairs.

"God's teeth, gel, I kin 'ardly believe me eyes. Lily, is it really you?"

She laughed. She had always like Jolly. "It is truly me, though I know I am older and I look different. I am here to see my uncle. Is there any chance he still lives in the room upstairs?"

Jolly shook his massive head, moving strands of curly black hair. "Sorry, miss. Ol' Jack moved out just about a year ago." He grinned, and she saw he had lost several teeth. "Got hisself some finer digs a few blocks down the street."

She perked up. "Can you tell me where?"

He gave her instructions and she hurried back out to the street. She climbed into the cab, gave the driver new directions, and the horse plodded, head down, to their new destination, a three-story wooden building with a sign that read, Mrs. Murphy's Boardinghouse.

"I'll be back as quickly as I can," she said as she climbed from the cab, then crossed to the door of the rooming house and walked in.

Worn board floors creaked beneath her feet as she moved toward the staircase. "Room 2C," she said to herself, remembering Jolly's instructions, lifting her skirts as she climbed to the second floor. The lodging house wasn't fancy, but it was far better than their garret room above the tavern, with flowered paper on the walls and an iron chandelier above the stairwell.

She knocked on the door of room 2C, but no one answered. She knocked again, heard footsteps, and a few seconds later, the door swung wide. Jack Moran stood in the opening, lean and wiry, his short, iron-gray hair sticking up all over his head as if she had awakened him from sleep—which she probably had.

Jack liked to gamble and drink, and though he had

modified his behavior while he was raising a child, it was likely he had returned to his former style of living. He wore only an undershirt and trousers, and he scratched the gray hair on his chest through the thin cotton fabric.

"Well, now, what's a pretty little thing like you doin' standin' outside my door?"

"Uncle Jack, it's me—Lily."

His eyebrows shot up and his light green eyes widened in disbelief. "Praise God, my little girl has come back to me!" And he swept her into his long, stringy arms and hugged her, and Lily hugged him back, and it felt so wonderful to be with him again after so many years, her eyes stung with tears.

"Well, come on in, my fine lass, and tell your old uncle why it is his good fortune that you've come to see him."

Lily let him lead her into the sparsely furnished apartment and felt a pang of regret that she had not come sooner. But over the years, the past had faded, her memories dimmed and part of her didn't want to relive that time in her life.

She glanced round the room that held a bed, a worn settee and a small wooden table and chairs. The room was tidy, as Jack had always been, and livable enough, she supposed. Uncle Jack made them a cup of tea on the coal burner in the corner and they sat at the table enjoying it while Lily told him about her life with the Caulfields and the plans she had to open her own business.

"I'm going to make hats, Uncle Jack. I've already signed the lease."

"That's my girl! Always knew you'd do all right for

yourself. You were a smart little thing, just like your father." The brothers had been close. Though Jack was the black sheep of the pair, he was as well educated as her father. He spoke well and read books in the original Latin, and though he survived by a life of crime, he had always been kindhearted, and being with him again Lily realized how much she had missed him.

"What about you, Uncle Jack? Are you doing all right?"

"I always do, lass. I scored a bit of cash a few months back, enough to keep my belly full and move in here. Been on the straight and narrow ever since." He grinned. "And I've got myself a lady friend. Her name is Molly. She's a pip, is Molly. So I guess you could say I'm doin' just fine." He eyed her with speculation. "You still haven't told me why you're here."

Lily took a breath. Careful to keep her feelings from showing, she told him about the Duke of Bransford and how she had met him, how he had saved her the day the carriage had overturned in the snow. She told him that they had become friends, and what had happened to the duke's late father.

"I am hoping you might be able to help him, Uncle Jack."

"Are you, now?"

"Will you talk to him at least?"

Jack smiled. "Fancy that—Jack Moran rubbin' elbows with some fancy aristocrat—a duke, no less. I'll talk to him, luv. You could ask me for just about anything, sweet girl, and I would do it for you."

Lily reached over and took hold of his hand. "Thank you, Uncle Jack."

But deep inside, she almost wished he had refused.

* * *

After his encounter with Lily in the carriage, Royal had postponed the meeting with Chase Morgan until the following day. He'd been too rattled, too bloody aroused, to do anything more than go home and pour himself a very strong drink. Mostly, he spent the balance of the day and half the night berating himself for taking advantage of Lily—again.

Royal leaned back against the seat of the less ostentatious, two-horse brougham he used most of the time when he was in London. He was on his way to Threadneedle Street, to the office of Chase Morgan Investigations.

Yesterday, when he had spotted Lily walking briskly down the street, his intentions had been strictly aboveboard. He had only intended to give her a ride, get her out of the rain. Somehow, the minute she stepped into his carriage, all his good intentions had flown straight out the window.

He sighed as the carriage rumbled along. There was something irresistible about Lily. He knew she believed that her beautiful, vivacious cousin far outshined her, but in her own sweet way, Lily sparkled.

Add to that, an attraction unlike any he had felt for a woman in years, perhaps never, and the combination was lethal. At least for him.

The building appeared up ahead, a narrow brick structure next to Applegarth's Coffee House. The conveyance rolled to a halt and Royal climbed down to the busy street that bore traffic through the financial heart of the city. He knocked briefly on the door. Morgan appeared and invited him inside and the men exchanged greetings.

Royal followed him into a private office with dark

oak-paneled walls, a low table and two leather chairs. A big oak desk and chairs sat in front of it. Both Morgan and Royal sat down.

"I appreciate your coming," Morgan began. "I've a couple of interesting things to report."

Royal settled himself in the chair. "And those things would be…?"

"To start with, Preston Loomis is actually a lowlife named Dick Flynn. Word on the street is his mother was a whore, though apparently he was quite fond of her. They say he began his criminal activities almost as soon as he could walk, picking pockets and petty thieving. As he got older, he started running Little Goes—illegal small lotteries. He was an extremely skillful cardshark in his youth and later, a master thief."

"Surely with all of that, we have enough to go to the police."

"Unfortunately, all of this is nothing more than hearsay. There is no way to verify the authenticity. Flynn was never caught, never even a suspect in a crime. Five years ago, he made a small fortune in a jewelry heist and then just disappeared. No one ever saw or heard of Dick Flynn again, but my sources say he's the man who calls himself Preston Loomis."

Royal sat in silence, digesting the information. "Loomis is really a criminal named Dick Flynn," he repeated.

Morgan nodded. "That's right. My people are usually reliable. They don't make mistakes or they don't get paid."

Flynn was a bad sort, but there was still no way to prove it.

"You said there was something else."

"Just that Flynn was a very dangerous man. Anyone who crossed him eventually turned up dead. There is no reason to believe that has changed."

Anger pumped through him. Flynn deserved to be brought to justice, not just for swindling his father, but for the murders he had committed or paid someone to commit. "I'll keep that in mind."

Rising from his chair, Royal extended a hand, which Morgan rose and accepted. "I appreciate all your hard work," Royal said.

"We still don't have enough to go to the police."

Royal's jaw flexed. "I'm well aware." He thought of Lily and her uncle and took heart that perhaps Flynn would be brought to justice in another way.

He looked into the investigator's chiseled face. "Leave it for now. I'll get back in touch if I want you to continue. Send your bill to my solicitor's office."

Morgan made a faint bow of his head. "As you wish, Your Grace."

Royal left the investigator's office and headed back to his town house. He had just enough time to change and travel to Meadowbrook for his meeting with Jocelyn's father. Royal ignored the tightness in his chest and the bitter taste in his mouth.

By the end of the day, he would be engaged to marry.

Twelve

~~~~~~~~~~~~~~~~

Royal arrived at his town house to find Sheridan Knowles lounging in a chair in front of the fire in the drawing room. His city residence also needed painting and updated furnishings, but it was in far better shape than the castle. His staff, however, had been cut to the bone: only a butler, a housekeeper, a cook, chambermaid and a single footman. Of course, there was a gardener, a groom and a coachman, but considering he was a duke, his staff wasn't much.

"I thought you were enjoying the country," Royal said to Sherry.

"It became quite tedious after you and your houseful of visitors left. I thought to entertain myself a bit in the city."

"I'm glad you're here. I could do with a bit of company. Unfortunately, I've got to change for a meeting with my future father-in-law."

"I'll come up while you dress, tell you what you missed while you were gone."

As if there was much to miss in the quiet village of Bransford.

Sherry followed Royal upstairs and tossed himself down on the padded bench at the foot of the four-poster bed while Royal changed into pale gray trousers and a velvet-collared navy blue tailcoat over a matching, double-breasted waistcoat. He had left the aging valet he had inherited from his father back at the castle, since he managed just fine without him. He had, however, interviewed the old man in regard to Preston Loomis and the late duke, his father, regarding anything the valet might have overheard, but nothing had come of it.

Sherry's voice drew his attention. "Well, now, let me see," his friend began, "what excitement have we had while you were away? Ah, yes, Mrs. Brown's cat had a litter of kittens and old Mr. Perry's goat wandered into Mrs. Holstein's bakery and ate half her morning's baked goods before anyone realized what was happening."

"Fascinating," Royal said dryly, but his mouth curved as he fastened the front of his trousers.

"Oh, and there was another robbery—a carriage was waylaid on the Pemberton Road. The occupant was divested of his purse but no one was injured. There is no way to be certain it is the same band of thieves, but it seems most likely."

"Not good news."

"At least it happened in another county. Perhaps the buggers will stay over there and leave us alone."

Royal grunted. "Someone needs to catch them."

"Yes, I spoke to the constable about it and he assures me steps are being taken."

Royal made no reply. It was hard to concentrate when

his mind was fixed on the task that lay ahead. He would have to play the eager suitor and it wasn't going to be easy.

And he would have to spend time with Jocelyn, which wasn't really so bad as long as her mother wasn't around.

He hoped he wouldn't have to see Lily.

"So…this is the day, is it?" Sherry lounged back on the padded bench. "I hope you know what you are doing."

"I hope my father knew what he was doing. I don't have any say in the matter."

"I know you believe that, but the fact is, your father is dead. You have your own life to consider, Royal. I can't believe the old duke would wish you to do something that might make you unhappy."

"My father's greatest desire was to rebuild Bransford Castle and restore our family's fortune. That is all that mattered to him. He would do anything to make that happen and he expected the same of me."

Sherry made no reply.

"Look, it isn't as if most people don't marry for the same sort of reasons—money, power, social position. Very few people are fortunate enough to marry for love."

Sherry sat up on the bench. "Ah, so you admit to having delicate feelings for Miss Moran."

Feelings for certain. Lust, need, physical yearning. He wasn't entirely sure what else was involved. "I admit I feel a strong attraction. That is all it will ever be and I intend to put an end even to that."

"Well, then, I wish you every success. You have made clear how important this is."

Royal glanced at the clock on the mantel. "I have to go." He picked up his coat and shrugged it on, then started for the door. "Perhaps I'll see you at the club later this evening."

"Oh, you will. I intend to regain some of the money I lost to that rogue, St. Michaels, the last time I was there."

Dillon St. Michaels was one of their closest friends. Along with Royal and Sherry, he was one of the Oarsmen, a group of former Oxford sculling team members who had, over the years, formed an invincible bond.

Royal left the bedroom and Sheridan followed him out. The ducal coach waited out front as the butler opened the door and Royal descended the steep front-porch stairs. "Can I give you a lift?" he asked Sherry.

"Not necessary. I'll see you tonight."

Royal climbed into the coach and fell heavily onto the seat.

His task was set, his duty clear.

"Meadowbrook," he called up to the driver and closed his eyes, dreading what was to come.

Lily answered with dread the summons she had received, and now stood in the sumptuous Scarlet Drawing Room with the duke and the Caulfield family. Half an hour ago, Royal had met with Henry Caulfield and formally asked for his daughter's hand. The meeting was over, the happy news just announced. All that remained were the final negotiations that would make the betrothal official.

Next to Matilda Caulfield, Lily stood with her spine erect, a smile pasted on her lips.

"I couldn't be happier, my boy!" Henry clapped Royal on the back. "You'll make a fine husband for my beautiful girl." Henry grinned, his bald head glistening in the gaslight of the crystal chandelier in the drawing room, lit to banish the darkness of the gray, dismal day.

Cousin Henry was a good foot shorter than the duke, with bushy brown muttonchop whiskers lightened by a touch of gray.

"Winston!" he called out to the butler through the open drawing-room door. "Fetch a bottle of my finest champagne. This calls for a celebration!"

Lily's stomach churned. She flicked a glance at Royal whose smile looked carved into his face.

The champagne arrived amid Jocelyn's and Matilda's joyous chatter. Lily nodded and smiled as if she could actually hear what they were saying through the buzzing in her ears. Henry stood next to Royal, the grin still fixed on his face.

Champagne goblets were filled and lifted in a toast and Lily forced herself to take a swallow, though it was difficult to get the bubbles past the thick lump in her throat.

Royal had looked at her only once, as she had offered her congratulations to him and to Jo. He'd been stiffly formal and utterly remote and Lily wanted to cry.

Instead, she drank champagne and listened to the plans being made for a huge engagement party.

"We can hold the ball here at Meadowbrook," Matilda said, her broad face split with a brilliant smile. "His Grace can make the formal announcement that night."

"I don't want to wait too long," Jocelyn said, eager to taste the sweetness of becoming the new queen of society.

"We'll schedule it for the end of next month," Matilda suggested, "if that is agreeable to the duke. That should be time enough to send out the invitations and make the necessary arrangements."

Royal gave a slight nod of his head.

Matilda turned to her daughter. "Oh, isn't it just wonderful, dear? Your father and I are simply thrilled for you."

Jocelyn looked up at the duke and smiled. "You've made me so happy, Royal."

His lips curved, and Lily found herself staring at them, remembering the heat of his mouth over hers, the erotic taste of him, the hot sensations his kisses stirred.

"As happy as you have made me," he said, bringing Jocelyn's gloved hand to his lips and kissing the back.

Lily felt sick to her stomach. She had known this was going to happen, known Royal had no more choice in the matter than she did. Dear God, how could she have been so foolish as to fall in love with him!

Her heart jerked. For the first time she realized it was true. She was in love with the Duke of Bransford, had been in love even before their heated encounter in the carriage. She had been mad to follow her feelings when she had known from the start the pain it would bring.

"Oh, it is just so exciting," Matilda went on.

"We'll have our solicitors work out the details," Henry said to the duke. "I believe the rest will occur in due course."

Matilda floated forward. "Would you care to join us for supper, Your Grace? It would certainly be our honor to include you."

"I'm afraid I have to decline. I have a previous engagement."

Her lips pursed as if she had bitten into something sour. "Another time, then."

"Of course," he said, but he didn't look too eager.

The conversation continued for another half hour.

During that time, Lily made her farewells and escaped upstairs. Forcing down her emotions, she quickly penned a note to Royal about the meeting she had arranged with her uncle, then tried to decide if she dared to give it to him now or wait and send it to his town house.

In the end, as she stood at the top of the stairs and heard him bidding his hosts farewell, she made her way down to the entry and waited out of sight in the hall. As Royal approached the entry, Lily hurried out of the shadows, accidentally stumbled into him and shoved the note into his hand.

"Forgive my clumsiness, Your Grace," she said.

His fingers closed round the note. "Not at all. It was my fault entirely."

Lily kept walking, disappearing back down the hall. Darting into a drawing room that faced the front of the house, she ran to the window in time to see Royal reading the note as he climbed aboard his carriage.

The message asked him to meet her at the Fat Ox Tavern in Bunbury, St. Giles, twelve o'clock noon on the morrow. At least in a place like that, she wouldn't have to worry about anyone seeing them together.

And Uncle Jack would be waiting, as he had agreed.

Lily found herself praying fervently the duke would not come.

Lily sat in a dimly lit corner of the Fat Ox Tavern next to her uncle Jack. Though the taproom was noisy, the air smoky, the table Jack chose sat slightly apart from the rest, in a quieter place where it was easy to speak and yet no one would be able to hear their conversation.

"You think he'll come?" Jack asked.

In her heart she believed he would. Royal wanted justice for his father. He would be there, even though Lily fervently hoped he would not.

It was a minute before the hour of noon when the duke walked into the tavern, tall and impressive, even in the plain brown riding breeches and full-sleeved shirt that flashed beneath his long brown woolen cloak.

He paused for a moment, waiting for his eyes to adjust to the darkness. Jolly approached him and pointed to the table they occupied at the rear of the tavern.

"Thank you," he said and started striding in that direction.

Jack looked him over as he approached, studying him with the skill of a confidence artist assessing his quarry. "Quite a looker, ain't he?"

She shrugged, but Jack had a way of seeing right into the heart of a person.

"Anything else you want to tell me, little girl?"

Lily steeled herself. "I told you everything, Uncle Jack. The duke is marrying my cousin. We're friends. That is all."

He didn't say more, just cast her a dubious glance and rose from his chair at the table.

"Jack Moran," he said as the duke walked up.

"Royal Dewar," said the duke, omitting the use of his title, which seemed appropriate under the circumstances. Jack hailed a serving wench with big brown eyes and even bigger breasts who fetched each of them a tankard of ale.

"Lily says you're a friend of hers," Jack said to the duke as they each took a seat. "Since I love the girl more than my own life, I'd be happy to help one of her friends. What can I do for you, Duke?"

The maid arrived just then, set the tankards of ale down on the scarred wooden table and Royal flipped her a coin.

"Thank ye, sweet thing," the tavern maid said with a grin, stuffing the coin between her plump breasts.

Royal took a drink, Jack did the same, and both men set their pewter mugs down on the table. "I'm hoping you may be able to help me see justice done," Royal said.

Jack chuckled. "Now, that would be a first."

For the next half hour, Royal filled her uncle in on Preston Loomis and how he had convinced an ailing old man to trust him with his fortune.

"He's right here in London," Royal said, "living off his ill-gotten gains. There's a good chance his real name is Dick Flynn. Have you ever heard of him?"

Jack's bushy eyebrows slammed together. "Flynn, is it? Oh, I've heard of the blighter. Knew him some years back. No loyalty, that man, not even to his friends. He was a bad sort, was Dick. I heard he was dead, killed by one of his own men."

"Perhaps. Then again, perhaps not."

Jack took a swig of his ale, set the mug back down on the table. "Old Dick always was a cagey sort. Wouldn't surprise me if he was still alive and kickin'." Jack scratched his chin, clean shaven in deference to his meeting with the duke. "So what did you have in mind?"

Royal leaned back in his chair, the ladder back groaning beneath his weight. "I'm not exactly sure. I hoped perhaps you might know a way we could get back some of the money he stole from my father."

Lily spoke up just then. "I was thinking we might do some sort of a lottery scam, Uncle Jack. Or perhaps a pyramid of some kind."

Jack's dark gaze turned razor sharp. "I have to be honest, luv, nothing I've done has been in the league with what you'd need for a man in Loomis's position. From what you say, the man runs in very high circles." He sipped from his mug of ale. "But I might know someone who'd be interested in the job."

"Who?" Royal asked.

"It isn't just a matter of *who*. It's a matter of *how*. Whatever scheme we came up with would have to be financed. There'd be a mob to hire, clothes to fit them out. We'd need people we could trust on the inside— that means you and some of your friends would have to get involved. Would you want to risk your sterling reputation, Your Grace, by throwing your lot in with a bunch of confidence men? You'd be ruined if something went wrong and you got nabbed."

Royal looked him straight in the eye. Lily had a feeling he'd do whatever it took to vindicate his father. "That's a chance I'm willing to take."

Jack nodded his approval. "Then maybe I know someone who could do what you need done—if the price was right."

"How much?"

"Half the take."

"Ten percent," the duke said.

"He won't talk to you unless you agree to help with the con and give him at least twenty-five percent."

Royal didn't hesitate. "Done."

Uncle Jack grinned. Lily had the feeling he'd been bored staying out of trouble for so long. "I'll send word as soon as I can set up a meet."

Royal rose from his chair. "I am indebted to you both."

Jack and Lily stood up, too. "Hold your thanks till all of this is done and you're countin' your money, Duke," Jack said.

Lily gathered her courage and looked into Royal's face. There was something in his eyes, something sweet and yearning that made her heart squeeze.

"Thank you, Lily," he said softly.

"You saved my life. I am glad to help."

He held her gaze a moment more, then whirled away and strode out of the taproom.

Lily sank back down in her chair, her heart beating heavily.

Jack eyed her with dark speculation. "So that's the way of it."

Lily's gaze remained on the doorway where Royal had disappeared. "Yes…" she whispered, knowing it was useless to deny it any longer. "I'm afraid it is."

Thirteen

"**I**'m bored." Jocelyn trailed a finger along the windowsill in her bedroom. "I want to go out and dance. I want to have fun and not come home until the wee hours of the morning."

"Well, what is stopping you?" Lily asked, not in the least surprised. "You have plenty of invitations."

A petulant pout rose on her cousin's lips. "I thought Royal would be inviting me out. He is my fiancé, after all."

"Not officially. Not until the engagement is announced."

"Still…we are going to be married and he ignores me completely."

"I'm sure he is just busy." Very busy, she imagined, plotting and planning with Uncle Jack.

She had received a note from her uncle just that morning, telling her he had arranged a meeting with a man named Charles Sinclair. Lily had searched her memory and come up with a vague recollection of a gentleman, perfectly groomed and nattily dressed, her uncle had told her was a friend. She remembered thinking he must be very rich to wear such handsome, obviously expensive clothes. The meeting was set for this afternoon at four o'clock at an inn called the Red Rooster.

Lily planned to be there.

"I want to go out," Jo continued. "Since the duke has made no effort to entertain me, I intend to entertain myself."

"Where are you going?"

"Lord and Lady Westmore's ball. I've heard it is going to be quite glamorous, and the guest list is extensive. Who knows who might be there."

"You'll be going with your parents?"

"Mother is going and of course you must come with us."

Her heart sank. "I was planning to work tonight. I have a number of orders to fill and I need to make more samples for the shop, as well."

"Don't be silly. You can work all day tomorrow. Tonight we are going to have some fun!" Jo whirled away, lifting her arms as if she was dancing with an invisible man.

Lily inwardly groaned. Fun to Jo was a lot different than fun to Lily. Still, if Jocelyn wished her to go, she would go. It was part of her job as Jo's companion and she would be forever grateful for the position.

Jocelyn grabbed her hands and pulled her up from the pink brocade chair. The entire room was done in pink and white, with ivory gilt furniture. It was frilly and a bit overdone and it suited Jo perfectly. "Come on, we need to figure out what we are going to wear."

Lily let her cousin lead her over to the huge armoire

in the corner. "I suppose—knowing you as I do," Lily said, "we definitely should get started." She smiled. "After all, there are only six hours left until it is time to leave for the ball."

Royal walked into the Red Rooster Inn and scanned the dark interior. The place was in Chelsea, a middle-class, nondescript neighborhood where their meeting would arouse little notice. The taproom was in the basement, brightened by a row of stained-glass windows near the ceiling to let in light and paneled in gleaming dark wood.

Royal was simply dressed, as he had been before, in dark brown breeches and a white lawn shirt. As he had been instructed, he walked through the taproom, which was mostly empty this time of day, toward a small room at the back.

Two men sat at a round wooden table. Next to them sat Lily. His stomach lurched. *Lily.* He hadn't expected her to be there. Dammit to hell, he appreciated all she had done, but he certainly didn't expect her to involve herself any further.

He clenched his jaw. What they were planning was not only illegal, it was dangerous. Chase Morgan had made it clear Loomis was a man who wouldn't hesitate to do murder.

He stopped as he reached the table. "Gentlemen. Miss Moran." She looked fragile and lovely and so sweet he wanted to lean over and kiss her. An ache welled up inside him. Ruthlessly, he tamped it down.

The men rose to greet him. "Royal Dewar meet Charlie...er...Charles Sinclair," Jack said, keeping the introduction simple. "I think Charles may be able to help you."

"Mr. Sinclair," Royal said with a nod. Sweeping off his cloak, he tossed it over the back of the remaining chair and sat down across from the men, trying to keep his eyes from straying to Lily.

"Time is precious to all of us, so I won't stand on ceremony," Sinclair said. "Jack and Lily have given me all the background information they have. We've been discussing several possibilities for how we might proceed to accomplish the end all of us desire."

Sinclair was well spoken, obviously educated and immaculately dressed in expensively tailored clothes. He was tall and imposing, with solid features and a leonine mane of silver hair, handsome for a man in his fifties.

"I didn't expect Miss Moran to be here," Royal said. "This is certainly no affair for a lady."

Jack and Charles exchanged glances. Jack just smiled. "My niece is an accomplished confidence artist. She was taught by Sadie Burgess herself, God rest her soul, and I am proud to say that in her day my niece was one of the best. Lily might be a little out of practice, but with a bit of work, she'll be good as ever."

Royal stared at Lily. In the light of the candle on the table, he could see faint color creeping into her cheeks. It was impossible to believe she had ever done anything that required deception. Lily wasn't meant for the sort of life her uncle led. He couldn't possibly involve her in this.

"I can see what you're thinkin'," said Jack. "My girl's shy—always has been. That's part of the reason she's so good. No one figures her for a con. She just doesn't look the sort."

"I can do this, Royal," she said, reaching toward him across the table, her pretty sea-green eyes on his face. Just hearing his name, spoken in that gentle way of hers, sent a ripple of need coursing through him. The brush of her fingers against his skin made him go hard beneath the table.

"I want to help you," she said.

"No."

"If you want this to work," said Sinclair, "we're going to need the girl."

He shook his head. "It's too dangerous. Lily might get hurt."

Jack's bushy gray eyebrows shot up at the familiar use of her name.

"At any rate," Royal continued. "Because of her association with the Caulfield family, Miss Moran is fairly well known in society. She would undoubtedly be recognized."

"I would be disguised," Lily argued. "No one will know who I am."

"We need her," Sinclair pressed.

Royal would never know if his acquiescence came from his burning desire for justice or his equally burning desire for Lily. He selfishly wanted more time with her and this way he would get it.

"All right, but at the first sign of trouble, she's out."

"My feelins, exactly," said Jack.

"Then it's settled," Sinclair finished. "There are things we'll need to do. We'll need to hire the right people to help us…a group of actors who specialize in this sort of thing. This is where Jack shines. He's well respected in the business and his friends are extremely loyal. Can you get a mob together for us, Jack?"

He nodded. "I can."

"They'll need to be fitted out properly—that means clothing fine enough to allow them to enter the circles in which Loomis hunts for his prey."

The reminder that his father was one of Loomis's victims tightened Royal's jaw. "I'll cover that expense and whatever else we might need." He couldn't afford it, God knew. He was barely getting by as it was. But he wanted Loomis to pay and he figured he would manage somehow.

"We'll need people on the inside who are willing to help and can be trusted," Sinclair continued. "That part is up to you, Your Grace. Do you think you can manage?"

Royal thought of Sherry and knew he could count on him completely. And along with the viscount, he was fortunate to belong to the small fraternity who called themselves the Oarsmen.

One of the members, Jonathan Savage, had referred to them as the Whoresmen, but that was in their younger, wilder days.

There were six of them together now, men from the original team who had become fast friends, in truth as close as brothers. As soon as the weather warmed, Royal and the rest of the Oarsmen would be back in their low-slung, sculling boats—single-man boats these days—enjoying the exercise, the feel of muscles lengthening and tightening as they pulled on the oars, the thrill of the sleek boats skimming over the water. They often rowed against each other, betting or simply taking pleasure in the day.

They were men Royal could count on—even for something as dangerous as this.

"I can get the people we need," he vowed. "It won't be a problem."

Sinclair just nodded.

"What will you be doing?" Royal asked him.

Sinclair flashed a dignified, confident smile. "One of the things at which I am best. I shall be tracking our quarry. Before we begin, we need to know everything there is to know about Preston Loomis—his likes and dislikes, how he spends his money, how he spends his time, his sexual preferences—everything—down to the smallest detail. And particularly his vices. Those are the things we shall most likely prey upon."

Royal was impressed. Clearly, Sinclair was a professional. Still, it was far too soon to think they might actually succeed.

Sinclair straightened in his chair. "One last thing. Jack brought me a business proposition. Are we clear on the terms?"

"I front the money for what we need and give you access to Loomis. You get twenty-five percent of whatever we come away with." Assuming they got anything at all.

"All right, then, if everyone understands his task, we'll meet back here at the same time a week from today. Will that give you each enough time?"

Jack and Royal nodded.

"Once we have the information we need," Sinclair finished, "we can decide which con to use and where Lily would be most useful."

Royal didn't like the sound of that, but for the moment, he held his tongue.

Sinclair rose to his feet. "If you all will excuse me, I'm

afraid I have another appointment. I shall see you again next week." Charles Sinclair turned away from the table and began moving purposely toward the door of the taproom. As soon as he disappeared, Royal turned to Lily.

"I don't like this, Lily. I would never forgive myself if anything happened to you."

Her gaze held his. "Wouldn't you?" she asked softly. In the light of the candle her skin looked iridescent, her lips a delicate rose.

"No..." he replied in the same soft tone, unable to look away from her lovely pale eyes.

Desire pulsed through him. Damn, he couldn't seem to control himself even with her uncle sitting right beside her!

"Lily'll be all right," Jack assured him. "We'll both look out for her."

Royal tore his gaze away from her and simply nodded. He dared not look at her again. If he did, he would sweep her up and carry her out of there. He would take her straight to his bed and make love to her until both of them were too exhausted to move.

Hell and damnation! His infatuation for Lily was even worse than he had believed. He shoved himself up from his chair.

"Again I thank you for your help. I'll see you both next week." Turning, he strode out of the inn without looking back, afraid of what would happen if he did.

Lord and Lady Westmore's ball was exquisite. Jocelyn was impressed by the lavish bouquets of white chrysanthemums in huge pots along the mirrored walls of the ballroom. The entire chamber had been decorated to look like a fairy-tale castle, with a mural on one wall and hundreds of candles burning in tall, tiered candelabra. Overhead, crystal gaslights hanging from the molded ceilings cast a soft glow over the women in their elegant silk and satin gowns, and the men in black evening wear.

In a plum silk gown with a lighter-plum overskirt scattered with brilliants, Jocelyn stood next to her mother, entertaining a small group of male admirers that included Viscount Wellesley and several of Wellesley's friends, in particular, a magnificently handsome man named Jonathan Savage.

Savage was black-haired and olive-skinned and oddly disturbing, a man on the fringes of society, her mother had warned her, not the sort Jocelyn should ever be drawn to, and yet he was intriguing.

Dillon St. Michaels was among the group, a big man, the sort who always seemed to have something witty to say. He was handsome and charming, even managing to wring a laugh from her mother, nearly an impossible feat.

From the corner of her eye, she caught sight of another group of men deep in conversation. One stood out from the rest, his shoulders wider, his features more defined. She recognized Christopher Barclay and thought what a fine male specimen he was. She couldn't help admiring the confident way he moved, the rich timbre of his voice, and his eyes... Her breath caught as she realized he was watching her just as she watched him.

Ridiculously, her heart started pounding. She couldn't seem to drag her gaze away, and when his mouth curved as if he knew, a rare flush began to rise in her cheeks.

That smug look sent a jolt of indignation shooting through her. How dare he look at her that way! As if he had some sort of claim on her simply because he had kissed her! Why, the man had barely a nickel to his name! He was a barrister still striving to make himself known, certainly not someone *she* would be interested in.

She jerked her attention back to the men around her, smiled at Savage until he had no choice but to ask her to dance. A waltz was playing and as he whirled her around the floor, she saw that he was a very good dancer. Jocelyn gave him a brilliant smile as they waltzed past Christopher Barclay and she was delighted to see the smug smile slip from his face.

A scowl rose instead and Jocelyn inwardly smiled. Served him right, she thought. He was hardly her social equal. Once she was a duchess, she would give him the cut direct.

She held on to the thought as she and Savage finished the dance and he returned her to her mother.

"A pleasure, Miss Caulfield."

"Indeed, Mr. Savage."

Mother was scowling, not the least pleased to see her dancing with a man of such sordid reputation. Jocelyn ignored her. She wasn't interested in Jonathan Savage or any other man. She was soon to become a duchess. That was all that mattered.

Growing bored with the men's adoration, she glanced round the room in search of Lily, spotted her in conversation with the Dowager Countess of Tavistock, Royal's aunt Agatha, soon to be Jocelyn's aunt, as well. She should say a polite hello but she wasn't going to. At least for tonight, she would leave conversing with an old woman to her cousin, who laughed at something the dowager said and actually seemed to be enjoying their talk.

Jocelyn immersed herself in the dancing, partnered with a dozen different men, each time casting Christopher a triumphant glance, which seemed to make his hard jaw look even harder.

Beginning to tire of the game, she excused herself to the ladies' retiring room, but instead walked down the hall into an empty salon where she wouldn't be seen, then out onto the terrace for a cooling breath of air.

Careful to remain in the shadows around a corner out of sight, she made her way over to the balustrade that looked down into the garden. She was enjoying the hum of crickets and the reviving cool night air, when she felt a pair of hands settle on her waist and a man's hard body behind her. The squeak of outrage rising in her throat was silenced by a pair of familiar lips tracing a pattern on her collarbone.

"So…you like to dance, do you?"

His masculine scent filled her senses. The hard length of his body surrounded her, pressing her up against the balustrade. She should be outraged at his boldness, his incredible audacity, ought to turn and slap his handsome face. Instead, she stood there helplessly, letting him kiss the back of her neck.

"I've missed you," Christopher said softly, turning her around and into his arms. "I've thought of our kiss a hundred times."

Then his mouth settled over hers and he was kissing her and all she could do was sway against him and slide her arms around his neck. He demanded entrance to her mouth and when she parted her lips, his tongue swept in, taking her deeply, as if it was his right.

A little whimper escaped. Desire flooded through her, making her limbs feel weak. If he hadn't been holding her up, she wasn't sure she could have remained on her feet.

"It seems you like kissing, too," he said against the side of her neck, nipping an earlobe. "I'm not surprised...a woman as full of passion as you." He bit down on the lobe, then eased the pain by taking the sensitive bit of flesh into his mouth and sucking gently.

Jocelyn moaned.

"You're beautiful and fiery," he said, claiming her mouth again, kissing her until she felt light-headed. "You're also spoiled and selfish, the kind of woman a man needs to take in hand."

Her foggy mind cleared just enough to know she'd been insulted. "How dare you say such a thing! I should slap you for your insolence."

He chuckled. "But you won't, will you? You aren't sure I won't slap you back."

Dear God, it was true. Christopher Barclay was an unknown commodity, volatile, yet always tightly controlled.

He bent his head and kissed her again, gently this time, softening his words. "I would never hit a woman, certainly not one as lovely as you. Not even if you deserved it." He lifted his head, and a corner of his mouth edged up. "A good hard spanking wouldn't be out of the question, however."

"How dare you!"

His jaw hardened. "I'd dare a lot more if I could afford you—which we both know I can't. You'll marry far above me. I hope you at least get a real man for your money."

"Why, you—"

Cutting off her reply, he turned and left her there on the terrace, alone and fuming in the shadows. Knowing he was right.

She would never marry Christopher or any other man of his lowly social position. But the laugh would be on him when her engagement to the duke was announced.

There was no doubt of Royal Dewar's masculinity. He was a magnificent man, unbelievably handsome and amazingly virile, a fact she had discovered during their brief afternoon kiss. The tall male body pressing into hers had been as solid as granite, and so was his quite impressive male anatomy, if the tight fit of his riding breeches could be deemed any indication.

Jocelyn's gaze moved to the French doors leading into the drawing room. Christopher Barclay stood next to the Countess of Wren, a lovely woman in her thirties, his head bent toward her in intimate conversation. A stab of jealousy went through her, along with a renewed shot of temper.

Jocelyn moistened her lips, tasting Christopher there, feeling the same sweep of desire she had felt just moments ago. She watched his mouth curve into a seductive smile and her own lips began to curve. Christopher Barclay would never make a suitable husband. But then Jocelyn wasn't interested in marrying him—not when she could marry a duke.

Marriage wasn't an option, but there was no reason she couldn't take the man as a lover.

Jocelyn was used to getting what she wanted. And tonight she had discovered how badly she wanted Christopher Barclay.

Fourteen

Lily yawned as she stood in the bedroom unlacing Jocelyn's corset. Outside the window the sky was a mottled gray, sunrise less than an hour away. Lily was tired clear to the bone. For hours she had been forced to dance and converse with people she had only just met. Amazingly, she had enjoyed herself.

Perhaps it was the unusual attention she had received from Viscount Wellesley and his group of friends, who had kept her well entertained all evening. Perhaps Lord Wellesley had guessed her feelings for the duke and felt sorry for her. There was a kindness in Sheridan Knowles she found extremely charming.

The other men in the group were an interesting mix. Wellesley had said they had known each other since their days at Oxford, that all of them, including the duke, had been members of the Oxford sculling team. They had beaten Cambridge soundly in '45, he had said with a grin and obvious pride, winning the renowned Oxford and Cambridge Boat Race.

"Are you finished yet?" Jocelyn's voice jolted her from her thoughts.

"Very nearly." Lily tugged on the corset strings, loosening the laces, hearing Jocelyn's sigh of relief.

"Thank God. I can finally breathe." She inhaled deeply as if to confirm the fact. "It was quite an exciting evening, wasn't it?" Jo turned to face her. "Even *you* looked as if, for a change, you were enjoying yourself."

Lily smiled. "To my surprise, I was." Perhaps because Royal wasn't there and she didn't have to bear the agony of seeing him with Jo.

"As usual, my fiancé was nowhere to be seen." She stepped free of the corset that had fallen to her feet, picked it up and tossed it onto the bed. "Royal wasn't there, but Christopher Barclay was."

In the middle of hanging up Jo's plum silk gown, Lily stopped and turned. "Not *the* Christopher Barclay. Not the Number Ten Kisser, Christopher Barclay."

"That is the one…and I stand by my former assessment."

Lily's eyes widened. "Don't say you kissed him again—not after you've promised to marry the duke."

Jocelyn grinned. "Actually, he kissed me—at least at first."

"Jocelyn!"

She hoisted her chin. "Not only did I kiss him, I've decided to have an affair with him."

Lily just stood there, alarm sweeping through her. "But you can't possibly! You can't take a lover until you have given the duke an heir. And there is the not-so-small matter that your husband will expect you to be a virgin."

Jo just shrugged. "It's the 1850s, Lily—not medieval

times. I shall simply make certain the duke never knows the truth. Besides, Royal is hardly pure. He has had any number of mistresses—I know that for a fact."

Lily didn't doubt her. Jo had a way of ferreting out information. On top of that, Royal was an extremely virile man—as she knew from personal experience. There was no doubt he could have any woman he wanted.

The thought sent a little stab of jealousy shooting through her.

"You won't say anything, will you?"

Lily shook her head. "You know me better than that. You're my cousin. I would never repeat anything you told me in confidence." No matter the distance between herself and the Caulfields, she had always been loyal to them. Lily couldn't imagine where she might be now if they hadn't taken her in off the streets.

"Have you…have you made an assignation with Barclay?"

"Don't be silly. He hasn't the slightest notion. When I am ready, I shall let him know."

"Perhaps he will refuse. Once your engagement is announced, Barclay will be honor-bound to—"

"I don't intend to wait until I am officially engaged. The engagement ball is more than a month away. I intend to have Christopher very soon."

Lily couldn't believe it. "What if you are found out? The duke might break off the engagement."

Jo pulled her nightgown on over her head, let it fall down over her voluptuous curves. "I doubt it. He wants my money, not me. And if I am going to be married to a man who merely tolerates my existence, a man who will bed me simply because it is his duty—then I am going to know true passion with a man I desire before I am wed to him."

Lily said nothing. It was simply inconceivable that her cousin would make Royal a cuckold even before they were married. And yet, she had come to understand a bit about passion. With the right man, it was an emotion nearly impossible to resist.

And Jo might well be right about the duke. Lily thought there was a very good chance Royal would marry Jocelyn whether she was a virgin or not. He had made a vow to accept the marriage his father had arranged and rebuild the Bransford fortune.

Lily didn't believe there was anything Jo could do to make him break his word.

Royal sat in a private room at White's, surrounded by his closest friends. All of them had arrived precisely at the appointed time, 8:00 p.m.

Sherry was already in London, so was Jonathan Savage, third son of the Earl of Greville. Dillon St. Michaels lived in the city full-time, with the exception of an occasional excursion to his grandfather's estate in the country. Benjamin Wyndam, Earl of Nightingale, and his wife, Maryann, lived in a mansion in a fashionable Mayfair neighborhood. Only Quentin Garrett, Viscount March, heir to the Earl of Leighton, had ridden any distance in answer to Royal's summons.

Royal had no doubt they would come to his aid. Should they ask, he would do the same for any of them.

"All right, don't keep us in suspense," said St. Michaels, a big man, heavyset through the chest and shoulders, one hell of an oarsman. But then they all were. "What is it that is so all-fired important?"

"I hope it's something lurid," Savage said, lounging back in his chair, black hair gleaming, his fingers steepled lazily in front of him. "I find myself growing bored of late. Perhaps this will rouse my flagging spirits."

"Very little of yours ever flags," countered St. Michaels. "With your insatiable appetites, you walk around stiff as a pole half the time."

All of them chuckled. It was well known that Savage was the cocksman of the group. Being caught in a compromising situation last year with one of the young debutantes' chaperones had ruined what was left of his already sordid reputation.

"Perhaps Bransford wishes to cry off from marrying his delectable future bride," St. Michaels offered.

"I doubt it," said Savage. "I had the good fortune to dance with the lady last night and I can safely say, a man would be a fool to give up bedding a wench like that."

"We were speaking of marriage, Savage," Quent reminded him, speaking up for the first time. "There is a difference, which I am sure, deep down, you must know." As heir to the Earl of Leighton he carried the honorary title of Viscount March, but he preferred his friends simply call him Quent.

Quent had recently entered the marriage mart, though so far he hadn't met anyone who fit his exacting standards. Royal envied him being able to wed a woman he chose instead of one who had been chosen for him.

"I believe the matter we are here to discuss concerns the late duke, Royal's father," Sherry said, returning the men to the subject at hand.

The small group instantly sobered. All of them knew Royal's misfortune in inheriting a worthless dukedom and that because of it he would be marrying for money, wedding a woman of incredible wealth, a marriage his father had arranged.

"As you all know, over the last three years of his life, my father lost most of the Bransford fortune. That in itself is a tragedy of immense proportions. It seems, however, that the duke was not solely to blame. My father was acting in a diminished capacity. That is to say, his stroke left him less than capable of making financial decisions."

"Which is where a man named Preston Loomis comes in," Sherry added, having already been brought up to date early that morning.

"Loomis, you say? I believe I know the name," Nightingale said. "Met the chap at an affair last year, seemed a nice enough fellow."

"I'm sure he did," Royal said, his jaw going tight.

"Loomis is actually a con man named Dick Flynn," Sherry explained. "Basically, he bled the old duke dry and now lives in fine feather off Royal's inheritance right here in the city."

Jonathan frowned, drawing his winged black eyebrows together. "I think I also may have met him. Suave sort of fellow, charms all the older women?"

Royal nodded. "And apparently charismatic enough to convince my father to invest a fortune in what were nothing more than a series of well-planned swindles."

"Put simply, the poor man was duped," added Sherry. "It is one thing to make business decisions that turn out badly. It is another thing entirely to take advantage of a sick old man who is mentally incapable of using sound judgment."

"We all liked and admired your father, Royal," said Quent. "Loomis should be brought to justice."

"Unfortunately, there is no solid evidence," Royal said. "All we have are rumor and innuendo, no physical proof we can take to the authorities."

"Which means we will have to deal with the man ourselves," Sherry finished.

St. Michaels leaned forward. "Which begs the question…why have you brought us here? What can we do to help?"

Royal's gaze ran over the men. "As I said, we can't go to the police, but I may have come up with a way to get back at least some of what Loomis stole from my father."

Quent straightened, his lean, broad-shouldered build becoming more pronounced, his expression even more serious than it usually was.

St. Michaels rubbed his big hands together in glee. "Oh, joy, Savage may indeed be saved from boredom."

One of Jonathan's black eyebrows arched up and he looked askance at Royal. "I admit, this sounds intriguing. What role do you expect us to play?"

"To tell you the truth, I am not yet quite sure. I must warn you this could be dangerous. Rumor has it, Loomis won't stop at murder. And there is always the chance we'll be caught and if we are, our reputations will suffer."

Savage snorted. "That is hardly a problem for me."

"I'm in," said St. Michaels. "I could do with a bit of entertainment."

"Anyone wish to decline?" Sherry asked.

No one said a word.

Royal surveyed his friends, saw the resolve in their faces. "All right, then. I'll keep you posted. A week from now, I should know more. I'll let you know what I need."

The men relaxed. Sherry left to fetch a waiter for a fresh round of drinks and talk turned to less serious matters.

The stage was set. The cast assembled. Royal wondered how long it would be before the play began.

Fifteen

Lily sat nervously next to her uncle in the backroom of the Red Rooster Inn. Charles Sinclair sat across from them, his leonine mane of silver hair gleaming in the light of the candle in the center of the table. Royal would arrive any minute.

Lily steeled herself for his appearance, torn between despair and a ridiculous eagerness to see him. She wondered what he would say when he saw the way she was dressed—in flowing, bright-colored silk skirts that showed a bit of ankle, glittering fake gold jewelry and a glossy black wig.

Not pleased, she didn't imagine.

He didn't want her involved in this and today it would be clear how deeply she would be.

There was some comfort in that, she supposed, that he was concerned for her welfare. It was a notion she would hold on to as all of this progressed.

She smoothed the red silk blouse that was part of her costume, the gathered neckline modestly cut so as not to offend her hostess at whatever affair she attended. The skirt was even more colorful, a garment she had fashioned from scarves and scraps of diaphanous fabric. Though the skirt and blouse were of far better quality than the ones she had worn when she was sixteen, she wasn't used to the sideways glances and raised eyebrows she had garnered as she walked down the street.

It didn't matter. Once she immersed herself in whatever role she played, she became completely that person. And she had played the role of Gypsy several times before.

She sighed as she silently sat waiting. At least one good thing had come of this. After six lonely years, she had been reunited with her uncle. Uncle Jack was the only connection she had to her parents and the happy memories of her childhood. No matter the poverty she had suffered when she had lived with him, no matter the sort of life he led, she had missed him. And she loved him.

"There he is." Sinclair rose, along with her uncle, to greet the duke. Salutations were exchanged and Sinclair and Uncle Jack sat back down.

For an instant, Royal remained standing, his gaze riveted on Lily. Then the pieces fell together, recognition dawned and he hissed in a breath.

"Good God, I can scarcely believe it is you. I wouldn't have recognized you at all if I hadn't expected you to be here."

Jack gave up a rough chuckle. "She can play a dozen different parts. Girl has a real talent for acting."

But she hated every moment of it, hated the deception and being in the spotlight, and from his tight-jawed expression, she thought Royal somehow knew.

"She should be making hats," he said darkly, taking a seat across from her.

"Oh, she will be," Jack said. "Soon as we finish the job. Lily never was a quitter."

No, she had always seen the sham through to the end. They had to eat and this was how her uncle earned what little money he had. Of course, they had never tried anything as monumental as this.

"So what is the plan?" Royal asked.

Charles Sinclair spoke up in answer. "Before we come to that, you need to understand a bit about our mark."

"Loomis, you mean."

"Exactly so. On the surface, Preston Loomis is a rather dull fellow. He likes to gamble, but only in moderation. He enjoys betting on sporting events, though again, not overmuch. He drinks, but not to excess."

"Sounds like a bloody saint," grumbled Jack.

"What about women?" Royal asked.

"The man's no eunuch. He enjoys women, particularly beautiful ones, but he is careful to keep them at a distance. He's never had a mistress."

"Doesn't sound like an extravagant spender," Royal said. "Likely, he'll have at least a portion of the money he stole from my father."

"Most of it, from what I could discover. As I said, Loomis is fairly dull. It is Dick Flynn who is intriguing." Sinclair smiled as if he relished relaying the information he had gathered. "As you may know, Your Grace, Flynn's mother was a prostitute, but that was mostly a sideline. She made her living by reading palms and casting tarot cards, a trade she learned from an old Gypsy woman named Madam Medela who lived in the

Haymarket District. Flynn's mother went there for readings, herself, and she always took her son."

Royal flicked a glance at Lily, his gaze running over her Gypsy costume and straight black, shoulder-length wig—an item he had unknowingly paid for. "I gather his background figures into what you have planned."

"Precisely. You see, even after his mother died, Flynn continued to visit the old Gypsy woman, seeking advice on personal matters and ofttimes matters of finance. He returned to her house even after he became Preston Loomis."

"She still alive?" Jack asked.

Sinclair shook his head. "She died several years ago. Apparently, Loomis still laments her passing."

"The information you've collected is impressive," Royal said. "I'm still not certain how you plan to use it."

Sinclair flashed a self-satisfied smile. "We are simply going to provide Mr. Loomis with a substitute…Madam Medela's grand-niece, Madam Tsaya."

Royal's gaze swung back to Lily and she read the doubt in his face. "The man is a confidence artist. Won't he be suspicious that Madam Tsaya is a fake?"

Sinclair chuckled. "Ofttimes a confidence man is the easiest mark of all. To be successful, you must believe you are smarter than everyone else. Loomis thinks he is invincible. Add to that, he has never worked with a woman." Sinclair smiled. "And Lily can be extremely convincing."

Royal's jaw flexed. "Whatever he is, I don't think the man is a fool. I don't like involving Lily in something as dangerous as this."

Sinclair dismissed his protest with a wave of his

hand. "We've been through all that before. You want Loomis. This is the best way to get to him and we need Lily in order to see it done."

Uncle Jack broke in before Royal could summon another protest. "So what's our next move?" Jack asked with undisguised excitement. He had always enjoyed his work, Lily knew, even when one of his schemes had gone wrong and they had to go into hiding from the law.

"How we proceed from here is up to His Grace," Sinclair said. "We need to begin introducing Madam Tsaya into Loomis's social circles. After she attends her first party, she will undoubtedly be invited to others. She's an oddity, entertainment for people who live jaded, bored existences and have very little to keep themselves occupied. Jack, Lily and I will work out the details. You just get her invited and let Lily take care of the rest."

"How can we be sure Loomis will attend?" Royal asked.

"It's been a while since your father died. I have a feeling Loomis will be on the prowl for fresh game. The man is a professional. It is simply what he does."

Royal leaned back in his chair. "You seem to have everything worked out."

"That, sir, is what I do."

Royal rose from his seat. "It appears our business here is finished. I'll send word as soon as arrangements have been made." His gaze lingered a moment too long on Lily's face, making her heart start to clatter. "Miss Moran…gentlemen." Grabbing his cloak off the back of his chair, he swirled it round his shoulders and with long, purposeful strides, exited the room.

Lily let out a breath. She managed a shaky smile. "Well, it looks as if we are off and running."

"Indeed," said Sinclair.

"I've got us a mob," Jack said, "and they're being fitted out as we speak."

"Good work," said Sinclair. "Lily, you and I will go over the information I was able to collect on Madam Medela. You needn't claim to know her well since you are merely her grand-niece. Just let Loomis know you have inherited some of her same talents—except that you use the stars as your guide instead of a deck of cards. You have used that ruse before as I recall."

"Why, yes."

"It will give your story an intriguing twist."

Lily liked the idea. Since she loved the stars and knew most of the constellations by name, it wasn't a difficult thing to do.

More details were discussed and decided upon before Lily and her uncle made their way out to the street and Lily hailed a hansom cab to return her to the Caulfields' mansion.

Three days later a note arrived from Royal. Lord and Lady Nightingale would be hosting a soiree on Saturday next. Preston Loomis was listed among the invited guests. If he accepted the invitation, their plan would be set in motion.

Lily's stomach roiled with nerves at the thought of the performance she would have to give. Still, she was ready. She wanted to do this, wanted Royal to have the justice he deserved.

And she simply wanted to be with him. It was foolish, but there it was.

She couldn't stop a rush of anticipation, knowing she would see him again very soon.

The weather warmed over the following week. The early March air was still chilly that Friday afternoon, but Jocelyn welcomed the respite, however brief, from the bone-chilling cold.

Her spirits were high as she entered the private, curtained booth at Chez le Mer, an elegant restaurant known for its intimate dining rooms and its discretion.

It hadn't been difficult to find such a place. She had friends among the most sophisticated women in London. They gossiped about illicit affairs, who met who in places like Chez le Mer, secretly yearning to be one of the women who went there to meet her lover.

Jocelyn glanced up at the clock, her fingers drumming against the linen cloth on the table. She turned at the sound of Christopher's familiar deep voice. He was only a few minutes late and yet it annoyed her.

"So you are here at last," she said. "Don't you know it is impolite to keep a lady waiting? I was just about to leave."

"Were you, indeed?" Bending his dark head, he pressed a light kiss on her lips, and the taste of him filled her senses. The man had unmitigated nerve and yet Jocelyn didn't resist his attentions. She liked that she couldn't dominate him as she could others, that he didn't fawn over her the way most men did.

Except of course for her fiancé, who rarely paid her any attention at all.

The irritating thought bolstered her courage. She ignored a rush of nerves as Christopher took a seat across from her, pulled the bottle of champagne from the silver bucket beside the table and poured each of them a glass.

He lifted his goblet, waited till she lifted hers, then took a sip and savored the flavor. "An excellent choice. Knowing your tastes, I am not surprised." He set the glass back down on the table. "I am here at your invitation. I could be wrong, but I don't believe you suggested our meeting to enjoy the delicious food. Tell me, sweet, why did you ask me to come?"

"You don't believe in being subtle, do you?"

"Not really."

Jocelyn sipped her champagne, deciding how best to proceed. "All right, then, I shall tell you. I have given the matter a good deal of thought and I have decided I want us to become lovers."

His deep brown eyes darkened. His gaze moved over her face as if he caressed her and a little shiver went through her. "You certainly don't mince words."

"I don't see any point."

"Neither do I. But I admit you have taken me by surprise. You are a maiden yet. Or at least I believe you to be one. Your husband will expect you to come to him a virgin."

She colored faintly, but held her ground. "I shall marry for reasons other than passion. I would like to know true passion before that day comes. I believe I can know it with you."

A gleam came into his eyes and his nostrils flared. "You understand…given our circumstances…should we embark upon such a course, whatever happens between us will come to naught. Desire is all we will ever share."

She was on safer ground here. "The course of my life has already been decided. Desire is all I want from you, Christopher."

He studied her as if he was weighing the possible consequences before making a decision. Shoving back his chair, he rose to his feet. He caught her hand, drew her up beside him and straight into his arms.

"Desire and pleasure," he whispered against the side of her neck. "Those are the only things I can give you. If that is enough…"

Soft kisses trailed over her throat, raising goose bumps across her skin. Jocelyn dragged his mouth to hers for a wet, burning kiss, telling him with her lips and tongue that his offer was exactly what she wanted.

"When can we meet?" he asked between deep, drugging kisses that left her gasping for breath and her body on fire.

"Tomorrow night. I've taken a suite for our use at the Parkland Hotel under the name Mrs. Middleton."

He bit down on her earlobe as he drew her into the vee between his legs, letting her feel how hard he was. "Sure of yourself, weren't you."

She smiled wickedly. "I can't imagine a man of your sexuality refusing a woman he wants."

He laughed harshly. "I suppose there is no point in denying it." He kissed her again, taking her deeply with his tongue. He began inching up her heavy silk skirts, and Jocelyn knew a moment of uncertainty.

Christopher must have sensed it, for he paused, began to kiss her softly again. "So…you *are* a virgin."

She stiffened in his arms and her chin inched up. "I won't be after tomorrow night."

He laughed softly and Jocelyn relaxed back into his embrace. She kissed him again, opening her mouth so that he could taste her more deeply, and Christopher groaned. Lifting her skirts all the way to her waist, he slid his hands over the twin globes of her bottom. She could feel the heat of his palms through the thin fabric of her drawers and a soft ache throbbed between her legs.

"We'll take our time," he whispered. "I'll give you what you want—I promise you."

Jocelyn gasped as his hands eased beneath the waistband of her drawers, slid over her bottom to caress her naked flesh, gripped and lifted until she was riding his thigh and moaning softly.

"You've a good deal to learn, sweeting," he said, tilting her chin so that he could kiss her throat. "I don't think one night is going to be enough."

"No," she whispered, lacing her fingers in his thick dark hair. "I don't suppose it will."

Christopher's body tightened as he forced himself to end the embrace and move away. Setting her on her feet, he let her skirts fall back into place over her hips. "It's time for me to go. If I stay, I'll give in to my need and have you right here on the table."

Jocelyn's eyes widened at the vivid image. Unable to form a single word, she simply nodded.

"Is your carriage here?" he asked as he straightened his clothes.

"Yes, just outside."

"Then I shall leave you. I'll see you tomorrow night." With a last, hard kiss, he was gone.

For long moments, Jocelyn just stood there. She felt weak and dizzy, her body damp and throbbing. She had made the necessary preparations. Christopher had agreed. Now all she had to do was see it done.

She squared her shoulders. She wanted this—wanted him.

Tomorrow night she was going to have him.

Sixteen

◦◦◦

Saturday night arrived all too soon. Dressed in her Gypsy costume, posing as Lady Nightingale's special entertainment for the evening, Lily entered the elegant brick mansion through the servants' entrance. With a quick glance over her shoulder, she caught a wave from Uncle Jack, who would be waiting for her in the alley when her performance was finished.

Taking a breath to steady her nerves, Lily started along the hallway, passing the stairs to the kitchen, moving past the butler's pantry, stepping out of the way as a bevy of servants rushed by on their way to the drawing room where the party was being held.

She stopped a footman before he had time to escape, lowered her voice and slipped into the slight accent that she had used in the role long ago. "I am sorry to bother you, but I vould appreciate your help. Vould you pleaze tell Lady Nightingale Madam Tsaya has arrived."

She kept her voice husky and her cadence slow. She could do a very good Hungarian accent, but they had decided it should be kept to a minimum. If her great-aunt was Madam Medela, an old woman when she died, Tsaya would likely have lived in England for quite some time.

Standing in the shadows at the end of the hall, she could see into the entry, three stories high and crowned with a stained-glass dome. The walls were lined with marble busts of famous heads of state, and flowers in crystal vases filled the house with a fragrant scent.

Most of the guests had already arrived. At ten o'clock, Lady Nightingale would introduce her, telling those in attendance that she was a seer known for her ability to predict good fortune to certain lucky individuals.

At their weekly meeting at the Red Rooster, they had discussed Royal's plans to introduce Madam Tsaya into society and he had told them a little about the people who would be helping them. At various affairs, Royal's friends would attest that she had made uncanny predictions that had indeed come true.

Tonight she was going to predict good fortune for Lord Nightingale, her host, as well as a viscount named March. She wouldn't approach Preston Loomis—not tonight. With the help of Royal's friends, Loomis would be invited to other affairs where she would be included. In time, she would seek him out and begin to predict good fortune for him.

"Madam Tsaya! Do come in." Lady Nightingale, a small woman, lightly freckled and copper-haired, hurried toward her. She was young, no more than five-and-twenty, her smile so genuinely warm Lily found herself instantly at ease.

"My lady," she said with a slight curtsy.

"I am so glad you could come. Your name has come up quite often of late. It is said you have incredible powers."

"I am a Gypsy. Some of us can see things other people cannot. It is not so difficult as it may seem."

"Well, I could scarcely begin to predict who might or might not have good fortune." The little countess took her arm. "Come now, and I shall present you to my guests."

Lily felt a wave of nerves that made her stomach flutter. It had always been that way and yet, eventually, the feeling would pass and she would be able to do what she had come for. She let the countess lead her into the main salon, a spectacular chamber done in dark green and gold with molded ceilings and thick Persian carpets. Huge marble fireplaces warmed each end of the room.

Laughter and gaiety filled the air, along with the sound of music. The countess raised her hand as a signal to the orchestra playing in a corner of the drawing room, and the music instantly ceased.

"If I may please have your attention." Little by little the guests began to quiet until Lady Nightingale had their full attention. "Some of you may have heard of our very special guest tonight. For those of you who have not, it is my pleasure to present Madam Tsaya. Over the course of the evening, some of you may be lucky enough to have her seek you out. You see, Madam Tsaya has the ability to predict good fortune."

A rumble came from the crowd, followed by looks of interest. The countess turned the floor over to her guest. "Madam?"

"Good evening," Lily said. "It is my pleasure to be here. I hope I vill see good fortune for many of you tonight." She glanced round the room, spotted a number of familiar faces but, dressed in such wildly different clothes, her blond hair stuffed under the heavy black wig, she had no fear of being recognized.

As she moved beside the countess, she saw Sheridan Knowles standing next to Jonathan Savage and robust Dillon St. Michaels, men she had met at Lady Westmore's ball. St. Michaels conversed with an elegant young woman with honey-brown hair, while Savage spoke to a lean, attractive man with hard, carved features and a far-too-serious expression.

The men were Royal's conspirators, she knew, along with some she didn't yet know, perhaps the woman, as well. Her perusal continued past one guest after another and suddenly her breath caught. Tall and golden, the duke was impossible to miss in his black evening clothes. He chatted with his aunt, his head bent toward the elderly woman as he listened to what she said, but over her thin shoulders, his tawny gaze was fixed on Lily.

Her pulse kicked up, began to pound in her ears. For an instant, she couldn't look away. But if their plan was going to succeed, she needed to concentrate on her role, to forget the Duke of Bransford and become entirely Madam Tsaya.

Lily fixed a long-ago practiced, faintly mysterious smile on her face and returned her attention to Lady Nightingale, who escorted her round the room. The countess paused next to Lord Wellesley. "I believe, my lord, you have already met our guest, Madam Tsaya."

"Why, yes," said the viscount. "As a matter of fact, Madam Tsaya predicted I would win a wager I had made with Lord Nightingale, and so I did."

Two or three people turned at the announcement to

study her more closely. Lady Nightingale kept moving, guiding Lily through the crowd. "Mr. Savage…I believe you are also acquainted with Madam Tsaya."

He flashed a devilish smile, caught her hand, bowed over it and kissed the back. "Indeed, I am." She wasn't wearing gloves and she could feel the warmth of his lips against her skin. He was an incredibly handsome man, dark and mysterious, the exact opposite of Royal.

"The lady predicted my stallion, Black Star, would win at the racetrack," he said. "I bet heavily, and I won—just as she said."

"Astounding," said the countess.

Lily just smiled. From the corner of her eye, she saw Royal, closer now, his jaw hard as he watched her interplay with Savage. Jocelyn was nowhere to be seen. She was ensconced in a suite at the Parkland Hotel, waiting for her lover.

Lily still found it hard to believe. Not only was her cousin's engagement soon to be announced, she was a virgin. But Jocelyn had always been headstrong and spoiled, and Royal's inattention had wounded her pride.

The countess led Lily toward the tall man with the carved features she had noticed before.

"Madam, may I present you to Viscount March."

"How do you do, my lord?"

March made a faint bow of his head, causing a strand of dark brown hair to tumble forward. "A pleasure, madam."

Lily studied him for several long moments, her gaze going over his dark eyes and lean features. "You will be playing cards later at your club," she said as if it were a fact and not a question.

"Why, yes. I plan to stop by on my way home."

"If you play tonight," she told him, "you will win."

He chuckled as if he found her prediction amusing but didn't give it much credence. "I'll be sure to keep that in mind."

At their next affair, March would announce his good fortune in winning at his club—whether he actually went there or not. A time would come when they would have to be careful to make sure each prediction could be verified, but not yet.

The evening progressed and Lily settled more deeply into her role. The countess made a number of other introductions, then left her in the care of a group of young men who were instantly enamored of the exotic woman she pretended to be. The description she had of Preston Loomis fit a man standing a few feet away. In his early sixties, tall and silver-haired, he reminded her of Charles Sinclair, with the same sort of imposing presence. But Loomis's eyes were blue and not brown, and he boasted an elegant silver mustache.

She made no move to approach him, just kept her attention fixed on the young men in the group, smiling and laughing as if everything they said was utterly fascinating. She lowered her lashes and kept her mysterious smile in place.

"So…Madam Tsaya, may I ask if you are a married lady?" This from the son of a viscount who was introduced to her as Mr. Emmet Burrows. "Or is there some hope for us poor besotted fools?"

She mustered an uncertain expression. "I vas married once," she said gravely. "My husband passed to the other side three years ago."

"You have my most sincere regrets," Burrows said.

"So you are a widow," said another young man. "You must be very lonely."

She shrugged her shoulders. "One gets used to being alone."

"There is hardly a need for that," said Burrows, slim, blond and eager. "I would be happy to entertain you. Perhaps you would care to accompany me to a play."

Her soot-blackened lashes swept down. "I do not know you well enough. Perhaps at some time in the future." She gave him a look of encouragement before making her farewells and walking off toward Lord Nightingale.

She paused just in front of him. "My lord?"

He looked up as if he hadn't been expecting her, which she knew he had. Like the rest of Royal's friends, Nightingale was handsome, with his nearly black hair and hazel eyes. He seemed older than the others, though she knew he wasn't. "What is it, my dear?"

"It has come to me that should you wish to increase your fortune, you should buy stock in…" She leaned over and pretended to whisper the name, as if the information were for his ears alone.

"I believe I've heard of that company. I shall give it some consideration. Thank you, my dear."

She turned away, barely glanced at Loomis, who was staring at her with shrewd blue eyes. It wasn't the first time he had noticed her. Loomis had been watching her off and on since the moment of her arrival.

It appeared she had accomplished what she had come for. She had captured his interest. The game would continue from here.

Exhaustion began to set in, as it always did after a performance. Grateful it was finally time to leave, Lily excused herself to the ladies' retiring room, made her way to the staircase and headed upstairs.

Royal laughed politely at whatever it was Sherry said, excused himself and followed the slender, black-haired Gypsy out of the drawing room. All evening, he had watched her. With her exotic beauty and gaudy silk skirts, she had lured men to her like bees to honey.

He had known Lily would be disguised, but the woman at the tavern seemed a mild version of the creature here tonight. He couldn't believe the seductive smile belonged to his sweet Lily, nor the kohl-rimmed, pale eyes that made her look even more exotic. Like the rest of the men, he found himself mesmerized by her husky laughter and faraway glances. Though she never quite flirted, she left men staring after her wherever she went, drawn to her dark allure, wanting her in their beds.

None of them wanting her as badly as he did.

Jealousy burned through him as he followed her up the stairs. He saw her disappear into the ladies' retiring room and walked on past, waited out of sight until she reappeared then strode toward her, his temper rising with every step. This woman wasn't some mysterious stranger, she was Lily, and Lily did not behave the way this woman did!

His hand clamped around her arm and her eyes flew to his. She didn't say a word, nor did she protest when he led her along the corridor, checked to be sure no one saw them, hauled her into one of the bedrooms, closed the door and turned the key.

"What is it?" she asked. "What is wrong?" She looked up at him with her long, black lashes, her pale skin in contrast to her glossy black hair.

"What is wrong?" he repeated, his temper barely in check. "What is wrong is that you have spent the entire evening seducing every man in the drawing room. You have half the men here imagining you spread beneath them. You smile and tease and let them believe you are interested in their advances. The fools are half-mad with lust for you."

Instead of being sorry, her chin went up. "I am playing a role, *Your Grace*—in case you have forgot. The role of Gypsy fortune-teller. A role I am playing for *you!*"

Her lips were stained a lush ruby red and when she moistened them they glistened. His groin tightened. He went hard to the point of pain.

"Is that so? You didn't look like you were playing a role when Savage kissed your hand. You looked like you were enjoying his attention, as if you would welcome him into your bed!"

"What are you talking about?"

"And that little pip-squeak, Emmet Burrows. You had him salivating at the thought of what would happen when he got you alone."

"I just wanted to keep his interest. It is part of the game."

"Really?" He moved toward her, forcing her backward till her shoulders came up against the wall. "What about me?" He slid his hands beneath her heavy black hair. "Am I a game to you, too?" Tilting her head back, he crushed his mouth down over hers and for an instant, Lily went still.

Then she moaned and parted her lips and her small

tongue slid over his and any rational thought that remained inside his head slipped away. Desire crashed over him, burned through his blood. Lust sank its claws into his flesh and all he could think of was having the beautiful, exotic creature in his arms.

He plunged his tongue into her mouth, ravished her lips, cupped her breast through her thin silk blouse. Her nipple peaked instantly, pressing hotly into his palm. He pulled the string on the gathered neckline, drew the silk blouse off her shoulder. She was wearing only a chemise and he tugged it down as well, baring her lovely, apple-round breasts.

His body clenched as he bent his head and suckled her there, laved and tasted, turned to her other breast and ministered to it, as well. A soft moan came from her throat, urging him on, and her hands slid into his hair. She trembled as he nipped the rose-hued tip, circled it with his tongue, then pulled the diamond-hard point into his mouth. Returning to her lips, he drank from them as if they were nectar, breathed her in as if he couldn't get enough.

He was hard. Aching and throbbing with every heart-beat. Lifting her into his arms, he carried her over to the bed and settled her on the edge. He kissed her again, shoved up her bright silk skirts and began to open the front of his trousers.

She wanted a man. Well, he would give her what she wanted. He moved between her legs, looked up in time to see that she had pulled off her straight black wig. Silver-blond hair tumbled loose from its pins and cascaded round her slender shoulders. Soft tendrils framed her cheeks.

"Lily…" he said, the sight of her lovely pale face clearing some of the fog from his lust-starved brain. He stood there frozen, fighting to pull himself under control. "Good Christ…what am I doing?"

Lily looked up at him. "You are making love to me, Royal. I just wanted you to know it was me and not some other woman."

But in truth he had always known it was her. There had never been anyone else for him, not since the day he had met her.

"Lily…" he whispered, saying her name like a prayer, knowing it was Lily he had wanted all along, that the anger seething through him was jealousy, that he was furious she had given her attentions to every man but him.

Leaning down, he kissed her, more softly this time, nibbling the corners of her mouth, his tongue gliding over her lips. "Make me stop, Lily. Tell me you don't want this."

Instead, she reached up, looped her arms round his neck and pulled his mouth back down to hers. Parting her lips under his, she encouraged the hot thrust of his tongue. Royal kissed her deeply, his fingers sliding into her silky pale hair. When he looked at her now, he saw Lily, the woman he wanted far more than the Gypsy, the woman he needed above all others.

Her thin silk skirts had ridden up her legs. Nestled as he was between her thighs, he could feel her mound against his hardness. His erection throbbed, ached for release. He tried to tell himself to stop, but his will was gone, his thoughts only of Lily and being inside her.

He popped the buttons on the front of his trousers and freed himself, positioned himself at the entrance to her

YOUR PARTICIPATION IS REQUESTED!

Dear Reader,

Since you are a lover of fiction – we would like to get to know you!

Inside you will find a short Reader's Survey. Sharing your answers with us will help our editorial staff understand who you are and what activities you enjoy.

To thank you for your participation, we would like to send you 2 books and 2 gifts – **ABSOLUTELY FREE!**

Enjoy your gifts with our appreciation,

Pam Powers

SEE INSIDE FOR READER'S SURVEY

What's Your Reading Pleasure...
ROMANCE? _OR_ SUSPENSE?

Do you prefer spine-tingling page turners OR heart-stirring stories about love and relationships? Tell us which books you enjoy – and you'll get 2 FREE "ROMANCE" BOOKS or 2 FREE "SUSPENSE" BOOKS with no obligation to purchase anything.

Choose **"ROMANCE"** and get **2 FREE BOOKS** that will fuel your imagination with intensely moving stories about life, love and relationships.

FREE!

Choose **"SUSPENSE"** and you'll get **2 FREE BOOKS** that will thrill you with a spine-tingling blend of suspense and mystery.

FREE!

We'll send you 2 books and 2 gifts
ABSOLUTELY FREE just for completing our Reader's Survey!

YOURS FREE! *We'll send you two fabulous surprise gifts absolutely FREE, just for trying "Romance" or "Suspense"!*

YOUR READER'S SURVEY "THANK YOU" FREE GIFTS INCLUDE:

- ▶ 2 Romance OR 2 Suspense books
- ▶ 2 lovely surprise gifts

PLEASE FILL IN THE CIRCLES COMPLETELY TO RESPOND

1) What type of fiction books do you enjoy reading? (Check all that apply)
- ○ Suspense/Thrillers ○ Action/Adventure ○ Modern-day Romances
- ○ Historical Romance ○ Humour ○ Science fiction

2) What attracted you most to the last fiction book you purchased on impulse?
- ○ The Title ○ The Cover ○ The Author ○ The Story

3) What is usually the greatest influencer when you <u>plan</u> to buy a book?
- ○ Advertising ○ Referral from a friend
- ○ Book Review ○ Like the author

4) Approximately how many fiction books do you read in a year?
- ○ 1 to 6 ○ 7 to 19 ○ 20 or more

5) How often do you access the internet?
- ○ Daily ○ Weekly ○ Monthly ○ Rarely or never.

YES!
I have completed the Reader's Survey. Please send me the 2 FREE books and 2 FREE gifts (gifts are worth about $10) for which I qualify. I understand that I am under no obligation to purchase any books, as explained on the back of this card.

Check one:

| **ROMANCE** |
| 393 MDL EYKZ   193 MDL EYKD |

| **SUSPENSE** |
| 392 MDL EYKP   192 MDL EYUY |

FIRST NAME   LAST NAME

ADDRESS

APT.#   CITY

STATE/PROV.   ZIP/POSTAL CODE

Offer limited to one per household and not valid to current subscribers of Romance, Suspense or the Romance/Suspense combo.

Your Privacy – The Reader Service is committed to protecting your privacy. Our Privacy Policy is available online at <u>www.eHarlequin.com</u> or upon request from the Reader Service. From time to time we make our lists of customers available to reputable third parties who may have a product or service of interest to you. If you would prefer us not to share your name and address, please check here. ☐

▶ **DETACH AND MAIL CARD TODAY!**

© 2009 HARLEQUIN ENTERPRISES LIMITED
® and ™ are trademarks owned and used by the trademark owner and/or its licensee.
(SUR-RS-09R2)

The Reader Service — Here's How It Works:

passage. The bed was high, giving him perfect access. He spread her thighs wide apart, watched her lovely eyes slowly close as he eased himself inside her.

Reaching her maidenhead should have given him pause. Instead, he felt a wild exhilaration that no other man had possessed her. She belonged to him and had since the moment he had seen her lying like a silver-haired angel in the glistening white snow.

Royal leaned over her, braced himself on his elbows, kissed her deeply. As he drove himself home, a soft cry slipped from her lips. Lily froze at the painful breach of her womanhood, and Royal clamped down on the urge to thrust himself even farther inside.

"I'm sorry, love, I didn't mean to hurt you."

"I'm all right." Her body relaxed and she managed a tremulous smile that wrapped around his heart. "I wanted you to be the one."

"Lily…"

She moved just then, taking him deeper, and Royal groaned. His body caught fire at the feel of her gloving him so sweetly and the last of his control completely faded. Plunging wildly, he took her again and again, absorbing the pleasure that was sweeter than any he had ever known. To his relief and joy, Lily cried out his name, and her body clenched around him, her womb pulsing against his erection as she reached a shattering release.

Royal came an instant later, driving into her fiercely, his muscles straining as he spilled himself inside her.

His heart was pounding, his chest rising and falling. For several moments, neither of them moved. Then reality began to set in. The sound of the orchestra playing downstairs, an occasional burst of laughter.

Regret slowly filled him, replacing the euphoria of only moments ago. He could scarcely believe what he had done.

"Royal…" Eyes still closed, Lily sighed his name on a whisper of air and Royal felt a tightening in his chest.

Sweet God, he had taken Lily like some paid-for strumpet, both of them still half-dressed, lying across someone else's bed in a house where at any moment they might be discovered. Cursing himself, unable to believe he had lost control so badly, he eased himself from the warmth of her body though it took every ounce of his will.

Lily's eyes slowly opened. She watched him as he re-fastened his clothes and she began to do the same, pulling her chemise up to cover her lovely breasts, donning her scarlet silk blouse.

Royal moved to the dresser, poured water from the pitcher into the basin, dampened a linen cloth and returned to where she lay. Lily took the cloth and turned away to cleanse the virginal blood from her thighs. More guilt assailed him. He had taken what he wanted and there was nothing he could do to make it right.

Royal returned the soiled linen to the basin, walked back to where Lily sat on the edge of the bed. She looked lovely and fragile and he couldn't believe he had broken her trust and violated her the way he had.

"Lily…sweetheart, I am so sorry."

She held up a hand as if to halt his words. "Please, I beg you, Royal, do not say you are sorry."

"I ruined you, but I can't marry you. Of course I am sorry."

Tears filled her eyes and Royal's heart twisted. He

reached for her as she came up off the bed, but she only shook her head. "I don't want your pity, Royal. I never have." She fumbled with her clothes, finally got them all back in place. Grabbing her wig, she settled it on her head and began to stuff her pale hair up underneath.

She looked up at him. "I could have stopped you. You know that is true."

It was. He never would have taken her against her will. Lily had wanted him as much as he had wanted her. If anything, that made him feel worse.

"It is past time I left," she said. "I'll use the back stairs. My uncle will be waiting in the alley to see me home."

Royal just stood there, feeling more miserable than he ever could recall.

He watched her walk to the door, her silk skirts flowing round her ankles, her hair once more as black as midnight, but this time he wasn't fooled.

The woman was his sweet Lily. That had not changed.

Royal's chest squeezed painfully as he watched her walk out of the room and quietly close the door.

Seventeen

Dressed in a plain white cotton nightgown, Lily sat in the window seat of her bedroom. Tonight, everything in her life had changed. She was no longer a virgin and she was deeply in love with a man she could not have.

A thread of guilt trickled through her. She was Jocelyn's cousin, no matter how distant, and Royal would soon be Jo's husband. Perhaps she could have denied him if she had not been aware of her cousin's tryst with Christopher Barclay and that Jo held no true feelings for the man she would wed.

Perhaps if things were different, Lily would have done the honorable thing and turned him away, but she would never truly know.

A familiar light knock sounded, drawing her attention to the door. Jocelyn was home, the last person Lily wished to see. But the bedroom door swung open and there she was, sweeping into the room like the royalty she would one day become.

"Lily! I saw the glow of your lamp beneath the door. I am so glad you are still awake!"

Lily managed a smile. "You look radiant. Your evening with Barclay must have gone well."

Jocelyn beamed. "Lord—there are simply no words to describe it. Christopher was…he was… Passion is amazing, Lily. They try to keep us from knowing—our parents, the men we will marry. They don't want us to find out. A man can have any woman he wants, but a woman…a woman is supposed to remain chaste. It is so unfair, Lily."

Lily said nothing. Jo was right—it was unfair. And yet for Lily, there was no other man besides Royal she wanted or ever would.

Jocelyn sank onto the tapestry stool in front of the dresser. "It was fantastic, Lily. Christopher was so incredibly passionate and yet he was gentle." She looked up at Lily and grinned. "I picked the perfect man to be my first lover."

Lily swallowed, thinking she had picked exactly the wrong man to fall in love with. "What…what about Royal?"

"What about him? We are not yet wed. It is perfectly fine for him to do what he wishes until we are married—even after. Well, as far as I am concerned, it is perfectly fine for me, too."

Lily had no idea what to say. How could she criticize Jo when she and Royal had done the same thing?

"I wish I could describe it, Lily. There is this feeling that comes over you at the end… It's…it's like floating among the stars. It's like bursting into a thousand little pieces of sheer bliss. Lord, I never could have imagined."

Neither could Lily—until tonight—though she had read about it. "The French call it *the little death*."

Jocelyn turned, grinned. "Because it's as if you died and went to heaven."

Truly it was like heaven. But there was a price to pay for the pleasure. She had given a little part of herself to Royal, a part she would never get back.

"I just had to tell you, Lily. I was bursting to tell someone and there is no one else I trust the way I trust you."

Fresh guilt washed over her. From the moment she had left the house party, Lily had told herself what she had done was wrong. But every time she thought of Royal and the yearning she had seen in his eyes, the need that only she seemed able to fill, she couldn't make herself believe it. She refused to regret the brief moments of joy she had taken for herself.

But it *was* wrong, and deep down she knew it.

Jocelyn rose from the stool. "I had better get to bed. Mother thinks I went with the Stewarts to the Bergmans' ball. My maid will still be up, waiting to help me undress."

Jocelyn had lied to her parents. In order to begin her Gypsy charade, Lily had simply pled a headache and stayed upstairs in her room. As soon as the time was right, she had slipped down the backstairs and joined her uncle, who was waiting with a rented carriage in the alley behind the house.

Jo walked over and hugged her, taking Lily by surprise. "I just feel so wonderful."

Lily looked at her cousin, saw the blush in her cheeks and her brilliant white smile. "I get the feeling this isn't over. Surely you aren't going to meet him again."

Jo rolled her amazing violet eyes as if the answer were obvious. "But of course I am. I am not officially engaged. Until I am, I intend to do as I please." She grinned. "And it pleases me greatly to make love with Christopher Barclay."

Lily wished she could be so cavalier, that she could be with Royal again as they had been tonight and not feel the least bit guilty. "What…what if he gets you with child?"

Jocelyn arched a sleek dark eyebrow. "There are ways, Lily, to prevent such things. And Christopher is quite sophisticated in that regard."

Lily said nothing. Dear God, she hadn't considered until that moment, the consequences of what she and Royal had done. As far as she knew, Royal had taken no such precautions. Even now she could be carrying his babe.

Her heart lurched. Part of her was terrified of having a child out of wedlock. Another, deeper part secretly yearned to have Royal's baby.

Jocelyn walked out of the room, smiling and humming a slightly off-key tune. As the door quietly closed, Lily turned her cheek to the icy windowpane and felt the tears begin to slide down her cheeks.

Royal paced the floor of the study in his town house. After a sleepless night, he was tired to the bone, his hair mussed from running his fingers through it. He glanced up at the sound of footfalls, breathed a sigh of relief as Sherry walked into the room.

Sheridan's footsteps halted a few feet inside the door. "Good God, man, you look a fright. Has something happened? I thought things went very well last night."

Even his sigh sounded weary. "The evening went exactly as planned. At least for the most part."

"And that part has you looking like something the dog dragged in?"

Under different circumstances, Royal might have smiled. "I just didn't sleep very well."

Sherry nodded sagely. "You need a woman, my friend. Why don't we pay a call at the Blue Dolphin tonight? The women there are exquisite—and extremely skillful at what they do. I promise you'll feel better in the morning."

"I don't need a woman. I've already had a woman. That is the problem."

One of Sherry's light brown eyebrows went up. He propped a hip on the edge of Royal's desk. "I am all ears."

"I've ruined her, Sherry. I don't know exactly how it happened, but the deed is well and truly done." And though he had taken her virginity, all he could think of was having her again.

Sheridan shrugged. "So move up the wedding. If your heir comes a month early, no one will really care."

Royal made a sound of exasperation. "It wasn't Jocelyn, Sherry. It happened with Lily."

"Oh, dear."

"Quite."

"I suppose I should have known. You have fancied the girl from the start."

Royal raked a hand through his hair. "What the devil am I going to do? She might even now be carrying my child and there is no way I can marry her."

"I gather you took no precautions."

"None whatsoever. I was half out of my mind with lust. I don't know what came over me."

"I think that is fairly obvious. You didn't force her, did you?"

He was appalled. "Of course not! We have always shared a certain…attraction. Last night it got out of hand." Now, *there* was an understatement. He had never wanted anything as much as he wanted Lily. And when he had been inside her, her sweetness had filled him, touched him in a way he had never been touched before.

Sherry sighed. "Yes, well, sometimes these things happen. What we must decide now is how best to take care of Lily."

"She is completely innocent in all of this. Somehow I have to make things right."

Sherry slid down off the desk and paced over to the window. The garden was still barren, and not in the best condition. The grass was in need of clipping and wet leaves covered the gravel paths, but a weak sun slipped down through the naked branches, foretelling the coming of spring.

Sherry turned. "As you say, you must make things right and so there is only one thing to be done. You will simply have to find her a husband."

Royal's chest constricted. "How can I possibly do that? She has no money and I don't have enough to provide her any sort of decent dowry."

"No, but you will. As soon as you are married, you will have money to burn, more than enough to insure Lily marries well."

His stomach rolled. He couldn't imagine another man in Lily's bed, another man making love to her.

He hadn't realized Sherry had moved till he felt his friend's hand on his shoulder. "I can see this isn't what you want. I know you have feelings for the girl. Perhaps the money isn't so important. Perhaps you should marry her yourself."

Until that moment, he hadn't realized how badly he wanted to do just that.

He simply shook his head. "I can't. I made a vow. I promised my father and I won't break my word."

Sherry squeezed his shoulder. "Then we had best get started. We'll need to find someone suitable who will be willing—for a price—to overlook the fact that his bride is no longer a virgin."

Royal just nodded. His mouth felt dry. His heart pumped dully. He would come up with a list of suitable candidates and then go over the list with Lily. Whatever it took, he would make certain she got whichever man she wanted.

It was the least he could do.

Lily worked all week getting her millinery shop ready to open. She cleaned and rearranged, swept and organized, anything to keep her mind off Royal and what had happened at the Nightingales' soiree. For months, she had been fashioning hats, creating new styles, working till late into the evenings to make enough merchandise for the store she planned to open, enough to satisfy old customers and attract new clientele.

She glanced round the shop, pleased with the work she had done. The store was arranged to her satisfaction, the hats sitting in neat little rows: wide-brimmed bonnets, some with feathers, others trimmed with lace and ribbon, a cabriolet bonnet with false roses, lace caps in a dozen colors and several coal shuttle bonnets.

Proceeding to the desk behind the counter, she began the task of addressing notes to the ladies who had previously purchased merchandise, informing them of the location of her shop and the date it would officially open.

Her back was aching by the time she finished. She stretched and rose from her chair, glanced at the clock and saw that the afternoon had slipped away.

She couldn't put it off any longer. It was time to go back to Meadowbrook and make preparations for the evening ahead. Tonight Madam Tsaya was attending a ball given by Lord March's widowed sister, Lady Annabelle Townsend. The invitations made note of special entertainment in the form of Madam Tsaya, and apparently Preston Loomis had replied his intention to attend.

Jocelyn was invited and Lily meant to accompany her. As the evening progressed, she would slip away long enough to change into her Gypsy clothes then return downstairs as Madam Tsaya. She would appear briefly, make a few predictions to Royal's friends, then go up and change back into her ball gown for the balance of the evening.

Lily sighed. If only Royal weren't going to be there. If only she didn't have to see him and especially not with Jo. Her moment of madness was over. Both of them knew it could never happen again. Still, instead of regretting what had occurred as Royal did, Lily treasured the memory of the incredible moments they had shared.

Satisfied that all was in order in the shop, she locked the door, walked to the corner and hailed a hansom. She arrived at Meadowbrook to find Jocelyn taking her afternoon nap. Lily wished she could lose herself in sleep, but the moment she closed her eyes, Royal's handsome face appeared, along with burning memories of their passionate encounter upstairs at the soiree.

Instead of napping, Lily surveyed her wardrobe, which grew each time Jocelyn tossed aside a gown. She chose one she had altered but never worn, a sea foam-green taffeta the color of her eyes.

At the ball tonight, Uncle Jack would arrive with her Gypsy costume. She would meet him in the garden behind the house, then take the clothes upstairs to change.

The hours slipped past. Lily was nervous by the time Jocelyn had finally finished dressing in a plum velvet gown, and the two of them were ready to leave. Though Matilda Caulfield would be acting as chaperone for the night, Lily didn't think her brief disappearance would be noted. Neither Matilda nor her daughter paid much attention to Lily once they were caught up in the gaiety of the affair.

And tonight there would be entertainment in the form of Madam Tsaya. Lily couldn't stop a smile at the thought of what her cousin would think of the Gypsy woman who would be present at the ball tonight.

"Did the mark show up?" Jack asked. It was nearly ten o'clock, the night pitch-dark and windy. Her uncle stood in the alley next to the simple carriage the duke had rented for their use.

"Loomis is here. I saw him a little bit earlier."

"He's curious. By tonight, you'll have him hooked." Jack held out a small cloth bag that held her costume, and Lily took it from his long-boned hand. "You got my message? You know what you're to do?"

"I got your message." Pleading a stomach ailment, she

had avoided the weekly meeting at the Red Rooster. She simply hadn't had the courage to face Royal so soon.

"Just toss Loomis a bone or two," Jack told her. "Don't give him too much. Make him come to you."

She nodded. She knew how to handle a mark. Once she had started playing the game again, it hadn't taken long for her unorthodox education to come flooding back to her. She knew about Loomis's mother and that she used tarot cards and told fortunes, knew about the man's fascination with Madam Medela. She knew what to do to capture his interest.

She leaned over and kissed her uncle's whiskery cheek. "I have to go. I don't want to be missed."

Jack just smiled. "Good luck, luv."

But Jack Moran had taught her it wasn't a matter of luck. It was a matter of skill, and she had learned from a very good teacher, a friend of Jack's, an old con woman named Sadie Burgess who had a weak spot for children and especially a lonely little girl.

Lily waved goodbye, turned and hurried back to the house, slipped inside and headed up the backstairs. A few minutes later, she was garbed as a Gypsy in bright, fluttery silk skirts and on her way back down to the drawing room.

Lord March's sister, Lady Annabelle Townsend, stood waiting—the slender woman with the honey-brown hair she had seen at the Nightingales' affair. She was even prettier up close, with fine-boned features, a slim, straight nose and blue eyes.

"Are you ready?" Lady Annabelle asked, and the gleam in her eyes said she knew exactly what was going on. Lady Nightingale hadn't been informed of the scheme in which her husband was involved, but clearly this young woman knew. No shrinking violet, Annabelle Townsend seemed excited at the prospect.

For an instant, Lily broke the rules and came out of character. "Thank you for helping us, my lady."

"I am just Anna to my friends and since you are a friend of the duke's, I am more than happy to help. Come along…Madam Tsaya."

"I vill follow wherever you lead," Lily said with a smile, back in character again.

They made their way along the hall into the large, ornate ballroom, which was crowded with the social elite. Lily spotted Jocelyn across the way and next to her the man she would marry. Tall and golden-haired, the Duke of Bransford was magnificent, a fact proclaimed by the sideways glances cast by half the women in the room.

Caught in his spell, Lily stumbled, and embarrassed color flooded her cheeks.

"Are you all right?" Lady Annabelle asked.

Lily managed a smile. "I am fine. A misstep, is all."

Ignoring the duke, whose gaze was now locked on Lily, she followed March's pretty sister toward the stage where the orchestra was playing.

"Since we haven't much time," her hostess said, "I'll just jump right in." Annabelle climbed the steps to the stage, leading Lily by the hand. The musicians stopped playing and the room fell silent.

"Good evening, one and all." Annabelle smiled, waited for the last of the guests to quiet. "As you all know, we have a special guest in our presence tonight. I should like to introduce Madam Tsaya. If you are lucky, perhaps you will be one of those she chooses. Perhaps you will be the lucky one to have good fortune."

A round of applause went up.

"It is my pleasure to be here tonight," Lily said. Her glance strayed to Jocelyn, slid over to Royal, and some little demon sparked to life inside her.

She surveyed the crowd, taking her time, letting the interest build. Then she fixed her attention on the duke. "Congratulations, Your Grace, on your upcoming nuptials."

The crowd murmured then erupted. Everyone turned toward Royal, saw him standing next to one of the wealthiest young women in London and began noisily speculating on whether or not the Gypsy could be right.

Even from a distance, Lily could see Royal's jaw go tight. Jocelyn just grinned, thrilled to be the center of attention and with the bets that would be made as to whether or not she would become the next Duchess of Bransford. Jo tossed a triumphant glance at her archrival, Serafina Maitlin, whose sleek red eyebrows drew almost together.

"Well, isn't that something," Lady Annabelle said to the excited throng. "Already we have a prediction for good fortune. Perhaps, if we are lucky, others will also receive good news." Reaching over, she caught Lily's hand and led her back down off the stage. The orchestra resumed its playing, but the buzz continued in the ballroom.

"That was extremely well done of you," whispered Lady Annabelle.

"I am not sure His Grace would agree."

Annabelle just laughed. "If Royal is embarrassed to be marrying the lady, he should marry someone else."

Lily made no reply, but she thought she liked Lord March's sister.

Walking next to her hostess, Lily began making her way round the ballroom, hearing her name spoken in nearly every circle. Royal's friends had been doing their jobs. People were discussing Savage's horse race win, March's card win at White's and the bet Lord Welles-ley had wagered and won.

From the corner of her eye, she saw Preston Loomis in conversation with Lord Nightingale and realized the earl was telling him that he had indeed purchased the stock Tsaya had suggested and that, indeed, the invest-ment had paid off quite handsomely.

"How does she claim to do it?" Loomis asked, standing close enough that she could hear.

"I am not quite certain." Nightingale turned, indicat-ing Tsaya should join the conversation. "Why don't you ask her?"

Loomis arched a silver eyebrow. "And so I shall," he agreed congenially, reaching up to smooth his mustache. "Will you tell us, my dear, how you are able to know these things?"

Lily flashed her mysterious smile. "I learned much from my grandmother's sister, a Gypsy named Madam Medela. She also had the sight. I am sad to say she died a few years back. But unlike my great-aunt, Medi—that is what I called her—I see things in the stars."

Loomis stared. "You are related to Madam Medela?"

"As I said, she was my grandmother's sister. You have heard of her?"

"She was a friend of my mother's."

Lily nodded as if she wasn't surprised. "My aunt

helped many people." She stared at him, studied his face. "If you play cards with Lord Nightingale tonight, you will win."

It had all been planned ahead of time, of course. Even now Royal's friends were getting ready to play in a private salon—assuming Nightingale could convince Loomis to join him.

One of the earl's nearly black eyebrows went up in challenge. "Would you care to test the lady? I was just getting ready to join a private game."

Loomis glanced in her direction, but Lily was already slipping away. She had played her part. Now it was up to the men to play theirs.

She had just started down the hall when a man stepped into her way. She had noticed him when he came into the ballroom a few minutes earlier, young, no more than three-and-twenty, and dashing, with wavy dark hair and brilliant blue eyes. She was sure the ladies must all go atwitter when this one walked into a room.

His smile was as devastating as his eyes. "Well, look at this—it seems I am having my own good fortune, running into such a beautiful woman." He made her an extravagant bow. "Rule Dewar, at your service, madam."

Rule Dewar. She knew Royal had two brothers, but she had never met them. This one was probably the youngest. And in a different way, he was as handsome as his older brother.

"I am Madam Tsaya," she said, wondering if Royal knew his brother was there and if he had been told about their charade. The way those blue eyes seemed to be eating her up, she didn't think so. The younger Dewar was obviously enamored of the exotic Madam Tsaya.

"I know who you are," he said. "Though you are far too young to be addressed in such a manner. I should think you would prefer to simply be Tsaya. It is such a lovely name."

"You are very bold, my lord." She gave him what she hoped was a discouraging glance. "If you are looking for good fortune, tonight you vill have to look elsewhere."

She started past him, but Rule caught her arm. "Surely you aren't leaving. The night has only begun."

"Please, there are things I must do. I have to go."

His hand remained familiarly on her arm. "If you want to leave, I will be more than happy to take you wherever you wish to go. My carriage is just out front. Perhaps you would care to join me for—"

"Let go of the lady's arm." This from Royal, who had magically appeared in the hallway. Lily wasn't sure if she was happy he was there or if she was better off with the brother.

Rule released Lily's arm. "Well, if it isn't my big brother, interfering as usual."

"I didn't know you were in town."

"I had a couple of days off from school. I came with friends."

Royal glanced down at Lily and she felt the familiar curl of heat in the pit of her stomach.

"The lady has to leave," he said. "There is more going on here than you know. I'll explain everything later."

Rule's dark eyebrows drew together. There were questions in those fierce blue eyes, but also respect for his brother. His gaze swung from Royal to Lily and he flashed a mischievous grin. "Another time, sweet Tsaya."

Lily cast Royal a last fleeting glance, felt the heat in

those tawny eyes and jerked her gaze away. Hurriedly, she slipped off down the hall and headed up the back-stairs. Checking to be sure she wasn't seen, she ducked into the bedroom to change.

The pale green ball gown waited in the empty armoire and Lily hurried over to retrieve it. She slipped out of her Gypsy costume and stepped into the taffeta gown, discovering it was more difficult to refasten the buttons than it had been to loosen them. Lily cursed softly as she struggled, then jumped at the sound of the door swinging open behind her.

Relief filtered through her at the appearance of Annabelle Townsend walking into the bedroom.

"Here, let me help you."

"Thank you." As the lady worked on the buttons, Lily tugged off her wig and stuffed it into a small cloth bag. As soon as the gown was fastened, she raced over to the dresser and began to pin up her hair. She had worn it in a simple knot at the nape of her neck and she managed quite easily to return it to the straightforward but elegant style.

Pouring water into the basin, she washed the kohl from around her eyes, the soot from her lashes, and wiped away the last traces of lip rouge.

"My, that's quite a change," Annabelle said. "Still, you are lovely."

Lily flushed, unused to such praise. "Thank you."

"I suppose we had better get you back downstairs before you are missed."

Lily nodded. She started for the door, but Annabelle's voice stopped her. "Why are you doing this, Lily? My brother told me most of it—about Loomis and the swindle. I know how Quent and the others feel about Royal, but what about you? Why are you involved in this?"

Lily swallowed. How could she possibly explain? "The duke saved my life once. I owe him."

Annabelle eyed her shrewdly. "I see."

Lily wondered how much the young woman did see, and prayed she hadn't guessed that Lily would do just about anything for the duke.

"You'd better go," Annabelle said.

Lily nodded. "May you be blessed with good fortune, my lady," she said with a smile and hurried out the door.

She had almost reached the main staircase when Royal appeared in the hallway beside her.

"I need a word with you, *Tsaya,*" he said with only a trace of sarcasm in his voice.

"If you are angry because I mentioned your impending engagement—"

"This isn't about my engagement."

"I didn't encourage your brother. I wouldn't do a thing like that."

"It isn't about Rule, either. This is personal. I need to talk to you, Lily."

"Not tonight. There isn't time."

"It's important. When can we meet?"

She didn't want to talk to him at all, but she could tell by the set of his jaw, he wouldn't leave off until she agreed to hear what he had to say.

"Tomorrow. I'll be working in my shop all afternoon."

"All right. I'll stop by at the end of the day. There are things we need to discuss."

"I have nothing to say to you, Royal."

"Perhaps not, but I have things to say to you. I'll see you tomorrow."

Lily ignored the quiet thudding of her heart as he walked away. Smoothing her elegant taffeta skirts, she headed down the sweeping staircase. She was Lily once more. She wondered if Rule Dewar would have paid her the least attention if he had seen her as she really was.

At least her absence would go unremarked. Only Royal seemed to notice her.

And knowing he did only made matters worse.

Eighteen

The day seemed to go on forever. Lily had opened the shop for business that morning, though the official opening wasn't until next week. Every hat was perfectly in place, all the trim set out so the ladies could make their own personal choice of hats they might wish to design.

The shop was ready for business. Lily had even added a few homey touches to the tiny apartment upstairs: lace doilies on the arms of the settee, an embroidered linen tablecloth on the tiny oak table, several petit-point samplers hanging on the walls. The shop was ready. The apartment was prepared, though she wouldn't actually be moving in for some months yet, not until Jocelyn was married.

The thought sent a chill down her spine. Jo would marry the duke, though she didn't love him. The duke would marry Jo to gain her fortune. Sometimes the world was an ugly place, Lily thought.

She shook off the thought, determined to return to

her usual optimistic nature. Buoyed by the sale of a pretty silk bonnet during the first hour she was open, she didn't take much notice of the time until late in the afternoon. Worried that Royal would appear at any moment, growing more and more restless, Lily set aside the bonnet she was sewing and tried to read, one of her favorite pastimes, but it was impossible to concentrate.

By four o'clock she was pacing the floor, wishing she had never told Royal she would talk to him. Just when the tension seemed to stretch to unbearable limits, she spotted his tall figure through the mullioned panes on the top half of the door.

Lily took a deep breath, squared her shoulders and started walking in his direction. She paused as Royal walked in, ringing the bell above the door. He strode toward her, stopped directly in front of her, and suddenly the air in the room seemed to vanish. Her chest squeezed and it was difficult to breathe.

She forced herself to inhale a deep breath. "You came."

"I was afraid you wouldn't still be here."

"I told you I would be."

"Yes, you did, but I was afraid you might—"

"What is it you want… Your Grace?"

His tawny gaze darkened at the use of his title instead of his name. "I think we are far beyond that, sweetheart, don't you?"

Lily's cheeks flushed. About as far as a man and woman could get. "I thought that…that putting some distance between us might…might be wise."

His eyes bored into her. "If I had my way, there wouldn't be the slightest distance between us, Lily. I would bury myself so far inside you we wouldn't be able to tell where one of us stopped and the other began."

Her eyes widened and her cheeks burned. The words stirred an image so erotic dampness slid into her core. "Royal, please, you…you mustn't talk that way."

He sighed into the quiet inside the shop. "I know. It's just that when I see you, I seem to forget everything but having you again."

Her heart stuttered. He wanted her. But then, there had never been any question of that. She wondered what else he might feel for her, knew that whatever it was, it wasn't enough.

Lily bit the inside of her cheek to hold back tears. "Why are you here, Royal? What do you want?"

He reached out and caught her hand, brought it to his lips. She wore no gloves and the warmth of his mouth sent a curl of heat into the pit of her stomach.

"You know what I want—I want you, Lily. But that is not the reason I am here."

She couldn't look away from his handsome face, from the straight nose and sensuous lips, the solid jaw and the tiny indentation in his chin. "Why, then?"

Reaching into the inside pocket of his brown, velvet-collared tailcoat, he withdrew a sheet of paper and handed it to Lily. She frowned as she unfolded it and saw a list of five men's names. "What is this?"

"Those are the names of men who would make satisfactory husbands."

"*Husbands?* What are you talking about?"

"After what happened between us, Lily, you have no choice but to marry. Since I cannot be the man to see it done, I have come up with the names of eligible men who would be willing to wed you."

Lily just stared, unable to believe her ears. "I cannot credit you are saying this."

Royal caught her shoulders, his expression grim. "Listen to me, Lily. I've already spoken to each of these men. I didn't tell them your name, only that you were a lovely young woman who meant a great deal to me and would come to them with a sizable dowry. I told them the money would have to be postponed until after I am married, but as they are all in need of finances, it wasn't an issue for any of them. All of them agreed to the terms of the marriage."

Her teeth clamped together so hard her jaw hurt. She thrust the paper back into his hands. "You have gone too far, Royal Dewar. You are mad if you think I would even consider such a thing."

Royal straightened, making him seem even taller. "I am hardly mad. This is the only thing that makes any sense."

Lily clamped her hands on her hips, her temper barely in check. "It makes not the least amount of sense. I have a life, *Your Grace,* in case it hasn't occurred to you. I have opened my own shop. I have my own place to live. I don't need you or any other man."

He held the sheet of paper out to her. "Just take a look. That is all I am asking."

She stared at the paper in his hand, her temper nearly out of control. She snatched the list from his fingers and looked at the names, a couple of whom she recognized.

"I thought you said Emmet Burrows was a pip-squeak."

He cleared his throat. "I may have spoken too harshly. Besides, I thought you liked him."

"I don't even know him." She looked him in the face, her anger goading her on. "You want me to marry?"

"It's not what I want that matters. It is what has to be done."

"And I get to choose, is that correct?"

He swallowed. "I'll get you whichever man you want."

Lily pursed her lips, pretending to contemplate. "If I can have anyone I want, then I think I shall choose someone not on your list. I believe I will choose your friend, Mr. Savage. Can you get him for me?"

Royal's tawny eyebrows slammed together. "Savage! Now you are the one who is mad. The man is a dedicated rogue. He wouldn't be true to you for a moment."

She knew that, of course. Jocelyn had told her all about Jonathan Savage. "All right, then perhaps I'll have Lord March. He seems a nice enough fellow."

Royal's features went dark. "March is…March is too much of a perfectionist to make a good husband. He is searching for the perfect female and I doubt he will ever find one who meets his exacting standards. He would be a very bad choice indeed."

She tapped her chin with her finger as if she was thinking it over. "I can see where that might be a problem." She flashed a triumphant smile. "I have it! I'll marry your brother Rule! He is handsome in the extreme. He is young and I imagine quite virile. I suppose if I have to wed—"

"Not Rule! There is no way you are marrying my brother!"

She laughed then, because he was jealous, as she had hoped he would be. He didn't want her to marry his brother or any of his friends.

"You don't have to worry, Royal. I'm not going to marry anyone. I told you—I have a life of my own and I am quite content."

"But…but what if you are with child?"

"I'm not."

"You know that for certain?"

Her face went warm. Her monthly courses were hardly a subject she wished to discuss. "I am certain." She was sure she wasn't pregnant, though deep inside that same little part of her still wished she were.

Royal raked a hand through his hair, shoving the golden strands into slight disarray. "Well, that is one less worry, I suppose."

"I suppose," she said, wishing she meant it. "Now, if you are finished, I would like you to leave."

For several long moments he just stood there. She could feel his gaze burning into her. The air seemed to thicken and warm, seemed to swirl around them, pulling them closer together. The tension between them seemed almost a tangible thing, changing direction, turning into something else entirely. Her breathing grew shallow and so did his. Her heart was thrumming. His lion's eyes seemed to hold her rooted to the floor.

With a growl low in his throat, Royal reached for her, but Lily backed away. She couldn't risk it. A single kiss and she knew she would be lost.

"I…I want you to leave."

A tremor went through him and she realized how hard he was fighting for control. Royal took a shaky breath and nodded. "You are right, of course." Still he made no move.

"Royal, please…"

He studied her face a moment longer, taking in each

of her features, then wordlessly turned and started for the door. The bell rang as he opened it, and the moment he stepped outside, Lily burst into tears.

"She hates me. Every time I close my eyes, I see the hurt and disgust in her eyes."

"She doesn't hate you." Sherry lounged in a deep leather chair in front of the hearth. Cracks spidered the once-expensive leather, but the seat was still comfortable, and orange flames curled over the grate in the hearth, warming the study.

"She might be angry," Sherry continued. "After all, you did take her virginity without benefit of marriage— but she doesn't hate you. I am sure she appreciated your efforts to make things right."

Royal scoffed. "If she'd had a pair of sewing shears, the lady would have cut off my bollocks."

Sherry laughed. "So she wasn't impressed with our list."

"You might say that."

"I have to admit, the girl has more grit than I had believed. She's been doing a smashing job with this Tsaya thing. If you watch her working, you forget she's the sweet little lamb you ruthlessly seduced."

Royal grunted. "I appreciate the reminder."

Sherry just laughed. "You needn't look so guilty. The lady is far tougher than she appears. If she hadn't wanted you, you never would have had her."

It was true. Lily was tough and vulnerable at the same time, and she was the sweetest, most desirable creature he had ever known.

"At any rate," Royal continued, "she refused to consider marriage to anyone. She says she has her own life. She doesn't need a man to take care of her."

"Good for her. Of course, we all know it isn't true. There isn't a female on earth who wouldn't be better off under a man's protection."

Royal frowned. "Annabelle Townsend seems to do well enough."

"True, but Anna's late husband left her very well settled. The only income your Lily has is whatever she might earn from her millinery shop."

Worry swirled through him. He looked down at the stack of bills on his desk. The cost of the scam they were running had begun to add up. Yesterday, at Charles Sinclair's instruction, Jack Moran had rented an apartment for Tsaya. Very soon now, Sinclair believed, Loomis would wish to pay the Gypsy a call.

Along with those expenses and the staggering amount of money necessary to run a dukedom, he could barely make ends meet. At least the brewery he had built was doing well. Swansdowne Ale was gaining a reputation as one of the finest in England. Still, the costs of the endeavor had not yet been repaid. There was no profit yet, though he hoped that eventually there would be.

"Once Jocelyn and I are married, I will make certain Lily is well cared for," he vowed. "She is part of Jocelyn's family, after all. It would only be proper."

Sherry swirled the brandy in his glass, took a slow swallow. "Perhaps you could make her your mistress. That would solve any number of problems."

It wasn't the first time the thought had occurred, only the first time it had been put into words. Erotic images arose: Lily naked, awaiting him in the town house he rented for her; Lily lying on top of the bed, her slender legs spread wide to receive him, her breasts like ripe plums, inviting him to taste them. Desire stirred to life and the blood began to pool in his groin. Royal bit back a groan and forced the images away.

"If only I could." But Lily deserved a better sort of life than that and he was fairly certain she wouldn't agree even if he asked her. God's teeth, how had he let his feelings for her get so far out of hand?

Sherry started to say something, when a light knock sounded and both men glanced toward the door. The butler's gray head appeared in the opening.

"Your brother, Lord Rule, is here, Your Grace."

But Rule was already pushing his way into the study. Royal cast Sherry a glance, telling his friend without words that discussing his involvement with Lily was off-limits, even to his brother.

"So you are still in town," Royal said as Rule paused at the sideboard to pour himself a drink. "I thought you were heading back to Oxford."

"I've got a couple more days. I thought maybe there was a way I could help you with this Loomis fellow."

The night of the ball Royal had filled his brother in on the swindle Loomis had perpetrated on their father, Madam Tsaya's true identity, and how he hoped to get a measure of justice by regaining at least some portion of the money Loomis had stolen.

Sherry seemed to be contemplating Rule's suggestion, watching the tall, black-haired man over the rim of his brandy glass. "Perhaps Tsaya could predict you will get high marks in your final exams." He arched a light brown eyebrow. "You will, won't you?"

"I'll do well enough," Rule said. "I always have." The youngest Dewar brother had always been an extremely bright student. He had extended his studies, likely to avoid any sort of responsibility for as long as he could, but lately he was growing bored. He was ready to live his life. Royal just hoped the path he chose would be a wise one.

Royal straightened on the leather sofa. "Tsaya has been invited to a musicale given by Lady Severn at the end of the week. If you will be there, she could make the prediction then. The exams are coming up. You could return with the news of your good fortune shortly thereafter."

"I shall make it a point to attend Severn's ball." Rule grinned, carving a dimple into his cheek. "It shouldn't be an imposition. The countess is purported to be beautiful and her husband as old as Moses. They say she is quite inventive in bed and I should like nothing better than to find out."

Royal shook his head, but a smile lurked on his lips. "You are incorrigible, brother mine."

"And at my age, you weren't the least bit interested in women?"

He had been, of course. He'd had more than his share of ladies over the years. "Point taken." On Barbados he had kept a beautiful half-caste mistress. If he hadn't been short of funds, he likely would have set up a woman in London to see to his needs.

Lately, much to his surprise and chagrin, he seemed to have lost interest in the female gender.

Except, of course, for Lily.

The thought did not sit well.

"All right, then," Sherry said. "Royal, you will see Lily at your meeting Wednesday next, correct?"

A tightness settled between his shoulder blades. She would likely be there. He wished he wasn't looking forward to the meeting so much. "If she's not, Jack Moran will get word to her."

Sherry cast a pointed glance at Rule. "And we can count on you to attend the Severn affair?"

"Have no fear. Since my brother is determined the mysterious Tsaya is forbidden, I shall fix my attentions on the delectable countess."

Royal couldn't help a smile. Knowing his brother as he did, Lady Severn would no doubt wind up in his bed.

His thoughts returned to the upcoming event. Annabelle had managed to get Loomis on Severn's guest list. According to Charles Sinclair, it was just about time for Tsaya to start reeling the bastard in.

It was raining. Preston Loomis always hated going out in the rain. As he hurried toward his carriage, he glanced up from beneath the umbrella his butler held over his head into the sullen gray sky. Heavy drops of water managed to soak his expensive black evening coat. If there was a moon, he couldn't see it.

Grumbling, he climbed the iron stairs and settled himself inside the coach with a sigh of relief. Aside from the dismal weather, his life had taken an interesting turn of late. He had met a beautiful woman, in itself not particularly surprising. Since he had become a wealthy man, beautiful women often sought him out.

But this one was different. This one intrigued him as none had in a very long time. He wondered if she was merely a woman playing a role, doing her best to make a living as his mother had done, or if she was actually related to the one truly spiritual person he had ever known.

Tsaya claimed to be the grand-niece of Madam Medela, a Gypsy seer with the power to predict the future. Medela wasn't a con. In all the years he had known her, the old woman's advice had never failed him or his mother. Since her death, making his way in life had been far more difficult. Although he was a rich man now, he felt adrift, alone in a harsh world in which he had never truly belonged.

Was it possible the ancient Medela's grand-niece had inherited her same awesome powers? He tried to think back…the old lady had never talked about her family, though once she had said that her gift was passed down to her through the female side of her clan.

Was there a chance Tsaya could guide him, give him that feeling of control he'd had when her aunt was alive?

He had to know the truth.

The carriage rolled beneath the portico of the mansion belonging to the Earl and Countess of Severn. He passed through the receiving line and began making conversation with some of the guests. All the while his glance searched for Tsaya.

It wasn't until the first half of the musical entertainment was over, Signor Franco Mencini, an opera singer currently in vogue, that he saw her walk through the door.

Preston set his glass of champagne on a passing waiter's tray and started in her direction.

Nineteen

❧❧❧

Lily smiled at the circle of young men surrounding her. Well, not truly her, but the mysterious Gypsy, Tsaya, a group that included Rule Dewar. As they had planned, Tsaya predicted he would pass his school examinations at the top of his class.

Rule had been far better behaved tonight, no longer the brash, overbold rake used to getting what he wanted from a woman, but a polite young man who treated her with respect. She wondered what Royal had said to keep his brother in line.

Royal. He was here tonight, though his unofficial fiancée wasn't. Jocelyn was meeting her lover at the Parkland Hotel, and Lily discovered she was jealous. Jo was bold enough to act on her convictions. Lily wished she were daring enough for an assignation with Royal.

Unfortunately, her sense of honor would not let her, though her heart and body wanted to make love with him above all things. Jocelyn was, after all, her cousin, and no matter the lack of feelings Jo had for Royal, the pair was soon to wed.

Lily turned away from where the duke stood in conversation with his friend, darkly handsome Jonathan Savage, determined to keep her mind on the job she was there to do. From the corner of her eye, she spotted her quarry and he was coming her way. As tall, imposing, silver-haired Preston Loomis walked toward her, Lily smiled and excused herself from the group of young men, giving him a chance to seek her out.

Loomis stopped directly in front of her. "Madam Tsaya. It is good to see you."

"You, as well, Mr. Loomis."

"I wanted to let you know that your prediction came true. I won quite handsomely at cards the night I played with Lord Nightingale. You seem to have an interesting talent."

"I am fortunate, I suppose. I am able to help certain people, and the hostesses at these affairs pay me well for entertaining their guests. Still, at times it seems more a burden than a gift."

"In what way, may I ask?"

She toyed with a fold in her gaudy silk skirts. "Though I predict only good fortune, I sometimes see things I would rather not."

"You have made a prediction for me. Do you see bad things in my future?"

She looked up at him, studied his face, noticed the way his mustache followed the line of his upper lip. "I see nothing tonight." She continued to watch him, closed her eyes a moment, opened them and gave him the news they had planned. "Soon you will meet someone…an older woman. I do not understand what it means, but your fortune will be enhanced by this woman."

He smiled. "Is that so? It will be interesting to see if you are correct."

"You said you knew my great-aunt."

"She and my mother were quite good friends. When my mother died, Madam Medela and I continued our friendship. I am surprised she never mentioned you."

"I was only a child when I knew her. Mostly I have lived with my mother on the Continent. I have only been back in London for the past few months."

"Your aunt was an amazing woman."

"I have only the shadow of her talent. Still, if I feel a connection to someone, as she did to you, my skills can be quite useful." There it was—she had dangled the carrot in front of his nose. It remained to be seen if he would take it.

"By useful, do you mean profitable?"

She shrugged her shoulders, making the red silk of her blouse slide sinuously across her bosom. "If destiny wishes, it can be so." She gave him a fleeting smile. "Now, if you will excuse me, I have other guests to whom I must speak."

"Of course." He made a slight inclination of his head. "Perhaps we will talk again."

Lily made no reply. He needed to come to her and she dared not make it too easy. Moving across the room, she paused next to Lady Annabelle, who drew her into her circle of friends and began to chat with her as if they were old friends—which, it seemed, considering their conspiracy, might actually come to pass.

* * *

Lifting her full, moiré skirts out of the way, Jocelyn hurried up the carpeted staircase of the Parkland Hotel. Though a gas chandelier burned overhead, the lobby was dimly lit. Perhaps other patrons wished to keep their identity secret.

With the hood of her cloak pulled over her head, Jocelyn hurried along the hall, skeleton key in hand. At the door to her bedroom suite, she fumbled, trying to push the key into the lock. The door swung open before she could manage and Christopher Barclay stood in the opening.

"You're late."

She brushed past his tall figure as she swept into the room. "Only an hour or so."

Christopher caught her arm and turned her to face him, sending the hood of her cloak tumbling backward. "The rest of your dandies might enjoy waiting on your every whim, but I do not. If you say you will be here, you had better be on time."

Jocelyn gasped as he hauled her into his arms and his mouth crushed down over hers. His kiss was hot and hard, his tongue demanding entrance, then plundering the inside of her mouth. This wasn't the tender lover who had taken her virginity, and it occurred to her that he was angry.

"I—I had trouble getting away," she explained as he pulled the tie on her cloak and tossed it away. "I didn't mean to keep you waiting." The words whispered out on a breath of air as he kissed the side of her neck, deftly worked the buttons at the back of her gown.

Christopher's dark head came up. "Perhaps you were busy entertaining your duke."

The words stunned her, though they shouldn't have. Everyone in London was talking about the Gypsy woman's prediction, wondering if the heiress and the Duke of Bransford would soon be engaged to wed.

"It isn't official. The announcement is yet some weeks away."

"So it's true."

She shrugged the shoulders left bare by the cut of her ball gown, though at Christopher's harsh regard she hardly felt nonchalant. "A marriage of convenience, nothing more."

"Which is exactly what I am to you—a convenience."

Her gaze met his. She saw the sparks there and the undisguised heat. "You knew it would come to this sooner or later. Have you changed your mind?"

A slightly mocking smile curved his lips. "Why would I do that? I have the use of your luscious body, and both of us can continue to enjoy the pleasure we get from each other."

"That…that is true." And yet there was something in the way he said it that bothered her.

Jocelyn didn't have time to ponder as he continued undressing her, stripping away her gown and petticoats, untying her corset and tossing it away, tugging her chemise off over her head. He turned her toward the mirror above the dresser, moved behind her and began to fondle her breasts. There was something incredibly erotic about seeing herself naked while Christopher remained fully clothed, and a spiral of heat curled low in her belly.

"Ripe," he said, cupping the heavy globes. "Like plump, delicious melons." He squeezed and lifted, and her nipples stiffened, rubbed deliciously against his palms. She felt his mouth against the nape of her neck, then his teeth biting down on an earlobe.

Pleasure tore through her, sent a flood of dampness into her core. His hand skimmed over her belly, traveled through the moist, dark curls between her legs, and a finger slipped inside her. Jocelyn trembled.

"Tell me what you want," he commanded, sliding the finger a little deeper, moving it over the bud at the apex of her sex. He rubbed and she bit her lip to keep from begging him for more.

"Tell me what will please you, Jo." Aside from Lily, he was the only person on earth who dared to call her that. But then Christopher dared just about anything.

He nipped the side of her neck to regain her attention. "What do you want, Jocelyn? How shall I take you?"

His finger probed and she quivered. "Deeper," she whispered. "Faster. Please don't stop."

He laughed softly and his hand fell away. Angry at the way he toyed with her, Jocelyn opened her mouth to rain down an angry retort. The words died on her lips as he shrugged out of his coat and began to strip away his neck cloth. He removed his shirt and shoes and the balance of his clothes and walked toward her, as naked as she, a magnificent specimen, his body lean and fit and as solid as granite.

He was hard, rampantly so, his member thick and heavy, straining upward from the nest of dark curls between his legs. If she hadn't known how good it would feel to have him inside her, she might have been frightened by the size of him. He stopped in front of her, cupped her face between his hands, tipped her head back and claimed her mouth in a deep burning kiss.

Jocelyn moaned. Her arms slid around his neck and she clung to him, absorbing his musky scent, her nipples tingling where they pressed into his chest. Christopher kissed her one way and then another, hot, wet, drugging kisses that left her mind spinning and her knees weak. She barely noticed when he turned her to face the mirror, urged her forward till her palms settled on the tapestry stool in front.

She started to rise, unsure what he meant to do, then felt him behind her, urging her legs apart, setting his hands on her hips.

"I'm here to bring you pleasure. That is what you want from me, and I intend to give it to you." His hand roamed over her bare bottom, making her skin tingle.

She gasped as he found her passage, positioned himself and surged forward, impaling her completely. He paused a moment, giving her time to adjust, then reached around and began to stroke the nubbin at her core. Streaks of sensation flashed through her, and intense, scorching heat. Christopher started to move and pleasure washed through her, and a need so powerful she moaned.

The pinnacle loomed ahead, the place of sweetness and light he had taken her to before.

"Chris…!" she cried out as he thrust into her again and again, driving her toward the promise of fulfillment, pounding relentlessly, taking her hard and deep. He thrust into her until she reached her peak, and tumbled into a shattering climax before allowing his own release.

She was barely conscious when he withdrew from inside her, turned her around and gathered her into his arms.

For an instant he just held her. She felt the press of his lips against the top of her head, then he straightened away.

"There is much more I can teach you—if that is still your wish."

She gazed up at him, the sweetness of their coupling still humming through her veins. "You know it is."

Christopher bent his head and pressed a tender kiss on her lips that seemed in contrast to his demanding lovemaking of moments ago.

In silence they both began to dress. As soon as he had finished, Christopher helped her button and straighten her garments, moving with a brisk efficiency that told her just how much practice he'd had. Once she was properly clothed, he turned and strode to the door.

"Send word when you wish another lesson." Then he turned the handle and walked out of the suite.

Jocelyn stared at the place he had been. Her body still pulsed from his touch. Pleasure still warmed her insides. Christopher had fulfilled his part of the bargain. He had behaved exactly as she had intended.

She didn't understand why it bothered her so much that he had left her the way he had.

Preston Loomis sat brooding in front of the fire in the study of his Mayfair town house. As he stared into the flames behind the grate, images of Tsaya slipped through his head. With her light eyes and pale skin, she looked nothing at all like Medela. Even the straight black hair didn't match the coarse gray strands that belonged to the Gypsy. But Medela had been an old woman when he had met her as a boy. She was an ancient, wrinkled creature when she died.

Was it possible they were related? The connection was distant. It was possible, he supposed.

His head turned at the ring of footsteps outside the study door.

"Come in," he called out to the man in the hallway, Barton McGrew, his man of affairs—or at least that was the title Preston had given him. But Bart's job had nothing to do with pushing papers around a desk. He handled whatever Preston needed done and nothing was too much to ask.

"Pour yourself a drink and sit down."

McGrew did as he was told, filling the crystal glass a little too full, then sipping the extra so that it didn't spill onto the expensive Persian carpet. Bart might have only the barest social polish, but a man like him was invaluable.

"What can I do for you, boss?" McGrew heaved his bulky frame into the chair across from where Preston sat on the leather sofa.

Preston had known Bart for years. The two of them had grown up together in a sleazy neighborhood in Southwark. McGrew was the only man who had known him as the infamous Dick Flynn. Aside from his mother and perhaps the old Gypsy, Medela, Bart was the only person in the world Preston completely trusted. Mostly because the big looby was somewhat bird-witted and, except for his loyalty to Preston, entirely without scruples.

And he depended on Preston for everything.

"There is a woman…" Preston began. "She uses the name Madam Tsaya. I want to know everything about her."

"How do I find her?"

Preston gave him the address he had obtained from Lady Severn, a house in an unremarkable neighborhood in Piccadilly.

"I'll do my best." Tilting the glass up and draining the contents, Bart shoved himself up from the chair and lumbered toward the door.

Preston watched him walk into the hall, thinking what an incongruous picture he made, perfectly dressed in the expensively tailored clothes Preston had bought for him, his short brown hair parted in the middle and neatly slicked back. At the same time, his big, ruddy features and lumpy broken nose were as coarse as those of the burly dockworker whose bastard son he was.

McGrew closed the door and Preston returned his attention to the flames curling over the grate, but he couldn't keep a small portion of his brain from straying to the beautiful and mysterious Tsaya, and wondering what Bart would find out.

Lily arrived a few minutes late for their weekly Wednesday meeting at the Red Rooster Inn. Shoving back the hood of her cloak as she headed down the stairs into the basement taproom, she hurried toward the room at the rear of the inn. The men at the table rose as she entered: Charles Sinclair, Uncle Jack and the duke.

Lily ignored a little pinch in her chest at the sight of him, so tall and incredibly handsome, and fixed her attention on the person who remained seated, a small woman with silver hair pulled back at the nape of her neck, a sturdy, attractive woman in her fifties.

Her name was Molly Daniels, Jack had told Lily, a

very good friend of his. More than a friend, in truth, for she and Jack were lovers. Lily couldn't help noticing the way he looked at her, with a sort of softness and pride. She belonged to him, that look said, and there would be hell to pay should any man try to take her from him.

Lily started to smile, would have if her gaze hadn't strayed at that moment to Royal. Unlike Jack, his features were carefully schooled into blandness, and Lily hadn't the slightest notion what he was thinking.

"Lily, meet Molly," her uncle said by way of introduction.

"It's a pleasure to meet you, Mrs. Daniels," Lily said.

"Same here, but it's just Molly. Always has been. Your uncle Jack's real proud of you, luv."

Lily turned a smile in her uncle's direction then Charles Sinclair began the meeting.

"It would appear things are going exactly as we've planned. Loomis has made contact. He'll be trying to discover whether or not Tsaya is real or merely playing a role in some sort of operation. His man, Barton McGrew, handles anything of a personal nature Loomis might require. Fortunately for us, McGrew isn't long on brains. He's a dangerous man, though, utterly without conscience, and he will do anything Loomis asks."

"McGrew will be going to Tsaya's flat," Jack added. "Dottie Hobbs is there, acting as Tsaya's housekeeper, and she'll know what to say."

Dottie was one of *the mob,* people Jack had brought in to play different roles in the con. Her daughters, Darcy and Mary, would be Tsaya's cook and chambermaid during the day, the minimum household staff for someone of the middle class, which Tsaya purported to be, all of them dressed in freshly starched servants' garb at Royal's expense.

"You don't expect Lily to stay there, do you?" he asked, his expression changing from bland to worried. "You said yourself, this man, McGrew, is dangerous."

"She needs to drop by as Tsaya as often as possible," Sinclair said. "She needs to be seen going in and out."

"I don't like it," Royal said darkly.

Lily tried not to notice the way the indentation in his chin became more pronounced when his jaw was clenched, the way his eyes kept straying toward her.

Jack's shrewd gaze swung toward him. "My girl knows how to take care of herself—leastwise most of the time."

It was a not-so-subtle message that Royal was more a threat to Lily than McGrew. A muscle bunched in his cheek but he made no comment.

"When do I go in?" Molly Daniels asked, speaking up for the first time.

Royal answered, "Annabelle Townsend has a friend, Lady Sabrina Jeffers, the daughter of a marquess. Annabelle trusts her entirely and the girl has agreed to help us. Lady Sabrina has convinced her mother to hold a soiree the end of next week. The marchioness has invited Tsaya—who seems to have become all the rage. Tsaya's name is mentioned on the invitations and Lady Sabrina has made certain to include Preston Loomis on the guest list."

"I daresay, your friends have been quite useful," Sinclair said. "Let us hope they say nothing that will get back to Loomis."

"My friends are extremely loyal, and they all had a great respect for my father. They'll keep silent."

Sinclair nodded, seemed satisfied. "All right then, the soiree should do nicely. If Loomis knows Tsaya will be there, odds are he will come. And since he is expecting to meet an older woman who will enhance his fortune, we shall make a point to see that he does."

Sinclair explained that the plan was for Molly, heavily aged by theatrical paint, to be introduced as an eccentric, extremely wealthy, dotty old woman—the sort ripe for a man like Preston Loomis.

Sinclair turned his attention to Molly. "Lady Sabrina will introduce you as Mrs. Hortense Crowley, a friend of the family's just arrived from her estate in York."

Molly grinned. "Oh, I can't wait. I love a good part and this one's a pip."

Royal eyed her with uncertainty. "Are you sure about this, Mrs. Daniels? Mrs. Crowley would…well, there is the problem of the way she would speak."

Molly straightened and one of her silver eyebrows arched up in disdain. "Are you implying, young man, that I am anything other than a lady of the upper class?" The words were perfectly intonated and spoken with a haughty demeanor that could only belong to a well-bred lady.

Royal laughed and Lily found herself smiling as well. "You have my most humble apologies," he said, playing along with the role. "I cannot imagine what I was thinking."

"It takes a bit of practice," Molly said in her natural voice, "but it's not so hard—once ye get the 'ang of it." She added the cockney to show him how versatile she was, and Royal laughed again.

"I think our friend Loomis is in trouble," he said.

"My Molly's got real talent," Jack said proudly.

"So I see, but won't Loomis find out the Crowley woman doesn't actually exist?"

"He has no reason to doubt the word of the daughter of a marquess. York is a very good distance away, and though the jewels she will be wearing will be paste, they'll look real enough to be convincing."

The meeting continued until the details were all worked out. Once Loomis met Molly—Mrs. Crowley— an old woman who could enhance his fortune as Tsaya predicted—he would be convinced the Gypsy was real. Sinclair believed Loomis would seek Tsaya out for more advice and the Gypsy would very gladly give it.

The meeting adjourned and Lily rose from the table. Royal looked as if there was something he wished to say, but with Jack and Molly protectively surrounding her, he merely stepped out of the way.

As they walked toward the door, Lily forced herself not to look back at him and instead walked out of the inn.

Twenty

It was overcast and cloudy as Lily walked beside Jack and Molly to the cab stand. They waited until she was able to hail a hansom then waved goodbye as the carriage rolled away.

She was headed back to her millinery shop, where she had been working most days, though the shop wouldn't be officially open till Monday. She kept several versions of her Gypsy garb there and she needed to change before making the trip to the small house in Piccadilly that had been rented for Tsaya.

She was climbing the stairs to the small apartment on the second floor when she heard a knock on the door to the shop. Hoping it was a customer, she hurried down then came to a sudden halt at the sight of the tall blond man on the opposite side of the mullioned panes.

Her heart took a leap and started thrumming. Lily took a deep breath, unlocked and opened the door.

"What's happened?" she asked, and though she

didn't invite him inside, he brushed past her into the shop. "Is it Loomis? Has something gone wrong?"

"I don't want you going to Tsaya's house, not when McGrew will likely show up there."

"I have to go. I have to make it look real."

He blew out a breath, shoved a hand through his hair. "I never wanted you involved in this, Lily. If I'd truly understood the risks you would be taking, I never would have started this."

"But you did start, Royal. And we've gone too far to stop." She looked up at him, saw the worry in his eyes. "I won't be alone when I'm there. Dottie Hobbs will be there. She is staying in the house until this is over."

"I don't want you getting hurt, Lily, and I'm afraid that's going to happen."

In truth, she was already hurting, but it had nothing to do with their confidence scheme.

"I'll be fine. So far everything has gone exactly as we've planned. As long as we do what needs to be done, that isn't going to change."

Those golden eyes ran over her face. "Everything in my life has changed," he said softly. "It changed the day I met you." And then he reached for her and drew her into his arms, bent his head and very softly kissed her. "I'm tired of fighting what I feel for you, Lily. I need you so much."

Lily's eyes slid closed and she swayed against him. She knew what they were doing was wrong and yet it felt so good to be held by him, to feel the warmth of his lips, the solid strength of his body. Deep, seductive kisses had her clinging to his shoulders, ravishing, mind-numbing kisses made her forget all the reasons they should stop.

Instead, when he lifted her into his arms and started

for the stairs, Lily slid her arms around his neck and let him carry her up to her apartment.

The door was partially open. Royal nudged it wide with the toe of his boot and strode across the tiny living room into the bedroom. When he set her on her feet and started kissing her again, the last fleeting thoughts of protest died away.

Royal kissed her as if he couldn't get enough of her, as if he wanted to absorb her into his very skin. Hot, wet kisses rained over her neck and behind her ears. Tiny shivers moved over her skin as he drew an earlobe into his mouth and nibbled gently. Ripples of pleasure poured through her. Heat and need rose up, and burning desire for the man she loved.

The front of her gown tipped forward and she realized he had unbuttoned her dress. His mouth scorched a path across her shoulders, over the swell of her breasts above her corset. He dispatched the gown and petticoats with a skill that made her a little uneasy, but as he unlaced her corset and slid her drawers down over her hips, the thought melted away.

She stood before him naked except for her blue satin garters and white silk stockings, and his gaze fixed for an instant on the pale, downy curls above her sex.

"I've imagined this," he said between soft, coaxing kisses. "Imagined seeing you in nothing at all. Imagined making love to you slowly and completely as I should have done the first time."

She trembled as he knelt in front of her, untied her satin garters and began to roll down her stockings. A gasp escaped as he cupped her bottom and pressed his mouth against the sensitive bud at the entrance to her sex.

"I've dreamt of tasting you, giving you pleasure this way." And then, shockingly, his tongue found its way through her curls, and even as she tried to push him away, pleasure swept through her, so fierce and hot she thought she might faint.

A whimper escaped. "Royal..."

He steadied her, but didn't stop, just settled his mouth over the swollen bud, laved and tasted until the pleasure was so intense, so incredibly sweet, she cried out his name. Her body drew as taut as a bowstring. She felt as if she were breaking apart as a shattering climax hit her, pulsed out through her limbs. Dear God, she had never felt anything like it.

She was limp and pliant in his arms as he carried her over to the bed and settled her on the mattress, left her for a moment to strip off his clothes. She roused herself enough to watch him walk toward her, felt a renewed hum of excitement at the width of his powerful shoulders, the way they veed to a narrow waist and slim hips.

A light furring of golden hair covered a chest that was solidly muscled. Long, sinewy legs carried him to the bed, a heavy erection riding against his flat belly.

He was big and hard, and just thinking of having him inside her made her squirm on the mattress. Royal came up over her, bent his head and captured her lips.

"Lily..." he whispered between fierce, plundering kisses that heated her body and scorched through her blood. All she could think of was Royal and how much he wanted her and how much she wanted him.

"It won't hurt this time," he promised as he bent to her breasts and began to suckle the fullness. His teeth grazed the crest, turning her nipples diamond hard, and her skin seemed to burn.

"Please…" she whispered, urging him to take her, desperate to feel his powerful erection moving inside her.

Royal kissed her again and parted her legs, forming a cradle for himself, positioning his shaft at the entrance to her passage. She was wet and ready, slick and welcoming, and as he promised, when he thrust deeply, this time there was no pain, only delicious sensation, overwhelming heat and a need so fierce she bit down on her lip to keep from crying out.

His hips moved, setting up an erotic rhythm that had her whole body tingling. The heavy thrust and drag of his shaft seemed to have no end, stirring the pleasure, making each second more intense. Lily wrapped her legs around his muscular calves and arched upward to receive each of his penetrating thrusts.

His taking was relentless, driving harder and faster until Lily reached the pinnacle and soared out over the edge. Her body tightened around him, urging him to follow, and Royal's muscles clenched. At the last instant, he withdrew from her body as he reached a powerful release.

For seconds they lay together, their hearts beating in unison. Then Royal lifted himself away and lay down beside her, curled Lily spoon fashion against him. He kissed the top of her head, then tucked her securely beneath his chin, and Lily wished they could stay this way forever.

They must have slept for a time, for she awakened to the brush of his mouth against her shoulder, the press of his arousal against her thigh. They made love slowly this time, and there was a sort of desperate sadness about it. Their affair couldn't continue. This had to be the end. But the thoughts burned away in the incredible heat, and when she reached release, it was as powerful as before.

They slept again and by the time she awakened it was dark outside. Dear Lord, she had to get back to Meadowbrook. She still lived with the Caulfields and they would begin to be concerned.

Her cousin's image rose into her mind, along with a shot of guilt. Lily slipped from the bed only to discover Royal sitting in a chair across the room fully clothed. She grabbed her silk wrapper from the foot of the bed and hurriedly pulled it on, trying not to think of the intimate things they had done. But a warm blush rose into her cheeks.

"I—I have to get home. I'll go to Tsaya's tomorrow."

He came toward her like a lion on the prowl. "I don't want you going there at all. I want to keep you safe. I have been thinking on this a great deal, Lily." He looked down at her, his gaze on her face. "Once I am…financially settled, I intend to see you well cared for. I'll make certain you have everything you want."

She frowned. "What are you talking about?"

Royal reached for her, drew her into his arms. "This thing between us, Lily, it isn't going to go away. I'll find a place where we can be together. I'll take care of you, sweetheart. You won't have to worry about a thing."

She struggled to make her mind work, to make sense of what he was saying. The fog slowly cleared and anger rose in its place.

Lily stepped out of Royal's embrace. "Are you… are…you saying you wish me to become your mistress?

You are going to marry Jocelyn and I am to be the other woman?"

"That's not how it is between us and you know it. My marriage was arranged before my father died. Jocelyn gets the title she wants and I get the money I need to rebuild my family's fortune. You've known that from the start. I am trying to find a way for us to be together."

Her eyes welled. She *had* known. The plan had been set the day she had first seen him kneeling beside her in the snow. And yet she hadn't been able to keep herself from falling in love with him.

She swallowed past the bitter lump in her throat. "I have a life, Royal. I told you that before. I wanted you and I am not sorry for what we have shared. But I won't become your paid-for woman. I won't walk around ashamed of who I am."

He reached for her. "Sweetheart, please…"

Lily backed away. "What happened today is what we both wanted. But this has to be the end of it, Royal."

"Lily…" There was something in his face, something deep and yearning.

Lily struggled to ignore it. "Give Jocelyn a chance," she said, having to force out the words. "Perhaps you will discover a way for the two of you to make your marriage work."

He glanced toward the window, seemed to be fighting for control. When he turned back, his jaw was set in a determined line she had begun to recognize. "I am sending a man to the house in Piccadilly, someone who can look out for you if there is trouble. He can be Tsaya's butler or footman, or whatever it is you wish to call him."

"I told you, I don't need—"

"He'll be there tomorrow. Let Mrs. Hobbs know he is coming." With a last glance her way, he turned and strode out of the apartment.

Lily heard his footsteps on the stairs leading down to the shop. "Lock the door behind me," he called over his shoulder and then he was gone.

Tears blurred her vision. She told herself she would not cry, but the wetness seeped down her cheeks.

Barton McGrew knocked on the door of the small house in Piccadilly where Madam Tsaya lived. He could hear footsteps inside the house, then muttering on the other side of the door. When it swung open, a heavyset woman wearing a mobcap and carrying a broom stood in the entry.

"May I help you?"

"Heard tell there was a woman here could predict the future. I was hoping she could help me."

The stout woman looked up at him, moving a strand of mouse-brown hair streaked with gray that had slipped from beneath her cap.

"That'd be my employer, Madam Tsaya. I'm her housekeeper, Mrs. Hobbs. But Tsaya don't tell fortunes— she just sees things sometimes. If she sees something good, she lets the person know."

"I'd sure like to meet her. What time do you think she'll be back?"

She shrugged her plump shoulders. "You never know with Tsaya. She's real independent. Comes and goes as she pleases."

"You think I might wait a while, see if she comes home?"

"What's your name?"

"Bart McGrew. Me mother's took sick. I'm real worried about her. I thought the lady might be able to tell me if me mum is gonna get well."

He tried to look worried. He figured the mention of his mother might soften the old bag up. From the way she seemed to be thinking it over, he thought it just might work. The Hobbs woman scrunched up her nose as she surveyed the cut of his clothes: the expensive tailored trousers, dark brown tailcoat and matching waistcoat that Dick had bought for him. The boss took real good care of him. And he took real good care of the boss.

'Course, he had learned to call him Preston, the way he liked, but deep down, Bart would always think of him as his boyhood friend from Southwark, Dicky Flynn, who'd taught him how to survive in the streets.

"I suppose I could make ye a cup of tea," the stout woman said. "But ye can't stay long. I've got to get back to work."

The old gal wanted company. He'd figured that right off. And he wanted some answers. Be interesting to see what he could learn.

They went into the kitchen and he sat down at a small round table while she set the teakettle on the stove.

"If she can tell fortunes, how come no one's heard of her till now?"

"I told you, she can't tell fortunes. She just sees things sometimes. And she only just got to London two months ago. Afore that, she lived in France." The teakettle whistled and the woman poured the boiling water into a china teapot.

"Where's her husband now?" he asked, trying to sound casual.

"Poor man died a few years back. Left her enough to take care of herself, but I guess she wanted to come back here where she'd lived as a girl." She poured the tea into two cups, added a lump of sugar to each one, carried them over and set them down on the table and sat down across from him.

He wasn't that good at making conversation, so he just sipped his tea, wishing she'd put in a second lump of sugar, and let her rattle on. She talked about the weather, said her big toe was aching, a sure sign of a storm. She chattered about the chambermaid who was working upstairs and about the cook who hadn't shown up that morning.

"I thought Tsaya would be back by now," she finally said, "but like I told ye, the lady's real independent-natured so you never know." She got up and carried her cup over to the counter, came back and took his before he was quite finished.

"You'll have to come back, Mr. McGrew. I'm sorry, but I have to get back to work."

He heaved himself up from his chair. He'd found out what he'd come to learn. "My thanks for the tea, Mrs. Hobbs. But I don't think I'll be coming back."

She smiled with approval. "Best just to hold good thoughts for yer mum and take real good care of her."

Bart just nodded. His mum was a whore, same as Dicky's. But at five years old, she'd run off and left him to fend for himself. If it hadn't been for Dicky and his mother, he would have been dead afore the end of the year.

Bart buried thoughts of the mother he'd never known

and left the house, happy with the job he had done, always eager to please his friend.

Royal glanced up from the Swansdowne Brewery ledgers in front of him to see Sheridan Knowles strolling into the study as if he were the one who owned the house. He walked behind Royal's chair and looked down at the leather-bound book sitting open on the desk.

"You might want to turn it round if you actually intend to read it."

A flush rose beneath the bones in his cheeks. He'd been staring at the pages for the past half hour, but he couldn't seem to focus on the finely scrolled numbers his accountant had penned there. "I was just getting to it."

He turned the heavy volume to face him, hoping the afternoon would prove more worthwhile than the morning. Sherry ambled over to a nearby chair and threw himself down, tossing one long leg over the padded leather arm.

"Still having female trouble, I gather." His friend eyed him with the keen instincts that served him well and made Royal want to hit him.

"Let's just say that although your idea of making Lily my mistress had a goodly amount of merit, Lily didn't see it that way."

Sherry chuckled. "I don't see any scars."

At least none that showed, Royal thought. And yet all morning he had been thinking of the way it had felt when he'd made love to her, as if he was exactly where he was supposed to be, as if there were no better place on earth.

"I take it your brother went back to school," said Sherry.

Royal nodded. "Rule left a few days after Lady Severn's affair."

"I got news from the country. Thought you would be interested."

"What is it?"

"That band of outlaws struck again, a carriage belonging to Lord Denby this time. His wife was inside, scared the bloody wits out of her. Took her jewelry and the coin in her purse, but did her no physical harm."

"That's something, I guess. Dammit, we need to stop them."

Sherry sighed. "I daresay I wish we were there. We'd deal with the rotters ourselves, get rid of them once and for all."

"I can't leave—not in the middle of this thing with Loomis."

"I know. I just hope no one gets hurt while we're busy playing cat and mouse here in the city."

Royal got up from behind his desk and walked over to the hearth, turning his back to the flames to warm himself against the cold that had slipped in with the fog that morning.

"This thing with Loomis…" he said. "I've been thinking about calling it off."

"What?"

"Sinclair says Loomis and McGrew are dangerous. Morgan said the same. I'm not sure the risk is worth it. Someone might get hurt."

Sherry fixed him with a stare. "That *someone* you're worried about wouldn't be Lily, would it?"

"She's a likely target. If Loomis finds out who she really is—"

"Once this is over, Tsaya will disappear forever, and Lily will be completely out of danger. Give it some time, Royal. Tonight is the Wyhurst soiree. Once Loomis meets our Mrs. Crowley, things are going to move a whole lot faster. We'll reel Loomis in like a fish on a line. You'll have at least a portion of your father's money returned and the justice he deserves."

Justice. He wanted that above all things.

Royal released a breath. "All right, we'll see how things progress. If it looks like Loomis is taking the bait, we'll keep going."

"Good lad," said Sherry, coming up from his chair. "You never were much of a quitter." He started for the door. "I'll see you tonight." A light brown eyebrow arched in question. "I presume you are going to be there."

"I'm accompanying Jocelyn and her parents. I figured it was time I faced my situation and tried to make the best of it." Though it was a bitter pill to swallow and not his idea but Lily's.

Still the concept was sound. His engagement would be announced in only three weeks. He needed to focus his attention on the woman he would wed and look for a way they might find some bit of happiness together.

Royal wished he felt more enthusiasm for the notion.

Twenty-One

Jocelyn stood next to their hostess, Lady Fiona Wyhurst, a rotund little woman with red hair fading to gray and a very large bosom, which she did her best to disguise beneath the modest sequined bodice of her shot-silver ball gown.

Her daughter stood beside her, Lady Sabrina Jeffers, a beautiful, willowy blonde that Jocelyn had seen on occasion but never met. Sabrina was polite enough, Jocelyn supposed, yet there was a certain aloofness about her, a self-assurance that said she belonged to the aristocracy. Each lift of her golden eyebrows seemed to say *I am the daughter of a marquess. I am someone special.*

Then again, perhaps it was simply that Jocelyn never liked a woman who was nearly as beautiful as she.

Sabrina caught sight of the Gypsy woman who had become society's latest amusement and gave the small group a faint, parting smile.

"If you all will excuse me, I believe I see our special guest for the evening, Madam Tsaya." Sabrina turned and drifted away with a grace Jocelyn envied. Still, it was *she* who was marrying a duke, not the willowy blonde.

Royal stood on her opposite side and Jocelyn turned to face him. "I hope you're enjoying yourself, Your Grace."

He looked down at her and smiled. "Of course I am. I am escorting the most beautiful woman in the room. How could I not be?"

She almost blushed, a rare occurrence for her, but the duke so rarely paid her a compliment, she felt slightly giddy. He was, after all, one of the most eligible bachelors in England and by his presence at her side tonight, he was letting all of London know his intentions.

Standing in the same circle, her mother flicked Jocelyn a conspiratorial glance, then focused her attention on the duke. "They are playing a waltz, Your Grace. My Jocelyn so loves to dance."

He smiled. "Then it is fortunate I reserved several dances on her card and I believe this is one of them." He extended an arm and she rested her fingers on the sleeve of his black evening coat. "Shall we?"

With his impressive height, golden eyes and golden hair, he looked stunning. But then he always did. Dozens of eyes followed them as they made their way through the crowd and a little thrill went through her that once they were married, this sort of attention would always be hers.

They had almost reached the dance floor when her gaze happened to light on Christopher Barclay, standing among a group of his friends. She was always a little surprised to see him in such elevated circles and yet there was something about Christopher that demanded acceptance and respect. With his drive and determination, she had no doubt he would become one of the most successful barristers in London, and connections among the social elite would surely be helpful.

Still, he would never be a truly wealthy man.

And he would never be a duke.

She kept her eyes on Royal as she walked past him onto the dance floor and moved into position in front of her partner, resting her hand on his wide shoulder. The orchestra began the waltz and Royal swept her into the dance with unerring grace. Still, she couldn't keep her glance from straying to the dark-haired man who was her lover.

He was scowling, she saw, his face as black as thunder. He had no right to be angry and yet it gave her a jolt of satisfaction to know he was jealous. She lost track of him as the waltz progressed and fixed her attention on her future husband. She wondered what it would be like to make love with him, wondered if he would be able to rouse her passions as her current lover did.

But even as she smiled up at him, thoughts of Christopher intruded: the determined press of his lips, the hot way they moved over hers, his white teeth grazing her nipple, his hands on her hips as he bent her over and drove himself inside her from behind.

Jocelyn stumbled.

Royal caught her before she could fall. "All right?"

She managed a smile, but it wasn't easy. "I must have stepped on something. I am fine." But a sensual rash spread over her breasts, and perspiration trickled between her breasts. It infuriated her to discover that just the memory of Christopher's lovemaking could have so much power over her.

It wasn't supposed to happen. *She* was the one who

was supposed to be in charge, the one in control. Christopher Barclay was no more than a dalliance, an affair that would be over the moment she deemed it so.

She repeated those words several times through the evening, and yet several hours later as she stood next to her father and spotted Christopher talking to her archenemy, Serafina Maitlin, jealousy burned into her stomach like a red-hot coal.

How dare he? If he thought for a moment he could sleep with Serafina and also with her, he was sorely mistaken!

Taking several deep breaths, she brought herself under control and returned her attention to her father, who rarely attended these affairs and had come tonight only because the duke was joining their party and strictly to please her.

"Bransford has been quite attentive this evening," he said, obviously pleased.

Jocelyn nodded. "As he should be. After all, we shall be officially engaged in only three weeks."

Her father smiled. "Your mother and I couldn't be more pleased."

Jocelyn managed to keep the smile on her face, but even as they continued to converse, she was thinking of Christopher, determined to talk to him, set him straight on the conditions of their arrangement.

Most importantly that while they were lovers, there would be no other women!

Dressed as Tsaya, Lily chatted with Lady Annabelle Townsend and Lady Sabrina Jeffers, coconspirators in their scheme. Lily tried not to notice Royal standing next to Jo, but it was impossible to do. Had it been only three days since she had lain with him? Since they had made passionate love in her tiny upstairs apartment?

She tried not to recall the ease with which he had undressed her, the skillful lovemaking that gave evidence to the number of women he'd had. She tried not to be insulted by his indecent proposal that she should become his mistress, but she couldn't help wondering if the attention he had paid her was merely a diversion, a source of entertainment while he awaited his beautiful bride.

"Tsaya, I believe you've met Lord Wellesley." Lady Sabrina's voice pierced the haze of her thoughts.

Lily turned toward him, jangling the gold bracelets on her wrists. "We have met. It is good to see you, my lord."

He made a faint bow. "You, as well, Madam Tsaya."

"I believe Lady Sabrina and I are being summoned," Annabelle said good-naturedly. "I'm afraid you will have to excuse us." The ladies departed, leaving her to chat with Royal's best friend.

"How are you holding up, love?"

Her gaze strayed to Royal for a single telling instant. "Well enough. Loomis is here. Mrs. Crowley is here. It should be an interesting evening."

"Indeed." His gaze lit for a moment on Royal, just as hers had done. "If he could change things, he would."

"Perhaps." But she was no longer certain. In three weeks' time, Royal would become formally engaged to the wealthiest, most beautiful woman in England. If he could change things, would he actually wish to marry a woman who came to him with nothing? One who had lived on the streets for a time, surviving by her wits, by trickery, theft and deceit? A woman whose body no longer held surprises for him? It was difficult to believe.

"Loomis is talking to Mrs. Crowley," the viscount said, his gaze on the pair not far away. "Let's get a little closer, see if we can hear what they are saying?"

Lily turned her attention to the stoop-shouldered old lady who had arrived earlier. Molly Daniels was totally unrecognizable as the woman Lily had met at the Red Rooster Inn. Gowned expensively in dove-gray silk, she wore a sparkling diamond necklace that even keen-eyed Preston Loomis wouldn't recognize as a fake.

As planned, Lady Sabrina had introduced Mrs. Crowley to her guests as a family friend from York, and Molly seemed to have had no trouble keeping up her end of the conversation with the group of women she met. She had also conversed with Wellesley and Savage, who pretended to be acquainted.

Chatting casually as they strolled, Sherry led Lily to a spot near where Preston Loomis stood next to Molly, who was grinning up at him like a half-witted fool. She was shaking her head, her silver hair dimmed to a lackluster gray, the faint lines in her face etched deeply into wrinkles.

"Now…what the devil was I saying…? Something about clothes, wasn't it? Or were we discussing my cotton mills?" She wore too much powder and her cheeks were a little too rosy, as if she had drunk a bit too much champagne. "Lately, it seems harder and harder to recall."

Loomis gave her a reassuring smile. "We were discussing the lovely gown you are wearing, madam, but I believe you did mention something about a mill."

Her heavy gray eyebrows drew together. "Can't recall what it was. Probably talking about coal. My late husband, Freddy, was fascinated with coal. Bought two new mines just before he passed away, God rest his soul."

Loomis's interest was clearly piqued. "Is that so? I, too, am interested in mining. Perhaps we could discuss the subject on another occasion."

Mrs. Crowley grinned. "Just like my Freddy. You even look a little like him—younger, of course, but just as handsome as my Freddy."

Preston was smiling, continuing to converse with Molly as Sheridan led Lily away.

He chuckled softly. "I think our Mrs. Crowley has snared herself a rabbit."

"My uncle says she is the best confidence woman he has ever met."

"She certainly seems to know what she is about. Loomis was practically salivating."

Lily turned just then, peered through her heavy black bangs to see Jonathan Savage approaching.

"All seems to be going well," he said, flicking a glance to where Loomis still talked to Mrs. Crowley. He was the exact opposite of Royal, black-haired and dark-eyed, no golden angel, but devilishly handsome.

"I think I had better mingle," Lily said, for Loomis had ended his discourse with the wealthy widow and might wish to seek Tsaya out. She paused to say hello to Lord Nightingale and his wife, who were congenial, as always. Then someone tapped her shoulder.

Lily turned to see Royal's aunt Agatha, Lady Tavistock, standing beside her as if she had appeared out of nowhere. "Might we have a word, my dear?"

A trickle of unease slipped through her. "As you wish," Lily said with a slightly thicker accent than she had been using thus far.

Lady Tavistock led her a few feet away where they

could be private. "That is quite a marvelous costume, my dear, but I wonder why it is you are wearing it?"

Lily's stomach turned over. Dear God, was it possible the dowager countess had recognized her?

She took a deep breath and tried to bluff it out. "I am afraid I do not know vhat you mean."

"Well, I am quite certain you do, my dear, and I would like to know what sort of nonsense my nephew has involved you in that would require you to dress like a Gypsy."

Fortunately, Lord Wellesley appeared just then. He smiled down at Lady Tavistock. "I see you have met Madam Tsaya. Is she predicting good fortune for you?"

"She is predicting that my nephew is in a great deal of trouble. As I imagine you and the rest of his friends are also a part of this, you may explain to me exactly what is going on and why Royal has involved this lovely young woman in one of his outrageous pranks."

The viscount looked at Lily over the frail old woman's head, caught her arm and laced it through his. "Come with me, my lady. You will probably disapprove, but perhaps, once you understand, you might even be willing to help."

He cast Lily a glance that said *what else can I do?* and led the dowager away. Lily breathed a sigh of relief that she didn't have to deal with the problem and nearly collided with Preston Loomis, whose light blue eyes were practically dancing.

"I met her, Tsaya. The old woman you told me about."

Lily collected herself, nodded sagely. "It was foretold. I saw it—as I sometimes do."

"I wish to meet with you," Loomis said. "When can that be arranged?"

This was it. It was happening just as they had planned. She frowned, pretended to think when she might be free. "Tuesday would be a good day." Monday was the official opening of her millinery shop, plus she didn't want to seem too eager. "You may come to my house in Piccadilly. At noon would be best." She gave him her address and Loomis nodded.

"All right, Tuesday. I look forward to seeing you then."

"I cannot say for certain I will have more to tell you. But there is a chance."

He smiled with obvious anticipation, tilting the ends of his mustache, and made an inclination of his head. "Till Tuesday. Have a good evening, madam."

It was done. She would begin making financial predictions for Loomis. In the beginning, those predictions would pay off. In the end, if all went well, Loomis would learn a very costly lesson.

She looked over to where Royal had been standing next to Jo but saw neither one of them. Her heart sank. Had they slipped off somewhere together? Was Royal kissing Jocelyn, touching her? Her cousin had not spoken of her second rendezvous with Christopher Barclay. Was she tired of the man already and eager for someone new?

And what of Royal? When Lily had refused to become his mistress, had he simply turned to the woman he would soon make his wife?

And if they were together, how could she fault them?

She glanced round the drawing room, but they were nowhere to be seen. Ignoring the sick feeling in her stomach, Lily hurried along the hall toward the servants' stairs at the back of the house, needing to go up and change out of her Tsaya costume and leave the soiree.

She wouldn't return downstairs as Lily. Since Jocelyn and her parents were escorted tonight by the duke, Lily had pretended a headache and stayed home. Only Tsaya had come and as soon as she changed, she hurried out of the house to meet her uncle in the alley behind the stable where he waited in his rented carriage to escort her home.

Molly was with him, she saw when she reached them, both of them excited by the success of the evening.

Lily thought of Royal, ignored the pain in her heart and climbed inside the coach.

Jocelyn saw Christopher escaping through the French doors out onto the terrace. She watched him for a moment, heart pounding as she waited to see if Serafina Maitlin would join him.

But the redhead was busy entertaining a group of male admirers and didn't seem in a hurry to leave.

Excusing herself to the ladies' retiring room, Jocelyn fled down the hall and slipped out a side door into the shadows of the terrace. A few feet away, Christopher stood alone in the darkness, the tip of his cigar glowing in the inky solitude of the night.

Jocelyn readied herself as she approached him, her temper climbing with every step. He turned at the padding of her soft kid slippers on the flagstones and leaned back against the balustrade, clamping the cigar between his straight white teeth.

Jocelyn reached up and jerked it out of his mouth, tossed it out into the garden.

One of his dark eyebrows went up. "I see you are in one of your moods."

"What were you doing with Serafina Maitlin?"

"I was entertaining myself while you preened and flirted with the duke."

"I wasn't preening. And what do you mean by entertaining yourself? If you think for one minute I am going to stand by and let you seduce that woman into your bed while you are making love to me—"

Christopher caught her arm and jerked her hard against him. "You think I was trying to seduce her? You little fool. You're the woman I want in my bed. You, Jocelyn—with your tantrums and your fancy airs. I want to fuck the insolence out of you. I want to take you until you admit I'm the only man you need."

Shock held her immobile. "Why, you…you crude, arrogant—" Her tirade ended as the passion in his words began to reach her. He wanted her. Only her.

She stared at the hard set of his jaw, the compelling planes of his face, unable to look away. His dark gaze bored into her, daring her to finish what she had started to say. Instead, her fingers curled into the lapels of his coat and she went up on her toes and kissed him.

Hard arms clamped around her and Christopher's mouth crushed down over hers. He kissed her as no other man ever dared, holding her spellbound, unable to escape the powerful force he exuded.

The kiss went on and on and yet it ended far too soon. Both of them were breathing hard when Christopher broke away.

"Go back inside, Jo," he said gruffly, "before I take you right here on the terrace."

She just stood there, her legs trembling beneath her full skirts, a little whimper caught in her throat.

"Go," he said, more gently this time. "For both of our sakes."

Jocelyn turned and fled. Something was happening to her. Something she didn't understand.

And she had never been more terrified in her life.

Twenty-Two

❧◆◆◆❧

Monday was the official opening of the Lily Pad. On the sign above her door in smaller letters it read, Fine Millinery Goods, and Lily grinned every time she looked up and saw it.

At the end of last week, she had hired a shopgirl named Flora Perkins to work a few hours each day so that she could leave the establishment if needed, and also have more time to sew. Lily hoped eventually she would have enough business to need an assistant hatmaker and she could train Flora for the job.

This morning the gangly, carrot-haired girl had arrived at ten, giving Lily plenty of time to reach the house in Piccadilly for Tsaya's noon appointment with Preston Loomis.

There was a man in the house when she arrived. Dottie Hobbs said his name was Chase Morgan. Dressed in her black wig and Gypsy skirts, Lily pushed through the swinging door and jerked to a halt at the sight of Royal sitting at the kitchen table.

A little shiver of awareness went through her that she determinedly ignored.

"What are you doing here?" she asked, hoping he wouldn't notice the slightly breathless note in her voice.

"Morgan was busy. I came in his place."

"But…but…you can't be here. If Loomis sees you, he'll recognize you. For heaven's sake, you're the Duke of Bransford."

But he wasn't dressed like a duke. Instead, he wore the plain brown riding breeches and simple white lawn shirt he wore to the inn. As her gaze ran over the magnificent width of his shoulders and angled down over his narrow hips, she thought that he looked even better today than he had in his evening clothes at the Wyhurst soiree.

"I'll stay in the kitchen out of sight," he promised. "But I'll be close by if you need me. If Loomis threatens you in any way, just call out."

Lily set a hand on the silky garment flowing over her hip. "I don't need your protection, Royal. I am quite capable of taking care of myself."

His lips faintly curved. "Perhaps. You never fail to surprise me, sweetheart. But just in case, I am staying."

Lily opened her mouth to argue, but only a sputtering sound came out. Spinning round, she marched out of the kitchen, passing Dottie Hobbs headed in the opposite direction. The door swung closed and Dottie laughed at something Chase Morgan said. Lily heard the sound of cups rattling as Dottie busied herself making him tea.

Trying not to think of him with Jo the night of the soiree, Lily walked into the parlor and plopped down on the sofa. The black wig itched, and every time she moved, the charms jangling on her bracelet grated on her nerves.

Silently she cursed. She was doing this for Royal, but at the moment, she had no idea why. Royal might be a duke, but he was no longer the image of the perfect man she had once believed. He was arrogant and domineering, stubborn and overprotective and used to getting his way. Why, the man would be impossible to live with. She pitied her poor cousin, once she was his wife.

Lily sighed as she leaned back on the horsehair sofa. She rarely lied to herself, as she was doing now. Royal might have his faults, but so did she, and no matter how pigheaded he was at times, she was still in love with him.

Not that it would do her the least amount of good.

Glancing over at the clock on the mantel, she saw that it was almost noon. Through the lace curtains, she watched Preston Loomis climb the front-porch steps right on time and knock on the heavy wooden door. Lily waited as Mrs. Hobbs went to let him in, then stood up as he entered the parlor.

"Mr. Loomis, please come in." Lily motioned for him to join her at a small round table with a red fringed cloth draped over the top. Twin high-backed chairs encircled it, and both of them sat down.

"I appreciate your seeing me, Tsaya." Loomis smiled. He had very large teeth, she noticed as she hadn't before since they were hidden by his mustache. His coat and trousers were perfectly pressed and his silver hair gleamed. "You don't mind my calling you that, do you? Your aunt and I were very good friends. I feel as if we are friends, as well."

He was such a smooth talker. It was no surprise he was extremely good at his work. "I am flattered. If it is your wish, to you I am merely Tsaya."

He nodded, obviously pleased. His gaze roamed over her face, taking in the straight black hair and fringe of bangs that covered her forehead. "Your eyes…they are quite an unusual shade of green and your skin is very pale for a Gypsy."

She shrugged, shifting the scarlet silk blouse across her shoulders. "My father was a *gadjo,* a Frenchman."

He stared at her across the table, his pale blue gaze piercing. "I came in the hope you might be able to advise me. What have you seen?"

Lily straightened in her chair. "Not much. A boat race, only. Bet a good sum, for you are destined to win."

"What sort of boat race?"

"Four men. Friends and rivals. They will race on the Thames sometime soon. The black-haired man will win."

Loomis seemed impressed. "How do you know these things? How can you be sure they are true?"

She had been waiting for this. The stars would give her predictions more credence. "If you were here at night, I would show you." She rose and walked over to the writing desk along the wall, opened the fold-down top. Drawing a rolled-up parchment from inside, she returned to the table.

"What is it?" Loomis asked.

She unrolled the parchment. On it were drawings of the night sky over London at different times of the year. "At night, I look at the stars. Here…do you see this?" She pointed at one of the constellations. "This is the dog. Next to him, the hunter. At night, I look into the stars and study the patterns and when I do, sometimes images come into my head."

He was frowning. "Medela did not do this."

"No. It was something my mother taught me. It helps me to see more clearly. Mostly, I meet someone and something will occur to me, but for a clearer picture, I turn to the stars."

He seemed to mull that over and Lily held her breath, praying he would be intrigued.

The frown lines faded from his forehead. "Tell me more about this race."

"I know only that the man who wins will make you money sometime in the future."

"Are you talking about some sort of investment?"

She pretended to think. Then nodded. "Yes, I believe it will be something like that."

Loomis rose from his chair. "I'll see what I can find out about the race. If you are correct, I shall return." He set a pouch of coins on the table in front of her. "Good day, Tsaya."

She inclined her head. "Mr. Loomis."

Lily waited until he left the house, then hurried into the kitchen, slamming into Royal as she shoved open the swinging door.

He caught her when she stumbled, and a frisson of heat rolled through her. "Easy, sweetheart." Still on alert for any sign of trouble from Loomis, his body hummed with its last remnants of tension.

He tipped his head toward the parlor. "From what I could hear, it sounded like Loomis believed it completely."

"He asked questions. I gave him the answers he wanted to hear."

He smiled. "You're amazing."

Her cheeks warmed at the compliment. Lily steeled

herself. "I told you, you didn't need to be here. Loomis was completely the gentleman."

His smile slipped away. "This time, perhaps. But if he wants to meet with you again, I'll expect you to send word. And I'll want to know if his henchman, McGrew, shows up here again."

She opened her mouth to tell him she had no intention of encouraging him to come back, when she felt his solid grip on her arm. "I'll end this, Lily, I swear. I'm not going to let you get hurt."

Her heart squeezed. She couldn't mistake his concern. Whatever he felt for her, he didn't want anything happening to her.

If only all of this was over. But they were in too deep to quit. Uncle Jack and Molly would get a share of any monies recovered from Loomis and she knew how much they were counting on the funds. She wanted to do this for them. And for Royal. She had no choice but to do whatever he asked.

"All right, I'll send word. Otherwise, we'll talk at the Red Rooster."

He released his hold on her shoulder. "That's my girl."

She *was* his, utterly and completely. She wondered if he knew. For a moment, he just looked at her and she thought he might say something more. In the end, he made a slight bow of his head. "I shall see you at the meeting tomorrow."

Lily just nodded.

Royal escaped out the backdoor, the way he had come, and Lily breathed a sigh of relief. Her heart was pounding. Her palms felt damp. Her body still thrummed from their single brief moment of contact. Sweet God, she couldn't be in the same room with the man without wanting him to kiss her—and far more than that.

Footsteps sounded and Dottie burst through the swinging door. "Good Lord, isn't that man quite something? Made me want to swoon like a maiden." Dottie cast a yearning glance at the door through which Royal had disappeared.

"Quite something, indeed," Lily said, trying not to smile.

She thought of the lengths Royal was willing to go in order to protect her, and wished she understood what it meant.

Royal sat at their usual table in the taproom of the Red Rooster Inn. Lily sat across from him, looking so beautiful it made his chest hurt.

"So everything went as planned," Charles Sinclair said, looking to Lily for confirmation.

"The meeting went smoothly," she said. "Unless something goes wrong, Loomis is in for the duration."

"And you mentioned the boat race?"

"I told him the black-haired man would win, just as we discussed."

"I'll speak to Savage and the others," Royal said, "get things organized. The Oarsmen race whenever they need a little competition, so it won't be unexpected."

"So Savage will win," Jack Moran said, almost gleeful at the prospect of Royal losing. He wondered how much Lily's uncle had guessed about his relationship with Lily. *Past* relationship, he corrected. Whatever Jack knew or thought he knew, it was clear he disapproved.

And rightly so.

Royal looked over to where Lily sat across the table and found her watching him. Her cheeks colored prettily and she quickly glanced away. His groin tightened. God's blood, he wanted her. He couldn't stop thinking of making love to her, imagining her slender body moving beneath him with such unschooled passion, her sweet little cries of pleasure.

"So Savage understands what we have planned?" Sinclair asked, putting an end to his musings.

Royal nodded. "After the race, he'll talk to Loomis, mention that he makes high-interest, short-term loans to a group of Americans. He'll offer Loomis a chance to join in and if he agrees, a week later, he'll have his money back plus a very sizable profit."

"That ought to impress him," said Sinclair.

Royal scoffed. "Unfortunately, it's money I'll have to pay."

With an air of confidence, Jack leaned back in his chair, tipping it up on two legs. "Don't worry, lad, you'll get it back—and a handsome sum to boot."

Perhaps he would, Royal thought, but there was a very good chance the entire scheme would fail and he would wind up losing money he could ill afford.

"You're saving me for last," Molly said. "Ain't that right?"

"Savin' the best for last, sweetness," said Jack, whose chair thumped back down on the floor. He slipped an arm round Molly's waist and gave her a hug.

"We will work out the details as we go," said Sinclair. "Until then, let us focus on the race and the investment we want Loomis to make."

They discussed a few more possibilities, but Jack

and Molly had an errand to run, so they made their farewells and prepared to leave. "Charlie, will you see Lily
gets to the cab stand?"

"It would be my pleasure."

Jack and Molly left the inn and the three who
remained finished making plans for the race and figured
out how to make certain Loomis heard about it.

"All right then," Sinclair said, rising to his feet. "With
that settled, our meeting is concluded." He pulled out
Lily's chair and helped her rise. "Come, my dear, I'll
walk you to the corner."

She nodded, barely flicking Royal a glance. Each
week, they came and left separately. Royal waited a
few minutes for Lily and Sinclair to climb the stairs
to the street, then started up behind them. By the time
he reached the corner, Lily stood at the cab stand,
waiting for a carriage. Sinclair was disappearing down
the street.

He told himself to turn and walk the other way, but
his feet refused to obey. Lily spotted him and froze as
he started striding toward her. He didn't see the skinny
boy who darted into his path until they had collided.

"Beg pardon, milord," the boy said, spinning round
to dash off in the opposite direction. Lily's hand shot out
and caught the back of the lad's ragged coat, bringing
him to a sudden, sliding halt. Royal stepped in front of
him, further blocking his way.

Lily's glance went from the boy to Royal. "I believe
you must have dropped this, Your Grace." She held up
the pouch of coins that had been in his inside coat pocket.

"Blimey..." the boy said, wide-eyed, "yer good. I
didn't feel a thing."

"What the devil…?" Royal stared down at the leather pouch Lily held out to him.

"He's a cutpurse, Your Grace." She handed him the pouch, then turned back to the boy, who looked up at her with huge, frightened eyes. He couldn't have been more than eleven or twelve, small for his age, and utterly skin and bones.

"Who taught you," she asked, "Harry O?"

The boy started to run again and Royal caught his shoulders and brought him to a struggling halt. "Easy, lad."

"Who?" Lily pressed.

The boy ceased his struggles and just stood there looking defeated. "Fast Eddie. But I been on me own fer a bit."

"Men like Harry and Eddie teach boys the trade. They learn to steal then exchange their ill-gotten gains for a bit of food and a place to sleep."

"Are ye gonna call the coppers?"

Royal felt a wave of sympathy for the ragtag boy. "What's your name?" he asked.

"Tommy. Me name's Tommy Cox. I won't do it again, milord—I give ye me word."

"Where are your parents, Tommy?" Lily asked softly.

The lad just stood there, his head hanging down, brown hair falling forward, covering a pair of sugar-bowl ears.

Royal tugged on the back of the boy's dirty tweed coat. "Answer the lady, lad. Where are your mother and father?"

He swallowed so hard his throat moved up and down. "I don't remember me da. He died when I was small. Me mum got sick and died a few years back. Ye gonna call the coppers?"

Lily looked up at Royal, silently beseeching him to let the boy go.

"Not this time," Royal said. "But if you keep up this kind of behavior, Tommy, sooner or later, you'll wind up in prison."

Lily caught the boy's arm. "Listen to me, Tommy. My name is Lily Moran. I own a hat shop in Harken Lane called the Lily Pad. It's just off Bond. If you need something to eat or a warm place to sleep, you come and see me, all right?"

Tommy looked up at her, his eyes even bigger, and filled with something that looked like hope. "Ye mean it?"

She smiled. "I mean it, I promise."

"Whot about me dog? I don't go nowhere Mugs ain't welcome."

Royal hadn't noticed the ugly, brown-and-white mutt until it trotted over and sat down at the boy's feet.

Lily pretended not to notice how bad the dog smelled or the splotches of dried mud and offal on its coat. "You can bring Mugs, too."

For the first time, Tommy smiled. Lily saw it, and the tender expression on her face made something tighten in Royal's chest. He caught the boy's hand and dumped a handful of silver into his grimy palm. He didn't dare risk a gold sovereign. A boy his size could be killed for something as valuable as that.

Tommy grinned up at him. "Thank ye, sir." He turned to Lily. "I may come see ye, miss. I may hold ye to yer word."

Lily smiled at him. "You do that, Tommy."

The boy dashed away, his mangy dog at his heels, both of them vanishing round the corner.

"If he shows up, he'll probably steal you blind," Royal said, but he couldn't pull his gaze from Lily's face, and pride rose inside him at what she had done.

The tilt of her chin held a trace of defiance. "I lived in the streets once. My uncle was good to me, but we were poor. I was a cutpurse and a thief. I know what it's like to go hungry."

His chest squeezed. She was so brave and so sweet. He simply couldn't help himself. Leaning toward her, he bent his head and settled his mouth over hers. Right there on the street next to the cab stand, he kissed her.

For an instant, Lily stiffened, then her mouth softened under his and she kissed him back, her slender body swaying toward him. Arousal shot through him and the blood seemed to burn through his veins. Desire hit him like a fist, numbing his brain and making him go rock hard. In an instant he was lost.

It was the press of Lily's hands on his chest, pushing him away, that brought reality crashing in. Her cheeks were flushed, her breathing a little too fast.

"I—I can't do this, Royal. I can't…can't be your mistress."

He swallowed, wanting her so badly he ached. "I know."

Her eyes welled, brimmed with tears. "There's something I need to know, Royal. I know I have no right to ask, but…are you…are you and Jocelyn…"

He frowned. "Are we what…?"

"Did you make love to her, Royal?"

"Good God, no!"

Lily looked down at the slender feet peeping out from beneath the hem of her skirts. "I thought…at the ball the other night…you both disappeared and I…" She looked up at him. "You're an extremely virile man, Your Grace, and men have needs. Since we can't…can't be together, it seemed only logical that you would—"

"It didn't happen, Lily. I am surprised you thought Jocelyn would be willing."

She shrugged and glanced away. "The two of you are going to be married. It wouldn't be the first time a man took his wife before the wedding."

"Not this man," he said, and realized how little he desired the woman destined to become his bride.

Lily just looked at him. "And yet you took me," she said softly.

A cab appeared just then, the bay horse plodding up in front of the stand. There was no time to explain and he had no idea what he would say if he tried.

"I have to go." Lily made her way toward the door of the carriage. Royal helped her inside and paid the driver the fare.

"Will you come to the race?" he found himself asking.

Lily leaned out of the cab and for the first time, she smiled. "I wouldn't miss it for the world."

Royal just stood there, captivated by that smile, wondering how he was ever going to give her up.

Then he remembered the vow he had made to a father who lay dying, and knew he would have to find a way.

Preston Loomis shifted in his chair in front of the fire. A dying March would soon blossom into April. Spring couldn't get here soon enough for Preston. He hated the damnable cold, hated the fog and the rain.

Maybe he would take some of his recent earnings and

slip off to Italy or Spain, someplace warm. He smiled at the notion, knowing he would never actually go. He was a Londoner, no matter the rotten weather.

He looked up at the sound of a man's gruff voice, saw Bart McGrew standing in the doorway.

"Come in and get warm," he offered. "It's bloody cold out there."

Bart lumbered toward him, set himself in front of the hearth and turned his back to the fire to warm himself. "'Twas warmer today than yesterday. Maybe winter's finally on the way out."

"I hope so." Preston shifted on the brocade sofa, trying to find a comfortable position, which seemed harder to do every year. "So what have you learned about the old woman, Mrs. Crowley?"

"I asked round like you said. Found a few what knows her. She's from York, they say, stayin' with Lady Tavistock, the countess, ya know? I guess they're friends."

"I know who Tavistock is." And it was rather ironic that the late Duke of Bransford's aging aunt was going to provide a second tasty morsel to add to Preston's already overflowing coffers—in the form of her friend, Mrs. Crowley.

"So you ran across nothing untoward about her, no hint of anything amiss?"

Bart shrugged his beefy shoulders. "She's a dotty ol' bat, half-addled in the brain. Lots of money, they say, and not much kin to help her spend it."

"No children?"

"None I heard of. Old man Crowley left her a bloody fortune and she's still got most of it. I guess he owned mills and such, and some kinda factory."

Coal and cotton and who knew what else, according to Mrs. Crowley.

"Nice work, Bart."

The big man nodded, pleased at the compliment. He turned and headed for the door.

"Oh, there is one more thing," Preston said, stopping him before he reached it. "There is a boat race coming up. It's some kind of sculling match between four men. I want to know who is racing and when."

Bart grinned. "I already know when it is. Race is set for Sunday next, if the weather ain't too poor. Starts at Battersea, goes round the bend toward Putney. After church. One o'clock off the mark. Be lots of folks there, bettin' and such."

Preston rarely questioned Bart's information. The man had developed a network of servants round the city, all with an ear for gossip, and Bart paid them handsomely for information.

"You did well, my friend. Let me know the names of the men who will be racing as soon as you know."

Bart just nodded. As he ambled out of the drawing room, Preston picked up the book he had started to read. His mother had taught him the basics of reading and ciphering, all she had ever learned. She had made him promise to learn more, said it would pay off in the future.

His mother, as usual, was right. The tutor he had hired with the first money he made had not only schooled him, but educated him in the ways of a gentleman. Preston mingled with the upper crust as if he were born there and no one questioned whether he belonged or not.

And he had a knack for persuasion. They called a

man a confidence artist because he could win a person's confidence long enough to steal his money.

Preston chuckled. Once he won old lady Crowley's trust, she wouldn't know what hit her.

Twenty-Three

❧∽❧∽❧

They got lucky. Sunday was the prettiest day they'd had so far this year, perfect for a boat race. Royal stood in a circle with Sherry, Jonathan Savage and Quentin Garrett, the other Oarsmen who had come to race. The winter had been long and cold and all of them were looking forward to being on the water again, to limbering up muscles that hadn't been worked since the fall.

Four single-seat sculls waited on the muddy bank of the river flowing through Battersea Park on the outskirts of London. A group of friends and acquaintances stood at the edge of the water, mingling with people who had simply heard about the competition and were eager for an excuse to get out in the sunshine.

Royal spotted Lily standing next to Jocelyn. She wasn't there as Tsaya. She was simply Lily, looking feminine and pretty, and so sweet something twisted inside him. She and Lady Annabelle stood in a circle talking to Lady Nightingale, Lady Sabrina, Aunt Agatha and the old woman, Mrs. Crowley.

Royal smiled fondly at his aunt. After she had heard the story, Aunt Agatha had, amazingly, been eager to join in their plan. She had been suspicious of Preston Loomis from the start, she had said, had tried to warn William, her nephew, the duke, but by then he had been sucked under Loomis's spell. She hadn't known the confidence man had been responsible for depleting much of the Bransford fortune. She was furious and eager for justice once she found out.

Aunt Agatha laughed at something Molly Daniels said, an odd pair if ever there was one. But the women seemed to be getting along very nicely and the sparkle in Aunt Agatha's eyes said she was enjoying the entire adventure.

"It's time we got the race under way." This from Quent Garrett, who had stripped off his coat and now stood near the boats, barefoot, in breeches and a full-sleeved shirt. Savage and Sherry did the same, and Royal joined them, stripping off his socks, boots and jacket, and handing them to Sherry's valet, who collected all of the garments and carried them into the tent that had been set up as a place to change at the end of the race.

St. Michaels wasn't racing today. Along with several volunteers, he would be officiating at the finish line. Nightingale would remain at the starting point, keeping an eye on Loomis, assuming he appeared. There was no way to know for certain, but Lily was convinced he would be there.

Royal looked over at the slender woman gowned in peach silk. Wisps of silver-blond hair had escaped from beneath her wide-brimmed straw bonnet and floated seductively around her heart-shaped face. She was smiling at something Lady Annabelle said, her cheeks flushed an enchanting shade of rose. A pang of longing went through him and a jolt of desire so strong his whole body tightened.

Inwardly he cursed.

"Come, lads." Sherry slapped him on the back as he started toward the river. "Time to race."

Like the others, Royal was eager for the match. He wanted to win today, wanted to win for Lily, but instead he would lose to Savage. It galled him, though he might have lost anyway. The men were evenly matched. If the outcome weren't set, any of them might be the winner.

As it stood, Savage would win and the rest of them would race hard for second place. They would give it their all and do their best to win. That was the fun of the sport.

Sherry grinned. "I shall see you all at the finish," he challenged as he reached his boat.

"All you will see is my stern," Quent countered, the red in his dark hair glinting in the sun.

"You will both see mine," Royal promised, grinning as they made their way toward the water.

As they checked their equipment a final time, making certain the smooth spruce oars were properly placed and the brass oarlocks would hold securely, Royal couldn't resist a glance over his shoulder. Jocelyn waved, but it was Lily who drew his attention, Lily and the smile he knew was meant for him alone.

Wishing it didn't please him so much, Royal shoved his long, sleek scull into the water, jumped in, settled himself in the sliding seat and took hold of the oars.

Lily watched Royal and the Oarsmen as they expertly lined themselves up for an even start in the water. The crowd muttered then fell silent, waiting for Lord Nightingale to pull the trigger on the starting gun. Preston Loomis, the gathering's latest addition, stood next to the earl, a relief to all of them. Nightingale had worked hard to strike up a friendship with the confidence man and it seemed he had succeeded.

Lily stood close enough to overhear some of the men's conversation. They were talking about the race, then a wager was made. Nightingale bet on the duke, Loomis bet on Savage.

Lily hid a smile. Savage would win, of course. And when he mentioned the business deal Tsaya had told Loomis about, Loomis would make the investment, which, like the wager, would also pay off. If all went well, Tsaya could expect a message from Loomis requesting a meeting in the very near future.

She watched the four boats in the water, her gaze honing in on Royal as if he were a magnet and she a splinter of steel. The men were racing as a means to an end, but also for the fun of it. All of them were grinning as they sat in their long, skinny little boats. It seemed a miracle they could keep their balance and not topple into the water.

"Gentlemen, are you ready?" Nightingale stood in his place atop a boulder at the edge of the river.

"Ready!" came the four men's reply in unison.

The earl fired the starting gun, the sound echoing down the channel. The crowd sent up a cheer and the boats were off. Oars stroked through the water; paddles flashed as the men put their backs into the rhythm. Each rower fought for the lead, digging deeply and with perfect precision.

Lily's heart leaped with excitement. Oars dipped and

sliced, carrying the boats along the slightly more-than-two-mile course toward the small town of Putney, the sleek sculls moving with lightning speed as they skimmed over the glittering surface of the water.

Like the others, Royal bent to the task, his long legs working the slide that moved the rolling seat, biceps bulging, straining against the seams of his fine lawn shirt. The fabric, wet with perspiration and nearly transparent, stuck to the bands of muscle across his broad back and clung to his narrow waist.

Her pulse quickened. She remembered the feel of those muscles tightening beneath her fingers as he moved above her, thrust deeply inside her. A sweep of heat settled low in her belly. A flush crept over her breasts and moved up her throat. Lily took a steadying breath and forced the memory away.

Conversation swirled around her. "The duke is magnificent," said the Marchioness of Eastgate. "All those lovely muscles and that beautiful golden hair."

"That black-haired devil is also quite something," said Lady Severn. She was a striking brunette married to a man forty years her senior, and there was a lot of gossip about the countess and younger men. "Yes, isn't he? Savage, I believe is his name."

"I know all about him." The marchioness arched a dark red eyebrow. "The man's behavior borders on scandalous. I wouldn't want my Serafina anywhere near him."

"Well, I should say not," a third woman said.

Lily couldn't help wondering what sort of things Jonathan Savage had done to earn his black reputation. Being the son of an earl was all that allowed him to continue in society.

"Lord March is quite a catch," Lady Severn continued, the cluster of heavy dark curls on her shoulder moving as she turned to watch him. "The viscount is handsome and extremely wealthy. I hear he has entered the marriage mart."

Always on the hunt for a husband for Serafina, Lady Eastgate pursed her lips. "I wonder if he likes redheads."

All of them laughed and the cluster of women moved off toward the river as the boats traveled upstream.

Jocelyn reached over and clutched Lily's arm. "This is so exciting. Do you think the duke will win?"

Lily managed a smile. "I am sure he will." Like everyone else, her gaze remained riveted on the sleek boats slicing through the water, the precision-like dip and sway of the oars. "Lord March says the entire race takes only about twenty minutes. Then they turn round and row with the current back down to the park."

They were racing as part of the plan, but nothing said spectators and racers alike couldn't enjoy themselves. Earlier, tables had been set up and covered with linen cloths. A group of servants Lord Nightingale had provided busied themselves setting out an amazing array of food.

Lemonade, kegs of ale and jugs of wine sat next to trays overflowing with cold lamb and roasted beef, small meat pies, fresh-baked breads, Stilton and Cheshire cheeses. A sinful selection of candied fruits and custards, black-currant pudding and lemon tarts all vied for space on the table.

And the day was altogether glorious. Lily flicked a glance at Jo, was intrigued to see her scanning the crowd as if she searched for someone.

"Who are you looking for?" Lily asked.

Jocelyn glanced away. "Why, no one in particular. I just wanted to see who was here."

But her pink cheeks and evasive manner said it wasn't the truth. Jo had been acting strangely ever since the Wyhurst soiree. That night, Lily had believed it was because of her cousin's involvement with Royal. But he had denied an affair.

She looked at Jocelyn, whose violet eyes again skimmed the crowd. "Is it Barclay?"

Jo's gaze whipped toward her. "No, of course not!"

"Are you still seeing him?"

Jocelyn shook her head. "Not lately. I am not entirely certain I wish to continue the affair."

"Why not? I thought you said he was an amazing lover."

She shrugged as if the matter held not the least importance. "The man is too cocksure of himself by half. I am not certain I wish to involve myself further." But clearly, she was looking for him there in the park.

It made no sense and yet, where her cousin was concerned, things ofttimes did not.

Lily looked back at the river. The men were just disappearing round the bend out of sight. Their return would be more leisurely, perhaps half an hour from now. While they waited, Lily and Jo wandered among the crowd, all of whom were rooting for their favorite and eager to learn who had won. Afterward, they would enjoy the sumptuous luncheon provided by the racers.

Lily tried to hide her anticipation at seeing Royal, perhaps even talking to him.

But it was not easy.

* * *

Savage had won, of course. The men arrived to a hail of cheers. Nightingale made the formal announcement and Savage received hearty congratulations from friends and acquaintances, which he accepted with a mischievous twinkle in his nearly black eyes. A few minutes later, the men disappeared inside the tent to change out of their sweat-damp garments into fresh clothing.

Lily wandered about for a while, paused to speak to Lady Annabelle and Lady Sabrina. From the corner of her eye, she noticed Preston Loomis in conversation with doddering old Mrs. Crowley and almost smiled.

Loomis was taking the bait, a trifle at a time, just as they planned. As the minutes lengthened, she looked past him in search of Royal and spotted him standing next to Jocelyn and her mother.

Lily's heart sank. She should have known the duke's attention would be directed toward his future wife. Hadn't she been the one to suggest that very thing? She'd been a fool to imagine he might seek her out and, even if he did, what good would it do?

He wasn't hers and never would be. She had to stop dreaming about him, mooning over him like a lovesick fool. Adjusting her straw bonnet against the April sun, she wandered off toward a line of trees away from the river. She didn't notice she wasn't alone until a man stepped out from behind a tree and started walking toward her.

She had seen him earlier, conversing with Lady Annabelle and Lady Nightingale, but she didn't know his name.

He smiled as he approached. "You're Miss Moran,

are you not?" He was young, just a few years older than she, sandy-haired and attractive.

"I'm Lily Moran, yes. Have we met?"

"I am sorry to say I haven't had the pleasure. I know it is not the proper thing, but I saw you earlier and I simply couldn't leave without introducing myself. Phillip Landen, Viscount Hartwell, at your service. I hope you will forgive my ill manners and grant me a few moments of conversation."

He seemed so genuine. And who was she to quibble about a breach in manners, she who had once picked pockets for a living.

"It is a pleasure to meet you, my lord."

"And you, Miss Moran."

They talked for a while, about the weather, about the boat race, the sort of conversation a man would have with a woman he had only just met.

They traveled a shady path through the trees, taking a circuitous route back toward the festivities. Before they got there, the viscount paused and turned toward her. "I realize I am being quite forward, but I am the sort of man who knows what he wants, and I want very much to see you again. I understand you live with your cousins, Mr. and Mrs. Caulfield. Is there a chance I might call on you at your residence?"

"You are right, my lord—you are quite forward. And also quite well informed."

"I have never been particularly shy."

A faint smile blossomed. "I can see that."

"Would Monday be convenient?"

The eagerness in his voice had her looking up at him.

It was rare a man approached her. "I—I am not sure. As you say, we have only just met."

And she had enough problems without adding more. As attractive as the viscount was, she simply wasn't interested.

She started to politely decline, when a familiar deep voice rumbled toward her. "As a friend of Miss Moran's family, I am afraid I shall have to decline for her, since the two of you have not been properly introduced. Perhaps if you spoke to Mr. Caulfield, he would be willing to arrange an introduction at some later date."

Lily stared at Royal in amazement. He was about to become engaged to another woman. He had not the least say in her affairs and never would! How dare he have the cheek to interfere!

She turned an overbright smile on the viscount. "I own a millinery shop in Harken Lane, just off Bond. If that does not offend your noble sensibilities, my shop opens at nine in the morning. Perhaps you will drop by sometime."

The young viscount beamed. "I shall make a point of it." He made an extravagant bow. "A pleasure meeting you, Miss Moran."

"You, as well, my lord." Lily managed to keep her smile firmly in place as the viscount ambled away. She was still smiling when she felt Royal's fingers wrap around her arm, turning her to face him.

"What the devil are you doing?"

"I am doing exactly as I please. I was enjoying a pleasant conversation with a handsome man. What is wrong with that?"

"You don't even know him."

She lifted her chin. "I do now."

"You are encouraging him? Clearly he wishes to pay you court. You said you had a life of your own. You said you weren't interested in marriage."

"I am not utterly opposed to it, either. But should I wish to wed, it would be to a man of my choosing, not yours!"

Royal's golden eyes glittered, his temper barely in check. "And what do you think he will say when he finds out you were once a cutpurse living on the streets?"

The words hit her like a blow. He knew her innermost secrets. She had never dreamed he would use them against her.

He looked as stricken as she. "I'm sorry, Lily. I didn't mean that. Please forgive me, I just—"

"You are right, of course. The man is a viscount, after all. I am sure he would be appalled at the very notion of a woman with my sordid past."

"Lily, please—"

"On the other hand, perhaps I shall tell him and see what he has to say." Whirling away, she lifted her skirts out of the way and started marching back toward the group she had come with.

Royal caught up with her in two long strides. "I didn't mean it, dammit. I don't care about your past and if a man cares for you, neither will he. I just…I didn't want you to see him."

Lily ignored him, something she wouldn't have done even a few weeks ago. But she was a woman now, no longer a girl—Royal had seen to that. She owned her own business and had begun to earn her own living. She was starting to make her way in the world—and she was learning to stand up for herself.

Royal hurried to keep up with her. "Lily, wait!"

Sheridan Knowles walked up just then, interrupting whatever Royal wanted to say.

"Your fiancée is looking for you," Sherry said to Royal with a pointed glance Lily's way. "She is angling for an invitation to the opera. I think she wants to be seen in the ducal box. She is hoping you will escort her and her mother."

Frustration tightened Royal's features. Clearly he wanted to stay and yet he had no choice but to leave. "We aren't finished, Lily."

"Oh, but we are," she said sweetly.

A muscle bunched in his cheek. Turning away, Royal started walking toward the woman he would marry. Lily watched Jocelyn take his arm and her bravado slowly faded. Seeing Royal with Jo made her heart hurt. All she wanted to do was go home.

But she had come to Battersea with the Caulfields. She would have to return with them. Lily steeled herself to reenter the group and had nearly reached them when Quentin Garrett, Lord March, walked up beside her.

"Perhaps…Miss Moran, you would care to join me in a glass of lemonade," he said gently, offering her his arm. "It's a bit warm out today."

"Thank you, that would be lovely." Grateful for the reprieve, she accepted his arm. She wasn't sure how much Royal's friends had guessed about the two of them, but the men were a protective lot, and whatever they thought, they had been good to her.

Taking comfort in Lord March's escort, she let him guide her toward the punch bowl.

Twenty-Four

Monday was a busy day at the millinery shop. Lily took several orders and also spent time working on the hats she had sold and currently needed to complete.

"I'll be leavin' now, miss." Flora, her helper, stood in the doorway of the backroom, where Lily sat working. It was already two o'clock. "I'll be back in the mornin', miss."

"Thank you, Flora." She watched the red-haired girl leave, grateful for the help, but she was always glad when the shop was hers alone.

It was late afternoon the next time the bell above the door rang. As Lily emerged from the back, she was surprised to see Phillip Landen, Viscount Hartwell, walk into the shop.

Wishing she hadn't been quite so impulsive at the picnic, Lily pasted on a smile and started toward him.

"Good afternoon, my lord."

He swept his beaver hat from his head. "Good afternoon, Miss Moran." His hazel eyes appraised her, then shone with appreciation. "My, don't you make a lovely picture."

A blush began to rise in her cheeks. "Thank you, my lord."

He glanced round the shop. "It is unusual for a young woman to own her own business. I admire your initiative."

She couldn't help a smile. "It's been a dream of mine for some time."

He meandered round the narrow interior, studying a bonnet here, a lace cap there. "Quite nice work, I should say. Though I am certainly no expert on ladies' hats. Do you make them yourself?"

"Why, yes, I do."

His smile was slightly lopsided, she saw, which made it somehow charming. "I believe I should like to purchase one of your lovely creations for my mother. Which one do you think she might like?"

She walked over to where he stood peering at a row of bonnets that included a pale green silk and one of pearl-gray velvet with burgundy ribbons. Several straw bonnets sat on the shelf below.

"It is difficult to know a woman's tastes," she said.

"Mother is quite conservative in her clothing. And pretty much everything else." This was said with one of his charming, lopsided smiles.

Lily smiled back, but a ripple of unease began to surface. Royal's words popped into her head. *What do you think he will say when he finds out you were once a cutpurse living on the streets?*

She reached up for a cream silk cap trimmed with Belgian lace. "This one might please her. It is a simple design, which makes it versatile and not offensive, and size shouldn't be a problem."

He took the hat from her hand, held it up to examine it. "I believe you have come up with the perfect choice." He smiled down at her. "Thank you, Miss Moran."

Lily escorted him to the counter where he paid for the merchandise and she put it into a pretty paper hatbox. The viscount continued to watch her, and as she sensed his growing interest, the more difficult it was to look at him.

"Is something wrong?" he finally asked. "You seem troubled of a sudden."

"I...I am sorry. It is just...I do not wish to encourage your interest, my lord, when it cannot be returned."

He frowned. "And why is that?"

"It seems more than clear. Because you are a viscount and I am merely a shopkeeper."

He reached over and caught her hand. "You are far more than that. You are lovely and intelligent, and yet I can sense your gentleness. You are someone I would value knowing. The rest is unimportant."

Perhaps to him it would be, but certainly not to his mother or the rest of his family.

"I appreciate your kindness, my lord, but I do not think it is a good idea for you to return."

He studied her for several long moments, searching for what lay beneath the surface of her words. "For now, I shall bow to your wishes, Miss Moran. But I am not a man to give up easily." He plucked the box off the counter. "I am certain my mother will be pleased with the hat."

Setting his own hat on his head and tapping it into place, he crossed to the door and pulled it open, and disappeared out of the shop.

Lily breathed a sigh of relief. Even should his words prove true and her past not be a hurdle, she wasn't interested in the young viscount. Her heart still yearned for Royal and until that pain went away, she simply couldn't entertain thoughts of another man.

Lily returned to work in the back of the shop, greeted several other customers and sold one of them a lovely straw bonnet. She was surprised to realize it was almost closing time.

How quickly the time seemed to pass! She supposed it was the result of doing something one so enjoyed.

She busied herself preparing to close out her daily accounts when the bell rang once more. As Royal walked into the shop, her heart did an unwanted skip. She told herself she was still angry at him for the cruel things he had said, but when she saw the misery in his face, her heart simply melted.

Royal stopped in front of her. He cleared his throat, looking nervous, as he rarely did. "I came here to apologize. I'm sorry, Lily. I didn't mean those things I said. I never cared about your past, and any man who holds feelings for you won't care either. I was jealous. I know that is no excuse, but it's true."

Her eyes welled.

He caught her hand and brought it to his lips. "I would cut out my heart before I would purposely do anything to hurt you."

Her throat tightened. She loved him so much. "Royal…" And then she was in his arms, clinging to him as he clung to her. He leaned toward her and she felt his cheek against hers.

"I'm sorry," he said softly. "Please say you'll forgive me."

"It's all right, Royal."

"Any man would be lucky to have you. Any man."

She tried to smile. "It doesn't matter. It only matters that you cared enough to come."

He drew away to look at her. "I care, Lily. I care far too much." She couldn't resist the soft brush of his lips, the gentle way they settled over hers. It was a tender kiss that held a trace of longing and ended far too soon.

"I ache for you, Lily. You're all I can think of. I don't know how I am going to make a life without you."

She swallowed past the lump in her throat, her heart beating painfully. "Sometimes we have to do things we don't want to. That is just the way life is." She had learned that lesson when she was twelve years old and her parents had died, when she'd had to steal in order to eat.

Royal lifted his hand to her cheek. "My solicitor came by this morning. He says the tenants have signed a petition demanding improvements be made to their homes." He looked into her eyes as if he willed her to understand. "I can't let them down, Lily. I'll have to borrow the money to see it done and eventually I'll have to pay it back."

She forced out the words. "As soon as you are…married, you'll have all the money you need."

He swallowed. "I know. I just…I wanted you to understand."

Her throat ached. "I do understand, Royal."

And it was breaking her heart.

She went back into his arms and Royal just held her. She was still clinging to him, pressing her cheek into his shoulder when the bell rang. Lily jerked out of his embrace and Royal stepped away, but it was too late.

Jocelyn and Matilda Caulfield stood frozen in the doorway, both of them wide-eyed with shock.

"Well, I daresay, this is certainly unexpected." Matilda's eyebrows climbed to her forehead.

"Please, you must let me explain—" Royal started.

"Do not further insult me by lying." Matilda's condemning stare moved to Lily. "I should have known. Once a mongrel, always a mongrel."

Royal stiffened. "None of this is Lily's fault. I took advantage. I am entirely to blame. Lily is innocent in any of this."

It wasn't true. She was at fault in everything that had happened. Guilt and shame washed over her. "I am sorry, Jo. I never meant to break your trust."

Jocelyn ignored her. Instead, her furious gaze fixed on Royal. "I will not take her leavings. I will not marry a man who does not want me."

"He's a man, dear heart," Matilda said flatly. "Men have needs. Your cousin was simply available to fulfill them." She returned her hard gaze to Royal. "This marriage is going forward exactly as planned. Whatever has been going on between the two of you is over as of this minute. Do you understand?"

Royal's jaw hardened. Lily read his anger and realized he was about to call off the wedding.

"The duke was merely amusing himself," she said, stopping him before he could speak, knowing he would regret the words the instant they were spoken. "I never meant for anything like this to happen and neither did His Grace." She turned to Jo. "You are the woman he wants, Jocelyn. You always have been."

Jo sniffed, flicked a glance at the duke, but seemed somewhat mollified. He was simply a man, her expression said, and easily led astray. She had never considered Lily any sort of competition and she did not now.

"From this day forward I shall expect your full attention," Jo said. "We shall start with the opera tonight. I should like very much to sit in the Bransford box."

Royal made no comment, but a muscle ticked in his cheek.

"And you, young woman," Matilda said to Lily. "It is past time you moved out of our house. I believe you mentioned there was an apartment above the shop."

Lily just nodded, misery washing over her in waves. "I will be gone by tomorrow."

"Good riddance," said Jo, though Lily thought she heard a note of regret in her cousin's voice. Jo depended on Lily, who was her closest confidante. Lily felt the loss, too. Once they had been friends, a relationship Lily had managed to destroy.

"Then we are all in agreement," Matilda said firmly. "What happened here shall go no further." She fixed her cold stare on Royal. "I shan't mention this deplorable display to Mr. Caulfield, and your engagement to my daughter shall stand. The announcement will be made at the ball Saturday night, as we had planned."

Royal straightened to his full height. He didn't look at Lily but instead made a bow to Jo. "My apologies, Jocelyn. I never meant to embarrass you and I shall not do so again."

"Whatever you do after we are wed, I shall expect you to do it with discretion."

Royal curtly nodded.

Nothing more was said as the group, including the duke, turned and walked out of the shop. Lily watched Royal escort the women to their carriage then climb into his own.

As the vehicles rolled away, Lily's eyes welled with tears and the ache returned to her throat.

Inside her chest, her heart completely shattered.

"What do you mean he is indisposed?" Sherry spoke to Royal's butler. He and Dillon St. Michaels stood on the front porch steps of the Duke of Bransford's town house. "What is the matter with him?"

"His Grace is…well, he is not himself today. It would be better if you came back on the morrow."

Sherry caught the little man's shoulders, physically moved him aside and stepped into the house. Something was wrong—he could feel it. He strode down the hall toward the study, St. Michaels at his heels, but no one was there.

"Upstairs," Dillon said and Sherry nodded.

"Wait, I beg you." The butler threw his slight body between them as if he meant to sacrifice himself. "You mustn't go up there."

Which only made Sherry more determined. "Come on." The men brushed past, taking the stairs two at a time then heading down the hall to the master's suite. St. Michaels slammed a meaty fist against the door several times, but got no answer.

Sherry turned the knob, found the door unlocked and

walked into the room. Royal was sprawled on the sofa in front of the fire in the corner, an empty bottle of brandy lying on the table, a half-filled glass in one hand.

"Go away."

"Good God—you're bloody foxed," Sherry said. "What in blazes has happened?"

Royal straightened a little, sloshing brandy over the rim of his glass. "I am getting married, that is what has happened—to the wrong woman."

"That is old news, my friend," said St. Michaels. "And certainly not what has driven you to drink yourself into a drunken stupor."

Royal grunted. "I have given it my best effort, I admit. Unfortunately, I am not nearly—" he hiccupped "—drunk enough."

Both men rolled their eyes.

"Matilda Caulfield found us together in Lily's hat shop." He sloshed down a gulp of brandy. "Jocelyn was with her."

"Jocelyn didn't call off the wedding?" Sherry asked, more than a little surprised.

Royal shook his head. "Her mother wouldn't let her." He gulped down more brandy. "I should have ended it no matter the cost. Lily is ruined because of me. It is my duty to make things right."

"You can't afford to marry a woman without two farthings in her purse," said St. Michaels, being practical for once. "You're a duke, man. You have duties, responsibilities."

Royal sat forward on the small settee, hung his head and raked his hands through his hair. "I know."

"What did Lily say when this happened?" Sherry asked.

"She told them it was her fault. She said she meant nothing to me, that she was only an amusement. She took the blame entirely and I let her."

"You had no choice," Dillon said.

"There is always a choice," muttered Royal.

"What's done is done," said Sherry. "At least you needn't worry about Lily's reputation. The Caulfields can't afford for any of this to get out."

"I suppose that is something," Royal reluctantly agreed.

"You'll get through this." St. Michaels rested a wide hand on Royal's shoulder. "Life is full of these little ups and downs and somehow we manage to survive them."

Sherry leaned down and plucked up a note carelessly tossed onto the table in front of the sofa. "What is this?"

"Matilda wants to move up the wedding." Royal sighed. "I think she's afraid something else will go wrong."

"Well, that is good news," said St. Michaels. "You'll have your wife's money sooner rather than later and let's face it, you need it."

"Money," Royal said with disgust. "That's what it always comes down to. Sometimes I envy the beggars on the street."

Sherry ignored him. Royal was drunk and in love and the combination was lethal.

He plucked the glass out of his best friend's hand. Royal didn't seem to notice. "Get some sleep. You'll feel better in the morning."

When Royal made no reply, just slid down on the sofa, closed his eyes and began to snore softly, Sherry tipped his head toward the door. "Time to go."

Dillon nodded, glanced down at his rumpled friend. "There is a man I do not envy."

Sherry grunted. "Remind me never to fall in love."

Lily stood behind the counter in the Lily Pad. So far today business had been slow and she was grateful. Flora had left at two, working with only a few sideways glances at her employer's puffy, swollen eyes and wan complexion. At least she hadn't pursued the matter and asked embarrassing questions.

Lily yawned behind her hand. She hadn't slept all night. Whenever she closed her eyes, she saw Matilda Caulfield's cold, hard, accusing eyes. *Once a mongrel, always a mongrel.*

The lump returned to Lily's throat. She had never been truly accepted by the Caulfields, particularly not Matilda. Though she was an earl's great-granddaughter, the same as Jo, Lily's branch of the family had been disowned years ago.

She tried not to think of Jocelyn and the blow she had dealt her. So what if Jo had a lover? What Jocelyn did was her own business. Lily lived by a different code of morals, and being intimate with the man her cousin was to marry wasn't acceptable in any way.

Exhausted and depressed, barely enough energy to make it through the day, she wandered over to a chair behind the counter and sank down wearily. How in heaven's name had her life spiraled so far out of control?

Morose as she pondered her situation and bone deep in guilt, she started at the sound of a knock at the backdoor. Lily pushed to her feet and forced herself to move on legs that felt leaden. Turning the key in the lock, she opened the door and looked down to see a raga-muffin boy standing in the alley at the back of the shop.

"Ye said I could come. Did ye mean it?"

It was the urchin, Tommy Cox. Along with his mangy brown-and-white dog. For the first time that day, something brightened inside her. "I meant it. Come in, Tommy."

Looking at the skinny youth reminded her of the years she had lived a life much like his. She remembered how terrified she had been after her parents died and she had gone to live with her uncle. She remembered how Uncle Jack had taught her to be strong and how, little by little, she had become confident and fearless, and how she had survived those days.

She stood back from the door, allowing Tommy and Mugs to come into the backroom of the shop. "Are you hungry?" He was thin to the point of gaunt. She thought that at the mention of food, his mouth started to water.

"I could use a bite o' something. Might ye have a scrap for Mugs, too?"

Emotion swelled in her chest. As hungry as he was, he was still concerned for his dog. "I'll find something for both of you. Stay right here."

Beneath the dirt, he was a handsome boy, she thought as she hurried up the stairs. If no one helped him, sooner or later he would become a hardened criminal or forced into a life of prostitution. It was fear of the latter that had driven Uncle Jack to find a place for her with her cousin.

Heaping a plate with hard-crusted bread, Gloucester cheese and gingerbread, she returned downstairs. Tommy and Mugs stood exactly where she had left them, close to the door in case they needed to run.

She cleared her sewing off the table and set the platter of food down in front of them. "Go ahead. Help yourself."

A grimy hand shot out and grabbed a hunk of cheese and a slice of bread. Part went to Tommy, the other to Mugs. In seconds, the food disappeared as if it were never there. Lily would have offered him more, but she was afraid his empty stomach would rebel and he would get sick.

Instead, she poured him a glass of lemonade from the pitcher she kept in the back of the shop. Tommy swigged it down in a couple of hearty swallows.

"Good?" she asked.

The boy just nodded, his cheeks still bulging with the last of the gingerbread. She noticed less of that had gone to Mugs.

"You can stay the night, if you like. I could make us some stew for supper and we could have chocolate and cakes in the morning."

Tommy's eyes rounded. "Ye'd make me supper?"

She nodded. Her heart was beating oddly, filled with pity and something more. "And chocolate in the morning, and it's a lot warmer in here than outside."

Tommy looked to Mugs for advice. "Whatcha think, boy?"

The dog wagged its tail, making a thumping sound on the wooden floor, which must have been a yes, for Tommy grinned. "All right, we'll stay."

Something softened inside her. Perhaps Tommy had been sent to her in answer to her prayers. Here was a child who needed her. And Lily needed him.

"It's closing time. I'll just lock up, then make a quick trip to the grocer, see what I can find us to eat."

Tommy nodded. He smelled awful and so did his mangy dog. But a bath could wait. She wanted the boy to know he was welcome just the way he was. Eventually, if she was lucky, maybe he would come to trust her.

For the first time since Matilda and Jocelyn Caulfield had walked into the shop and found her in Royal's arms, Lily felt a kernel of gladness begin to grow inside her.

Jonathan Savage rang the bell on the elegant three-story brick house that belonged to Preston Loomis. Loomis's butler answered, a tall, dignified man with salt-and-pepper hair.

"May I help you?" the butler asked.

"My name is Jonathan Savage. I'm here to see Mr. Loomis."

"Mr. Loomis is expecting you. If you will please follow me."

He had sent word ahead, requesting a meeting to discuss the investment Loomis had made. The promise of money had a way of getting a rapid response.

Loomis rose as Jonathan walked into the drawing room, which was expensively furnished and done with exquisite taste. Amazing what one could do with a ducal fortune.

"I hadn't expected to hear from you so soon." Loomis strode toward him, an imposing figure with his silver hair and perfectly trimmed mustache.

"We got lucky. The borrowers received the money they were expecting far sooner than they had hoped. Which means they were able to repay the loan in very short order."

"I see. Would you care for a brandy?"

"I believe I would."

Loomis walked over to the sideboard and poured a portion of amber liquid into two crystal snifters. Jonathan accepted the glass and took a sip. The brandy was old and expensive, some of the finest he had ever tasted.

"Exquisite." He held the glass up to the light to assess the rich color. "I salute your taste in brandy, Mr. Loomis."

"I'm glad you like it." Loomis smiled, lifting the ends of his mustache. "All it takes is money."

Jonathan chuckled. Being the third son instead of his father's heir, most of the wealth he had accumulated had been earned. His shipyard, a failing endeavor he had inherited from his grandfather, had been reorganized into his most profitable concern. Other businesses he had purchased and restructured also made a handsome profit.

Jonathan took a swallow of his brandy, reached into his coat pocket and pulled out a bank draft for the amount Loomis had invested plus a thirty percent return. For Royal's sake, he hoped to hell they got the late duke's money back and all of this wasn't for naught.

Loomis eyed the bank draft with relish. "You will let me know if you run across another reliable short-term borrower."

"I will, indeed, though mostly I fund those loans myself." That was a total lie. He didn't make exorbitant loans, and though his reputation was as black as sin, he didn't steal other people's money.

Jonathan drained his glass and set it down on the polished mahogany table. "It's been nice doing business with you, Mr. Loomis."

"You, as well, Mr. Savage."

Jonathan left the house, climbed aboard his carriage

and instructed his coachman to make a stop at the Duke of Bransford's town house. From there he was headed to Jermyn Street for a visit with his current mistress.

He had played his role. Everything was set for the final act. He didn't care a whit for justice. He just wanted his good friend to get his money back.

Twenty-Five

Lily didn't go to the Red Rooster Inn on Wednesday.
It was simply too soon to see Royal after the terrible
scene in the shop. Instead, Molly Daniels arrived at her
door at closing time to fill her in on what had transpired
at the meeting.

Flora had already gone home. Tommy and Mugs had
left just after breakfast, too skittish to stay very long in
one place. But Tommy had promised to return for
supper and to spend the night. It was a beginning, Lily
hoped. Looking forward to their visit kept her from
thinking of Royal and helped ease the pain in her heart.

"I was just closing up," she said to Molly, glad for
the company. "It's chilly outside. Why don't you come
upstairs and we'll talk over a cup of tea."

Molly grinned. "A girl after me own heart." Her hair
was silver again, not the dismal gray, gleaming where
it showed beneath her bonnet, and when she smiled, it
was clear she had once been a very pretty woman.
Nothing at all like the crotchety old biddy she portrayed
with such skill.

They climbed the stairs to the tiny flat Lily occupied, and Molly settled herself on the settee in front of the small coal-burning hearth. Lily built up the fire, then went to put the teakettle on to boil. She filled a plate with cakes she had picked up at the bakery, thinking how much Tommy would like them. By the time she had finished, the kettle was singing. She returned with the tea and set the plate of cakes on the table in front of the settee.

"So tell me about the meeting." Seating herself in the chair across from her guest, she began to pour the tea.

"Well, the duke was there, of course." Molly accepted the cup and saucer Lily handed her and carefully stirred in a lump of sugar. "Such a handsome man, he is." She eyed Lily over the rim of her cup as she took a sip. "Though today he seemed a bit out of sorts. I think he was unhappy because you weren't there."

Molly Daniels wasn't a fool and clearly the older woman had sensed the attraction between them.

"The duke is to marry my cousin," Lily said carefully. "Whatever…friendship…we shared is over."

"I see."

A memory arose of the bitter scene downstairs and she felt a burning behind her eyes. Her throat swelled painfully and though she tried to hold back tears, several spilled over onto her cheeks.

Molly handed her a handkerchief she tugged out of her reticule. "It's all right, dear. Falling in love is nothing to be ashamed of. Sometimes it just happens, whether we like it or not."

Lily blotted the wetness from her cheeks. "I tried not to love him, truly I did. I have no idea how Royal feels about me, but—"

"Why, he loves you, dear heart. Anyone with two good eyes can see that."

Lily sniffed and blew her nose. She had no true notion of Royal's feelings, though she couldn't help hoping Molly was right. "It doesn't matter how he feels. He has to marry a woman of wealth. He made a vow to his father, and he desperately needs the money. His…his engagement to my cousin is being announced on Saturday night."

"Oh dear."

Lily swallowed past the tightness in her throat. "A couple of days ago, Royal came to see me. My cousin and her mother found us together downstairs. I can hardly bear to think of it." She managed to hold back a sob, but more tears leaked from beneath her lashes. Though she hadn't meant to, Lily found herself telling Molly Daniels about the awful confrontation in the shop.

"Matilda said I was a mongrel, and she was right." She pressed the handkerchief beneath her nose. "Even if I were rich, Royal couldn't marry me—not after the things I've done."

"Now don't you go talkin' foolish. You were born a lady. Why, Jack says your grandma was the daughter of an earl. Nothing can change that. You had some bad times, but that was in the past. You're a lady now, just like you were before."

Lily looked at Molly through a mist of tears. "Do you really believe that?"

"'Course I do. And so does your duke or he wouldn't have fallen in love with you."

Lily made no reply. She might never know the depth of Royal's feelings, but she was glad she had confided in Molly. She needed a friend and it looked as if she had found one.

Feeling a little better and wanting to change the subject, she focused on the reason Molly was there. "So what happened at the meeting?"

"Well, things are still going well. Better than well, in fact. Charlie thinks you'll be hearin' from Mr. Loomis very soon."

"Why is that?"

"Because the duke's friend, Mr. Savage, paid Loomis a visit—a highly profitable visit. Loomis made money—just like Tsaya predicted. By now he's bound to be convinced she is truly Medela's kin." She laughed. "Loomis is a greedy bastard. He'll be wantin' to make even more and you're about to give him what he wants."

Lily smiled. "You mean you are."

Molly chuckled. "That I am. Me and Mrs. Crowley, and it's going to be our pleasure."

Lily couldn't help thinking how much she liked this woman and how glad she was her uncle had found her. "So what's our next move?"

"Nothing till you hear from Loomis. Once you do, you'll need to set up a meeting. Once it's done, send word to Jack and me."

But not to Royal, as she had once promised. Any communication between them was over.

"When Loomis meets with Tsaya," Molly went on, "she's to tell him Mrs. Crowley owns a company that manufactures guns and such, and it's going to make him very rich. Tell him her stock will double in a very short time. Tell him it has something to do with the

Americans and the turbulence going on in their country. Tell him to buy as much as the old woman will sell him."

Lily sipped her tea, pondering the plan. "The problems in America…that part is true, is it not?"

Molly nodded. "It's in the newspapers all the time. The north half of the country is afraid there might be a war with the south half over them owning slaves. Could be they'll want to arm themselves just in case—or at least that's what Loomis will believe."

"I see. Loomis will be convinced my prediction will come true because part of it *is* true."

Molly grinned. "Your uncle said you were a smart girl."

It was the way a successful con worked. Tell them three truths and then they'd believe the lie.

Molly finished the last of her tea, set the cup down in its saucer and rose from her place on the settee. "Keep in touch, luv. And don't believe for a minute you aren't equal to any fine lady in London."

Lily rose, as well. Leaning over, she gave the older woman a hug. "Thank you, Molly. For everything."

"Don't you worry, luv. We'll stick the bloody bastard good and proper. Your duke will get at least some of his money back."

But it wouldn't be enough. And there was the promise Royal had made to his father. They walked together downstairs and out to the cab stand. Lily waited till Molly was able to hail a carriage, then returned upstairs.

As she entered her tiny apartment, she thought of what Molly had said. Even if she was good enough to marry a duke, it wasn't going to happen.

Lily's eyes burned. After Saturday night, Royal would belong completely to Jo.

* * *

Jocelyn shoved her key into the lock and entered the suite she had rented at the Parkland Hotel. She was nervous. She wasn't used to the feeling. But Christopher was due any moment and there were important matters she wanted to discuss.

She tossed off her hooded cloak and began to pace the floor, the skirts of her scarlet-trimmed green velvet gown swirling around her feet as she turned. Back and forth, back and forth. She glanced at the clock. Christopher wasn't late. She had gotten there early.

Her nerves kicked up even more. It was ridiculous. Of course he would be happy at the news. He would be eager, ecstatic. Even if his feelings for her were uncertain, he would want the money.

Unconsciously, she frowned. The notion didn't sit well, though with Royal it didn't matter. Their relationship, such as it was, was strictly a matter of business. With Christopher…well, with Christopher it was different. Though she had fought against it, somehow her feelings had gotten involved.

A key turned in the lock and the door swung open. Christopher Barclay walked into the suite, looking as handsome and unruffled as he usually did. His dark eyebrows arched up at the sight of her. Clearly, he was surprised to see her there awaiting his arrival since she was perpetually tardy.

"You're early. Whatever you wanted to talk about must be important. Or are you simply randy for another bout of lusty sex?"

Jocelyn blushed. Christopher never minced words and yet somehow she found his candor refreshing. He strode toward her, caught her shoulders and hauled her against him. His mouth came down and he kissed her, roughly at first, then more gently, a thorough taking that had Jocelyn swaying against him, eager to feel his skillful hands on her flesh, eager to have him inside her.

Christopher stepped away. "Perhaps we should talk first. Otherwise it might not happen. Why did you ask me to come, Jo? Your note said it was important."

Jocelyn paced away from him, her nervousness returning. Christopher wasn't like any other man she knew, and as certain as she was, there was always a chance—

She shook her head, turned and walked back to where he stood. "I've decided I am not going to marry the duke."

Surprised flared in his eyes, then he frowned. "Why not? I thought the arrangements had already been made."

"They have, but… The truth is, I do not care a whit for Royal Dewar and I am not going to marry him." She looked up at him, into his handsome, compelling face. "I thought that instead I would marry you."

Silence. Then a bark of laughter escaped through Christopher's hard mouth. "Have you lost your mind?"

Her stomach knotted. "I thought…thought you would be happy about it."

He stared at her for several long moments, then turned and walked over to the window. Jocelyn could hear carriage wheels churning on the cobbled streets below. A newsboy hawked his wares.

Christopher sighed into the thickening silence, turned and walked back to her. "I can't marry you, Jo. I'm not what you want and never will be. I'd just be one of your lapdogs and that isn't going to happen. If things were different… If I had money and a title, perhaps…"

His jaw hardened. "The fact is I don't. I can't give you a single thing Bransford can. You'd be miserable and so would I."

Her eyes welled. She couldn't believe he was turning her down. He had bedded her, made love to her half a dozen different ways. How dare he refuse to marry her!

Fury engulfed her. Anger and humiliation.

Her hand snaked out and connected with his cheek so hard he stumbled backward. "I hate you!" she shouted. "I hate you, Christopher Barclay!"

Whirling away, she raced for the door. Jerking it open, she rushed out of the room without retrieving her cloak. What did she care if someone saw her? She had money enough to silence any wagging tongues. She could buy anyone and anything she wanted.

Tears blurred her vision and she stumbled, caught herself before she fell.

She could buy anyone.

Anyone—except Christopher Barclay.

Lily looked up as the shop door burst open and Dottie Hobbs rushed in, an apron still tied around her thick girth.

"Can't stay but a minute. Just wanted to give ye this." She handed a note to Lily. "Loomis came to the house looking for Tsaya. He wants to meet with her tonight. He left this note. Tsaya's supposed to send word to the address on the note if she agrees."

Lily opened the note, which asked for a ten o'clock appointment and gave the address for her reply. It was nearly two in the afternoon. "Good grief, he didn't give us much time."

She glanced into the room at the rear of the shop.

Seated in a chair, tendrils of carrot-red hair spilling from her mobcap, Flora hummed as she sewed flowers onto the brim of a blue velvet bonnet.

"Flora, I need to run upstairs. I'll be back in just a few minutes."

Flora nodded and Lily hurried up to her flat to pen a note from Tsaya agreeing to the meeting. A second note went to Uncle Jack, telling him Loomis had made contact and that she had agreed to a ten o'clock appointment.

She sanded the notes, folded, and sealed them with wax, then headed back downstairs.

"Loomis's address is on the one you brought," she told Dottie, handing her the original message along with the ones she had just penned. "See that he gets my reply. The other note goes to Molly and Jack."

"I'll see to it meself, miss."

"Thank you, Dottie." The woman hurried away.

Flora finished at two and departed, leaving Lily to pace and worry and wish the time would pass more swiftly. Toward the end of the day, a matronly woman walked into the shop, the grocer's wife, Mrs. Smythe. She commissioned a dress cap of white Belgian lace, perfect to wear, she said, to her grandson's christening. As soon as Lily finished taking the order, she locked up the shop.

Tommy and Mugs arrived at the backdoor just after dark. Lily was always relieved to see them. She knew what it was like on the streets. She worried about the boy's safety and prayed he wouldn't get into trouble.

"I have to go out for a while after supper," she told Tommy. "But I won't be gone long."

"Where ye goin'?" he asked.

"I'm meeting a man to talk about the stars."

"I used to look at 'em with me mum. She used to make up stories about them."

Lily smiled. "If you watched the stars, you must have lived in the country."

He nodded. "Till Mum took sick. After she died, I come to London." He was looking past her, she realized, and turned to see what had captured his gaze. It was a small, leather-bound book of poetry, sitting where she had left it on the table.

"I never thought to ask…can you read?"

"Me mum taught me. She didn't have no formal schoolin', but she were real smart. She were a chambermaid in a big country house and the housekeeper taught her."

She walked over to the book of poems, brought it over and handed it to Tommy. "You might enjoy reading this while I'm out."

Tommy grinned. He had a nice wide smile and eating a proper amount of food was beginning to fill out his thin face. He took the book from her hand as if it were made of precious stones. "Thank ye, miss. I'll take real good care o' it."

Lily had fixed the boy a pallet in the backroom to sleep on. As soon as Tommy had eaten, he sat down on the pallet, Mugs curled up beside him, and began to read the book by the light of an oil lamp.

Dusk became nightfall. It was nine o'clock by the time Lily was dressed in her bright silk Gypsy garments and ready to leave the shop. Tommy and Mugs were asleep on the pallet as she whirled her cloak round her shoulders and tied the string beneath her chin. Drawing the hood up to cover her straight black hair, she headed for the cab stand.

It wasn't long before a plodding horse pulling a hansom appeared at the corner. As the vehicle rolled toward the small house in Piccadilly that belonged to Madam Tsaya, Lily thought of Preston Loomis and ignored the thread of worry that slipped down her spine.

Christopher Barclay sat alone at a corner table at White's, his gentlemen's club, an untouched glass of brandy in front of him. If his stomach hadn't been tied in knots, he might have gotten drunk. As it was, just thinking about it made him queasy.

For the past two days, he hadn't been able to eat, hadn't been able to sleep. All he'd done was think of the reckless little witch who had managed to enchant him.

God's blood, what had possessed him to get involved with the girl in the first place? He had known it would only lead to trouble. But a stiff cock had little conscience and he had wanted her as he couldn't remember wanting a woman.

He glanced up as a familiar masculine face came into focus: straight nose, black hair, brilliant blue eyes.

"Mind if I join you?" Rule Dewar stood next to him at the table, a glass of brandy in his hand. A Dewar was the last person Christopher wanted to see, but Rule and Christopher's younger brother, Lucas, were of an age and they were close friends.

"I thought you were in school."

"I finished the last of my classes. I'm out of there for good and damned glad of it." He pulled out a chair but didn't take a seat, just stood there waiting for an invitation Christopher wished he didn't have to give.

"I don't mind, but I warn you, I'm not in a very good mood."

Rule sprawled in the chair, drink in hand, his intense blue eyes searching Christopher's face. "Unless you lost a bundle at the gaming tables, I'd say the cause is a woman."

Christopher just grunted.

"Is she married?"

"Might as well be."

"Don't tell me you're in love."

The word made his stomach tighten. "Lust, maybe. A case of overinfatuation. Whatever it is, it's worse than an ague and I'll be glad when it's over."

"That bad, is it?"

Christopher took a drink of his heretofore-untouched drink. Rule Dewar was the last person he should be talking to. "Worse."

"If she isn't actually married, why don't you do something about it?"

"Nothing I can do. The lady is out of my league. I've no fortune to speak of. No title. If I married her, I'd never be her equal. She's worth a bloody fortune and she believes it gives her license to own the world. She'd try to own me and I'm not willing to let that happen. I'd end up no more than a bad decision she would always regret."

Rule took a sip of his drink. "The last thing a man needs is a woman who holds the purse strings."

"Doesn't seem to bother your brother." The minute the words were out, he wished he could call them back.

Rule seemed unfazed. "I guess you've heard the

rumors. Everyone in London seems to know Royal is to marry the Caulfield girl, though it won't be official until the announcement is made this Saturday night. That is one of the reasons I came to London."

Christopher said nothing, but his stomach churned.

"As for my brother, he really has no choice. He's the Duke of Bransford, after all. Got to have an heir and all that. Besides, he made a vow to our father. He intends to use his wife's money to rebuild the family fortune."

Christopher sipped his drink. "She'll make him dance for every penny. She's that kind of woman."

"Then she doesn't know the man she is going to marry. Royal will control the money as soon as the vows are spoken. As his wife, she'll have little say about what he does with it."

Christopher clamped down on a bitter laugh. *You don't know her like I do,* he thought. Jocelyn was spoiled and selfish and she would make the duke's life miserable. A man would be a fool to think he could tame a creature like that.

But, by damn, he wanted to be the man to try.

His fingers tightened around the glass. It wasn't going to happen. Jocelyn didn't love him. He wasn't sure she was capable of that kind of emotion, and it would take that and more for a marriage with such a difficult woman to work.

He downed the last of the liquid in his glass, set it on the table and rose from the chair.

"Nice talking to you, Rule. Give your brother my regards." *And my eternal sympathy for the life of hell he is about to embark upon with Jo.*

Twenty-Six

❧⟳❧

It was almost ten o'clock. When Lily arrived at the house, Dottie was busy in the kitchen. She had delivered Tsaya's reply to Preston Loomis and left the note for Jack with Molly at the flat the two of them now shared, a circumstance Lily wholeheartedly approved.

She glanced at the clock. Loomis would be arriving any minute. She walked over and pulled out the rolled-up astronomy chart showing the position of the stars. She knew why Loomis wanted to come after dark. He wanted to watch her, see how she worked.

She almost smiled. As a little girl, she had been fascinated by the stars. Her father had taught her the names of each constellation and how to locate them—assuming it was clear enough to see them, which it usually was at their cottage in the country.

Here in London, the sooty air, low-hanging clouds and fog kept the sky mostly obscured. Not tonight. The wind had come up this afternoon, blowing away the soot and cleansing the air. The sky was black as pitch, the stars sparkling like diamonds, which, she was sure, was the reason Loomis had chosen tonight for his visit.

She made a last quick check of her appearance, tugging the black wig into position and straightening her red silk blouse, then headed for the kitchen to make certain Dottie was ready to receive their visitor.

Pushing through the swinging door, she froze at the sight of Royal Dewar standing exactly where he had been the last time Loomis paid a call, dressed in the same simple, masculine garments as before.

"You…you shouldn't be here. How…how did you know Loomis was coming?"

"Molly sent me a note. She didn't like the idea of your being here with him alone."

"I'm not alone. Dottie is here."

He scoffed as if to say, *Two women are not much better at defending themselves than one.* "I'll wait back here out of sight, as I did before."

"But—"

A knock on the door ended the argument. Exasperated and resigned, Lily took a breath, turned and walked back into the parlor while Dottie went to answer the door. The housekeeper showed Loomis into the sitting room and Lily rose to greet him.

"Mr. Loomis… Good evening."

"It is good to see you, Tsaya."

"You, as well. Would you care for tea? Or perhaps something stronger?"

"Nothing tonight." Instead, Loomis's gaze lit on the charts spread open on the table. He walked in that direction. "You were preparing to use these tonight?"

"The sky is clear, as it rarely is in the city. I hoped to renew myself, perhaps be granted the gift of a vision."

He smoothed his silver mustache. "You were right about Savage. The investment I made with him paid off quite nicely."

She made a slight bow of her head.

"Are you ever wrong?"

"I do not speak if I am in doubt."

He flicked a glance toward the darkness outside the window. "Would you mind if I watched you work?"

She shrugged as if it didn't matter. "If that is your wish." Making her way out of the parlor, she paused to retrieve her cloak, then led him into the entry and down the hall to the back of the house. On the porch, she wrapped her hands round the railing and looked up into the darkness.

"How does it work?" he asked as he walked up beside her.

Lily kept her eyes on the sky. "First you must search for the Star of the North. It is the center of all things." She pointed. "There, do you see it?"

His gaze followed where she pointed. "Yes."

"To the left is the shape you English call the Plough. There are seven brilliant stars in the group."

"I think I see it."

"On the other side of the Star of the North there are five stars in a group—do you see them?"

He frowned but kept looking, finally saw the constellation she was trying to show him. "I see them."

"Those stars form the figure of a woman. The Greeks call her Cassiopeia, the vain queen. Because she was so obsessed by her beauty."

He chuckled. "I had no idea you were so enlightened."

She shrugged. "These things I learned from my mother. The stars are a great comfort to me."

"And a great adviser?"

"At times." She turned back to the sky. For long minutes she remained silent, concentrating on the blackness above the earth, the distant, twinkling prisms. Loomis seemed content just to watch her.

More time passed. Finally, she let her posture relax. "Come. It is time we went back into the house."

Loomis said nothing as they traveled the length of the hall, but the moment she stepped into the parlor, he asked the question she had hoped to hear.

"What did you see?"

Lily gave him her mysterious Tsaya smile. "I pictured you there among the stars. In my mind, the old woman appeared beside you—you know her name."

Loomis subtly straightened. "Mrs. Crowley, I believe is her name."

She nodded. "This woman…she owns many companies, but one will make you rich."

"Which one, can you tell me?"

"Guns. I saw rifles, rows of them. It has something to do with the Americans. A struggle there could lead them to war and they will need weapons. The old woman… invest all you can and you will make a fortune."

"Are you certain of this?"

She shrugged. "It is written in the stars. That is all I can say."

She could almost see his mind working, remembering the predictions she had made, how they had all been correct, trying to discover any way he could have been tricked. But Royal's friends were the cream of British society and Loomis would never imagine they would be involved in any sort of swindle.

"I shall think on what you have said."

"I warn you, this will happen soon."

He nodded. "Thank you for seeing me, Tsaya."

She made a faint bow of her head. "Good evening, Mr. Loomis."

The rings on her fingers danced in the lamplight as he caught her hand. "Preston," he softly corrected, pressing a kiss against the back. "We have become friends, have we not?"

Lily suppressed a shudder. "Friends…yes." She retrieved her hand and forced herself to smile. "Good night…Preston."

Through the window, she watched him descend the front-porch stairs and climb into his carriage. She waited till the carriage disappeared, then blew out a relieved breath and walked into the bedroom to pull off her itchy black wig. Though she wasn't quite sure why, it bothered her for Royal to see her dressed as Tsaya. Perhaps she didn't want to remind him of the life that she had once led.

Slipping the pins from her hair, she shook out the long blond strands and tied them back with a ribbon. Certain Royal had not yet left the house, she steeled herself to face him and walked down the hall to the kitchen. When she shoved through the door, she was surprised to discover that Dottie was gone and Royal stood in the kitchen alone.

"Mrs. Hobbs's youngest daughter is sick. She needed to go home and check on her. I told her you were safe as long as I was here. I told her I would see you home."

Tension tightened her shoulders. "But you can't possibly do that. What if we are seen together? Dear God, getting caught together in the shop was bad enough."

He blew out a breath. "I blame myself for that, Lily, and everything else that has happened between us. If I had left you alone in the first place—"

"The blame is hardly yours alone. What happened... it was like a train that kept speeding faster and faster and couldn't be stopped."

And the attraction was still there, his golden eyes said as they traveled over her face and the length of her bright silk garments, as strong as ever, maybe stronger.

He reached out and touched her cheek and she felt the heat of his fingers as if they burned her. "You look beautiful, even in your Gypsy clothes."

She only shook her head. Just looking at him made her want him, made her heartbeat quicken and her body soften, preparing itself for him.

"There are things I would say to you, feelings I would share if I could."

She nervously moistened her lips and his gaze sharpened. She fought to ignore the charged energy between them, vibrations so strong they seemed tangible. "Whatever we feel, we have to ignore. We've sinned enough, Royal."

"If we sinned, why did it feel so right? Why is it I want to make love to you again? Why is it I dream of the way it felt to be inside you? Of simply holding you in my arms?"

Her eyes teared, and her body wept for him. She wanted him to touch her, make love to her. No matter the cost. No matter how wrong it was.

"I wish I were stronger," she said, realizing that where Royal was concerned she hadn't the least strength of will. "I wish I could walk away from you, but I can't."

She moved closer, reached up and cupped his cheek. Going up on her toes, she kissed him, a gentle, sweet kiss filled with longing and goodbye. It deepened, grew more fierce, and suddenly she was swaying against him, silently begging him for more.

She had made a vow to forget him, but now she found she could not keep it. When Royal tried to ease away, Lily would not let him.

"After tomorrow, there will be no turning back. This is our last chance to be together. I want this night, Royal. I need you this one last time."

For an instant, he stood frozen. He was fighting a battle he could not win, a battle that demanded surrender. She heard his deep groan, signaling defeat, and then he was sweeping her up in his arms, carrying her out of the kitchen, down the hall to the bedroom that belonged to Tsaya.

He shoved open the door with his foot and set her on her feet. He couldn't seem to undress her fast enough. He jerked the ribbon on her red silk blouse and shoved it down off her shoulders, planted his mouth over her nipple and groaned at the taste of her breast. He suckled her there, and heat tugged low in her belly. All the while his hands stayed busy, working the tabs on her bright silk skirts, shoving them down, along with her pantalets.

He paused long enough for her to step out of them and shed her satin slippers while he frantically tugged at his own clothes, the black knee-high boots, his full-sleeved shirt and breeches. Naked, he stood before her and she marveled at the beauty of his lean, broad-shouldered build, the bands of muscle across his chest and the rampant fullness of his sex. He was big and hard and she wanted to feel him inside her.

His hot gaze skimmed over her, making her nipples peak and distend. Dampness seeped into her core and fierce, aching desire.

"If I could," he said, "I would make love to you every night for the rest of our lives," he said, and then she was back in his arms and he was kissing her, claiming her with his mouth and tongue. Deep, scorching kisses burned through her, wild, hungry kisses that seemed to have no end.

Lifting her up, he carried her over to the bed and settled her on the mattress, then came down on top of her. He laved her breasts and suckled her, grazed her nipples with his teeth, and desire clenched deep in her belly.

Kisses trailed over her neck and her shoulders, moist lips burned a trail past her navel. She cried out as his mouth settled over the entrance to her sex and he tasted her there. Sensation rocked her and waves of pleasure shot through her.

Royal laved and caressed her until she was trembling all over, her hands fisted in the bedsheets. A powerful climax shook her. Sweet pleasure rolled through her in long, endless waves. She thought that he would take her, ease the ache she knew he felt. Instead, he lay down beside her, lifted her and set her astride him.

He ran a finger along her cheek. "It's your turn to ride, sweet lady."

Her heartbeat quickened. Awareness of the hard male

body beneath her sent a flood of arousal into her blood. He was giving her control, allowing her to do whatever she wished. She could feel his rigid sex against the inside of her thigh, see the rapid rise and fall of his muscular chest.

She watched his face as she eased herself farther down his body, kissed his flat stomach, bent over and tentatively touched his shaft with her tongue.

"Lily, you don't have to—" He broke off with a groan as she took him into her mouth, began to lick and taste him, learning what gave him pleasure as she went along.

He hissed in a breath. "Sweet God, Lily." His whole body jerked as she cupped him in her hands, and a heady sense of power filled her. And a love for him so deep, tears burned her eyes.

"You have to stop, love," Royal said thickly, his voice low and husky. "I want to be inside you and if you keep that up—"

She gasped as his hands spanned her waist and he lifted her astride him, settled her over his hardened length. For the first time, she realized what he had meant. *It's your turn to ride, sweet lady.*

Her excitement grew as she slowly sank down on his rigid shaft. He was thick and hard and she didn't stop until he filled her completely. A shudder rippled through her as she rose and sank down again, rose and sank down.

"Lily…" he said and she could feel the tension in his lean, hard body.

Heat crawled through her, prickled her skin. His breathing grew shallow as she moved faster, took him deeper, rode him harder. Her heartbeat thundered. Her breath quickened and her insides started to quiver. She felt his muscles tighten, felt his body jerk as he reached release and Lily started coming. Fierce sensation, pleasure deep and saturating, washed through her. Lily moaned and cried out Royal's name as joy and sorrow combined, along with a feeling of sweet fulfillment.

For long moments, she lay slumped over his powerful chest, their bodies still joined. She wasn't sure how long she stayed there. Perhaps she even slumbered, for when she opened her eyes, she felt his hands smoothing over her hair.

She started to tell him she loved him, but the words remained locked away. There was no future for them. It wouldn't be fair to Royal and it wouldn't be fair to her.

Instead, when he rolled her beneath him, his body hard once more, she locked her arms round his neck and began to match the rhythm he set. Her mouth found his and she kissed him. The night belonged to her.

She would pay for her sins on the morrow.

Twenty-Seven

$\sim\!\!\sim\!\!\sim\!\!\infty\!\!\Longleftrightarrow\!\!\sim$

Music drifted into the street in front of the Caulfields' sumptuous three-story brick mansion. Golden light spilled through the windows, and elegantly attired guests formed a line at the entrance to the house. As the big black ducal coach rolled beneath the portico pulled by four matched gray horses, a remnant of the days before his father had lost his fortune, Royal steeled himself.

From this night forward, his life would no longer be his own. Marriage was a duty he had accepted, a price he had agreed to pay, and he would do what was required of him.

He would marry Jocelyn Caulfield and claim her fortune, and in return, she would become the Duchess of Bransford. She would give him heirs and somehow he would find a way for them to build a life together.

It didn't matter that he was in love with another woman. In the world in which he lived, marriage had nothing to do with love.

And though the fact had been apparent for weeks, he

had only just discovered the depth of the love he felt for Lily Moran.

He straightened at the feel of the carriage wheels rolling to a stop.

"It appears we have arrived." Aunt Agatha's fragile voice drifted toward him from the opposite side of the carriage where she sat next to his brother Rule.

"So it would seem," Rule said dryly as the door swung open and a footman in powder-blue livery and a silver periwig stood rigidly awaiting their descent.

Royal stepped lightly to the ground, turned and helped Aunt Agatha down. Taking her arm, he escorted her slowly along the red carpet toward the ornate, white-painted front doors.

The Caulfields greeted their guests in the high-ceilinged entry. Black-and-white marble floors gleamed beneath their feet.

"A pleasure to see you, Your Grace," Matilda Caulfield said, her eyes gleaming with an anticipation she made no effort to hide. She smiled at his aunt. "You, as well, Lady Tavistock."

Though it was difficult to imagine Jocelyn's rare beauty coming from her slightly rotund mother, the evidence of Matilda's parentage was there in the arch of her fine dark eyebrows, glossy mahogany hair and the perfect shape of her lips.

"Welcome to Meadowbrook," Henry Caulfield said to Royal warmly.

"Thank you, sir. I believe you've met my brother Rule. He is just returned from university."

"Of course. Good evening, my lord," Henry said to Rule, who made a snappy bow.

"Mr. and Mrs. Caulfield, a pleasure to see you again."

Royal turned his attention to Jo. "Miss Caulfield, you are looking exceptionally lovely tonight."

"You as well, Your Grace." She was lavishly gowned in violet silk the same shade as her eyes. Ringlets of thick dark hair nestled against her bare shoulders, gleaming in the light of the gas chandelier. Royal thought she had never looked more stunning.

They spoke a moment. His future wife was friendly, her manner gracious, and yet he sensed a turmoil in her he had never witnessed before. Perhaps it was the result of finding him with Lily in the hat shop, but he didn't think so. Jocelyn was completely sure of herself and her appeal, and certain of what it was she truly wanted.

He couldn't imagine her having the slightest doubt of his interest in her or the finalization of their marriage.

Other guests arrived, demanding their hosts' attention. Royal moved toward the stairs, Aunt Agatha on his arm, her cane in one knobby hand. Giving her the time she needed to handle the double sweeping staircase, they climbed to the floor that housed the magnificent ballroom, Rule close behind them. Finished with his schooling at last, the youngest Dewar appeared to be looking forward to the evening ahead.

Royal just wished it was over.

Jocelyn stood next to her mother, a smile pasted on her lips. Her chest ached. She felt like crying. It was ridiculous. Tonight should be the happiest night of her life. In a couple of hours, her engagement to the Duke of Bransford would be announced and she would be crowned the future queen of society.

Her mother was already beaming, imagining her own moment of triumph, the elevated social position that being the mother-in-law of a duke would bring her. Her father was laughing and smiling, so proud of her, thrilled she would soon become the duchess he was certain she was born to be.

Everyone was happy.

Everyone but Jo.

And all because Christopher Barclay had rejected her.

Only days ago, she would have been furious at the thought that a lowly barrister with no money and little social position would have the gall to refuse her offer of marriage. She would have been livid, as she had been the day she had stormed out of the Parkland Hotel.

Since then, the anger had faded and the pain had set in. It was deep and abiding, an ache so fierce she could barely sleep, barely eat. Her mother thought she'd been beset by nerves, worry about her upcoming engagement.

Thank God, she would never know the truth.

In the past few days, Jocelyn had thought of Christopher a thousand times. She had tried to convince herself it was impossible that she could have fallen in love with him. She didn't even believe in love.

But the pain in her heart was real and her feelings for Christopher had only deepened since that day. She respected him, she realized, for being man enough to stand up to her. Man enough to turn down an offer that told him nothing of her feelings. An offer he believed was little more than a whim.

Perhaps at the time, it had been.

Since his refusal, she had thought of him constantly. She had listened for any thread of gossip about him, scoured the newspapers for articles that mentioned his name. In a discussion of a case he had won, the *London Times* praised him for his abilities as a barrister and predicted he would go far. Christopher was smart and strong and yet she knew he could be tender.

Her heart hurt. She had spent hours telling herself she only wanted him because she could not have him. Now she knew she wanted so much more. She wanted Christopher to love her. As deeply as she was in love with him.

Her throat tightened. It was all just so unfair!

She felt trapped and confused. Part of her wanted to call off the wedding. Another part warned that if she did, she would be left with no one. Christopher had laughed at her offer of marriage, and should she repeat that offer, would likely do so again.

The evening slipped past. She danced with Royal three times, danced with his darkly handsome younger brother, Rule, danced with half the eligible bachelors in London, smiling all the while, pretending to be happy, working to look gay and sophisticated. She tried not to glance at the door, tried not to wish that Christopher would appear. She tried not to hope he would rush in and demand she cry off with Royal, tell her he had changed his mind. Tell her that he loved her and truly wanted to marry her.

Instead, she saw her father and mother approaching from the opposite side of the ballroom. From another direction, Royal walked toward her. It was time to announce their engagement.

"The hour has come," the duke said softly, offering her his arm. "I believe your parents have something of importance they wish to announce."

For a single, mad moment, she wanted to bolt for the door. She wanted to run away, hide until this nightmare was over.

Then she spotted her archenemy, Serafina Maitlin, standing near the platform where the musicians were playing and the announcement would be made. Her eyes were saucer-round as she watched the duke escorting Jocelyn and her parents toward the platform and realized exactly what it meant.

Anger turned Serafina's face bright red. Her mouth thinned into a brittle line and her eyes seemed to glitter. Jocelyn's doubt slipped away at the sight of her rival's jealousy.

By heaven, she would do it! She would become a duchess! She would show them! She would show all of them!

And especially Christopher Barclay!

Standing near the mirrored wall at the end of the ballroom, Preston Loomis spotted the old woman he had come there to see. Next to the Dowager Countess of Tavistock, Hortense Crowley was a gnarly old woman, wrinkled and slightly hunched over. More importantly, her mind was as old and fading as the rest of her.

He made his way in the old woman's direction, setting his empty punch cup down on a passing waiter's tray.

Around him, the crowd was murmuring, discussing the formal announcement that had just been made—the Duke of Bransford's engagement to the wealthy heiress Jocelyn Caulfield. It came as little surprise to anyone. The betting books were full of wagers. The duke was nearly bankrupt. The Caulfield girl came with a fortune. Royal Dewar had no real choice.

Preston managed to keep a satisfied smile off his face. His own coffers were overflowing, thanks to the most successful confidence scheme he had ever managed to accomplish. With the size of his fortune, he never had to work another day.

But the thrill of success came as much from the challenge a mark presented as it did the money. He focused his attention on old lady Crowley, who had moved a little away from the countess and now stood unsteadily next to a potted palm. Preston fixed a smile on his face and moved toward her.

"Mrs. Crowley, a pleasure to see you again."

She frowned, drawing her busy, dull gray eyebrows together. "Do I know you?"

A trickle of annoyance filtered through him. He wasn't used to being forgotten. "Why, yes. We've met on several occasions. My name is Preston Loomis. You may recall, I remind you of your late husband."

She looked up at him and her eyes brightened. "Indeed! Mr. Loomis, of course. Why, you're a dead ringer for my Freddy when he was your age."

They talked for a while, saying nothing of importance, just giving her time to relax in his company and get things moving in the direction he wanted.

"Do you follow the newspapers, Mrs. Crowley?"

She shook her head. "Never had much use for them. My Freddy did, though."

"I understand your husband was in the business of making armaments, among other things."

"Guns, you mean?"

"Why, yes."

She nodded, moving gray strands of hair that had escaped her silk cap. "Now that you mention it. Built rifles, he did. Foreigners are interested in rifles these days."

"I have an interest in weaponry, myself, at least as an investment. Would there be a chance I might participate in some way in the ownership of the plant?"

She stared off into the distance, said nothing for the longest time. Then she blinked and seemed to refocus. "You want to buy some stock?"

"I might consider it, yes. Though I would need to see the facility, of course."

She nodded sagely. "Of course. My Freddy always said never buy a pig in a poke. Why don't I have my solicitor pay you a call? Stevens is his name. Good man is Stevens."

Preston handed her an embossed white card with his address printed on it. He hoped the old bat would stay lucid long enough to remember why she had it.

"What's this for?" She waved the card around as if she were trying to dry the ink, and his hopes sank.

"You were going to give it to your solicitor, Mr. Stevens. Tell him I am interested in buying stock in your armaments factory."

"Guns, you mean?"

He barely hung on to his temper. "I would appreciate it if your Mr. Stevens got in touch." Once he did—if he did—Preston would take care of the rest.

The old woman tucked the card into the velvet reticule hanging from her arm, turned and ambled away without so much as a by-your-leave.

Preston blew out a frustrated breath. Perhaps he would never hear from her man.

Then again, the Gypsy had never been wrong.

An image of her appeared in his mind, lovely and exotic, her pale skin and light eyes a delicate contrast to her black hair and midnight eyebrows. An unexpected trickle of desire slipped through him. It was a rare thing these days. Perhaps along with their business dealings, they might make another sort of bargain.

Inwardly, he smiled. Then he brushed the thought away. At present, it was money he wanted, not the girl.

All in due time, he told himself.

All in due time.

Royal was finally able to escape his fiancée and their well-wishers and make his way to the safe haven of his friends.

"Congratulations," Nightingale said, the heavy gold and ruby ring on his right hand gleaming as he took a drink of champagne. "You will soon be one of us married folk."

Royal just nodded. He would be married, but Night had been fortunate enough to marry for love.

"Cheer up, old man," Quent said, a smile lifting the corners of his mouth. "You would have had to wed sooner or later. A man needs an heir and all that." This from a man who had just entered the marriage mart. Royal wondered how he would feel a few months from now.

"She's a lovely little piece," drawled Savage. "You're wedding the toast of London. Bedding her should be entertaining. That is some consolation."

Royal turned and looked back at his future bride. In her violet silk gown, her glorious mahogany hair gleaming, she was impossibly beautiful. She stood there like the duchess she would soon become, surrounded by a sea of admirers: envious young women, and men who thought that somewhere down the road there was a chance she might take one of them as a lover. For clearly her marriage was one of convenience.

Sherry's hazel gaze went in the same direction and he leaned toward Royal, the friend who knew his heart. "There is always the chance your fair lady will change her mind and the two of you can still be together."

Royal couldn't help hoping that would happen, even as he felt guilty for the thought. Lily deserved a husband and family. If he truly loved her, he would leave her alone.

Dillon St. Michaels walked up to the group just then. He took one look at Royal's solemn expression and sighed. "At least your money problems will be solved."

That much was true. And since Matilda Caulfield pressed for the wedding to take place just three months hence, he wouldn't have long to wait.

Other friends arrived in the circle, Lady Annabelle Townsend and her friend, Lady Sabrina Jeffers. They both professed their profound good wishes and best regards for Royal and Jocelyn's happiness, but both the women's eyes seemed to hold a trace of pity. Surely they didn't know the way he felt. Then again, women had sense of such things.

Royal straightened. It wasn't fair to Jocelyn to harbor these feelings for Lily. It was time he tucked them away. He had duties, obligations. And soon he would have a wife and family to care for. Lily would always remain in his heart, but from now on, only he would know the truth of how he felt.

Royal managed a smile he hoped looked more genuine than those that had come before. "If you ladies and gentlemen will excuse me, it is time I joined my beautiful future wife."

All of them looked at him. Annabelle summoned a smile, but no one said a word.

Lily couldn't sleep. By this late hour, Jocelyn and Royal had announced their engagement. She slid out from beneath the covers, crossed to the door of her flat and descended the stairs to the shop. Creeping quietly to the backroom, she looked in to see Tommy next to Mugs on the pallet she had fashioned for them. Earlier, she had made him the offer of a bath and amazingly he had accepted.

"A bath?" His dark eyes widened. "You mean with real hot water?"

Lily laughed. "Hot and steaming."

"Blimey, I can't remember me last hot bath."

"And I got you some clothes and a new pair of shoes so you would have something clean to put on after."

He stared up at her with big, awestruck brown eyes that turned slightly misty. "Someday I'll repay ye, miss, I swear it on Mugs's life." The dog whined as if he wasn't too sure about that, and Lily smiled.

"Someday I'm certain you will."

Tommy fetched the copper bathing tub off the wall where she kept it and they heated hot water on the tiny stove in the backroom of the shop. She set the clothes on the counter, hoping they would fit, and closed the door, giving him the privacy he needed. Lily smiled as she listened to his off-key singing of some bawdy sailor's song.

The bath was a lengthy affair, which meant he was

enjoying himself. When he finished, he came out of the room dressed in a pair of brown twill trousers and a muslin shirt that were only a little too big for him.

His grin went from ear to ear. "The clothes is great, miss. Loose enough so's I can grow some and they'll still fit."

"You look very dapper." She glanced over at Mugs, pleased to see the dog had also got a bath.

Later, as usual, boy and dog had lain down on the pallet—this time between clean sheets.

"Now, ain't this the life?" Tommy shoved his hands behind his head. "Me and Mugs clean as a whistle, our bellies full and a warm place to sleep. I can't thank ye enough, miss, for all that ye've done."

"There's something else I would like to do, Tommy—if you will let me. I spoke to one of my customers, Mrs. Symthe, the grocer's wife. She said she and her husband are in need of a hardworking, trustworthy young man to handle deliveries for the store."

He sat up on the pallet. "Trustworthy? Ye don't mean me?"

"Well, you would be, wouldn't you? If you had a job, you wouldn't have to steal. Mr. Smythe would pay you a fair wage and you and Mugs could live in the room above the stable where the delivery cart is kept."

That was the difficult part, giving up Tommy's company. Whenever he was there, it helped to keep her mind off Royal and his upcoming marriage.

"Blimey, miss, I ain't never had a real job. Ye could trust me, fer sure. I wouldn't steal a thing."

"And you could still come over," she added. "We could still have supper together whenever you wished."

Tommy grinned. "I'd be pleased to take the job. When do I start?"

"Monday morning, if you're ready. I'll go with you to see the Smythes, help you get settled in."

Tommy laughed. "Ain't it somethin'. Me first real job—and all because I picked some fancy duke's pocket."

Lily's couldn't help a smile. But thoughts of Royal crept in and her smile slowly faded. "I'll see you in the morning, Tommy." She reached down and ruffled the dog's furry coat. "You and Mugs sleep well."

He closed his eyes, but the grin remained on his face. Lily smiled as she left the backroom and headed up to her apartment.

Now, hours later in the middle of the night, as she stood in the doorway watching them, she felt a soft tug at her heart. She sighed into the darkness. Tommy and Mugs slept soundly, but for her, sleep would remain elusive. Perhaps in time, she would be able to put her love for Royal behind her, but not tonight.

Not tonight.

Lily ignored the pain in her heart as she turned toward the stairs and headed up to her empty bed.

Twenty-Eight

───❦❦❦───

Four days had passed since the engagement ball. A cold April wind scoured the air and blew bits of paper into the street. Soon the daffodils would be in bloom, but today an icy chill blew in off the Thames.

A few blocks from the river, inside the big brick building that housed the Hawksworth Munitions Factory, Royal stood next to Benjamin Wyndam, Lord Nightingale, behind a glass window three stories above the main floor of the plant.

Situated in the Tooley Street area not far from the docks, the location had been chosen for the easy distribution of the products being made. Nightingale owned the plant. He chuckled as he watched the two men walking the floor three stories below, moving along the assembly line, one thin and dark-haired, the other sporting a thick, silver mustache.

"Loomis keeps nodding his head," Night said. "The man who is with him must be good. I think our friend is buying whatever the fellow is selling."

"He's saying something to the effect that batty old Mrs. Crowley's plant is worth far more than she knows. With the Americans on the verge of war, the stock Loomis is buying will soon be worth a fortune."

"Who is he?"

"Jack Moran calls him Gulliver. He's a member of *the mob*—a group of actors who do this sort of thing for a living."

Nightingale shook his head, dislodging a strand of heavy dark hair. "Watching the ease with which a man can be duped gives one pause. I can certainly understand how your father fell victim to this sort of swindle."

"I guess we'll find out if Loomis is as gullible as the rest of us."

Nightingale looked back down at the men, who kept moving along the line, pausing here and there to examine one of the rifles being made, apparently pleased with the quality, which, of course, was excellent. "So far, it would seem he is."

Though the plant was highly profitable, Night was thinking of selling it. The notion of making weapons just didn't sit well, he said.

Royal watched the men below. When Loomis and Mrs. Crowley's solicitor had arrived, no one had approached them. Everyone continued to work, ignoring them as if the solicitor had some sort of permission. Later, when Loomis discovered who the real owner was, Nightingale would simply say that his plant manager hadn't been working that day. He was sorry, but he knew nothing about any visitors.

Royal watched Preston Loomis leave the plant and wondered if he was convinced, and if so, how much stock he would purchase. Once the money was received by the man named Gulliver, it would be turned over to Charles Sinclair for distribution.

Then everyone would disappear. Tsaya would vacate the house in Piccadilly and Mrs. Crowley would no longer exist.

In a few more days, all of this would be over.

Royal felt a pang of longing. He wished he could talk to Lily, discuss what was going on. Instead, he followed Nightingale out of the office and the two of them headed downstairs.

It was nearly closing time when Lily heard the bell ring above the door. She set her sewing aside, rose from the chair and walked out of the backroom. She froze at the sight of her cousin standing in the middle of the shop.

She swallowed, for a moment unable to speak. "Jocelyn... I—I am surprised to see you." That was an understatement. The last time Jo had been there, Lily had been wrapped in Royal's arms.

Jocelyn twisted the embroidered handkerchief she held in her hand and Lily realized her cousin was as nervous as she.

"I need to speak to you, Lily. There is no one else who will understand. No one but you. Please say you will talk to me."

Lily didn't hesitate. If Jo had come to her after all that had happened, it had to be important. "Of course. Why don't I lock up and we'll go upstairs. I'll make us a nice pot of tea."

Jo just nodded.

Lily closed up quickly, then led Jocelyn up the stairs to her flat and put the teakettle on to boil. While the water heated, they sat down in the parlor in front of the small, coal-burning hearth.

"What is it, Jo? I can tell you are upset. What can I do to help?"

To Lily's amazement, Jocelyn's beautiful violet eyes filled with tears. Since Jo never cried, the impact was startling.

"I've done the most foolish thing." She glanced up, used the handkerchief to dab the moisture from her eyes. "I've fallen in love, Lily. Like a green girl in from the country, I have let down my guard and allowed a man to capture my heart."

Lily's chest tightened. Had Jo fallen in love with Royal? Was that the reason she had come to Lily?

She swallowed. "Royal?" she asked.

Jo's head came up. "No, of course not. You are the one who is in love with Royal. It is Christopher. Christopher Barclay."

Lily's heart began to pound. She could scarcely believe what her cousin was saying. It wasn't like Jo to let her emotions rule her. Not like her at all. "How does…how does Christopher feel about you?"

Jocelyn dabbed at her eyes. "That is the problem. Christopher doesn't…he doesn't love me."

"Are you certain?"

She sniffed. "Not entirely. I mean, when we are together, he seems…he seems to care very much, but when I asked him to marry me—"

"You asked Christopher Barclay to marry you? But you are engaged to the duke!"

"I wasn't at the time. But that is hardly important."

It seemed incredibly important to Lily.

"The point is, Christopher refused my offer. He said I would regret it later. He said…he said he wouldn't be one of my *lapdogs*." She started to cry, and no matter what had happened between them, Lily's heart went out to her. She knew the pain of loving someone. And it was clear this wasn't one of Jocelyn's famous ploys to draw attention. Her cousin's heart was clearly broken.

Lily hadn't realized Jo was capable of such deep emotion. It made her begin to see her cousin in a completely different light.

"I don't know what to do, Lily. I ache to see him again. I can't eat. I can't sleep. If I had known I would feel this way, I…I… Drats, I don't know what I would have done. All I know is that I love Christopher and I want him to love me back." She looked up, tears glittering on her thick dark lashes. "Please, Lily, tell me what to do."

Lily came out of her chair, crossed the small space between them and sat down next to Jo on the settee. She took hold of her cousin's hand. "What you have to do, Jo, is tell Christopher the way you feel."

Jo shook her head. "He won't believe me. He'll think I'm just saying the words in order to get my way."

She had a point. Jo had a history of behaving in whatever manner necessary to get what she wanted. "Then you will have to find a way to prove it. You will have to give Christopher a reason to believe you are truly in love with him."

"How do I do that?"

Lily squeezed Jo's hand. "I can't tell you what to do. You will have to figure that out for yourself."

"I don't know, Lily. What I do might not matter. He might not care for me in the least."

"I suppose that could happen. But if you discover he really doesn't want you, then he isn't the man you want, either."

Jocelyn seemed to mull that over, then her head came up. "You are right. I shall find a way to prove my love for Christopher. If he doesn't want me…if he doesn't want me—" She broke off and started to weep. "If he doesn't want me, I shall simply curl up and die."

Lily's heart pinched. She knew exactly the way her cousin felt. She wondered if Jo had begun to understand how Lily felt, as well.

A special meeting had been called. Lily had received the note requesting her attendance just that morning. Standing on the street in front of the Red Rooster Inn, she drew her cloak a little tighter against the wind, opened the door and walked inside.

As she descended the stairs to the taproom and crossed to the room in the back, she could hear the joviality in the air. Molly's laughter rang out, followed by Uncle Jack's chuckle of mirth. Charles Sinclair spoke gaily, saying something Royal answered with a smile in his deep familiar voice.

Anticipation made her heart pound. No matter how wrong it was, she ached to see him again.

As she walked through the door into the backroom, every eye turned in her direction.

Uncle Jack beamed. "There's my girl!" He came to his feet along with the other two men.

Molly shot up beside him. "We did it, luv! We fooled the bloody bastard out of a soddin' fortune!"

Her eyes widened. "Then it worked? Loomis came up with the money?"

"Indeed he did, my dear," said Sinclair. "He was so impressed with the factory, he bought twice as much of Mrs. Crowley's worthless stock as we figured he would. Even after we take our cut, His Grace will get back a very sizable chunk of his father's money."

Pure joy bubbled inside her. A laugh came from her throat. Their plan had worked! They had done it! "That is wonderful news! Wonderful news, indeed!" For the first time, she allowed herself to look at Royal.

There was a smile in his golden eyes that seemed meant just for her. It was a sweet, yearning smile that made her knees turn to jelly. Inside her chest, her heart trembled. It wasn't fair that one particular man could have such an effect on her.

His gaze lingered a moment, then he straightened and his features became remote.

"Everything you did was perfect, Lily. Tsaya was amazing. Molly was magnificent as old Mrs. Crowley, and Jack's man, Gulliver, delivered the final blow. Loomis bought the whole package. He was so certain Tsaya's prediction would come true, he invested nearly half his fortune."

Lily's eyes misted. "I am so happy for you…Your Grace."

His gaze found hers. "I owe it all to you, Lily. If you hadn't introduced me to your uncle, my father never would have gotten the justice he deserved. Thank you." He turned to the others. "Thank you all."

"This calls for a celebration," Jack said. He waved at a barmaid in a mobcap, who ambled over to take their order. "Drinks all round—on me!"

"Not a chance," Royal said. "Today the bill is mine."

All of them cheered. The laughter and gaiety continued. It was a great day for everyone.

Everyone but Lily.

Still, she had learned to celebrate the small victories in life and this definitely was one. They drank and ate and talked. Loomis's bank draft had been cashed as soon as it was received and the money dispersed as agreed. Mrs. Crowley had disappeared and Molly and Dottie Hobbs had taken care of closing up the house in Piccadilly. And there was no way for anyone to locate a solicitor name Stevens.

"It's over," Royal said. "We can all go back to our lives and feel that justice has been served."

"Hear, hear!" said Jack, lifting his mug in a toast. "And we'll all have coin in our pockets!"

Lily raised her glass with the rest, but her lips trembled. She was no longer welcome at the Caulfields'. And now that the charade was over, she might never see Royal again.

Preston Loomis sat in his favorite chair in front of the fire, a satisfied smile on his face. The *London Times* sat open on his lap. All week he had been scouring the newspapers, reading the articles that dealt with the problems in America.

Things were ratcheting up between the northern states and those in the southern part of the country. Both sides were quietly arming. The states in the North had factories that could eventually be refitted to produce weapons, but the southern lands were mostly agricultural.

Both would need to be prepared, just in case. They needed armaments and as of last week, he was in the armaments business in a very big way.

His smile widened.

Finishing the paper, he started at the sound of his butler's voice coming from the doorway.

"I am sorry to bother you, sir, but Mr. McGrew is here to see you."

Bart McGrew lumbered into the study. Preston started to smile, but the tension in Bart's ugly face put him on alert.

He set the paper aside and rose from his chair. "What is it?"

"I took the message to the Gypsy's house like ye asked."

He had sent word to Tsaya, eager for a meeting. "Yes, and what did she say?"

"She weren't there, boss. She's gone."

"Gone? What do you mean, gone?"

"She's a Gypsy, boss. I guess she packed up and left. Servants is all gone, too. Ye know how them people are."

He sighed. They were a footloose bunch, and unreliable. He should have expected this sort of behavior and yet he was sorely disappointed.

"There's more bad news."

Preston arched a sterling eyebrow. "And what is that?"

"After I left her house, I went by to see that fellow Stevens what works for old lady Crowley. Just to be on the safe side, ye know."

"That was very good thinking."

"I went to the address on the card he gave ye. No one there's ever heard of a Mr. Stevens."

Loomis's jaw tightened. "That is not possible."

McGrew made no reply and his lack of a response said more than words.

"Surely you are not thinking… It isn't possible. It is simply some sort of mistake. Go down to the factory, ask the manager how to find Mrs. Crowley's solicitor. If that doesn't work, find the old woman. She has been staying with Lady Tavistock for the past several weeks."

"Already done that, boss. Manager never heard of Stevens. Matter of fact, he never heard of Mrs. Crowley."

Preston's stomach rolled. "What…what are you talking about?"

"Manager said the Earl of Nightingale owned the plant and had for years."

Preston swallowed, the sick feeling in his stomach causing the bile to rise in his throat. "That can't be true. Find Mrs. Crowley. Go to the Countess of Tavistock's residence. Someone there will know—"

"Talked to her ladyship's cook, Mrs. Harvey. She says the old woman and Lady Tavistock only just met at some fancy affair. The old woman seemed a nice person so her ladyship invited her to stay a while before she went back to her home up in York. She left a couple days ago."

Preston's hand unconsciously fisted. It couldn't be true and yet his instincts were screaming that he had been had. "No…"

Bart said nothing. He had always been thorough. There was no need to belabor the point. Both of them knew exactly what had occurred.

"I want them found," Preston ground out, his jaw clamped so tight he could barely speak. "I want all of them found! I want to know who did this and I want my money back!"

"I hear ye."

"Can you do it? Can you find them?"

Bart straightened to his full height and squared his thick shoulders. "Ye can count on me, boss. I won't let ye down."

The big man turned to leave, and Preston sank back down in his chair. He'd been well and truly conned. He wouldn't have believed it was possible. In his business, he was the best of the best, the elite of the elite. No man was his equal.

His jaw tightened. Obviously, he was wrong.

The question now was who had done it and how he would make them pay.

This time it was more than money he wanted.

Twenty-Nine

Somberly dressed in dove-gray velvet trimmed with dark green silk, Jocelyn stood at the door of the modest town house owned by Christopher Barclay.

It was Saturday morning, two weeks since her engagement had been announced. It had taken her that long to figure things out, summon her courage and act. Her gloved hand shook as she lifted the brass knocker and rapped on the door. Inside her chest, her heart pounded as if she had run all the way from her home.

In a way she *had* run. Run from the meeting she had requested with her parents to inform them of her decision. Run from the horrified looks on their faces when, in as calm a manner as she could manage, she had told them she was ending her engagement to the Duke of Bransford.

"What are you talking about?" Her mother's eyes went saucer-round. "We are already making arrangements for the wedding."

"It's all right, Matilda," her father said. "It is simply

a bout of nerves. All young brides go through this sort of thing. In time, Jocelyn will realize—"

"What I realize, Father, is that money and social position are simply not enough to make me happy. I am in love with another man, Father. And though I am not…not certain of his feelings for me, I am certain I will not settle for marriage to a man I care nothing about."

Her mother sank onto the sofa, taking shallow breaths and fanning her flushed face with her hand. "You cannot do this, Jocelyn. You cannot throw away everything you have worked for, everything you have ever wanted."

"I am throwing away everything you and Father wanted me to have. Until now, I didn't realize it wasn't what I wanted at all."

Her mother gazed beseechingly at her husband. "Talk to her, Henry. Make her understand. She cannot do this. She simply cannot!"

"Your mother is right, dear heart. Consider your position. You are soon to be a duchess. You can't think to throw that away. And there is the duke to consider. What would he say if he found out what you are thinking? Why, the man would be devastated. Give yourself some time, dearest. In time you will come to see reason."

Jocelyn shook her head. "It is too late for that, Father. I sent word to the duke this morning."

"Dear God in heaven." Her mother's fanning increased.

"Unfortunately, Royal has already left for the country. It may take a day or two, but soon my letter will reach him. He will know the truth of my feelings and that will be the end of our engagement."

Her mother's face was so pale Jocelyn began to fear for her well-being.

"She needs a drink of water," Henry said. "Ring for one of the servants, Jocelyn—before your mother faints."

Jocelyn hurried to the bellpull and an instant later a bevy of servants appeared to fetch whatever was needed. It wasn't long before the color began to return to her mother's pale face.

"We'll be ruined," she said, making a whimpering sound into the handkerchief Jocelyn pressed into her hand.

"It's all right, my dear," Henry said to her, patting her pudgy fingers. "We'll find a way out of this. It's amazing what money can do."

And what it could not, Jo thought morosely as she stood now in front of Christopher's door, praying he was there. She wasn't sure how long her courage would last, or what she would do if he rejected her again.

The door swung open just then. It wasn't the butler, but Christopher himself who stood in the opening, hard and dark and sinfully handsome.

"Jocelyn…what the devil…?"

"Could I…could I speak to you for a moment?"

"Good God, Jo." He hauled her quickly inside. "This is a bachelor household. What if someone sees you?"

"I don't care. I… Please, I have something to say and I am hoping you will listen."

He sighed. "I shouldn't. I know damn well I shouldn't be listening to a word you say." But he led her into the drawing room and plunked her down on the sofa.

It was a pleasant room, she noticed vaguely, not shabby in the least, but tastefully done in rich masculine tones of dark brown and forest green. For an instant, she allowed her gaze to drink him in, the lean, solid build, the dark hair and intense brown eyes. His carved features carried the stamp of intelligence. His jaw was set with implacable resolve.

Her heart twisted. No matter what she said, he wouldn't listen. He wouldn't believe a word. He understood her better than anyone she had ever known, and yet he didn't know her at all.

Her heart was pounding, her stomach tied in knots.

"Why did you come here, Jo? You wanted another tumble before you took your vows with another man?"

"No, I…" Her throat tightened. She didn't know where to begin. "There aren't…aren't going to be any vows. There isn't going to be a wedding at all. I—I broke off my engagement."

His dark brows arched up. "What are you talking about?"

"I sent a letter to the duke. I told my parents I was ending our betrothal. I don't care about being a duchess. I just…I want to be with you, Christopher."

For an instant, surprise flashed in his face. Then his features hardened. "Tell him you made a mistake. Tell him it was just bridal nerves."

Her eyes welled. She shouldn't have come. "I told him…I said I was in love with another man."

Christopher's jaw tightened. He reached out and gripped her shoulders, hauled her up off the sofa. "You little fool. Do you know what you've done? You've thrown away everything—cast aside everything you ever wanted."

She lifted her chin and looked at him through a veil of tears. "Did I? Perhaps I discovered being a duchess wasn't as important as I had imagined. Maybe I found out it wasn't as important as loving someone."

For a moment, his hard look softened. "Jo…" His hand came up and gently touched her cheek. "Even if you…have feelings for me, it couldn't possibly work. I couldn't give you the life you want. I would only make you unhappy."

"Would you?"

"If we married, in time, you would regret it."

She could feel his implacability. He was refusing her again. "I love you. I would never regret it."

A muscle jerked in his cheek. "Someday you would wish you had married the duke."

She kept her head high, but tears washed down her cheeks. "Then you truly don't want me."

Christopher swallowed. She could feel the tension in the hands that gripped her shoulders. He stood there for long moments that seemed like hours, his eyes locked with hers. Then a low growl came from his throat and he hauled her into his arms.

"You think I don't want you?" he whispered against her cheek. "I want you more than I want to breathe. I'm crazy in love with you. Sweet God, Jo, you think I don't want you? I've never wanted anything as much as I want you." And then he kissed her, a deep, fierce, burning kiss that said all the things she wanted to hear.

Jocelyn wept as she clung to him. "I love you, Christopher. I love you so much. We can make it work, I know we can."

He kissed her again, then pressed his lips against the top of her head. "I'm not a rich man, Jo."

"You will be—once we are married. I know I am spoiled and used to getting my way, but—"

He cupped her face in his hands. "If we marry, I will spoil you far worse than you are already."

She smiled up at him through her tears. "I trust you, Christopher, as I've never trusted anyone before. I trust you to make me happy."

He eased her back into his arms. "I may be the biggest fool in London, but, by God, Jo, I'm going to marry you."

Her heart filled to overflowing. Tears of joy rolled down her cheeks. She couldn't remember ever being happier than she was in that moment.

Or more in love.

Or more certain she had done the right thing.

It was Saturday, two weeks after Royal and Jocelyn had announced their engagement. At that final meeting at the Red Rooster Inn, Uncle Jack had insisted Lily take her share of the money they had collected from Preston Loomis. Though she tried to refuse, Royal had insisted and she had finally given in.

The money went into the bank as a cushion should her business run into unforeseen problems. So far that hadn't happened. Her shop was doing well, her patronage growing.

At the grocer's just down the block, Tommy Cox was doing a bang-up job as a delivery boy—or so Mrs. Smythe reported. On the surface, her life seemed to be going very well.

On the surface.

Underneath, her heart was broken and she wasn't sure it would ever be whole again.

Lily ignored the ache in her chest as she closed up

the shop, ending another workday. She turned at the sound of a knock at the backdoor leading into the alley and smiled, certain Tommy had come by for supper. He had been there just last night, but he and Mugs were always more than welcome.

She hurried in that direction, opened the door and gasped at the sight of a huge, hulking figure standing on the back step.

"You Lily Moran?"

"Why, yes, that's right. Is there something I can do for you?"

His eyes gleamed. "It ain't me ye need to do for. 'Tis me friend, Dick Flynn."

Lily screamed as the man grabbed her arms and yanked her out of the shop into the alley. Dear God, Dick Flynn! Preston Loomis had found her out! Fear tore through her, making her heartbeat thunder. She searched for courage, and began to struggle against his brutal grip. She tried to kick him, but her heavy skirts got in the way. She tried to bite the big, meaty hand locked around her neck, twisted and turned, used all the tricks she had learned as a child on the street.

For an instant, she broke free, whirled and raked her nails down his puffy, florid face and turned to run.

"You little wench!" In an instant he was on her, cursing, calling her names she hadn't heard since she had lived the life of a thief.

She screamed again as a beefy fist rushed toward her, striking her jaw so hard, pain shot into her head. Another blow split her lip, slinging blood all over. Her head spun. Lily tried to get away, but her vision began to blur. Her gaze narrowed and faded until there was only blackness.

* * *

Royal leaned back against the seat of the ducal traveling coach. The gold-painted emblem on the side was chipped and fading, the red leather seats beginning to crack, a reminder of why he had gone to London.

Why he was marrying an heiress.

He blew out a breath. His task was complete. It was time he went home. After Jack Moran had handed Royal the lion's share of the money they had collected from Loomis, he had stayed in the city to clear his father's debts. He had paid off the majority of the bills that were owed, keeping enough in reserve to expand the brewery he had founded, which he still believed would prove a sound investment.

Though most of the money was gone, he felt he had served his father's memory well. There wasn't enough left to refurbish Bransford Castle but at least the family's good name had been restored.

He stared out the window of the carriage, seeing little more than a blur of green, not really noticing the budding leaves on the trees or the tiny spring flowers blooming in the grass on the rolling hills.

Instead, he was thinking of Jocelyn and his upcoming wedding. Thinking that he had done his duty, no matter how painful it was.

He refused to think of Lily. That time was past and remembering only brought pain.

He was deep in concentration when the sound of hoofbeats reached him. Galloping horses, men riding hard behind the carriage. Royal bolted up in the seat, his senses on full alert.

"Outlaws!" the coachman called out, whipping the

four matched grays into a gallop that surged to a flat-out run. Pistol shots rang out. Royal took a quick look out the window, cursed at the sight of four mounted riders bearing down on them, reached beneath the seat and dragged out the long-barreled Adams .44 cap-and-ball revolver kept there for protection.

The hoofbeats grew louder. Royal leaned out the window and saw the men getting closer. All of them wore handkerchiefs tied over their noses and mouths, all rode hard and were rapidly gaining against the cumbersome carriage.

Royal swore another curse. The highwaymen who had been roaming the countryside. Damnation! He hadn't expected an attack in the broad light of day.

The coach rocked and swayed. The coachman fired three shots from his revolver and one of the outlaws cried out. Royal watched him teeter on his horse, then slam headlong into the dirt, but the other men kept coming.

Leaning out the window as the carriage careened down the road, Royal took careful aim and pulled the trigger. He fired a second shot and then a third. The damn gun was bulky and inaccurate. He'd had his eye on a new Beaumont-Adams, a much-improved design. Now he wished he had spent the money.

Several more shots rang out, one splintering wood on the side of the carriage. In better days, he would have had footmen at the rear of the coach, all armed for protection. But there was no money for that now.

Royal took aim and fired and another man went down.

"Leave 'em where they lay!" shouted the taller of the remaining pair, the leader, it seemed, who aimed his weapon and fired off several rounds.

"I'm hit!" shouted the driver, his gun flying out of his hand. The coach careened right, tilted to the left and nearly toppled over. Royal fired his last two shots before the rig began to slow. It was clear the man in charge barely hung on to the reins.

Royal steeled himself. The coin in his purse was all he carried. The rest was safe in his London bank account. He wore little jewelry, just his father's emerald ring and the pocket watch his brother Reese had given him as a gift one Christmas before he returned to his duties in the army.

The coach continued to slow, rolled to a jerky stop, and the riders rushed up, pulling so hard on their horses' reins one of the animals whinnied.

"You inside! Come out of there! Do it now!"

His weapon was empty. His man was wounded and in need of attention. He had no other choice.

The door jerked open and the leader, a barrel-chested man with long black hair and a handkerchief tied over his nose, motioned for him to come down. Royal descended the iron steps and stood in front of him.

"I'm afraid you won't get much." He handed over his pouch of coins. "That's all I have with me."

The leader reached down from his saddle and snatched the bag from his hand. For the first time, Royal realized the second man led an extra horse. "Get mounted. Yer comin' with us."

"Like bloody hell I am."

"Ye will or ye'll die where ye stand." The leader aimed the pistol directly at Royal's heart.

He looked up at his coachman, who slumped against the seat, his coat covered in blood. No help would come from there.

"Unhitch the team, Oscar," the leader instructed his partner, a man with kinky brown hair and side-whiskers. "We don't want 'em comin' after us." He turned back to Royal. "Get aboard that horse. Do it now."

There was nowhere to go, no place to run. He had to go with them, but if he remained alert, perhaps he would find a chance to escape along the road.

Oscar swung down from his horse, went over and unhitched the team, which trotted off down the road. The outlaw returned, grabbed him by the front of his coat and swung him around to bind his wrists behind him. Royal seized the opportunity, swinging a fist into the man's ruddy face and knocking him several paces backward.

Royal had boxed at Oxford and later for sport. He ducked Oscar's blow and swung another punch that doubled the outlaw over, the blood of battle beginning to surge through his veins. A pistol shot rang out and both men halted, breathing hard, their fists still clenched.

The leader steadied his pistol. "Unless ye want to die right here, ye'll mind yer manners."

Oscar swore foully and spit blood into the dirt. Picking up the rope, he bound Royal's wrists behind him. As soon as Royal was securely tied, Oscar threw a punch that hit him hard in the face. A second blow knocked him to his knees.

"That's enough," the leader said. "Get him up on that horse."

"Come on, Blackie. Let me hit him a couple more times."

"I said it was enough."

As he was jerked toward the horse, Royal shook his

head to clear the buzzing in his ears. "Where are you taking me?"

Blackie grinned, his big teeth flashing. "Ye've an appointment with me boss, Bart McGrew, and he don't like ta be kept waitin'."

Thirty

Lily awakened lying on a cold stone floor. Her jaw ached, her lip hurt and her head throbbed. She moved a little and bit back a moan. Blinking into the fading light in the stone-walled room, she tried to recall what had happened.

She had been abducted.

Loomis had found out she was Tsaya. He had sent one of his henchmen to fetch her and now here she was God only knew where.

She forced herself into a sitting position, closing her eyes against the pain in her head, and leaned back against the wall to survey her surroundings. She was alone in what appeared to be a basement. Giving herself a few minutes to collect herself, she pushed shakily to her feet, stood there a moment to steady herself, then moved along the wall to explore the mostly empty room, searching for a passable way to escape.

There were small windows near the ceiling that let in a meager amount of fading sunlight. She spotted an empty crate and pulled it up to one of the windows, but discovered it was nailed tightly shut. She peered through the grimy glass, trying to figure out where she was, but there was nothing familiar about the buildings, though it looked as if she was still in London, perhaps in a manufacturing district.

The windows were too small to provide an avenue of escape and the area seemed to be deserted. Perhaps in the morning, there would be people about and she could break the glass and cry for help. With a resigned sigh, she climbed down from the crate and continued her surveillance.

There was a screened-off area to the left. She moved in that direction, walked round the screen and found a chamber pot and a table with a basin, glass and pitcher of water sitting on top. Her captor had seen to the necessities. She wondered what Loomis intended and tried not to shiver.

The minutes ticked past. Only the faint haze of dusk remained to light the basement. Fortunately, a lantern sat near where the empty crate had been, along with sulphur heads to light it. She struck the coated wooden stick against the stone floor and frowned at the smell as she lit the wick. The flickering yellow flame helped to push away the fear that churned inside her.

An hour passed and then another. She guessed it was somewhere near ten, perhaps eleven o'clock when she heard a commotion outside her door.

She gasped as the heavy wooden portal swung open and two men stood in the shadowy corridor outside, one with woolly brown side-whiskers, the other with dirty, long black hair.

"Ye've company, wench." The black-haired man shoved a bound man into the basement, hard enough that he landed facedown on the floor. "And a fancy duke, at that."

In the glow of the lantern she caught the gleam of thick blond hair. "Royal! Oh dear God!"

"Ye can't get away. Ye can try but it won't do ye any good. Ye can yell all ye want—ain't no one ta hear ye."

She had already figured that out.

"Might as well make yerself comfortable till the boss shows up in the mornin'." He laughed, slammed and locked the door, the sound reverberating across the room as Lily scrambled to kneel beside Royal.

He groaned and she saw that he had suffered several blows himself. His face was scraped, his jaw bruised and his eye beginning to swell. Clearly, he had made an effort to escape.

He rolled onto his back, his hands, tied behind him, making the task difficult. His eyes widened as he realized it was Lily who bent over him. "Lily!" He struggled against his bonds, shaking with rage, his bound hands fisting, tugging at the rope in an effort to break free. "I'll kill him! As God is my witness, I will!"

She smoothed locks of heavy blond hair back from his forehead, soothing him a little. "I'm all right. Just lie still while I untie you." He calmed a bit more, but his breathing remained rapid, telling her how angry he was.

She worked on the rope, finally managed to loosen the knots enough to free his wrists. He came to his knees in front of her, stared at her as if he couldn't believe she was actually there.

Very gently, he caught her chin and examined her

damaged face. "Who hit you? I swear I will beat him within an inch of his life."

"It might have been McGrew. I heard he was big, and this man certainly was. But that isn't important. What's important is getting out of here."

"He didn't touch you. He didn't—"

"No."

His voice gentled. "Does it hurt very badly?"

She took his hand, set his palm against her cheek. "It hurts, but not so much now that you are here."

Seated on the floor, Royal eased her into his arms, nestling her against him. "I've been such a fool." He shook his head. "This is all my fault. I never should have let you get involved. I should have known something bad would happen."

Lily told herself to move away from him. Royal belonged to someone else. Instead, she leaned closer, desperate to have his arms round her, share some of his strength. She had no idea what was going to happen. There was every chance Loomis would kill them.

He hugged her one last time, then rose to his feet. In the flickering light of the lamp, he began to prowl the basement.

"The windows are all nailed shut," she told him. "And at any rate, they are too small to get through. I thought of breaking one of them and shouting for help, but there is no one around to hear."

He grunted. "Only whoever is outside making sure we don't escape."

"I wonder how Loomis discovered we were the ones who took his money."

He returned to the place beside her and eased her

back into his arms. His lips brushed her forehead. "I don't know. We hired a lot of people. Maybe one of them overheard something, went to Loomis with the information in exchange for money."

"I don't think so. My uncle knew all of them personally. In the confidence business, a man's word is his bond. He can't make a living if he can't be trusted."

"Then perhaps Loomis threatened one of them, forced the man to talk. Somehow he put the pieces together and it led him to us."

Mentally, she ran over the list of people involved and her thoughts settled on Dottie Hobbs. Bart McGrew had seen Dottie at the house and she wouldn't be hard to find. A threat against Dottie's daughters might have forced her to speak.

"What are we going to do?"

He caught her hand, laced her fingers with his and raised them to his lips. "Wait. That's all we can do. Wait and see what Loomis has in store for us. Once we know his plans, we can figure out what to do. In the meantime, word will get out that we've been taken. People will be looking for us." He smiled softly. "After all, I am a duke."

Lily made no reply. Since the day she had fallen in love with him, she had wished with all her heart that he was not.

Sheridan Knowles knocked hard on the door to the residence belonging to Jonathan Savage. When the butler opened the door, Sherry strode into the house without waiting for permission.

He paused at the bottom of the stairs. "Where is he?"

"In his rooms, my lord, but…"

Sherry took the stairs two at a time.

"You can't go in there, my lord! Mr. Savage isn't alone!"

Sherry kept walking. He turned the handle on the bedroom door and shoved it open, walked into the bedroom.

"Sorry to bother you, old man, but Royal's in trouble and we need your help."

The bedcovers stopped moving. Jonathan cursed and the dark-haired beauty he was with ducked her head beneath the sheets.

"Give me five minutes," Jonathan growled.

"Make it three," Sherry said, striding back out in the hall. He had sent messages to the others, to Night and Quent and St. Michaels, as soon as word of the high-waymen's attack and Royal's abduction had reached him. It wasn't until Lady Tavistock had come pounding frantically at the door of his town house that he realized Loomis was behind the attack.

"Someone has kidnapped the duke!" the frail old woman had said. "You have to find him! You have to help him!" She trembled as Sherry led her over to the sofa and eased her down on the cushions.

"Tell me what happened." In reply, the countess handed him a note demanding ransom in an amount that was exactly double the money Loomis had lost on the phony stock purchase. Clearly the events were connected. The last line read: *No police or the duke is dead.*

Sherry took hold of the countess's frail, trembling hand. "It's all right, my lady, we'll find him. That I promise." And he had prayed with everything in him that they would.

Now, standing in Savage's drawing room, he turned at the sound of boot steps, looked over to see his friend in a shirt and riding breeches striding into the room, his black hair still mussed from his interrupted tumble.

"What's happened?" Jonathan asked.

"I'll explain everything on the way to Night's. My carriage is right out front."

They left the house and headed for the meeting he had set up with the others. Certain Loomis was behind the abduction, and in possession of the note naming the spot where the ransom money was to be paid, Sherry was convinced, if they put their heads together, they could figure out where the man was holding Royal.

Jack Moran paced back and forth across the small apartment he and Molly shared.

"You might as well stop pacing," Molly said. "It won't do a lick of good."

"If he hurts her…if the whoreson harms one hair on her pretty head—I swear I will cut off his bollocks and stuff them down his bloody throat."

Molly walked over and put her arms round Jack's neck. "We just played him a little wrong, is all. We thought he'd take his losses and that would be the end of it. Who'd 'a thought he'd go after Lily?"

"I should have known. He's bloody Dick Flynn, ain't he? I should have known he'd take it personal."

"You may as well stop blaming yourself. The important thing now is how do we get her back."

Molly had stopped by to see Lily at the hat shop earlier that evening. When she arrived at the alley door, she found it wide open. There were signs of a struggle and blood on the jamb. Lily was gone, but she hadn't let them take her without a fight.

"We'll find a way to get her back, luv," Jack promised. "I've got every bloke in the mob and every other sharper I know working to find her. Sooner or later, one of them will stumble onto something."

"I bloody well hope it's sooner," Molly said.

"So do I, luv. So do I."

Lily and Royal huddled on the rough stone floor, their arms wrapped around each other, sharing their body warmth. Though both of them were exhausted, neither was able to sleep. Their future was too uncertain.

"There's something I need to say to you, Lily." Royal eased a little away. "Something I've wanted to say for a very long time."

His serious expression made her heart start to pound. "What is it, Royal?"

"I love you, Lily. I can't say when it first happened. It just seems like I've always loved you. I wanted to tell you a dozen times, but the way things were…" He shook his head. "The way things were, it just didn't seem right."

Her eyes filled. "I love you, too, Royal. I think I fell in love with you the first time I saw you—that day you rode up on your big gray stallion and rescued me in the snow. No matter what happens, I don't regret a single moment I've spent with you."

He drew her closer. "If we get…when we get out of here, I'm breaking my engagement—as I should have done before."

She was gripped by a wild surge of hope and a jolt

of fear for Royal. "You have so much to lose. If Jocelyn refuses to cry off, the scandal will be unbearable. Her father might even sue for breach of promise. You can't afford that, Royal."

"I don't care about the scandal or the lawsuit or anything else. Jocelyn doesn't love me and I don't love her. In the eyes of God, you are already my wife." He reached out and touched her cheek. "The moment I saw you in this awful place—the terrible fear I felt when I realized your life was in danger—that is the moment I understood. That is the instant I realized what was truly important."

The tears in her eyes began to slip down her cheeks. "Royal…"

"The money isn't worth it. Not even the pledge I made to my father. I can't do something every fiber of my being tells me not to."

She brushed at the wetness on her face. "I know how much your word means, Royal. If you break your vow, part of you will always feel guilty."

"Perhaps. Even if that is so, it doesn't matter. Nothing matters but the love I feel for you, Lily." He took hold of her icy hands and smiled into her face. "Once this is over and I am free to wed, I will ask the question that is in my heart."

She swallowed past the ache in her throat. "And I will give you the answer I long to give."

Royal leaned over and very tenderly kissed her, careful of her swollen lip and battered face. It was a sweet, innocent kiss, yet even in the damp, musty basement her heartbeat quickened. Under different circumstances, the kiss might have led to more, to touching, to caressing, to making love.

"We had better stop," Royal said gruffly. "I am beginning to think of what I would do to you if this were our wedding night, and that is not going to happen here."

Arousal trickled through her, along with a thread of curiosity. "If it were our wedding night," she said softly, "what would you do?" Even with his battered eye and the purpling bruise on his jaw, he was the handsomest man she had ever seen.

She moistened her lips and his gaze heated. He took her hand, turned it over and began to trace small circles in her palm. "First, I would remove your wedding garments, one piece at a time."

A little tingle went through her, radiating from her palm.

"I would take my time undressing you, admiring your beautiful body. Once I had you naked, I would kiss you all over, kiss you in places that would make us both tremble."

Her mouth went dry. They might not live long enough to have a wedding night. She wanted to experience it now.

"What else would you do?" she asked almost too softly to hear.

His eyes darkened. The gold in them seemed to glitter. His hand moved over the bodice of her gown, cupped the fullness and squeezed gently. "I would take each of your lovely breasts into my mouth and I would suckle you, taste your firm little nipples." Which tightened and began to throb. He pinched the ends through the fabric and she moaned at the slice of pleasure that cut through her.

"What...what else?"

His breathing quickened as he began to enjoy the game. "I would carry you over to the bed and set you down on the edge of the mattress. I would part your pretty legs and kneel between them. I would lick and taste you…here." He found the spot between her thighs and pressed, and she felt the heat even through her petticoats. "I would tease and stroke you until you found your pleasure."

She trembled, her heart pounding wildly. Every part of her was throbbing. "Would you come inside me then?"

"I would want to." His voice sounded rusty. "Perhaps I would fondle you a little more before I entered you."

"No…" She shook her head. "I would need you right then. I would want to feel you. I would want you to fill me completely." She reached for him, felt the thick hard ridge pressing against the front of his trousers, and Royal's whole body tightened.

"If that was your wish, then I would come inside you. I would fill you so deeply we would both be as one."

She hadn't realized his hand was beneath her skirts, hadn't felt him part her drawers until his fingers slid inside her. Lily softly moaned.

"Then I would take you with fierce, pounding urgency. I would take you until you cried out in fulfillment."

His words and his talented hands had her suspended on the edge. In seconds, his skillful stroking sent her over the precipice into blissful abandon. Lily cried out and clung to him, shaking all over, caught in thrall by the sweet, roiling sensations.

Royal leaned over and very softly kissed her. "Only after you reached fulfillment a second time would I allow myself to join you in release."

Lily slumped against him, pleasure still coursing

through her. She hadn't meant for things to go so far and yet she wasn't sorry. Not when their life might end at any moment.

"There is so much to show you," he said softly. "So much pleasure to be found…once you are mine."

But that day might never come and both of them knew it.

Lily shivered in the darkness.

Exhausted but content in a way he had never been before, Royal eased Lily from his arms. The first light of dawn was breaking outside the window. Quietly, he crossed to the windows and climbed atop the crate to look outside in search of a landmark that might help him discover where they were being held.

To his amazement, he recognized the tower above Night's armaments factory. They were somewhere near Tooley Street, not far from the docks.

"What do you see?" Lily asked from behind him, her voice still edged with sleep. At least one of them had gotten some rest. He smiled to himself, happy to have given her that gift last night.

"I believe our friend Loomis has a keen sense of irony." He pointed out the window. "That tower is on the roof of Nightingale's armaments plant."

Her pretty green eyes widened. "You think he chose this place as a sort of just-deserts for the crime of duping him?"

"Probably." He stared back out the window. "It will soon be full light. People will be going to work. We're pretty far away, but we could break the glass, hope someone might hear us shouting."

"You could try it," came a deep voice from behind him. "If you do, one of my men will come in here and shoot you."

Royal turned, spotted Preston Loomis and jumped down from the crate. A huge, beefy, rough-looking man dressed in expensively tailored clothes stood beside him. It had to be Bart McGrew.

"I imagine neither of you is feeling quite so smug this morning."

Standing next to Royal, Lily stiffened. "Clearly, we underestimated you—Mr. Flynn."

A nerve ticked in Loomis's cheek. "Dick Flynn died a long time ago. It's Preston Loomis you need to fear at the moment." He studied Lily, his silver eyebrows drawing together. "So this is the real you. Too bad. I found myself quite drawn to you as Tsaya. So dark and exotic, beautiful in a strange, ethereal sort of way. Now you are merely a woman."

Loomis turned toward the big oaf of a man in the doorway. "But perhaps my friend McGrew might enjoy a taste of you."

Royal fought a blinding wave of fury. He stepped in front of Lily. "I'm the one you want, Loomis—the only one. Lily was just an innocent party."

"Not so very innocent, as I recall." He returned his attention to Lily. "I am curious, though, how was it that you knew about Medela?"

Lily flicked Royal a sideways glance, warning him not to mention the others. "It was merely an accident," she told Loomis. "As the two of us inquired of your interests and your past, her name came up. It was said you were intrigued by her. The idea of Tsaya came from that."

It was mostly a lie. Lily was protecting her uncle and his friends. Royal's admiration for her grew. Whatever happened, he knew for certain the decision he had made last night was the right one. He prayed he would have the chance to make her his.

"Since we are airing our curiosities," Royal said, "I would like to know how your man here, McGrew, came to be involved with the highwaymen roaming the countryside near Bransford Castle."

The huge man grinned. "Come to me whilst the boss was there scamming the old duke. Thought how ripe the place was for the pluckin'."

Loomis cast a contemptuous glare at McGrew. "You knew I wouldn't approve of something so risky. Now that I know what you have been up to, you are finished with it. Is that understood?"

McGrew studied his big feet. "Aye, boss."

"Besides, we shall be leaving England once this is over. It is too dangerous for us here now."

McGrew just grunted.

"What do you want from us, Loomis?" Royal asked.

"Why, I want my money, of course. Isn't it always about the money?"

"I used to think so. Not anymore."

"Well, as of yet I am not that enlightened. I want all you took from me and more. Your aunt, Lady Tavistock, has been contacted. If the ransom is paid, perhaps I will let you go."

So Aunt Agatha was also in peril. It made his stomach knot to think of any harm coming to the frail old woman who had come to mean so much to him. As for letting them go…clearly, it wasn't the man's intention. Loomis wasn't foolish enough to leave witnesses who could see him and Bart McGrew hang.

"My aunt will pay," Royal said. "She is not in the financial straits that I am."

"Well, that is good news."

"I ask that you do not harm her."

"I don't see any need for that." He tilted his head toward the door, motioning for McGrew to step out of the room. "And while we await that occurrence, I shall leave you." His gaze fixed on Lily. "*Adieu,* Miss Moran." He made a mocking bow to Royal. *"Your Grace."*

And then he was gone.

Royal turned to Lily and saw the pallor of her face.

"He is going to kill us," she said, reflecting his very thoughts.

Royal eased her into his arms. "Not if we don't give him the chance."

Thirty-One

~~~❦❧~~~

The plan was simple. They had spent hours trying to come up with something better, but their options were sorely limited. Finally, Lily had convinced Royal to let her lie on the floor and pretend to have fallen ill. Royal would shout for help and when the guard came into the room, he would hit the man over the head with the board he'd pried off the crate.

The plan wasn't particularly inventive, but Lily thought it might just work.

"Are you certain you can do this?" Royal asked.

She only laughed. "When I was with my uncle, I used to pretend to have fits to get people to throw us coins. Just promise me you will forget what I look like while I am doing this."

Royal kissed her cheek. "There isn't a single thing I ever want to forget about you, sweeting."

Lily smiled. Lying down on the stone floor, she nodded that she was ready, and Royal started shouting.

"Something's wrong with Miss Moran!" He pounded

frantically on the door. "She needs help! Please! I think she might be dying! Someone please help her!" It took a little more pounding and more of Royal's shouting demands before the sound of heavy boots rang out in the corridor outside the basement.

As soon as the lock began to turn, Lily took a deep breath and started shaking. She rolled her eyes back in her head until the whites were all that showed, opened her mouth and let her tongue hang out. She knew how awful she looked—as if a demon had possessed her. As if she suffered some kind of unearthly fit.

The iron latch lifted. The door burst open and the man with the woolly side-whiskers ran into the room. For an instant, he stood transfixed at the sight of her writhing, squirming and gagging on the floor. In that instant, Royal stepped out from behind the door and slammed the heavy board, full force, on the top of his head. The guard went down like a sack of grain.

"Come on!" Royal grabbed Lily's hand and hauled her to her feet. They raced for the doorway and scrambled out of the room into the passage. Tugging Lily behind him, Royal made it only a few feet into the dimly lit corridor when he jerked to a halt in front of the man with the long black hair.

A pistol pointed at Royal's chest. "Now, where do ye think yer going?" The gun held steady. He peered over Royal's shoulder toward the door to the basement room. "Hey, Oscar, you all right?"

A groan was the outlaw's answer.

Standing behind Royal, Lily could feel the tension in his tall, hard body as he weighed his options. She thought he might have attacked his opponent if Oscar hadn't come out of the room behind them just then, rubbing his head and swearing.

"Go on! Get back in that room!" the black-haired man commanded, the pistol held firm.

Sick and disheartened, Lily turned and started back the way she had come, brushing past Oscar, who caught hold of her arm.

"Hey, Blackie—whatcha say we keep this 'un for a while?"

"Not a chance!" With a growl of rage, Royal charged. Drawing back a fist, he hit Oscar so hard he went flying against the wall. "Leave her alone!"

Coming up behind the men, Blackie slammed the barrel of his pistol against the back of Royal's head.

"Royal!" Lily screamed as Oscar grabbed her again and Blackie hauled Royal through the basement door and dumped him nearly unconscious onto the hard stone floor.

"Bring the wench," Blackie said. "I could use a bit of entertainment."

"Lily!" Royal staggered to his feet, but it was too late. The door slammed closed. Oscar used the heavy iron key to turn the lock and shoved it into his pocket.

"Royal!" Lily struggled, but the arm around her waist only tightened.

"Ye might as well take it easy, pet. One way or the other, me and Blackie's gonna have ye."

Royal pounded on the door and shouted her name, and for an instant, Lily broke free. She stumbled and nearly went down.

"I said, bring the wench!" Blackie commanded as Oscar hauled her back to her feet.

"Better do what he tells ye, pet. Blackie's got a real

mean temper." Shoving her in front of him, Oscar urged her down the passage.

Behind her, Royal's shouting had ceased. Inwardly, Lily smiled. He had found the gift she had left for him.

As frightened as she was, she wasn't nearly as afraid as she'd been just moments before.

Royal grabbed the iron key Lily had shoved beneath the door. *My sweet little pickpocket.* His heart squeezed hard with love and fear for her.

Fighting the fury that threatened to swamp him, he waited for the men to move far enough down the passage that the basement door was out of their sight, then stuck the key into the lock and turned. He grabbed the board he had fashioned as a weapon, opened the door and stepped out into the corridor. Men's laughter echoed farther down the hall, along with Lily's cries of protest.

A fresh wave of fury hit him. With iron resolve, he headed silently in her direction. He might not live past the next few minutes, but he would die before he would let them hurt Lily.

Up ahead, a door appeared near a turn in the corridor. He listened, but no sound came from inside. Moving quietly onward, he paused when a second door appeared. It wasn't tightly closed and in the glow of a lamp, he caught a glimpse of the men inside.

"We'll start with yer shoes and stockings," Blackie commanded. "Ye can take 'em off first. Then ye can pull up them skirts and take off your drawers."

Royal fought to hang on to his temper. He needed his wits about him if they were going to survive. He raised his makeshift weapon. Blackie was armed. If he could get hold of the man's pistol they might have a chance.

He took a breath, prepared to rush into the room. A soft footfall reached him. Royal heard the sound of male voices coming from farther down the passage. He pressed himself into the shadows, his senses, already on full alert, kicking up even more.

"I hear something," a man whispered, and the familiar deep cadence of Sherry Knowles's voice nearly undid him.

Royal felt a powerful sweep of relief as he silently made his way down the hall. "Thank God you came!" He gripped his friend's arm and Sherry gripped his.

"Royal! Hell's teeth! Are you all right?"

He brought his finger to his lips and pointed down the passage. "They've got Lily. Come on."

A few feet behind Sherry, Savage, Nightingale and Quent moved quietly forward. Each of them carried a gun. Quent pulled a second weapon from the inside of his coat, a small pocket pistol, and pressed it into Royal's hand. "She's your lady. You'll need this."

Royal just nodded. They moved into position as he reached the door. Raising a booted foot, he steeled himself, kicked open the door and leveled the revolver at Blackie.

"Back away from her," he said with deadly calm. "Do it now."

Lily let her skirts fall back into place, her hands shaking.

Sherry aimed his weapon at Oscar. "Step away from the girl. Move over there by the wall."

Lily backed away from the men. Her face was the color of paper, and Royal itched to pull the trigger.

Oscar did as he was told, his eyes darting back and forth between Royal and the men.

"Very carefully," Savage ordered, his gun trained on Blackie, "pull that pistol out of your belt and set it on the floor."

At the thump of the weapon landing on the stones, Lily made a strangled sound and raced to Royal, who caught her in his arms. She was shaking. Her distress stirred his anger all over again. "Are you all right, my love?"

She looked up at him, her eyes glistening with tears. "I am fine now that you are here."

"We need something to tie them up," Quent said, moving past Royal into the room. In minutes, he had located a length of rope. Drawing a knife from his boot, he cut it in half and tossed the other half to Night. "Make yourself useful."

Nightingale chuckled and set to work on Oscar, binding his hands behind him while Quent tied Blackie's wrists good and tight.

"All right," Royal commanded the outlaws as soon as the task was completed, "I want you both to move very slowly down the hall toward the entrance." He flicked a glance at Sherry, who backed out of the room, leading the way. Savage and Night escorted the outlaws along the passage toward the stairs and Royal and Lily fell in behind them.

They climbed the rickety wooden stairs to a dusty, board-floored entry that led out the front door of what appeared to be an abandoned warehouse. They had just started for the horses when a fancy black carriage rolled to a stop in the street.

"It's Loomis and McGrew!" Royal warned.

"It's a trap!" Blackie shouted before the barrel of Savage's gun slammed down on the back of his head.

Night dragged the other outlaw behind a row of empty barrels, but it was too late.

Already out of the carriage, Loomis ducked behind the wheel while McGrew pulled a pistol and fired. Quent and Sherry both fired back, their gunshots echoing against the buildings. McGrew returned fire, his shots pinging against the brick walls, but Royal and Lily, Savage and the others had all taken cover and the shots fell harmlessly around them.

Savage pulled off several rounds and so did Nightingale. Royal took careful aim, fired the pocket pistol and the huge man went down. Several more gunshots slammed into the carriage near where Loomis was hiding.

"Hold your fire!" Loomis shouted. "I'm coming out!"

Royal kept his weapon aimed at the mustached man. "Step into the open, Loomis. Put your hands in the air."

Shoving his hands into the air, Loomis rounded the carriage and moved into the middle of the street. Royal and the others came out of their positions of cover, their pistols aimed straight at him, Night pushing Oscar along in front of him.

Once it was clear the men weren't going to kill him, Loomis turned and hurried to his fallen friend.

He knelt over McGrew's huge, unmoving body, tears welling in his eyes. "You've killed him. You've killed Bart."

"No, Loomis," Royal said as he and Lily approached. "You were the one who killed him. You did it years ago when you decided to steal other people's money."

Loomis made no reply. For several moments he

remained over the body of his friend, then woodenly, he walked away and simply stood there.

It was over.

"I'll fetch the other one," Savage volunteered. Gun in hand, he headed back toward the warehouse where Blackie lay moaning just outside the front door.

"How did you know where to find us?" Royal asked Sherry, who grinned, showing a couple of crooked bottom teeth.

"Your aunt Agatha. She got a ransom note telling her how much the kidnappers wanted and where to deliver the money. She did as she was instructed—except that she wasn't alone. The four of us followed her. We waited for the man Loomis sent to pick up the money and—with a little persuasion—he told us where you were being held. I didn't realize Lily had been abducted, as well."

Sherry leaned over and kissed Lily's cheek. "I'm glad you're safe, sweeting."

"Thank you for coming," she said. "Royal is lucky to have such wonderful friends." She moved toward Royal and his arms closed around her.

"It's time someone went for the police," Quent said, turning to round up his horse. He had taken only a couple of steps when a commotion down the street drew their attention. A hansom cab, traveling at breakneck speed and rocking perilously back and forth on its two wheels, came to a sliding halt in front of the warehouse. A police wagon followed, overflowing with uniformed police.

Jack Moran leaped out of the hansom, spotted Lily and started running, followed by a frazzled-looking Molly Daniels.

"Lily! Lily!"

"I'm all right," she said, letting the two of them envelop her in a big worried hug. "Bart McGrew is dead and Loomis has been captured."

"Praise God," Molly said, rolling her eyes toward the heavens.

One of the policemen spotted McGrew's body lying in the street and headed in that direction, while several more rushed toward Royal and the group in front of the warehouse.

"All right, now, what the devil is going on?" one of the policemen said.

"It's a long story, Officer," Royal told him. "I'm the Duke of Bransford. Miss Moran and I were abducted against our will by the man lying in the street and this man here." Sherry shoved Loomis forward. Just then Night and Savage appeared with the outlaws in tow.

Royal looked at the policeman, whose eyebrows had climbed nearly to his forehead. "My friends and I will be happy to explain everything."

"I should say so," the officer said grumpily and for the first time, Royal smiled.

Thirty-Two

For the next half hour, Lily, Royal and the others explained to the police everything that had happened over the past three days, leaving out, of course, any mention of Tsaya and the swindle. They weren't worried about Loomis bringing it up. It would only add more fuel to the case against him.

When the conversation came to a close, McGrew's body was loaded into the police wagon and Loomis was taken away in chains.

Lily turned to her uncle, who stood with his arm around Molly. "How did you know where to find me, Uncle Jack?"

Molly answered for him. "Jack put the word out on the street, said he'd pay a good sum for any information about the kidnapping of his niece, or where Preston Loomis might be holding her."

"'Ol Mickey Doyle came through for me," Jack added proudly. "Wouldn't even take the money—not when you were my kin. Said two or three others had helped him figure it out. A good bunch, they are."

The chatter continued, all of them grateful for Lily and Royal's safety and Loomis's arrest. But Lily was rapidly tiring, which Royal seemed to guess.

"If you all don't mind, I'd like to see Miss Moran home." His gaze found hers across the distance between them and her heart swelled with love for him.

"Afterward," he said, moving closer, his eyes on her face, "there is a matter of grave importance I need to attend."

Freshly bathed and dressed in clean clothing, Royal knocked on the door of the Caulfields' mansion. He had sent word ahead, asking to speak to both Jocelyn and her parents.

"Do come in, Your Grace," the butler said. "I am afraid Mr. and Mrs. Caulfield are out at the moment, but Miss Caulfield awaits you in the drawing room.

Royal took a deep breath. He wasn't sure what sort of histrionics he would be facing. He just knew he would do whatever it took to be free to marry Lily.

Jocelyn rose from the sofa as he walked in. She was dressed more somberly than he would have expected, in a gown of dark green velvet and a simple white lace cap.

"Your Grace," she said, dropping into a curtsy.

"You're looking very well," he replied, but then she always did. "I appreciate your seeing me on such short notice."

She glanced down, seemed inordinately nervous. "I realize how upset you must be. A note was hardly the way to handle the matter. I would have spoken to you in person, but you had already left for the country."

He frowned, not quite following the conversation. "I beg your pardon? Did you say you sent me a note?"

"Why, yes… To Bransford Castle. I assumed you had received it. I thought that was the reason for your visit."

"No, I'm afraid that isn't why I am here. Before we begin, why don't you tell me what was in the note."

"Oh dear."

She had forgotten to offer him a seat or any sort of refreshment. Instead, both of them remained standing, which was fine with him.

Jocelyn bit her lip. She subtly squared her shoulders. "Well, I suppose there is no easy way to say it. Therefore I shall simply come out with it. I am ending our engagement, Your Grace. I realize you will be losing a great deal of money. I know about the promise you made your father, but there is simply no help for it. You see, I have fallen in love with another man."

He stood there stunned. "You are breaking our engagement?"

"I have already informed my parents. They, of course, were extremely distressed, but in time they will come to accept matters as they stand."

"You are ending our betrothal," he repeated dumbly, his heart beginning to pound.

"That is correct. So you see, you aren't really breaking your vow. You cannot marry me if I refuse to marry you."

Elation poured through him and he fought not to grin. "No, I don't suppose I could."

Her dark eyebrows drew slightly together. "So you are not terribly upset?"

He managed to keep his relief from showing. Insulting the lady was never part of his plan. "It isn't as if we were ever in love."

"No, it isn't. In truth, there is a very good chance you are in love with someone else." She cast him a look from beneath her thick dark lashes. "I realize money is an issue but I thought, perhaps, now that you are free, you might wish to marry my cousin."

Something seemed to lodge in his chest. "I've come to realize money isn't the most important thing. As to marrying your cousin..." He did grin then. "I would wish that very much." He caught her by surprise when he leaned over and kissed her very soundly on the cheek. "I didn't love you before, Jocelyn, but I love you now. You have just blessed me with the most precious gift I have ever received."

Jocelyn returned his grin. "Then we are of a mind?"

"We are, indeed. If I may ask, who is the lucky man?"

"Christopher Barclay. I believe you may know him."

"We've met on occasion. He seems a good man."

"A very good man." She glanced away, then looked back at him. "In the past few months, I, too, have come to understand that money and social position aren't the most important things. It is a hard lesson for someone like me."

"It is difficult for most of us."

"Then perhaps, one day, after all of us are wed, we might become friends."

Royal smiled. "I would like that, Miss Caulfield. I would like that very much."

Royal left the house with one thing on his mind—asking Lily to marry him. Though the afternoon was almost over and dusk beginning to fall, he didn't intend to wait. He had waited far too long already.

As his carriage rolled to a stop in Harken Lane, he saw that the light was still on in Lily's hat shop, her slender figure moving behind the counter inside. Royal wiped his damp hands on his trousers, took a deep breath and opened the door. At the sound of the bell, she whirled to face him.

"Jocelyn is marrying Christopher Barclay," he blurted out, not at all the speech he had planned. "You are mine, sweeting. Will you marry me?"

There was a woman at the counter and she stood there stunned as Lily let out a very unladylike cry of joy, lifted her skirts, rounded the counter and rushed straight into his arms.

"I love you, Royal Dewar, I love you! And I can't wait to marry you!" And then he was kissing her and they were laughing and when he looked up, the woman at the counter was wiping tears from her eyes.

He was once more engaged—this time to the right woman.

And unlike before, this time he couldn't wait to get his bride to the altar.

Thirty-Three

The wedding at the end of May was a simple affair—at least by ducal standards. Neither Lily nor Royal had wished to wait an entire month, but Aunt Agatha had said that Lily deserved a wedding befitting the duchess she would become and insisted on paying for the entire affair.

During that month, the gardens at Bransford Castle had been trimmed and planted and returned to the way they were before they had fallen into shambles. Yellow crocus and purple pansies bloomed along the pathways and all of the trees bore lovely green leaves.

Standing on a snowy linen runner placed between rows of white lawn chairs, Lily stood next to her uncle as the wedding march began.

"Are you ready, little girl?" Jack asked, offering her his arm.

Lily gave him a teary smile, grateful to have him back in her life. "More than ready." The month she had waited to be married had been the longest of her life.

She rested a white-gloved hand on the sleeve of his

coat and they started down the aisle. As she gazed out
over the group of people who had come to help them
celebrate the marriage, she felt a surge of gratitude.
Silently, she thanked Royal's friends and family who
had accepted her so readily as the woman who would
become his wife.

She felt only a little shaky as she continued down the
aisle, passing the rows of guests. All of Royal's closest
friends were there, the Oarsmen, they called themselves:
the Earl of Nightingale, wickedly handsome Jonathan
Savage, ever-serious Quentin Garrett, charming Dillon
St. Michaels and dashing Sheridan Knowles.

Rule Dewar was there, grinning as she passed. Only
Lord Reese, Royal's middle brother, was missing, still
away at war.

A little farther down the aisle, she spotted Molly
Daniels seated next to Tommy Cox. Royal had given
Tommy a job at the castle and he and Mugs were
thrilled to be back in the country. Lily was thrilled to
have them there.

Tommy waved as they passed, while Molly smiled
and dabbed at her eyes.

Jocelyn was there, a surprise, but a welcome one. She
sat next to handsome, dark-haired Christopher Barclay,
her fiancé. That morning, she had sought Lily out the
moment she had arrived at the house.

"Royal invited us," she had said nervously, a rare occurrence for Jo. "You and I are family. I hope you don't
mind my coming."

Lily's eyes welled. She leaned over and hugged her
cousin. "I don't mind. I am delighted you are here."

Jocelyn stayed in the duchess's suite to help Lily

change into her wedding dress: a cream silk gown she had fashioned for herself, the skirt amazingly full, dropping into a vee at the waist, the square-cut bodice decorated with clusters of lace and tiny pearls. A gauzy net veil covered the pale curls resting on her shoulders, held in place by a small cap of cream lace dotted with the same gleaming pearls.

The altar loomed in front of her. Standing to the right was the handsomest man she had ever seen, the golden-haired duke who would soon be her husband. The tender smile he wore made her heart swell with love for him.

Uncle Jack paused in front of the altar, kissed her cheek and gave her over to the man she would wed. Lily cast her uncle a last warm smile, then her eyes filled with tears as Royal took her gloved hand and lifted it to his lips.

Together they turned to face the bishop.

"Dearly beloved. We are gathered together this day in the sight of God and in the presence of these witnesses to join together His Grace, Royal Holland Dewar, seventh Duke of Bransford, and this woman, Lily Amelia Moran, in the bonds of holy matrimony…"

Lily barely heard the words that followed. Her gaze and her heart were filled with Royal and the life they would share. She made the proper responses in all the right places at all the right times, thank God, pledged her troth and heard Royal's deep voice pledging his, and then it was over.

"You may kiss your bride," said the bishop. And when Royal took her in his arms and kissed her as if he would never let her go, she had no doubt that she well and truly belonged to him.

And tonight she would become his wife.

"I love you, Duchess," he said as they walked together down the aisle toward the wedding feast that had been prepared for them. "You're worth more to me than the entire Bransford dukedom."

Lily's heart swelled. She looked into his beautiful golden eyes and knew that he meant every word.

Epilogue

‹•∞•›

Bransford Castle, three months later

Lily snuggled closer to Royal's warmth. They had made love earlier and now she lay drowsily tucked into his side in the big ducal bed, where he insisted she sleep every night.

She felt his hand smooth over her tumbled pale blond hair and her eyes drifted closed. She knew she should get up. There was always a great deal to do, but fall was in the air and she was thinking that perhaps she would indulge herself a little this morning.

She snuggled closer, her hand skimming over the muscles on his chest. He felt so good, so solid and incredibly male. Her hand went lower, smoothed over his flat stomach, and her eyes widened. He was heavily aroused, his erection pressing against the sheets. Desire stirred as she imagined him making love to her once more before they were forced to meet the day.

"I believe we are of the same mind, Duchess," he said

gruffly as he came up over her. Then a firm knock sounded at the door. Royal groaned as the delicious possibility of lovemaking slipped away.

"Mr. Marlowe is here, Your Grace," said Greaves the butler through the door.

"Damnation." Royal sat up in bed, raking a hand through his hair.

Lily came fully awake and also sat up. "You've an appointment this morning?"

He leaned over and pressed a quick kiss on her mouth. "One I managed to forget. You're a beautiful distraction, Duchess, but a distraction just the same." Swinging his long legs over the side of the bed, he grabbed his dressing gown off the chair and slipped it on while Lily pulled on her blue silk wrapper.

"Mr. Marlowe? Isn't he the man you hired several months ago to oversee the brewery?"

He nodded, cinched the sash on his robe. "He's bringing me a six-month progress report."

Lily knew Royal's Swansdowne Ale was becoming more and more popular. In the past few weeks, he had been forced to hire several more employees just to keep up with the demand.

He flashed her a heated glance. "I guess what I had in mind will have to wait until tonight."

She reached toward him, ran a hand over the lapel of his dressing gown. "Or perhaps this afternoon," she teased with a hint of mischief that made his tawny eyes darken.

"I shall hold you to that, Duchess."

She yawned behind her hand, turned and headed for her own suite of rooms to dress for the day. "I needed to get up anyway. I promised myself I would answer Jocelyn's letter this morning."

In a hugely extravagant wedding, her cousin had married Christopher Barclay two months after Lily's marriage to Royal. In a recent letter she had written,

> I love being married to Christopher. He is ever attendant to my wishes, though when he sets his mind to something, he can be quite stubborn. Odd how that only makes him more attractive. He wants a son, he says, and he has devoted himself very thoroughly and entirely satisfactorily to making that happen. You shall be the first to know, dear cousin, should that blessed event occur.

Lily smiled, wondering which of them would conceive a child first, for certainly her own handsome husband also devoted himself to that endeavor.

Lily heard Royal's voice as she disappeared into her suite.

"Show Mr. Marlowe into my study," he instructed the butler. "See to his refreshment and tell him I shall be down very shortly."

"As you wish, Your Grace. And I shall send George up to help you dress." Royal watched the old man hurry off down the hall, far more fit than he appeared. George Middleton, his valet, appeared a few moments later as Royal finished shaving then wiped the soap and water from his face.

"Pick something simple, will you, George? I am in a hurry."

"Of course, Your Grace."

A few minutes later, dressed in a white shirt and brown trousers, a light woolen waistcoat and velvet-collared jacket, he headed downstairs.

Edwin Marlowe sat in a leather chair in the study, a lean man, impeccably groomed, with intelligent hazel eyes. He came to his feet as Royal walked in.

"Sorry to keep you waiting," Royal said with a smile. "I take refuge in the fact I am still a relatively new bridegroom."

"I can well understand, Your Grace. I have met your lovely new duchess."

The men sat down and chatted amiably for a while, then Marlowe retrieved the huge leather-bound volume he had brought with him and placed it on the desk.

"I am pleased to be the bearer of very good news, Your Grace."

Royal looked up at him. "So the brewery is doing as well as we expected."

"Not exactly, sir." He grinned. "Swansdowne is doing stupendously better than we ever could have imagined. In London, your ale is all the rage. They call it the nectar of the gods. Every pub in the city is demanding to increase their supply."

Royal felt a thread of satisfaction, followed by a leap of excitement. He had been right to begin the brewery. And now all his efforts were truly paying off. "We'll need to convert more of our fields to barley."

Marlowe nodded. "In the meantime, we'll have to buy grain from other growers."

"And the brewery is making enough that we can afford to do that?"

"More than enough. I don't believe you have yet

grasped the scope of your success, Your Grace. The Swansdowne Brewery is going to make you a very wealthy man. In fact, you are already reaping incredible profits."

Royal just sat there. It seemed they were well on the road to rebuilding Bransford Castle and the dukedom's fortune. He couldn't help thinking how proud his father would be.

And how thankful he was that he had followed his heart and married Lily, the woman he loved above all things and with whom he wished to share his good fortune.

For the next half hour, they made plans for increased production and distribution of the ale, and scheduled a meeting in London with his marketing manager to formulate a sales campaign. They were just finishing their discussion when a familiar soft knock tapped at the study door.

Royal walked over and opened it, not surprised to see his pretty wife, looking delectable and tempting, standing in the hallway.

"I am sorry to bother you, darling, but your brother Reese has arrived home unexpectedly." The worried look on her face told him something was wrong.

He turned to Marlowe. "I'm afraid we'll have to continue this at our meeting in the city. I appreciate all you have done."

Marlowe made a slight bow of his head. "I look forward to seeing you there."

As soon as the man disappeared down the hall, Lily caught Royal's arm. "Reese has been injured, Royal. His leg was damaged by cannon fire. He is home for good, darling. But it is clear he is not happy about it."

Royal took Lily's hand and gave it a gentle squeeze. "Well, then, we shall simply have to find a way to make him happy."

Hand in hand, they walked into the drawing room where Reese sat waiting. Tall and raven-haired, with the same intense blue eyes as Rule, Reese picked up the silver-headed cane lying next to him on the sofa and shoved himself to his feet.

"It's good to see you, Royal."

"Welcome home, brother." Royal strode toward him, clasped his shoulders and leaned in for a brotherly hug. "It's been far too long since we heard from you. All of us had begun to worry." No letters had arrived, not since a few months after the wedding. Royal had tried to discover what had happened to his brother, but had simply been told his location was unknown. All of them had begun to fear the worst.

"I'm home," Reese said, "as our father wished. Though I have no idea what to do with myself now that I am here. I imagine the old man is grinning as he peers down on us from heaven."

Royal laughed, glad to see that Reese, though not joyous, didn't seem quite as morose as Royal had feared. "You've met my wife."

He flashed her a brief smile. "Your very beautiful and charming wife. Congratulations. I can tell by the way you look at her that you are happy. Father must have chosen well."

Royal's gaze flicked to Lily, whose gaze flashed to his. Apparently none of Royal's letters had reached Reese, either. "It's a very long story. We'll tell you all about it at supper. In the meantime, it is your story we wish to hear."

And so Royal poured each of them a refreshment and they all sat down. For the next half hour, Reese talked of the war in the Crimea and the battles with the Russians and the grapeshot that had shattered a portion of his leg. He spoke of the months he had spent in a foreign hospital, unable to remember his own name. Once he had recovered enough to return to his regiment, he had been forced to leave the cavalry because of his injured leg.

"But you are feeling well now?" Lily asked.

Reese nodded. "Aside from a limp and a stiff leg that pains me on occasion, I am fine."

Royal took a sip of his brandy. "I presume you'll be moving into Briarwood, as father wished."

He sighed. "It's time, I suppose. I shall probably make the most inept farmer ever to grow a crop."

But Reese was the sort who excelled at anything he wanted to do. Athletic and intelligent, he would learn the business of farming—if that was truly his wish.

Still, there were the memories to conquer. Briarwood had once been the place Reese intended to make his home. An inheritance from their maternal grandfather, it was the place he had planned to live after he was married and starting to raise a family.

A military career did not preclude his taking a wife. He'd been in love with a girl named Elizabeth Clemens, the daughter of an earl who lived on a nearby estate. But her parents believed she was too young to wed. She would wait for him, she had promised when Reese was called to duty.

Instead, when he returned home on his first leave, he found his beloved married to another man.

Reese had never truly recovered from her betrayal. Nor had he ever forgiven her.

"One thing I can promise," Royal said to him. "If you grow barley, you'll have a buyer for all you can produce."

One of Reese's black eyebrows went up. "That sounds interesting. From the grin on your face, it would appear Bransford lands have once again begun to prosper. In truth, I am not surprised."

Clearly his brother was happy for his success, but Royal could see the resentment in Reese's blue eyes that life—and his father's wishes—had forced him into circumstances not of his choosing. Royal wondered if a wanderer like Reese could ever be happy in the sedentary world of a country lord.

Or if he was prepared to confront the fact of Elizabeth Clemens's long-ago betrayal when the mere mention of her name set Reese's teeth on edge. Royal wondered what his brother would do when he found out Elizabeth's husband of these past six years had died just last year.

Royal took a sip of his brandy, eyeing his brother over the rim of the glass. For the moment, he refused to worry about Reese's future. There would be plenty of time for that. Instead, tonight they would celebrate his brother's safe return, and Royal and Lily's joyous marriage.

Seated beside him on the sofa, his pretty wife looked up at him and his heart squeezed with love for this gentle, courageous woman he had wed. Royal clasped Lily's slender hand and said a silent prayer of thanks for the day he had found her in the snow.

DEANNA RAYBOURN

In Grimsgrave Hall, enigmatic
Nicholas Brisbane has inherited a
ruined estate, replete with uncanny
tenants and one unwanted
houseguest: Lady Julia Grey.

Despite Brisbane's admonitions
to stay away, Lady Julia arrives in
Yorkshire to find him as remote
and maddeningly attractive as ever.
They share the house with the
proud but impoverished remnants
of an ancient family: the sort who
keep their bloodlines pure and
their secrets close.

A mystery unfolds from the
rotten heart of Grimsgrave—
one Lady Julia may have to
solve alone, as Brisbane appears
inextricably tangled in its
heinous twists and turns.

Silent on the Moor

MIRA®

www.MIRABooks.com   MDR2614

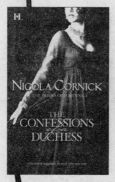  

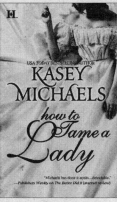

REQUEST YOUR
FREE BOOKS!

2 FREE NOVELS
FROM THE ROMANCE/SUSPENSE
COLLECTION PLUS 2 FREE GIFTS!

YES! Please send me 2 FREE novels from the Romance/Suspense Collection and my 2 FREE gifts (gifts are worth about $10). After receiving them, if I don't wish to receive any more books, I can return the shipping statement marked "cancel." If I don't cancel, I will receive 4 brand-new novels every month and be billed just $5.74 per book in the U.S. or $6.24 per book in Canada. That's a savings of at least 28% off the cover price. It's quite a bargain! Shipping and handling is just 50¢ per book.* I understand that accepting the 2 free books and gifts places me under no obligation to buy anything. I can always return a shipment and cancel at any time. Even if I never buy another book from the Reader Service, the two free books and gifts are mine to keep forever.

185 MDN EYNQ 385 MDN EYN2

Name	(PLEASE PRINT)	
Address		Apt. #
City	State/Prov.	Zip/Postal Code

Signature (if under 18, a parent or guardian must sign)

Mail to **The Reader Service:**
IN U.S.A.: P.O. Box 1867, Buffalo, NY 14240-1867
IN CANADA: P.O. Box 609, Fort Erie, Ontario L2A 5X3

Not valid to current subscribers of the Romance Collection,
the Suspense Collection or the Romance/Suspense Collection.

Want to try two free books from another line?
Call 1-800-873-8635 or visit www.morefreebooks.com.

* Terms and prices subject to change without notice. Prices do not include applicable taxes. Sales tax applicable in N.Y. Canadian residents will be charged applicable provincial taxes and GST. Offer not valid in Quebec. This offer is limited to one order per household. All orders subject to approval. Credit or debit balances in a customer's account(s) may be offset by any other outstanding balance owed by or to the customer. Please allow 4 to 6 weeks for delivery. Offer available while quantities last.

Your Privacy: Harlequin is committed to protecting your privacy. Our Privacy Policy is available online at www.eHarlequin.com or upon request from the Reader Service. From time to time we make our lists of customers available to reputable third parties who may have a product or service of interest to you. If you would prefer we not share your name and address, please check here. ☐

Harlequin® Historical
Historical Romantic Adventure!

Carole Mortimer's
debut Harlequin® Historical novel

THE DUKE'S CINDERELLA BRIDE

The Duke of Stourbridge thought Jane Smith a servant girl, so when Miss Jane is wrongly turned out of her home for inappropriate behavior after their encounter, the duke takes her in as his ward. Jane knows she cannot fall for his devastating charm. Their marriage would be forbidden— especially if he were to discover her shameful secret....

The Notorious St. Claires—
From plain Jane to society bride!

*Available September
wherever you buy books.*

KAT MARTIN

32609	HEART OF COURAGE	__ $7.99 U.S.	__ $7.99 CAN.
32554	SEASONS OF STRANGERS	__ $7.99 U.S.	__ $7.99 CAN.
32470	THE SUMMIT	__ $7.99 U.S.	__ $9.50 CAN.
32452	HEART OF FIRE	__ $7.99 U.S.	__ $9.50 CAN.
32383	HEART OF HONOR	__ $7.99 U.S.	__ $9.50 CAN.
32326	SCENT OF ROSES	__ $7.99 U.S.	__ $9.50 CAN.
32207	THE HANDMAIDEN'S NECKLACE	__ $7.99 U.S.	__ $9.50 CAN.
32199	THE DEVIL'S NECKLACE	__ $7.50 U.S.	__ $8.99 CAN.

(limited quantities available)

TOTAL AMOUNT	$ _____
POSTAGE & HANDLING	$ _____
($1.00 for 1 book, 50¢ for each additional)	
APPLICABLE TAXES*	$ _____
TOTAL PAYABLE	$ _____

(check or money order—please do not send cash)

To order, complete this form and send it, along with a check or money order for the total above, payable to MIRA Books, to: **In the U.S.:** 3010 Walden Avenue, P.O. Box 9077, Buffalo, NY 14269-9077; **In Canada:** P.O. Box 636, Fort Erie, Ontario, L2A 5X3.

Name: _____
Address: _____ City: _____
State/Prov.: _____ Zip/Postal Code: _____
Account Number (if applicable): _____

075 CSAS

*New York residents remit applicable sales taxes.
*Canadian residents remit applicable GST and provincial taxes.

MIRA®

www.MIRABooks.com

MKM0909BL